CW01662578

With or Without You

BOOKS BY DREW DAVIES

The Shape of Us
Dear Lily

With or Without You

DREW DAVIES

bookouture

Published by Bookouture in 2020

An imprint of Storyfire Ltd.
Carmelite House
50 Victoria Embankment
London EC4Y 0DZ

www.bookouture.com

ISBN: 978-1-83888-134-4
eBook ISBN: 978-1-83888-133-7

To Nanna.

PART ONE

The life-changing accident happened, as they often do, quite unexpectedly.

They were to head out for the morning. When Mrs Dixit came to collect her husband, he was straightening the only picture in their living room. It was a framed print of the long-windedly named *The Artist's Garden in Argenteuil (A Corner of the Garden with Dahlias)* by Claude Monet, but which they both called *the one with the flowers*. Mrs Dixit knew them to be dahlias – she'd worked in a florist shop after all – but her husband didn't, so 'flowers' they were. If she'd ever referred to the picture as *the one with the dahlias*, even clarifying it as *in the living room*, he would have looked at her in puzzlement, and possibly mild disapproval.

'It was crooked,' Mr Dixit explained. 'Off slightly.'

She shrugged in acquiescence, knowing this not to be true. What he meant was, the picture was cluttering up his nice clean wall, and had done for years. This, they would never agree upon: rooms needed pictures, one at the very least – which had always been her compromise. As payback, Mr Dixit was in constant battle with their correct hanging angle, regularly taking them off their hooks to see if they had discoloured his pristine walls.

Mrs Dixit stood back as her husband continued to tip the painting side to side, ever decreasingly.

'What do you think?'

'To the left,' she answered him. 'The right. Left. Right. Bit more left.' Each adjustment was so tiny it was practically negligible, and Mrs Dixit had to suppress a smile. She enjoyed teasing him like this, secretly. It cultivated fondness.

Mr Dixit ran a finger along the top of the picture's frame, and all affection for her husband dissolved.

'Huh,' he said, as if surprised about the lack of dust, although he shouldn't be; Mrs Dixit's cleaning hours each week were legion.

'Are you ready to go?' she asked, brushing away the imaginary dust from his finger with hers.

'After this,' he replied and kissed her hand.

The Dixits travelled to Stratford on the Central line, because Mr Dixit didn't like to drive in his own time. The couple sat quietly on the train carriage, covering their ears in sync whenever the scraping noise of the rails became too much for them, which was often. Mrs Dixit read a book about walking in nature, although they rarely walked in nature anymore, and Mr Dixit occasionally toyed on his phone. He was bidding on a set of six vintage polychrome model trains from a Midwest collector, and wanted to make sure he was still on top. He must have been, because he never grunted or sighed, his usual tell for a competing bid. Mrs Dixit, still reading, moved a hand to his left arm for moral support, and he squeezed her fingers with his bicep in reply.

When they arrived at their station, it was pleasingly empty. Eight a.m. on a brisk Saturday morning was never going to be busy, except perhaps at Christmas, and the Dixits would rarely venture into a shop post-October. It was now 20 February, the festive sales long over. They had come to look at a new washing machine in John Lewis, and the department store wouldn't be open for another hour. Being so early, to have the place all to themselves, very much satisfied them both. Once they'd entered the shopping mall, they walked along the empty main avenue, watching the assistants in the closed stores, unpacking boxes or squinting at cash registers. Some were dusting or hoovering, especially in the fancier stores.

'Must get a lot of street dust,' Mr Dixit noted, and his wife, lost in her own thoughts for a moment, and not understanding what he meant, nodded anyway.

They travelled up the escalators to the food hall and considered their options. Mrs Dixit was hungry, she'd gone to bed on a light dinner, but she let Mr Dixit make the final decision. Of the three places open, he chose the more upscale establishment, and bought two cappuccinos and two cheddar melt toasties, with a chocolate brownie to share. There was a lot of noise coming from the coffee machine: the barista thumping the stainless steel portafilter to loosen the spent granules, the loud frothing required to steam the milk – it made them both wince in unison.

Afterwards, they sat at a table in the unoccupied main dining area, still in their coats. If Mrs Dixit had known this would be the last meal she'd share with her husband that month, she might have appreciated it more. She would have tried to remember at least three things about his face in motion (the intelligent flick of his eyes, his jaw as he masticated, the way he cocked his head to ask 'too hot?' in relation to her coffee, and 'shall I get more?' when she spilt her sugar packet with a misjudged tear). Instead, she was distracted as the hot cheese from the toastie scalded the roof of her mouth. To cool her tongue, she made a sucking noise on each subsequent bite, much to the consternation of Mr Dixit – *why on earth was she making such a racket?* She stopped immediately.

At eight minutes to nine, they arrived hand in hand at the department store. The shutters were only half raised, and a security guard stood on the other side.

'We're not open for another ten minutes,' the guard said, through the shutters, although the Dixits knew the advertised time meant the store should be open in exactly eight. Mr Dixit nodded politely, however, and they waited.

*

Inside the store, the washing machine sales assistant wagged his index finger between the Dixits.

'And you are...?'

'Married,' Mr Dixit replied, and took his wife's hand again. She squeezed it. They were used to this rigmarole after nineteen years of marriage. Mrs Dixit was only eight years older than her husband, but most people presumed more, due to the uniform whiteness of her hair compared to his complete lack of grey. Mr Dixit's parents had emigrated to England from India, while his wife's family had rarely made it past the M25, their lineage not going much further either. This combination of an age gap and differing heritage often resulted in quizzical looks. An occasional concerned citizen asking Mrs Dixit if she was 'alright' – if Mr Dixit was bothering her? Or how it worked, the couple being from such different worlds? (For the record, they had both lived their whole lives in Chomley, a district in the north-east of London.) Not to mention the jokey comments about whether he was her 'toy boy'.

'Kids?'

They both shook their heads and hoped that would be enough.

'We want one that's as quiet as possible,' spoke Mr Dixit. 'Good value, eco-friendly, easy on delicates, but really, noise is our main concern.'

'Our neighbour,' Mrs Dixit chipped in. 'She complains about the spin cycle.'

This wasn't true. Mrs Rampersad, their upstairs neighbour, a retired postmistress, had never once said a word about their current washing machine, but it *was* very noisy, and how could they justify complaining about all the noise *she* made if they didn't replace it?

'This one is practically silent,' the sales assistant said, walking them to a machine.

'Can we turn it on to listen?' Mr Dixit asked.

The sales assistant blinked in surprise.

'On a cycle, you mean? It's not hooked up to the mains.'

'A spin then?'

'It won't make the same noise without clothes inside.'

Mr Dixit looked bewildered. He was always good to his taxi customers, never overcharging them and going the extra mile when he could – often literally – so of course he expected the same in return.

'Why don't we put our coats in?' Mrs Dixit offered helpfully, starting to take hers off.

'Not possible,' the sales assistant replied, smacking the top of the machine, and making the Dixits jump involuntarily. 'You'll just have to take my word for it.'

That was enough. They left, Mr Dixit muttering about checking the *Which?* recommendations instead. The trip had been in vain.

As they walked back to the station, they were met by an opposite flow of oncoming shoppers. All the stores were open now, and loud pop music could be heard from each, the long avenue filling up with large groups and noisy couples, many with children, and the downstairs food court was already heaving.

'Not a minute too soon,' Mrs Dixit said, shaking her head in exasperation as they scuttled down the escalators to escape.

Back in their pebble-dashed house in Chomley, having just avoided the rain, Mrs Dixit made a tuna and cucumber sandwich for her husband to eat at work. He was planning a long shift, returning after 10 p.m. She gifted him the wrapped sandwiches, and reminded him to check the air pressure in the tyres of his cab. Mr Dixit, on his phone, grunted – Mrs Dixit wasn't sure if it was in response to her, or because he'd been outbid. Perhaps both. A few moments later, she heard the garage door open, and his taxi pull away – the amber sign switched on for customers – and it would be the last time she could remember her husband having any agency of his own.

At just after 5 p.m., she received the call.

'Mrs Dixit?'

'Yes,' she replied, uncertainly. Why didn't people ever announce who they were anymore?

'I'm afraid I have some bad news about your husband,' the unknown person said. A woman.

Already Mrs Dixit's brain started to mangle the message. She reflected afterwards it was probably an act of self-preservation. A way for the mind to buy more time to process.

'My husband's at work,' she garbled, 'but you can leave him a message.'

She already knew that she was responding nonsensically – on some level, she understood.

'No, it's *about* your husband. He's been in a car accident.'

She didn't say anything for some time.

'Mrs Dixit?'

'Who is this, please?' she asked, finding her voice at last. There was a slight tone to it now, not fear, but annoyance. Because surely this was a mistake, or a ruse, or both?

'It's Nurse Bletchley, at Chomley hospital. Your husband is in a critical condition. Is there someone who you can ask to help you get here?'

Mrs Dixit considered this question. Was there someone? Not the neighbour, Mrs Rampersad, that was for sure. Mr Dixit would hate her getting involved in his business. Mrs Dixit could ring her sister perhaps, but wasn't she away?

'I'll take a taxi,' Mrs Dixit replied, and on saying the t-word, she thought of Mr Dixit's polished black cab, pulling out of the garage, sliding away from her, disappearing down the street. Tears welled in her eyes, and she wiped them away.

'Good,' said the voice on the phone. Nurse something. 'Come straight away.'

The phone went silent. Mrs Dixit held it by her side for a few moments, and then placed it on the cradle. When she picked it up again, she dialled a number from memory.

Cliff answered immediately, his gruff smoker's voice reassuring.

'Chomley Taxis. Pick-up address?'

'Cliff, it's Wendy.'

'Alright, Wendy? You want me to pass you through?'

'No, Cliff, there's been an accident.'

'I'm sorry. You want me to let Naveem know? Nothing serious, I hope.'

'It's *his* accident.' She wondered why he didn't already know. Surely, they had radios, someone would have called it in? 'I need a taxi, Cliff. Naveem's in hospital.'

'Oh, Wendy. That's why he's not been in my ear! I thought he was having a kip! I'm putting the word out to the other drivers. Someone will be right over. Is there anything I can do? Do you want me to come to the hospital?'

'No – thank you – the taxi is perfect,' Mrs Dixit replied, and laughed, because she felt she was being unnecessarily rude to Cliff, but couldn't help it.

'Of course. There's someone five minutes away.'

After thanking him, she put the phone down, and thought, *five minutes*? Five minutes to do what? Pack some clothes perhaps. What had the nurse said? What condition was he in? She cradled her face with her hands and let out an annoyed 'huh' sound, but it was much more animalistic than she was prepared for, more of a Wilhelm scream, and that amount of noise from her small person was unnerving. She stood, staring at the wall, and tried to sense what she should do next. Go back to sleep, she realised.

Curl back into bed. To wake refreshed, with everything resolved or undone.

A taxi beeped, and for a second Mrs Dixit imagined she'd been given God's pardon, or she'd daydreamed the nurse calling after all, but when she hurried to the window, she could see it was not Mr Dixit waiting in her driveway of course, but some unknown driver, and the harsh reality set in anew.

Mr Dixit was asleep. That's what it looked like at least. He always slept on his back, and although he rarely snored, he *grumbled*. Now, he was silent. There was only the beep of the machine nearby, keeping him alive.

'How long does a coma last?' Mrs Dixit asked, once the doctor had gone.

'Days, weeks, months?' the nurse said with a shrug, although her eyes were very kind.

'But on average?'

'They can still hear everything, you know,' the nurse replied, sidestepping the question. They both watched Mr Dixit, as if they would catch him eavesdropping. 'It's important you talk to him on your visits.'

'About what?'

'Whatever you like. What you've been up to? Keep him included. Helps with recovery.'

Mrs Dixit mulled this over. She had a habit of grinding her teeth when she concentrated; 'bruxism', it was called.

'Some people bring a stereo,' said the nurse. 'Did your husband like music?'

'Bossa nova,' Mrs Dixit replied, flatly, and then remembered her husband was possibly listening. 'Brazilian music from the fifties and sixties. He's a collector,' she announced, more brightly. 'All his albums are on vinyl though.'

'Maybe you could play him a selection on your phone? Make a playlist?'

'I don't think he'd like that. Too tinny. He's very particular about sound quality.'

The nurse smiled professionally. She'd spent enough time on this patient today.

'Can I ask one more thing?' Mrs Dixit touched her forehead.

'Of course.'

'What am I supposed… to do?' The nurse gave her a quizzical look. 'I mean, is there anything I can actually do? Other than wait? There must be something?'

The nurse patted Mrs Dixit on her shoulder.

'Stay strong, for his sake.'

'How?'

The nurse smiled again, one that signalled the imminent termination of their interaction.

'Imagine what your husband would do if it was *you* lying there,' she said, squeezing Mrs Dixit's shoulder as she left.

He'd wait too, she supposed. And probably check on his eBay bids.

Mrs Dixit ran a bath when she returned home. It was too hot initially, so she left it to cool.

I should call his mother, she thought, and normally the idea would make her recoil. Now though, she felt nothing.

Her own parents had been gone almost a decade, dying three months apart, her father from prostate cancer, and her mother, it seemed, from a lack of will to carry on alone. Not that Mrs Dixit had ever been close to them. She quietly blamed them for her inherent shyness and standoffishness – they seemed critical of everything she did, never accepting her marriage, and blatantly favoured her younger sister, keeping a cool distance from their eldest daughter right up to their deaths. It was one of the things which had bonded Mrs Dixit to her future husband, both having unfavourable parents.

Mrs Dixit dialled the number, noticing the absence of emotion. No anxiety at the dial tone. When a woman's voice picked up, her heart didn't even beat faster.

'Naveem's in hospital.'

There was a pause.

'I'm sorry, we are very busy,' the other Mrs Dixit said, and hung up.

Mrs Dixit put the phone down again and felt a surge of anger flowing up from her stomach, rushing through the arm still holding the phone, until she picked it up again and punched the redial button.

'A lorry hit him,' she said, more loudly this time. 'He has a head injury. He's in a coma.'

There was another pause.

'Which hospital?'

'Chomley.'

The phone went dead.

The bath was stone cold when Mrs Dixit remembered it, so she let out the water. She couldn't remember the last time she'd eaten.

1 day since the accident

In the morning, she showered and ate some toast. The bread caught in the rungs of the toaster, smoking and blackening, and the smoke alarm went off. Soon, there was the inevitable knock on the front door.

'I heard a wailin'' Mrs Rampersad said, one hand on the door frame for support. 'Where's what's-his-chops then?'

'He's away,' Mrs Dixit replied, not untruthfully, unready yet to reveal the true situation.

'Away, huh?' Mrs Rampersad raised her eyebrow. 'Where'd he go then?' She uttered, in a faux whisper, 'Did he leave you?'

Mrs Dixit frowned away this absurd suggestion.

'He's in the hospital,' she replied, reactively.

Mrs Rampersad nodded, and Mrs Dixit wondered if she'd heard her properly.

'In a coma,' she added.

More nodding.

'He had bleeding on his brain, it's very serious.'

Nod, nod.

'They're not sure when he will be conscious again.'

'Yes, yes.' Mrs Rampersad said. 'Terrible, these comas. Agnes Delores from church, her husband was in a coma too. Woke up lying on his secretary with his trousers down, a medical miracle!' She laughed, a dry, throaty laugh. 'If your husband's left you, there's no need to make up stories. Rejoice, I say.'

Mrs Dixit felt frustration prickle on her skin.

'My husband is in a critical condition. I have to visit him. Now. In fact, would you be so kind as to drive me to the hospital?'

It seemed the only way to make her understand the truth.

On the journey, Mrs Dixit realised her mistake.

'He can only have one visitor at a time,' she lied. It was brighter today, still overcast, but the clouds didn't seem to hang as ominously low.

Mrs Rampersad shrugged.

'I have a sudoku.'

*

Mrs Dixit sat next to his bed. His face looked serene, albeit slightly gormless. His eyelid twitched and for a moment she imagined he'd open his eyes. Mrs Dixit wasn't sure why, but she didn't feel *ready*. She would have worn nicer clothes for one. The shoes he liked – smart black ones, with a modest 31mm heel so she didn't complain about her feet hurting. Fortunately, though, the flickering subsided, and Mr Dixit continued on with his coma.

He was still handsome – his forty-eight years had been kind to him. There was his full head of hair, and his Romanesque nose. Yes, he was as short as Mrs Dixit – something he'd always been sensitive of – but really, everyone was the same height lying down.

She had never been conventionally attractive herself, but Mrs Dixit had good bone structure – even if her nose was slightly too pointy – and a naturally slender figure. She wasn't overly imaginative when it came to clothing, favouring warmth (she was usually cold, especially in her extremities) and natural, breathable, comfortable fabric over style. In her younger days, she'd often given people the impression she was more in control than she felt. In department stores, other shoppers would randomly ask her the location of things, and when she worked at the florist, people assumed she was the owner (so had Mr Dixit, initially). When she opened her mouth to speak, however, they seemed to quickly revise their estimation of her (except for Mr Dixit).

A new nurse arrived.

'Have you spoken to him?' she asked cheerily.

Mrs Dixit shook her head.

'There's not much to say,' she explained.

'I'm sure he'd like to hear it anyway.' The nurse made a note on her chart and left.

With a resigned sigh, Mrs Dixit looked around the room for inspiration. She found none. She glanced at the doorway, where she knew Mrs Rampersad was sitting in the hallway, in earshot, calculating numbers. It added to the pressure.

She opened her handbag, looking for something to read aloud, and found a packet of heartburn tablets.

'Indigestion relief,' she whispered quietly enough so she wouldn't be overheard, 'Peppermint flavour. Do not give to children under twelve years…'

In the car again, Mrs Rampersad was unusually silent. *Maybe this has been an inconvenience for her*, Mrs Dixit thought. *I must offer to pay for petrol.*

'How do you know he's not faking?' asked Mrs Rampersad finally. 'It's happened before.'

Mrs Dixit felt her jaw clench. *Ignore*, she thought.

'In Trinidad, a man was riding a motorcycle when he hit a school. No one was hurt, but he didn't want to pay the damage, so he lay in a fake coma for six weeks before escaping on a German cruise liner.'

'They have tests,' Mrs Dixit replied crisply.

'When do they say he'll wake up?'

'I'm not sure.'

'Don't they have tests for that too?'

They sat in a heavy silence all the way home.

The flat was so quiet, it seemed to be absorbing noise. Even the hum from the fridge was lessened. Mrs Dixit wandered through each room, looking for something to occupy her. In the bathroom, she scrubbed the toilet bowl with the brush. After washing her hands, she wiped down the place mats in the kitchen. She took a chair to stand on and dusted a spiderweb off the living-room ceiling. When that was done, she went down the basement stairs, vacuuming outside Mr Dixit's study, but not daring to go in.

Now everything was clean and tidy, she felt like buying fresh-cut flowers and placing them in each room. This impulse was met with a twinge of disloyalty to her husband. Mr Dixit disliked flowers in the house. It wasn't that he was allergic, he simply didn't appreciate them aesthetically. 'If I want to watch something slowly die, I can always look in a mirror,' he'd sniff. 'Save money too.' If it was up to Mr Dixit, even the painting in the living room would be less floral – bouquets of sprockets growing in the garden, instead.

Besides, she didn't have enough vases.

Three things unnerved her that night. A dreamt image of the study door very slowly opening. The real sound of a dog barking. The thought, as she lay, unable to get back to sleep, that Mr Dixit might return to the house without her knowing. In his hospital gown, his arms outstretched, as if he were a zombie. Walk slowly into the bedroom. Lie next to her. Why was that so frightening?

2 days since the accident

When she woke, a memory came to her, as if it had been waiting for its moment. A policeman explaining to her that Mr Dixit was not alone at the time of the accident. The 'not alone' had jangled in her ears.

'You mean a customer?' she'd asked.

'We're not sure yet.'

There had been so much going on, Mrs Dixit failed to give this exchange much thought.

Mrs Rampersad knocked on the door at 9.30 a.m. She was holding a tray covered in foil.

'It would be technically difficult to fake a coma,' she conceded, handing over the tray.

Mrs Rampersad followed Mrs Dixit into her kitchen. Mr Dixit would not have approved of the neighbour so brazenly walking in, but it felt good to have someone else's energy inside her home.

'I didn't sleep well,' Mrs Dixit confessed.

Mrs Rampersad, sitting herself at the kitchen table, sniffed. 'Were you thinking about finances?'

'Not particularly...'

'He won't be earning, lying there. It's practically a holiday. Will you have to go back to work?'

Mrs Dixit thought about the florist she used to work at, ten years ago, which was now a dry cleaner's you could also get your keys cut at.

'He's made provisions,' Mrs Dixit replied uncertainly. Instinctively, she knew it was not good to be talking about private matters so publicly. Mr Dixit would loathe it.

'Provisions, huh? That's nice. Very nice.'

This information seemed to put Mrs Rampersad at ease, and she leaned back in her chair. 'Men are a real mystery,' she said, opening her eyes wide.

Is she waiting for me to say something? Mrs Dixit wondered. After what seemed like a very long time, Mrs Rampersad hauled herself to her feet again.

'Do you need another ride to the hospital?' she asked.

'Thank you, I'll take a taxi.'

'Lucky you, with all those provisions.'

After her neighbour had gone, Mrs Dixit examined the baking tray. Under the foil was a kind of loaf. It smelled of ginger and oozed something sticky when prodded. She busied herself rearranging the fridge to accommodate the massive tray, realising it was the closest to content she'd been since the call from the hospital.

*

Len was the driver.

'It's a terrible, terrible thing.'

'Terrible,' she repeated.

'It could happen to anyone, at any time.'

'Anyone,' she mumbled. But it hadn't happened to anyone. It had happened to her husband.

'How are you taking it?' Len asked in his slightly farmer-y West Country accent, looking at her in the rear-view mirror, intrusively, she felt. Mr Dixit had not liked Len, historically. He said Len had a way of making people feel uncomfortable, and good ambience was vital, especially with the new customer rating systems.

How am I taking it? Mrs Dixit pondered. She wanted to say 'in my stride' but that didn't sound right. She was aware anything she said would be filtered back to the other drivers, and potentially Cliff at Control. Mrs Dixit regretted the taxi now, even with the inevitable discount. Mrs Rampersad was right, it was a luxury, and could she afford it? The documents she'd found had been inconclusive. They were insured up to the eyeballs for almost everything, except, it seemed, accidents at work. She should have taken the bus.

Len cleared his throat noisily.

'You don't think of Asians being in comas.'

'*What?*'

'In movies and TV. It's always white people, isn't it?' Mrs Dixit began to grind her teeth. 'But I guess statistically, based on population size, there's a much higher chance of an Asian going into a coma compared to a white person. If you think about it.'

Quickly, Mrs Dixit wound down the window, and the cold air was good.

*

Watching Mr Dixit lying there now, she realised she missed him. It was *unfair*. That was the word. To have him so near, and yet not himself. Mrs Dixit thought about crawling up beside him on the bed and lying with him for a few minutes, but she was disturbed by another new nurse.

'His mother was in earlier,' the woman said cheerily.

'Has she gone?' Mrs Dixit asked, panicked.

'I think so. It was an hour ago.'

Mrs Dixit sat back down again and tried not to appear flustered.

'My mother-in-law is a bit of a nightmare too,' the nurse added kindly.

'Did she say anything? About him?'

'No. She just sat. Very good posture.'

It was strange knowing that the other Mrs Dixit had been sitting in this very chair – it would have been the first time they were in the same room for fifteen years. A chill passed through Mrs Dixit's body.

'Don't forget to talk to him,' the nurse said, tucking in the sheet more securely. 'It really helps, you know.'

Alone, Mrs Dixit found it difficult to speak.

'I don't like Len either,' she said at last. 'His cab smells of feet.'

The bus ride home was full of schoolkids, so Mrs Dixit hid at the rear. They seemed to spill everywhere, these children, *squawking*. That was the word. The girls hit the boys; the boys brandished mobile phones at the girls with who-knows-what on the screens. Or they played loud electric music. Mrs Dixit spent the whole trip glaring so disapprovingly, it brought on a pounding headache.

*

Home, she closed the blinds against her headache and sat on the sofa. The silence engulfed her again, but surprisingly, it wasn't the relief she'd imagined.

If Mr Dixit was here, he might have rubbed her shoulders, massaged her temples, brought a cup of tea – no, she realised, he would have used the excuse of Mrs Dixit needing silence to go down to his trains. She mustn't over-romanticise him, turn him into someone he was not. The real version of her husband needed to be protected.

The phone rang, startling her, and she realised she must have been dozing.

'I've heard!' came her sister's voice.

'Yes, well…'

'Why didn't you tell me?'

Mrs Dixit knew why, but she didn't say. They both knew why.

'There's not much anyone can do,' Mrs Dixit explained, realising her headache was all but gone.

'If you'd like, I can get a babysitter for Henry, and come right over. We could have a girls' night in?'

Massaging her temple where the headache had been, Mrs Dixit gave a dismissive tut.

'No, no. I'm fine. I am.'

'If you're sure you're coping? It must have been such a shock. Have you heard about the woman he was driving?'

Woman?

'How do you know it was a woman?'

'It was in the *Chomley Gazette* today. The truck driver didn't have a scratch on him apparently. The passenger was a *doctor*. A female doctor. Isn't that terrible?' *My husband is in a coma*, Mrs Dixit wanted to yell, but didn't. 'There's a funeral soon.'

'Oh, she... I didn't know, she... How devastating. Poor woman. And her family...'

'Have the police been in touch?'

'They're sending round a constable, but they're understaffed, because of holidays, and those break-ins, so I won't hold my breath.'

'What if there are criminal charges? Negligence?'

'I thought it was the truck driver's fault?'

'Yes, but lawyers can always spin it their way.' Her sister changed her tone. 'Did he... I mean, *does* he have life insurance?'

'Of course,' Mrs Dixit replied, and then regretted being so vehement. She'd still not found those exact papers and reminded herself to call the insurance company.

Her sister was silent for a moment, but the sound of gears whirring was practically audible.

'Was he ever... you know... *controlling*?'

'What do you mean?'

'He always answered the phone when you were both in.'

'I don't see the issue with that.'

'But why wouldn't you *ever* answer it?'

'I'm not sure – maybe he was always closer to the phone...?'

The shameful truth was, Mrs Dixit made sure to screen calls through her husband, afraid it might be her sister ringing.

'He'd say you were busy.'

'Sometimes I was... I do have a life, you know.'

There was a vaguely judgemental silence.

'He didn't stop you from seeing us, then?'

Mrs Dixit laughed.

''Course not.'

This was true. Not that Mr Dixit actively encouraged seeing his sister-in-law either. He understood implicitly how complicated family could be.

'He never let you have a car of your own?'

'I never wanted my own. We have a car. Had one at least.'

transit. By her reckoning, the train was from the sixties, but that was a layman's guess. She placed the train on the kitchen table and rolled it forwards a few inches. Sometimes, Mrs Dixit had wanted to take a closer look at the model trains when they arrived, but she never dared ask. Mr Dixit would have given her the queerest of looks. Trains were his domain, to be shut away quickly in his study. She always suspected he felt there was something dangerous about his hobby – it being childish, obsessive, indulgent, a sign of a weak character and therefore important to be kept hidden. Mrs Dixit ached for her husband then, this man without toys of his own as a child, who coveted them as an adult instead.

Moments later, she found herself putting on shoes.

The nurse looked surprised to see Mrs Dixit back again so soon.

'Forgot something?' she asked.

'I wanted to sit with him.' Mrs Dixit found she was blushing.

For a while, she watched her husband's chest rise and fall as air was pumped into his lungs. Instead of finding this comforting, she worried each breath would be his last, so eventually she had to look away. Whatever she'd come to find was not here. The room contained his body, but where was *he*? Locked inside his mind, like the data on a broken computer? They could back up your hard drive, but what about your husband?

It wasn't only Mr Dixit who was imprisoned, it was their mutual history, their tacit agreements, their commitment to each other. Mrs Dixit had been older than him when they first met (*still was*, he would tease). She had always felt awkward around men; unattractive, shy. By the time she was thirty-seven, she'd given up hope of marrying. When romance had arrived – quietly, untheatrically – they'd tended to this tiny flame as if it was the most important thing in the world, which of course it was. But there were many things they'd never actively discussed. That, at twenty-nine when they'd first met, Mr Dixit was still a virgin. Why he had chosen to marry her, when he was younger, handsome? Was it their mutual reticence? The fact she was compliant to the ways he wanted his life to be – ordered, unfussed, isolated? Did he have a thing for older women in general? Whatever the reason, their life together had made her feel special. Without him, would she ever feel this way again?

She moved closer.

'Stop this,' hissed Mrs Dixit under her breath, 'just stop it' – but she wasn't sure if she was addressing her husband or herself.

3 days since the accident

The next morning, she climbed the hallway steps and knocked on Mrs Rampersad's door. She could hear calypso music playing, and smelt fried eggs and coffee.

'Could you drive me today?' asked Mrs Dixit, once the door opened.

'To the hospital?' Mrs Rampersad tied her dressing gown around her ample bosom.

'No,' Mrs Dixit replied nervously, 'Somewhere else.'

'Where then?'

Mrs Dixit clenched her jaw.

'I'm not sure yet.'

Mrs Dixit still hadn't decided on their destination by the time they were both seated in the car. Her face was flushed with embarrassment.

'Take your time,' said Mrs Rampersad charitably, removing a dog-eared sudoku magazine from the driver's seat pocket beside her. 'I don't have to be anywhere until lunch.'

'I need a place where I can think,' stammered Mrs Dixit.

'How about my church? Best place for it. God listens…'

'No,' Mrs Dixit replied quickly. 'But thank you.'

'I always think well in a library, but there are so many homeless people in there nowadays – and the smell!' Mrs Dixit baulked at her neighbour's lack of sensitivity. 'I have two overdue books, but I can't be messing with that, honestly!'

'Could we just drive? I think I'll know the place when I see it.'

Mrs Rampersad shrugged and with the sudoku magazine still on her lap, started the car, backing it out of the driveway. Mrs Dixit discretely kicked the takeaway food packaging away from under her feet and tried to relax.

'There,' she called, as they passed Chomley's only public art gallery.

'Wouldn't you rather go to a park?' suggested Mrs Rampersad, before shrugging and pulling over.

The art consisted of rope 'paintings'. Long lengths of rope twisted into coils and painted lurid colours.

'Seems a waste of good rope,' Mrs Rampersad muttered, only slightly under her breath. It was a sentiment that Mr Dixit would have shared, but even so, Mrs Dixit walked a few paces away from her neighbour to distance herself. More coiled rope. Different vivid colours. She tried to see something in the shapes. The coils could be waves on an ocean, except they were painted bright red, and when did you ever see red waves? The photocopied handout mentioned a connection to the past, human frailty, the plight of immigrants, but she couldn't see it herself. They were ugly, that was their problem. Art didn't need to be beautiful, Mrs Dixit understood that, but it shouldn't be this unattractive either. There was a line.

It wasn't working. The space, the light, the heavy hushed atmosphere – none of it. Mrs Dixit felt stifled, it was the same sense of claustrophobia she experienced at home.

'Can we go?' she asked Mrs Rampersad, starting to feel panicky and afraid she might be visibly sweating.

'I don't mind either way,' Mrs Rampersad replied. 'I've never understood what makes people want to look at things on walls. Dark little things on bright little walls.'

She chuckled to herself.

Half an hour later, Mrs Dixit dawdled at the hospital shop. Even though she wasn't hungry, she bought a chocolate bar, and put it in her handbag.

He was waiting, as he always was. There was a slight odour about him now. Not unwashed, just unmoved. The smell of stasis.

She felt mean-spirited, so she took his hand. It was strange, like a dummy's hand, but real. Heavy. His.

'I went to an art gallery,' she announced, and then wished she hadn't. It felt like she was bragging, or rebelling, because he didn't like her hanging pictures at home. She should have been here with him. Where had she been instead? Around a load of old rope. 'I don't want to go home,' she said, more quietly, and then, 'I miss you,' which was true. Mrs Dixit tried to picture her husband's eyes, although it was difficult. There was something about the consciousness held within them, an essence of aliveness, that defied memory. Instead, she brought her husband's hand to her face, and breathed in, and it was him, his smell, under all the anti-bacterial solution, under the scent of inertia, it still was. She wanted to cry, but the emotion felt tightly knotted inside her, crimson and electric violet. It would not yield.

Mrs Dixit held his hand like that until a nurse tapped her on the shoulder, startling her.

That night, she tried playing some of Mr Dixit's bossa nova records. She didn't have a favourite, so that made the selection easier. When the record began, she knew exactly which one it was. In her mind, she'd always called the album *annoying trumpet.* Nonetheless, she kept it playing as she washed her dinner dishes, hoping it would help. When it came to the lengthy instrumental solo, Mrs Dixit turned it off – she only had so much charity to give.

4 days since the accident

The following morning, the police made their visit.

'Sorry to have kept you waiting,' the younger, thinner one said. 'There's a prolific cat burglar doing the rounds in the area, I'm sure you've read about it.'

Mrs Dixit nodded, although she'd been avoiding the news for days.

'Your husband was driving his vehicle when an articulated lorry swerved into his path. The collision resulted in the death of the passenger, and so we wanted to ask you a few questions.'

She nodded again.

'How did your husband know the deceased?'

'Know her? I mean, she was a paying customer?'

The two policemen looked at each other.

'The thing is,' the older, fatter one said, 'the deceased was riding in the front passenger seat when the accident occurred. Without her seat belt. Would a passenger normally sit in the front of your husband's taxi?'

It felt like they already knew the answer, so why were they asking?

'Not that I know of,' she replied curtly.

'Did you ever sit in the front seat when your husband was driving? It's your only vehicle, am I correct?'

'Of course I'd sit in the front with him.'

Her mind was ticking over this new information. She needed time to process and she wanted the policemen to leave.

'Are you in touch with your husband's family?' asked the younger, slimmer one. And again, they already knew the answer. She was being prompted to confirm things they already knew.

'Naveem doesn't speak with his family. Not since… not since before our wedding, nineteen years ago. They don't approve.'

'But you did contact your husband's family? Recently?'

'I called his mother to let her know her son was in hospital, is that what you mean?'

'It's a terrible thing, this accident, it must be a terrible time for you,' said the older one, hanging his head and nodding in mock respect.

'What happened to the lorry driver?' asked Mrs Dixit.

'He is cooperating with our investigations, currently.'

'Will you be charging him?'

'I wouldn't like to say, at the present time.'

'It seems a pretty cut-and-dried situation to me. The lorry caused the accident. My husband is in a coma. A woman died.'

The police officers repeated their conspiratorial glance at each other.

'We are doing some routine checks – blood alcohol tests, analysing CCTV camera footage, assessing the vehicle mechanics before we make any assumptions.'

The other policeman cleared his throat.

'Naveem's mother – Mrs Dixit – seems convinced there was foul play.'

The present Mrs Dixit gritted her teeth.

'Foul play? How would she even know? She has nothing to do with Naveem.'

'Nonetheless, it's an avenue we have to explore.'

He tapped both knees with his knuckles as if that was that.

*

'What did they say?' Mrs Rampersad asked breathlessly, knocking on Mrs Dixit's door moments after the police had gone.

'His mother thinks someone might have tampered with the brakes,' Mrs Dixit said, rolling her eyes.

'I knew it! He was a dark horse, that husband of yours. You think he had connections with organised crime?'

'Of course not,' replied Mrs Dixit, bristling.

Although, it had to be said, Mr Dixit *was* very organised. It would be the sort of crime he'd naturally gravitate to.

Mrs Rampersad had to be politely manoeuvred out of the door, but not before she offered to drive to the hospital.

'I'll walk today, I think.' Mrs Dixit feigned a smile.

It took nearly an hour to get there. She'd assumed the exercise would clear her head, but it was the same as in the art gallery; expansiveness unnerved her, quietness was irritating. She didn't *want* to be alone with her own thoughts.

Watching him on the bed, Mrs Dixit tried to imagine her husband as a hardened criminal. It was impossible, he was drooling too much. Mrs Dixit wiped the saliva away with a tissue. She couldn't remember if the tissue was used or not, but really, did it matter? Hopelessness came over her in a great sudden torrent. She opened her bag, looking for something to take her mind off things, trying not to cry.

'He's doing much better,' a nurse said unexpectedly behind Mrs Dixit, almost making her drop the bag.

'How can you tell? Have there been tests?'

'His breathing has improved, that's always a good sign. Not to give you any false hope, but the doctor was pleased. How are you getting on?' the nurse asked. It was said in a way that wasn't soliciting an honest response, so Mrs Dixit complied.

'Fine. As best I can.' She looked her husband again. 'It's very surreal… all of this.'

'I know, I know. But he understands you're here, on some level.' Mrs Dixit nodded. 'It really does help if you talk to him.'

'I've tried, but I feel I'm not doing it right.'

'There's no right or wrong way. You can read the newspaper to him, if you like?'

'I've never liked reading aloud. Hearing the sound of my own voice.'

'Oh, don't,' replied the nurse, waving her hand. 'I hate mine. If I ever hear myself on answer message…' She scrunched up her face. 'Maybe tell him all the things he wouldn't listen to when he was awake. My husband could do with being in a coma sometimes, the way he's all in one ear and out the other!'

Mrs Dixit grimaced politely.

Back home, she was standing outside his study, her hand resting on the door handle, when the phone rang.

'She was sitting in the front seat!'

'How do you know?' Mrs Dixit asked of her younger sister.

'The CCTV. They've released some of the footage on the police website to encourage witnesses to come forward.'

Mrs Dixit felt her mouth become very dry.

'If they have the footage, why do they even need witnesses?'

'The CCTV doesn't capture every angle. The lorry obscuring things is an issue. Do you think he knew her? The woman?'

'Possibly. He had his regular customers.'

'You must find out.'

'Why?'

'To clear his name.'

'To clear it of what?'

Her younger sister lowered her voice.

'There are *rumblings*.'

Mrs Dixit caught the sound of her lower teeth squeaking against the upper ones.

'It's no one's business. He's not done anything wrong. The police said the accident wasn't his fault. They called back today and told me his brakes were fine.'

'Then there will be an obvious answer, won't there?' This sounded almost like a taunt, and Mrs Dixit didn't know how to respond. 'Anyway, I must dash. I have to return a coat to the shops.'

'Give Henry my lo...' started Mrs Dixit, but her sister had already cut her off.

She barely slept. At 2 a.m., she turned on her lamp and read. At 3 a.m., she had a cheese sandwich, in case it was hunger keeping her awake. After she'd brushed her teeth for the second time that night, she turned off her bedside light. There was a sensation, of being adrift in an inky black sea. Mrs Dixit reminded herself that there were people all around her. Mrs Rampersad in her bedroom directly above, probably no less than five metres away. Mr Dixit would say you could hear her bed springs creak, but when Mrs Rampersad had a boyfriend for a few months in the summer, the joke became too real. *What happened to him?* Mrs Dixit wondered, not sleepy at all. She considered taking out her iPad from its sleeve and going to the Police website, but that frightened her more than all the bottomless oceans put together, and she started counting backwards from one hundred instead. At zero, she let out a long sigh, and wiggled her toes.

5 days since the accident

Mrs Dixit woke with one lingering question on her mind: *what do Naveem's eyes look like?*

What do *his eyes look like?* she thought, blinking. She tried to picture them. The morning light filtered through the gap between the curtains. She hadn't closed them properly. Mr Dixit always liked the curtains drawn tight.

Brown, of course. Dark brown. Silly question.

She kicked her feet out of the bed, and slipper-less, and without stopping to put on her dressing gown, padded into the kitchen.

Mrs Dixit felt frazzled. She hoped a coffee might help, but it just made her edgy. Could she skip the hospital? Should she, when there were her sister's *rumblings*?

She took up Mrs Rampersad's mail when it arrived at just past 10.30 a.m. Bills and an envelope with American postage stamps.

'What's wrong with your hair?' Mrs Rampersad asked, opening the door.

'Nothing,' Mrs Dixit replied, smoothing it down with her free hand as she handed over the letters.

'It looks *distressed*.'

'I came to say I'll be making my own way to the hospital from now on. I appreciate your help, but I shouldn't be taking up all your time.'

Mrs Rampersad stared at her, and Mrs Dixit self-consciously patted her hair again.

'Fair enough,' Mrs Rampersad replied emotionlessly.

'I appreciate it though.' Mrs Rampersad nodded. 'Thank you for everything.'

'Mmmmhmmm.'

'I'm very grateful.'

'I'm doing some food shopping in half an hour. I can drop you at the hospital on the way.'

'Well, that's… it's kind of you, but…'

'No problem for me.' Mrs Rampersad said, giving a parting chuckle at Mrs Dixit's hair, before shutting the door.

'Your husband doesn't like me,' Mrs Rampersad announced as they drove.

'What... No... Impossible...' Mrs Dixit began, but she soon ran out of protestations.

'It's because I called his bossa nova "elevator music", isn't it?'

Mrs Dixit winced.

'He's very particular about things like that.'

'He started it. He called my 'lypso, a "racket".' She chuckled. 'He doesn't like strong women, does he?' Turning her head slightly to look out of the window, Mrs Dixit gave a half-hearted shrug. 'Domineering mother? Am I wrong?' Mrs Rampersad sniffed. 'I'm never wrong.'

They drove in silence for a few moments.

'How long have you been married?'

Mrs Dixit hesitated. If she started with the personal information, who knew where it would end?

'Nineteen years.'

Mrs Rampersad raised her eyebrows.

'Is he your second husband?'

'My first.'

'How old are you?'

Mrs Dixit felt the heat rise in her face, her worry confirmed.

'Fifty-eight.' Her cheeks were on fire.

Mrs Rampersad grunted.

'Married late then. You were lucky. How come you don't dye your hair? Put a nice colour through it? Take years off.'

Mrs Dixit felt even more tongue-tied now. She was sensitive about her hair. Her whole life it had been brittle, never taking to being coloured, and so when she started to grey in her forties, she was afraid the dyes might make it fall out altogether. Go grey or go bald seemed the only options, so she'd chosen to age naturally. It helped that Mr Dixit had never minded. 'Makes you look distinguished,' he'd told her, wrapping a white lock of hair around his brown knuckles. 'Like a surgeon general.'

'You can let me out here, if you like,' Mrs Dixit replied, a little too emphatically.

The car pulled over, and Mrs Dixit quickly got out, slamming the door in her enthusiasm to leave. She caught herself about to say, 'Love to Henry', she was in that much of a rush.

They were in the process of moving her husband when she arrived.

'Where are you taking him?' she asked the closest porter.

'Long-term care.'

'But they said he'll wake up any day now?'

The porter shrugged.

'Gotta move him,' he replied, blankly.

Mrs Dixit followed them as they wheeled the bed and the life support system down the corridor and into the new ward. The two porters found it challenging to keep the doors open and manoeuvre everything through cleanly, and Mrs Dixit had an impulse to help, but was afraid she might do something wrong, so she stood back and watched instead. At one point, they knocked into a door frame, and Mr Dixit's hand swung off the bed and hit the porter on the thigh. Mrs Dixit might have laughed if it wasn't so troubling.

The new ward had five other patients, all unconscious. Nevertheless, Mrs Dixit felt as if anything she said now would be overheard by these strangers, and it made her even more meek. Once the porters had checked everything and plugged all the cables in again, Mrs Dixit pulled the curtain around her husband's bed, and took his hand, the one that had fallen, stroking it gently.

'The nerve of that woman,' she muttered, but she couldn't think of anything else she wanted so publicly to say.

That evening, she heard the sound of a taxi in the driveway. Again, her heart fluttered before her mind could sanction reason.

At the window, she spotted Len stepping out of his cab. She let the curtain go. Had he seen her? The doorbell rang – she considered pretending she wasn't in, but of course the lights were on.

'Just thought I'd check up on you,' he said, when she finally did open the door, his West Country elongated vowels making Mrs Dixit's response even more clipped.

'That's very kind,' she enunciated.

Len was wearing a pressed shirt, Mrs Dixit noticed.

'Any news?'

'Nothing.'

'The waiting must be the hardest.'

Mrs Dixit shrugged.

'At least he's not in any immediate danger.'

'Is that what the doctors have said?'

'They don't say much, categorically. But he's not deteriorating at least.'

The phrase 'long term' pinged into Mrs Dixit's brain, as if it was written in hot pink neon.

Len nodded.

'At least you always know where you left him,' he said with a too-boisterous laugh.

'How's your wife, Len?' Mrs Dixit asked, when he'd finished.

'Fine. The same. Ah, I forgot – she made you something.' He rushed to his cab and brought back a baking dish covered with foil. 'Lasagne,' he said, passing it over. The dish weighed a tonne, Mrs Dixit almost dropping it.

'Thank her for me,' she said, once she'd recovered slightly.

'Will do, will do.'

There was something else he wanted to say, she could sense it. *Hurry up*, Mrs Dixit thought, *get it over with*. Her arms were already starting to tremble from the dish.

'You know how I am,' Len began, 'always like a joke, me. I might have gone a bit far with Naveem. On the day it happened. The accident. Making fun of his, you know, trains and things.' Mrs Dixit tightened her jaw. 'Thomas the Wank Engine, stuff like that. All in good fun, of course. I just hope it wasn't… distracting. He took things on too much. You're supposed to shrug that stuff off. But, Naveem…'

'Thank your wife for the lasagne,' Mrs Dixit said stiffly.

'If there's anything I can do – if you ever want to go for a drink and talk…'

'Goodbye now.'

She faked a smile and used her shoulder to close the door, before bending to put the dish hurriedly on the floor, so she didn't completely drop it. The last thing she needed was Len's wife's lasagne spilled all over her hallway carpet.

In the night, Mrs Dixit thought she heard a voice – or voices – above her through the floorboards. Loud. Frustrated. Instead of waking her up completely, she found the noise oddly calming, the soothing din sending her back to sleep.

6 days since the accident

In the morning, she took Mrs Rampersad's baking tray back up to her. She considered leaving it on the mat but knocked instead. There was no answer. She knocked again and waited, listening.

Nothing. Mrs Dixit turned, walked a few paces, before pausing and listening again. No sound. She was back in her own kitchen before she realised that she was still holding the tray.

Mrs Dixit rode the bus to the hospital again, but it didn't go well. The bus was late so she had to stand in the cold. When it finally arrived, the bus began on an alternative route due to roadworks, the driver pumping the brakes constantly and making all the passengers lurch in their seats. The bunch of Dutch freesias Mrs Dixit had bought at the florist before catching the bus were mangled by the time she reached her destination. Not that her husband would notice. In fact, she was counting on this – she knew it was unfitting to bring flowers, knowing full well Mr Dixit was not a fan, but it seemed inappropriate coming to the hospital each day and never bringing any. She was doing it as a show for the nurses, really.

It was better in the ward today, less daunting. Another of the male patients had guests, a wife and a son – sixteen perhaps. The wife smiled, but she was very blank behind the eyes, Mrs Dixit felt.

Taking the small vase she'd brought in her bag, Mrs Dixit arranged the flowers and filled it at the sink. The wife sat talking to her husband, leaning in, so her mouth was close to his ear. He was a big man, with wild eyebrows, and forearms like ham hocks. *What's she saying?* Mrs Dixit wondered. When she turned off the tap again, she realised the woman was praying.

She timed the bus home all wrong and was stuck with schoolchildren again. A boy bounced his bottom on a seated girl's knee, she snatched away his phone in retaliation, and then they tussled, screeching. None of the adults did a thing, staring stonily in front of them. Mrs Dixit marvelled at the freedom of the teens, to be loud, to be obnoxious, and yet, at the same time, to be practically invisible. She personally felt watched doing *anything*. Walking down the street, she felt judged by a thousand eyes. Closing her eyes now, she let the noise of the bus fill her mind. It was pleasant when you didn't resist. There was a fullness to the cacophony, a filling of the void inside her that felt settling. It made her almost miss her stop.

After she'd taken off her coat, she tried Mrs Rampersad again.

'Oh, you're up,' she said when the door swung open.

''Course I'm up,' Mrs Rampersad said, snatching back the tray. 'It's the middle of the afternoon, what do you take me for?' She was still wearing her bathrobe and slippers, however, Mrs Dixit noticed.

'Can I come in?'

Mrs Rampersad sniffed and turned, so Mrs Dixit took this as a sign she could.

They walked through the kitchen into the living room. The curtains were closed, and the TV was on silently – a game show. Mrs Rampersad flopped down onto the sofa and picked up the remote to raise the volume. Mrs Dixit sat in the armchair. She found it strange to be in the room above hers after all these years. She'd often wondered what it looked like. Now she was here, it seemed completely unexceptional.

Mrs Rampersad stared at the television. After a while, Mrs Dixit sat up and said, 'There's CCTV footage of the accident,' because really, it was her only news.

'Have you watched it?'

Mrs Dixit shook her head.

'Why not?'

'I don't need to see it. How would it help?' She looked at the TV again. 'There's the woman as well, the one who…'

'Does it show… you know? The impact?' asked Mrs Rampersad, leaning in.

'I don't think so. They've probably blurred it out.' But she wasn't sure, and this was one of the things that most scared her.

Mrs Dixit thought of her own living room below this one, the one she'd be returning to at any moment, and it surprised her how much the thought chilled her; even more, in some ways, than the CCTV footage.

But return she did. No sooner was she inside her own kitchen again than the phone rang.

'I've been ringing,' came her sister's voice, exasperated.

'I was out.'

'At the hospital?'

'At my neighbour's. A woman,' Mrs Dixit clarified quickly. She didn't want to add to those *rumblings*.

'Have you seen in the local paper? About the lady who died?'

'The doctor?'

'She was a podiatrist after all.'

'That's still a doctor.'

There was a pause, as if her sister was considering challenging this, but then thought better of it.

'The paper says she was in the passenger seat, so it's now on public record.'

'Well, she *was* a passenger,' Mrs Dixit responded curtly, knowing all too well what was to come.

'But sitting *beside* Naveem. What can it mean?'

'Sometimes passengers like to sit in the front,' said Mrs Dixit defensively.

'Why have a partition at all if the passengers are going to sit in *front*?' The way her sister said this made it sound almost vulgar.

'I really must start getting ready for the hosp—'

'I think you owe it to yourself to find out more.'

'*Owe it to myself?*' repeated Mrs Dixit incredulously.

'I'd want to know.'

'Know what?'

There was another pointed silence.

'The paper said there's to be a gathering for her…'

'I'm not going to some strange woman's funeral,' Mrs Dixit retorted loudly, and then, picturing Mrs Rampersad sitting directly above her, lowered her voice. 'This is Chomley, not some Hollywood movie…'

'Not her funeral, that's already happened. This is her memorial service at St Luke's. And it's open to the public.'

Mrs Dixit thought of the solemnity of the service, the stiff wooden pews, the smell of brass polish and damp, and cringed.

'I really must go,' she said. 'I have to visit Naveem.' *He's expecting me*, she nearly said, but of course he wasn't. 'Love to Henry.'

She was already putting the phone down when she heard her sister say:

'He's about to start karate classes…'

Oh well, whoops, Mrs Dixit thought, when the phone was safely back on its cradle.

That evening, returned from the hospital, and after a dinner of tomato soup and crackers, Mrs Dixit found herself once again standing outside her husband's study at the bottom of the basement stairs.

'It will need airing,' she said out loud, to no one in particular.

Turning the handle, Mrs Dixit pushed the door open a few inches. Quickly, she slipped her hand around the door frame to find the light cord. Her hand flicked it away by accident, so she had to wait for it to settle before trying again. The main light, when it did come on, was dim – Mr Dixit preferred special desk lamps when he was working on his trains.

Mrs Dixit pushed the door slightly wider, but still couldn't bring herself to step across the threshold. It *was* musty. She also caught the smell of metal and glue, a smell that was so *him*, it took her by surprise.

'Oh,' she said, ignoring the mustiness to breathe it in deeply.

At bedtime, she considered going to turn the study light off again but decided against it. Yes, it was a total waste of electricity – Mr Dixit would hate that – but for some reason it made her feel better knowing there was light in the room while she slept.

7 days since the accident

She was sitting next to his hospital bed the next day when she remembered about the study light still being on. Mrs Dixit reprimanded herself quietly.

The doctor had been explaining that Mr Dixit remained unchanged. *She* could have told him that.

When the nurse arrived, Mrs Dixit was fishing out a Fisherman's Friend mint lozenge from the packet.

'Have you spoken to him today?'

'The doctor? Yes, just now.'

'I mean your husband?'

Mrs Dixit experienced that bubble of resistance she'd always felt as a schoolchild when the teacher pressed her about some unfinished homework.

'I'm doing my best,' she said.

'I know you are.' The nurse smiled commiseratingly.

*

Mrs Rampersad's door swung open.

'Alright, alright! Where's the fire at?'

'Tomorrow…' said Mrs Dixit, still trying to catch her breath from the brisk walk from the bus stop. 'Could you drive me…'

'Can't tomorrow. I'm helping at my Bible Group.'

'Oh, of course.'

'Where were you planning on going?'

'Nowhere. It's not important.'

'You making a trip to that woman's service? No good would come of it. Let lying dogs sleep.'

'I wasn't…' but Mrs Dixit felt caught out. 'I need to *do* something.'

'Come and help at my group. We're giving out flyers on the high street.'

Mrs Dixit shook her head.

'I need to get out of Chomley.'

'No time for a holiday when your husband needs you.'

'But that's just it, he doesn't.'

'Needs you more than you realise.'

'How would you know?'

'I was married too. I know what it is to be with someone in sickness and in health.'

'Oh…' Mrs Dixit realised she didn't know very much about her neighbour, except what could be gleaned by the writing on her mail, and rare visits to her flat. 'Did he…?'

'He's alive, worse luck.' Mrs Rampersad gave a throaty chuckle. 'Fortunately, the Lord granted me a divorce long ago.'

'I see,' said Mrs Dixit. 'Thanks again, for all the driving. I hope you don't think I'm using you as a taxi service.'

'Makes no difference to me, as long as you help pay for petrol. Makes a change.'

'What does?'

'Speaking to you. I think this is one of the longest conversations we've ever had. I thought you both had it in for me. My calypso music being too loud. You'd blacklisted me.' She laughed.

Mrs Dixit shook her head in mock surprise, trying to hide the fact it was mostly true.

It was only when she was downstairs again that Mrs Dixit realised Mrs Rampersad had said 'let lying dogs sleep' and she'd not corrected her.

Later, she wasn't sure what to wear. Mrs Dixit knew how to dress in Chomley, or when she accompanied her husband on trips, such as to the Westfield in Stratford. But what did she wear on longer journeys by herself? She remembered her sister's words then: *was he ever… you know… controlling?* No, they'd simply made a protective bubble together. Inside the bubble, you could be as free as you liked. Within reason.

In the end, she wore her most basic navy coat, buttoned up to the neck. She wore a hat and scarf with a black and white houndstooth pattern. She also carried her handbag with the strongest straps in case someone tried to forcibly take it from her, most likely on a scooter. Here, she paused. Would it be better to take a handbag with weak straps? She didn't like the idea of being dragged behind a moving vehicle. She took the weaker-strapped bag instead.

Mrs Dixit took the bus to the tube station. She still didn't know where she was going ultimately, but she fancied Piccadilly Circus. She wanted to be lost in people. Feel the inky blackness pushed back by crowds.

At the tube turnstiles, she fumbled for her purse and her card dropped onto the ground. She picked it up again smartly, but the shock of it falling had jolted her: *where exactly was she going by herself?* Mrs Dixit thought of all the strange faces at Piccadilly Circus – they churned menacingly in her mind. What would Mr Dixit think, too? A poorly thought-out journey into the mania of Central London. He would not have approved. How she longed to go home, where it was safe.

It was then she remembered the light in the study was still on. That sealed the deal. She returned on the next bus.

Home brought no comfort. She'd been tricked, she realised, by her own sense of self-preservation. After she'd shut the front door, she went down and turned off the study room light. She was disappointed and muttered to herself tersely. 'Silly woman,' she said. 'Silly, weak-willed… hopeless!' Mrs Dixit could not stay here, would not. She checked her face in the bathroom mirror – it looked drawn and even more angled than normal, so she applied lipstick to distract and blush to soften her cheekbones. Then she put on her shoes again, picked up her bag and hurried out.

The policemen were waiting on the front step.

'I was about to knock,' the stouter one said. 'Glad we caught you.'

'Oh!' Mrs Dixit yelped – she'd had her head down and almost barged right into them.

'Didn't mean to startle you,' said the thinner one, although he looked as if he enjoyed it.

'I'm sorry,' Mrs Dixit replied, flustered.

'Where were you headed?'

'Um, well… probably to the hospital. I hadn't decided.'

'Your husband's not exactly going anywhere, I suppose.' The thin one laughed, and the fatter one shook his head in what seemed like exasperation. 'Can we come in?' he asked. 'We won't take a minute.'

'We have a question about the toxicology report.'

'What toxicology report?'

'Standard practice. It's usually for insurance reasons.'

'My husband isn't much of a drinker.'

The policemen looked at each other.

'There was no alcohol found in his blood. That's not the issue.'

It seemed the officers were trying to decide who should speak next. The heavier one took the plunge:

'Does your husband have a history of recreational drug use?'

'What, Naveem? *Drugs*? No,' Mrs Dixit shook her head in bewilderment. 'Actual drugs? He doesn't even like Horlicks anymore, because he says it keeps him up at night.'

'The thing is,' said the younger, thinner one, 'his tests showed some abnormalities.'

'Inhalants,' the fatter one said.

'What?'

'Huffing. Chroming. Sniffing.'

'That's street slang,' the thinner one clarified.

'*My husband does not do drugs*,' Mrs Dixit said perhaps too loudly.

The men glanced at each other as if to say, *poor dear*.

'Often the spouse or partner is unaware of the severity of the issue.'

'What issue?'

'Did your husband keep aerosols around?'

Mrs Dixit considered this.

'Not that I know of…'

The men nodded, as if this was what they expected.

'Often they'll buy them when they're out and do them right in the car,' the thinner one explained, the fatter one shaking his head ruefully. 'Did your husband spend a lot of time driving by himself?'

'He was a *taxi driver*,' Mrs Dixit almost shouted.

The men nodded again in sympathy.

'This must be quite a shock to you.'

'We can only imagine.'

'They can lead such normal lives, keep it from their loved ones.'

'Unless of course, something goes wrong.'

'Like a car accident,' added the other.

'Are you suggesting that Naveem…?'

'We're not suggesting anything at all, that's not our place. But it's fair to say we have some *concerns*.'

'*Troubling* concerns.'

'Is that why you're here today? To tell me how concerned you are?'

'We're here,' said the fatter one, straightening up, 'for a welfare check. Someone has suggested that you might… not be handling things… as best you could.'

'I'm handling things just fine,' Mrs Dixit said, flustered. 'Who told you I wasn't?'

'A concerned member of the public. To be frank, they were worried you might harm yourself.'

Mrs Dixit's mind raced. Not her sister, she wouldn't. *Who then? Ah…*

'His mother,' she said, tutting to herself.

'We are not at liberty.'

'What else did she say?'

'That your husband was possibly mistreated before the coma.'

'It's not an official statement,' the other officer clarified.

'By me, I suppose? That's ridiculous! I bet she told you I'm hysterical too. That's what she does, you know. She's toxic.' A new thought struck her. 'Have you told his mother about the inhalation… the drugs thing?' Mrs Dixit asked quickly.

'Yes, the other Mrs Dixit… Mrs Dixit senior… has been made aware of the situation.'

'What happens now?'

'Well,' they looked shiftily at each other again, 'maybe we can have a cup of tea?'

The policemen stayed for another half an hour, during which time they seemed to be trying to infer something, but Mrs Dixit wasn't sure precisely what. The thinner one asked to use the bathroom at one point, and she had the distinct impression that he might be going through the cabinet. Did they have to have a warrant to do that sort of thing, she wondered? Rummage.

When she came back from showing him to the bathroom, the larger officer was standing very near the cutlery drawer. Had he been going through the knives and forks? He did look shifty.

Eventually, still glancing around the house as if something or someone might burst out a cupboard at any moment, the policemen said their goodbyes, telling Mrs Dixit to call them if 'anything came up'.

After they'd left, Mrs Dixit picked up the phone to ring Naveem's mother, but she lost her nerve immediately. Nothing she could say would sway the woman's mind. Since their first meeting, Naveem's mother had considered the younger Mrs Dixit a threat, spinning whatever story she needed to undermine their marriage. Why should she be any different now?

The ward smelled like vomit. Mrs Dixit tried to ignore it, but it almost made her retch. The nurse came in, not the smiley nurse, or the curly haired one, but the one Mrs Dixit thought of as kind but serious. The nurse didn't mention the smell, and neither did Mrs Dixit. She wondered if you got used to scents like this, working at a hospital. But no, you could never get used to something like that, she decided. Could her husband smell it? Mrs Dixit watched him for a moment. His mouth was slightly ajar.

When the nurse left, Mrs Dixit moved closer to his bed. She placed her hands on Naveem's cheeks. The skin was hotter than she expected, and oily, as if he'd been sprayed with a clammy protective covering. She slid her fingers towards his nose, bunching the waxy skin on his cheeks and making his lips pout comically, grotesquely, letting them go as soon as she realised what she'd done. She did not step away though, not yet. Instead, she slowly hovered both hands near his eyelids, resisting the fear he might sense her presence and grab her by the wrists. She needed to see his eyes, it was a physical compulsion, she almost wasn't in control anymore – dark brown, yes, but what kind of dark brown? Were his eyes a uniform colour, or faceted with green, with grey, or even specks of gold? Carefully, she placed the tips of her fingers on his lower and upper lids, and gently prised them open. There was nothing, only a terrible white blindness. She gasped, taking a step back. The moment she did so, the answer came to her, making her feel ridiculous. His eyes were just the same, they'd simply turned backwards, rolled in their sockets. For a split second, she considered how she might encourage them forward – without hurting him of course – until she finally understood she'd gone too far.

She thought about going somewhere for dinner by herself, but the slight nausea as a result of the hospital smell had dulled any appetite.

Later, in bed, she couldn't sleep. Mrs Dixit had always prided herself on not taking up too much space. She was a small woman, and it was a large mattress – when Mr Dixit shared it with her, they barely ever touched. It was a sign of respect, allowing each other space. Tonight though, the mattress felt too big. Formidably so. She pulled the blankets up and wrapped them under her feet, so she was snugger, but it didn't feel snug, it felt messy. Mrs Dixit turned on the lamp and made the bed again. It was strange to slip into freshly made sheets, with the bed warm, as if some other person had been there only moments before. She lay in her bed, which suddenly didn't feel like hers anymore, as if the true owner would return and find Mrs Dixit lying there, and she realised this was exactly the kind of strange thinking the policemen would have been concerned about on their welfare check earlier.

Sighing, she took the notebook and pen from her bedside table and stared at the blank page. After much deliberation, she wrote down 'Camden Market' but crossed it out immediately, before turning the lamp off again and trying once more to sleep.

8 days since the accident

The next morning – it was a Leap Day, in fact – Mrs Dixit was guiltily trying to guess her husband's laptop password for the third time, when there was a knock at the door.

Mrs Rampersad stood in the hallway, jingling her car keys in the air. 'Where to?'

'Oh,' exclaimed Mrs Dixit, pleased, before remembering her manners. 'How did it go yesterday on the high street?'

Grunting, Mrs Rampersad shook her head.

'No one takes initiative anymore. If you do, you're branded *pushy*. Pushy? I don't want to be like those Jehovah's Witnesses, lurking outside train stations. If I'm gonna flyer, I'm gonna flyer, you know what I mean?' Mrs Dixit imagined what she'd do if she was walking down the high street and Mrs Rampersad tried to make her take a flyer. Probably dash into a shop until the coast was clear. 'People don't know what's good for them!'

Mrs Rampersad kept her boxes of flyers stacked in the shared hallway, much to Mr Dixit's constant annoyance. Mrs Dixit would always take a peek. *'On the wicked, God will rain coals of fire and sulphur! Psalm 11:6–7' 'You will never succeed in life if you try to hide your sins! Proverbs 28:13' 'Even the Demons believe–and shudder! James 2:19'*. Not exactly crowd-pleasing stuff, especially with the accompanying poorly photoshopped images of pitchforks and brimstone.

'Maybe we can take some flyers with us today,' offered Mrs Dixit generously, even though it was against her best impulse. 'We can leave them wherever we end up?'

'I suppose so,' Mrs Rampersad considered this carefully. 'Sinners *are* everywhere…'

'Perfect,' replied Mrs Dixit. 'I'll just go and get my coat.'

Mrs Rampersad closed the car door.

'Where are we going then?' she asked, breathing heavily as she organised her scarf around her neck and the swathes of dress fabric around her legs.

Mrs Dixit took out a piece of paper from her pocket and scanned it.

'I haven't fully decided,' she explained nervously.

Mrs Rampersad snatched the sheet of paper from her.

'Camden Market,' she read, raising her eyebrows. Under where it had been crossed out, Mrs Dixit had written it again this morning.

'If it's too far…?'

'Why do you wanna go there?'

'I'm not sure,' Mrs Dixit replied. 'I haven't been in years.'

Mrs Rampersad narrowed her eyes.

'We'll need to stop for petrol.'

'Of course, I have money.' Mrs Dixit patted her purse.

And with that, they set off.

'He ever… you know?' Mrs Rampersad asked, as they pulled away from the petrol station with a full tank.

Mrs Dixit shook her head, not understanding.

Making a fist, Mrs Rampersad punched the air.

'No!' Mrs Dixit said, horrified. 'He never touched me!'

'More common than you think,' Mrs Rampersad said, sniffing. 'Especially where I'm from.'

'In Trinidad?'

'No, Essex. I moved over from Trinidad when I was eight.'

'When did you… separate from your husband?'

'Fifteen years ago, thank the Lord.'

'Was he abusive?'

'Him? Never lifted a finger against anyone. Never lifted a finger at all. My husband was the laziest man I've ever met. He didn't want a wife, he wanted a second mother. One's enough. Two is greedy.'

'Where is he now?'

'Hopefully locked up somewhere. Good riddance.'

'You don't know for sure? But he's the father of your children!'

'He didn't behave like no father. A devil would take him over – that's the only explanation. He was too lazy to pick up his own shoes and yet come the evening, he'd be on me, humping away.'

Mrs Dixit wrinkled her face. They'd overstepped a mark, things had become too personal. Her husband would have thought exactly the same. She regretted their conversation and mentally willed it to stop.

'A devil indeed,' Mrs Rampersad muttered again, as she indicated left.

Parking was an issue. In the end, they left the car in a nearby supermarket car park, which made Mrs Dixit nervous.

'I can come back in an hour and move it,' Mrs Rampersad said, nonplussed, shovelling a wad of flyers into her bag.

Mrs Dixit wasn't sure where the markets *began*. North London's Camden was much busier than Chomley, even mid-morning on a weekday. Eventually, they found themselves on what felt like the main road, following a stream of people wrapped up in winter coats. It had rained overnight, and there were puddles in the gutters and a feeling of damp amid all the bustle.

Mrs Rampersad would pause whenever she came across someone handing out a flyer, observing their technique at a safe distance. This annoyed Mrs Dixit, who was keen to get on, but she stood by her neighbour and watched too.

One scraggly young man would thrust the flyers towards passers-by at groin level. People were caught unawares, so would take the flyer from him before they'd realised what they'd done. Often though, they'd drop them again a few steps later, a sight that made Mrs Rampersad grimace in sympathy.

'Monsters,' she murmured to herself.

Another youth, with a prominent neck tattoo of intertwined snakes, would try and strike up a conversation with his mark, smiling, teeth bared, the flyer seemingly an afterthought. Yet another held out the flyers statically, as if waiting for his relay team member to arrive and whisk the flyer off, his attention mostly on young women's behinds. Mrs Dixit had to do her best to keep Mrs Rampersad from marching up and telling him to mind his manners.

*

Camden Market proper, when they finally reached it, seemed to be mostly food and T-shirt stalls. The smell of sweet and sour sauce, vinegar, and fried oil permeated everything, as people jostled in or out of the catacombs.

'Where's a map?' asked Mrs Rampersad, looking around as if one would magically appear.

'Let's walk,' suggested Mrs Dixit. Her hands began to get painfully cold if she stood still too long.

Mrs Rampersad shrugged and started down one of the thoroughfares, her body lurching somewhat from the weight of the flyers in her bag.

'It's changed,' Mrs Dixit said. 'I remember it was all punk when I was here last.'

Mrs Rampersad grunted. Her lurch was becoming more and more pronounced.

'They'll take flyers about buying tattoos and burgers,' she said, obviously still hung up on what she'd witnessed before, 'but you can't *give away* personal salvation!'

'People do like burgers,' Mrs Dixit replied, starting to feel a little hungry herself.

They rounded another corner, and anxiety started to creep in. Whatever Mrs Dixit had come to find, it was still hidden. She imagined the impending drive home, the sense of failure, the visit to Mr Dixit later, where she would stew silently, until a nice nurse would say something to make her feel even more inadequate.

They stumbled upon a busy courtyard with food stalls and people sitting around eating on rain-soaked picnic tables.

'Let's go in here,' said Mrs Rampersad suddenly, pulling Mrs Dixit into a shop that was playing impressively loud dance music.

A girl, in what Mrs Dixit could only describe as 'space-aged' clothing, greeted them. It was not exactly clear what this shop was selling. Loud dance music? Futuristic clothing? On the sparse shelves there was a collection of random items – a backpack in neon colours with the googly eyes of a puppet, a display of Slinkys (Mrs Dixit hadn't seen one of those in *years*) and other strange bits and bobs. Most peculiar were the dancers – two girls above them in cages, gyrating their hips to the thumping music.

'Downstairs,' Mrs Rampersad called over the din, nodding towards an inexplicable escalator in the middle of the shop. Finding themselves in the basement, Mrs Dixit discovered it was the futuristic clothing the store mainly sold – possibly to wear on nights out clubbing? Mrs Dixit walked around the racks, inspecting the outfits that looked most outlandish. Puffed shoulders in mother-of-pearl, glittered sleeves, crop tops in PVC. The music pulsated all around her. Over in the corner, she watched as Mrs Rampersad left a hefty pile of flyers beside the ones for club nights and raves.

The music swelled, deafening, the bass rattling her bones, making her teeth feel funny. Mrs Dixit was about to head back up the escalator to escape the noise when something clicked inside her. *Here it is*, she thought, *this is what I was searching for*. More than the loud sounds, the bright colours – it was the strangeness of it all. The otherness. The anywhere but Mrs Dixit at home by herself, as her husband lay helpless.

She started to laugh.

Mrs Dixit felt guilty instantly, especially when she imagined what Mr Dixit would have made of the whole scenario. 'Looking for trouble', he'd have called it – which meant doing things the hard way, the unsafe way, the path less than optimal. What was the optimal way of doing things now, though? If only someone could tell her.

On the ride back to Chomley, Mrs Dixit couldn't be coaxed into any sort of conversation, so Mrs Rampersad carried it on by herself, commenting on the traffic, especially on reckless male drivers, muttering 'Heaven's be!' whenever one swerved into her path.

*

Mrs Rampersad dropped her straight at the hospital. Without her usual dithering at the café or the shop, Mrs Dixit arrived by her husband's bed, feeling relieved when she saw his familiar form. The other men in the ward were all sleeping or unconscious. It gave her the impression that they were in a dorm room, and a bell would be rung, and they would all start, waking up. She'd imagined bringing a bell, a big brass one, and clanging it loudly just to see.

Today, she watched Mr Dixit with mounting concern. Why wasn't he getting better? How could the doctors not tell her anything useful? Her mind kept flashing back to the Camden shop like a guilty secret. The noise, though, the sense of place and urgency. She understood why young people might want to wear those gaudy clothes and stand in a room filled with that obnoxious music. It helped fill the sad spaces between things, a kind of *exorcism*. She smiled, thinking Mrs Rampersad might enjoy that comparison, but caught herself. There would be no more inappropriate laughing today...

Mrs Dixit shivered, and pulled her least favourite Marks & Spencer's cardigan around her.

A nurse came in, checking one of the other patients, and Mrs Dixit pretended she was writing a message on her phone, so she didn't have to interact beyond a polite head nod. When the nurse left again, Mrs Dixit checked the time on her phone: she'd been there less than twelve minutes.

From somewhere in the room, she heard the sound of a whoopee cushion, or air escaping a rubber tyre. Or an old, unconscious man passing wind. It squealed extravagantly, luxuriously, before the room returned to silence. Mrs Dixit took one look around her and burst into peals of laughter. Not one man budged an eyelid.

*

She had to go to the bathroom to compose herself. Mrs Dixit was still sporadically laughing as she looked into the mirror to wipe her eyes with a tissue.

Returning to her husband's bed, she felt lighter. She took a deep breath, and wondered if she would laugh again, realising she was all laughed out.

'I went to Camden Market,' she said just loud enough for him to hear. 'Do you remember going there together? It's changed. Everyone still has weird piercings and tattoos, but it's mostly tourists now. I can't remember if you enjoyed it when we went there last, you've never been fond of markets. Always blocking up your routes, you'd say. Why close down a perfectly good road for some old stalls?' Her lips flickered with a smile. 'Why did we go to Camden all those years ago? I suppose it's because people don't look at you in a crowd. We could be invisible together, holding hands.'

She picked up his now and stroked it. 'Why *did* we go?' Mrs Dixit cocked her head, trying hard to remember. 'To look for records, I suppose.' This thought, although likely true, disappointed her. But then a flash of memory hit her. They were walking, hand in hand, when he stopped pointedly, to kiss her. On a bridge. Crossing the Camden Lock.

'You wanted to kiss me on a bridge,' Mrs Dixit said in a hushed, almost reverential whisper.

At home, she cooked herself some cod she'd defrosted from the freezer, and then opened all the windows to let out the trapped smell of fish. The fresh air was bracing.

She thought about the woman, the doctor in her husband's passenger seat, and closed the windows again quickly.

*

Just before bed, she opened the stack of mail that had accumulated over the past week. There was one large packet, which looked ominous. It was from the insurance company. They had reviewed the Dixits' account, but unfortunately Mr Dixit had not been keeping up with the payments, and so they would not be able to offer anything more. Their condolences. The letter was very official and final. Mrs Dixit stared at the sheet of paper. They must have made a mistake. Her husband was always so diligent with payments. She would call them first thing, although the thought filled her with dread.

In the middle of the night, she awoke thinking she could hear a noise, but possibly having dreamt it. She tiptoed out and checked the other rooms, but all was fine. After drinking a glass of water, she went to the utility cupboard, where they kept their tools, a stepladder and the drying racks. She took everything out, but there were no cans of solvents hidden in there, of course. She checked the back of the cupboard, feeling into the space that was too dark to see. Nothing. Mrs Dixit put everything back, shaking her head.

'Drugs,' she said, tutting to herself and closing the cupboard door, feeling vindicated.

9 days since the accident

In the morning, her sister rang.

'You sound tired,' she said.

'I barely slept,' Mrs Dixit replied.

'Everything must be wearing on you very hard.' Mrs Dixit thought back to the clothing store yesterday and felt a hot pang of remorse. 'Maybe we can go and have an afternoon out together?' her sister continued. 'Get a mani-pedi? My treat?'

'I don't think that would be appropriate in the circumstances.' Mrs Dixit felt another smaller jolt of remorse at saying no. 'Another time, though,' she lied.

'Of course.' Her sister was not able to disguise her relief. 'Did you see about the memorial service? Over a hundred people, the paper said, a lot of them her patients.'

'Mmm-hmm,' Mrs Dixit said, her stomach growling.

'She was married, and they had a daughter. It's such a tragedy.'

'So very sad,' Mrs Dixit said, tight-lipped.

'Maybe you could contact the husband? I'm sure he'd appreciate you reaching out.'

'Not after the media circus he's been through, no doubt. Poor man.'

'Have you spoken to any journalists?'

'Why would I?'

'Human interest story, about your plight?'

'My plight?'

'Might get you in one of the women's magazines. You should think about it.'

Mrs Dixit thought about warning her sister that if she spoke to a journalist, she'd never talk to her again, but she stayed silent.

'I have to go have breakfast,' she explained. 'Give my love to Hen…'

'Actually, Henry's here and he would like to say hello.'

Mrs Dixit felt tension in her chest, as if threaded strings around her ribcage had been tugged tighter.

'Hi,' came the high-pitched voice of her nephew, before she could protest. His voice triggered long dormant thoughts about her own children, how they might sound, or look, how they might behave in this world, when she still had hopes of having them.

'Hello,' Mrs Dixit replied, feeling cornered. 'How are you, Henry?'

'Good.'

There was a long, uncomfortable silence.

'How's school?'

Another interminable pause.

'Good.'

'Are you enjoying your karate class?'

'Sort of.'

More dead air.

'Can you put your mummy back on for me, Henry?'

'He's shy,' her sister began. 'He takes after you. That's why…'

'Must run,' said Mrs Dixit, putting the phone down quickly.

To punish herself for being so rude to her sister, she decided to do a deep clean.

Taking out her bucket with her yellow gloves from under the kitchen sink, Mrs Dixit attacked the kitchen, before blitzing the shower, bath, and toilet. By midday, every surface was gleaming, and she felt exhausted, but there was still the vacuuming to do, and she thought it was most orderly to start from the basement and work up. Once she'd carried the hoover down the stairs, however, she stood tentatively at the study door. Usually, Mr Dixit cleaned it himself, using only the mini hand-held vacuum so as not to disturb the trains and throw up unwanted dust particles. Would he object to her using the bigger machine? Still undecided, Mrs Dixit plugged the vacuum in at the wall and turned it on. The sound was courage-building. She didn't quite burst open the door, but opening it with some vigour, she quickly turned on the lights, and pulled the noisy machine through the doorway after her.

She'd only vacuumed a few feet when she looked up from the carpet, and noticed the main table. The contents were obscured by sheets of carboard, seemingly to protect what lay underneath. Mrs Dixit turned off the vacuum cleaner with the heel of her foot and stood before the cardboard layers. Carefully, she lifted off the closest panel. She gasped. Beneath, lay Chomley – a miniature version, but complex. There were tiny people, and a tiny park, with a tiny dog running on a leash. There were tiny trees, and shops, and the station, the tracks running through the town centre and around its circumference. There was so much detail, and it fascinated and worried Mrs Dixit in equal measures. When did he have the time? Whenever she was napping, or reading, or cooking, or ironing or went to bed early, of course – all the moments he could steal away without her noticing, which was often. Mr Dixit was careful never to seem too eager, but she'd always known on some level that this was where he most wanted to be. But to repair model trains, not to create… this… this piece of *art*.

Why hadn't he shown her his work? Didn't he trust her? Did he think she would mock him? It was beautiful! She felt frustration then, and an anger coiling around her spine, and Mrs Dixit was afraid she might smash something with her fists, so she trundled the vacuum cleaner out of the study quick smart, before any mishap could happen.

She was still in a foul mood by the time she arrived at the hospital. Restlessly, she sat next to her husband.

'The whole of Chomley…' she muttered under her breath.

'What?' came a man's croaky voice, startling her. She looked around nervously. All the patients were in their beds, seemingly asleep. Maybe she'd imagined it, or the noise had come from the hallway?

'Is there anyone… listening?' she asked uncertainly.

'We're all listening,' came the voice again, making Mrs Dixit jolt.

It came from the bed opposite; she was almost certain. He was sitting more upright than the others, with his hands on his chest as if he had closed his eyes for forty winks, rather than being unresponsively unconscious.

'What did you say?' she asked, watching for a reaction, but there was no tell-tale movement. 'I can see you,' she said, more loudly, emboldened.

Still nothing.

Mrs Dixit had to fight the urge to throw one of her shoes.

Later, at the nurses' station, she explained what had happened.

'Maybe a patient woke up?'

'Possibly.' The nurse, the Filipino one, looked doubtful. 'It could have been a groan? Are you sure he definitely spoke?'

'Yes, I am. In bed three. He said they were all listening.'

'Well, they can, you know. That's why it's so important that you…'

'Yes, yes, I know,' Mrs Dixit said impatiently, 'but what if he needs help? Locked-in syndrome or something?'

'Mr Klimt's vitals show no brain activity. He is in a vegetative state.'

'A vegetative state,' Mrs Dixit repeated.

'Which means he couldn't have spoken. Maybe it was someone in the corridor?'

'They'd have to be a ventriloquist, the way they threw their voice.'

The nurse took a deep fortifying breath. She was only a tiny thing, even smaller than Mrs Dixit.

'You know, it can be very lonely when your partner is in a coma. The mind can play all sorts of tricks. It's very natural. Are you getting out and seeing people? Friends and family?'

She thought of Camden then – a model Camden, with tiny food stalls, and tiny punks, tiny beer cans, and a tiny kissing bridge over a lock.

'I did hear him speak,' Mrs Dixit said contritely.

The nurse looked at her with a mixture of pity and disguised annoyance.

'If it happens again, let me know.'

They both gave tight-lipped smiles to each other.

She couldn't bring herself to open the front door when she arrived home. She stood with her keys in the lock, waiting for… *something*. Perhaps she could go to a restaurant by herself? She could choose anywhere, even spicy food, which Mr Dixit always avoided. But then she imagined being seated by herself, fending off the pitying looks from the other customers, having to wave down the waiter for more water – and the idea became repellent.

There was a loud noise upstairs, a clunk, and Mrs Dixit was relieved to be snapped out of her thoughts.

She went straight upstairs to her neighbour's flat. When Mrs Rampersad opened her door, she appeared flustered, her face beaded with sweat, her mouth full, so it took a few seconds of chewing before she could speak.

'I was wondering what to do about dinner,' Mrs Dixit said in the interim, 'I had some silly idea about inviting you to go eat somewhere, but I can see you've already cooked and I've interrupted you, I'm sorry.' She felt embarrassed; what if Mrs Rampersad thought she was fishing for an invite?

'I have church group tonight,' said Mrs Rampersad once she'd swallowed her mouthful. The smells of chicken, onions and spices wafted out of the kitchen. It made Mrs Dixit's mouth water.

'Oh, here?'

'Why not?'

'I didn't think you'd all fit.'

'What's that supposed to mean?' Mrs Rampersad was stony-faced.

'Around the table, I mean. That you'd have enough placings. I wasn't implying your kitchen is small. Or the church group is too big.' Mrs Dixit had begun to sweat too. 'If you need any extra plates or cutlery, let me know.'

'I'm fine.'

Mrs Dixit nodded, about to go. She noticed something then, behind Mrs Rampersad, on the table. A red candle. Next to a bottle of what looked like wine. And there were only two table settings. Was that crooning jazz she could hear?

Mrs Rampersad turned to see what had drawn Mrs Dixit's eye.

'Oh,' she started, as if she'd been caught out.

'Enjoy your... church group,' Mrs Dixit said, poker-faced.

'Yes... you see... we have...'

Mrs Dixit began to leave, miming tiptoeing down the hall.

'We're discussing Ecclesiastes...' Mrs Rampersad called after her.

'Ecclesiastes,' Mrs Dixit tittered to herself, as she continued down the stairs.

Eavesdropping kept her busy all evening. At 7 p.m., the front doorbell rang, and Mrs Dixit heard the shifting weight on the floorboards as Mrs Rampersad buzzed her guest in. The man (it was a man's laboured breathing) slowly climbed the stairs. Inside Mrs Rampersad's home, there was more squeaking of floorboards and then silence, broken occasionally by the squeal of chairs. Nine and ten came and went, with no one leaving. Mrs Dixit was practically giggling to herself, until she remembered that her neighbour's bedroom was directly above her own, and *those* noises she could do without. Fortunately, at 11 p.m., there was more squeaking and shuffling, and the deliberate sound of someone descending the stairs and the final clank of the front door as it was pulled shut on its lock. Mrs Dixit, already in bed, rolled her eyes to the heavens, and smiled.

10 days since the accident

She overslept. The phone roused her.

'Wendy Dixit?'

'Yes?'

'This is Shelly Marshall.' There was a pause, as if the caller was waiting for this to all make sense. When it didn't, the woman continued: 'I'm Penny Marshall's daughter?'

'I'm sorry, who?'

An intake of air.

'My mother was in your husband's taxi. During the accident. She…'

'Oh, yes! I'm so sorry about your mother.'

Shelly's voice grew softer. 'Thank you. I hope you don't mind me calling. I spoke to your mother-in-law, and she was kind enough to give me your details.'

'Naveem's mother gave you my number?'

'I wanted to tell you how sorry I am, about your husband.'

'Thank you, but it's nothing compared to what you've been through, I'm sure.'

'We've both lost people we love.'

Yes, but only temporarily in my case, Mrs Dixit wanted to say. This distinction was important to her, she realised. A phrase wafted back from her subconscious: 'vegetative state'. It made her think briefly of an old painting, where the face was made out of many different types of fruits and vegetables, a pear for the nose, cherries for lips, a cob of corn for the ear – and how Mr Dixit would hate the comparison…

'I wondered if you would like to meet for a coffee?' Shelly asked. 'We're linked in this strange way, and I thought it might…'

'I'm afraid I don't think that's possible, my husband is still in hospital, and I'm very busy with all the arrangements…' She felt guilty the moment she uttered these words. This poor girl had lost her *mother*.

'Okay.' The phone went silent.

'Again, I'm very sorry for your loss…'

'Have you watched the CCTV footage?'

'What?'

'The video that was released by the police…'

Mrs Dixit clenched her jaw.

'No, I haven't yet. How did you get Naveem's parents' number?' she asked, wanting to change the subject.

'I looked it up in the phone book. You're not listed,' Shelly added. Mr Dixit never wanted them to be added: 'creates more problems than it solves' had been his ruling.

'What did Naveem's mother say when you called?'

'She told me…' Shelly hesitated. 'She said sometimes she wished he'd died in the accident. That it would have made some things easier.' *How could his mother* say *that?* thought Mrs Dixit. *And to someone who'd just lost their parent?* She clenched her jaw so tightly, her teeth squeaked. 'And that she was worried about the level of care at the hospital – how they treat Asian patients like second-class citizens.'

'That's not true. Most of the doctors are Asian, anyway. Naveem *will* wake up, too. And once he does, we'll continue on.'

'That sounds nice,' Shelly said flatly. 'I'm sorry to bother you. I just thought if…'

'I can take your number,' Mrs Dixit offered, mostly so she wouldn't feel bad afterwards – writing it down on the pad next to the phone. Shelly also gave her work number at the DVSA, the local Driver and Vehicle Standards Agency.

'Goodbye then.'

After Mrs Dixit put the phone down, she hugged her arms around herself. It was as if a ghost had walked over her grave.

She sat down at the desktop computer in the alcove. Mrs Dixit did most of her internet browsing on her iPad, and rarely used the bigger machine. She didn't like the mouse in particular, she kept losing the cursor. As she waited for it to boot up, Mrs Dixit cleaned the keyboard with one of the cotton buds she kept in the desk drawer for just such an occasion. Once the computer was fully awake and operational, she brought up the browser window and searched for 'Chomley police website'. It took many attempts to find the right page, going round in circles until she struck on one that read: 'We Need Your Help'. There were four videos, two of fly-tipping suspects, one of the infamous cat burglar who was still at large, and one... she stopped short, hovering the mouse arrow over the video. There were two people sitting in a car. Naveem's taxi. It was grainy, but not so much she couldn't make out her own husband. It was definitely a woman sitting beside him, one with dark wavy hair.

In several rapid, ungraceful movements, Mrs Dixit managed to close down the browser and quickly shut off the computer completely.

Moments later, back in the kitchen and with no warning, she was sick in the sink. That wasn't altogether true – nothing of much substance came up – but after she had finished retching, Mrs Dixit sprayed everything down with bleach.

She was interrupted in her disinfecting by a knock at her door. Mrs Dixit quickly washed her face and dried it with the tea towel before answering – it was Mrs Rampersad, of course. Her neighbour nodded when she saw Mrs Dixit's watery eyes, as if this confirmed everything.

'I thought so,' she said. 'Tell me then, do *you* hear everything that comes through *my* floor?'

'Pretty much,' replied Mrs Dixit, too caught off guard to lie.

Mrs Rampersad took this information in gravely. 'They don't make houses fit for purpose in this country. Cardboard floors. People stacked on top of each other. Doesn't help you're like a church mouse down here.'

'The washing machine can be a bit noisy,' Mrs Dixit offered. Mrs Rampersad shook her head as if this didn't count. 'What about your complaints about Naveem's bossa nova?'

'That wasn't about the noise, it was the principle of the thing.' Mrs Rampersad sniffed. 'Like church mice, the both of you.'

It was true, the Dixits always tried to be considerate. Mr Dixit had mostly played his records in his study. They turned down the television low in the evenings, put on subtitles and whispered after nine, and rarely, if ever, had guests. They were proud of their conscientiousness, and judgemental of everyone else's apparent lack.

Mrs Dixit's eyes were still running.

'What's wrong with you?' Mrs Rampersad demanded. 'Is it food poisoning?'

'Perhaps,' Mrs Dixit said, sniffling. 'I think I need to get out of the house.'

'Art galleries, markets… Where to this time?'

Without hesitation, Mrs Dixit answered: 'Somewhere loud. The loudest place you can think of.'

'Why loud?'

'I don't know exactly…' Mrs Dixit stammered. She felt foolish asking now. 'I want to take my mind off my mind, I suppose. Drown out my thoughts.'

Mrs Rampersad raised a finger.

'I know just the place.'

As they were getting into the car, Mrs Rampersad asked: 'You bring money for petrol?'

Mrs Dixit patted her bag, and happy with that, her neighbour heaved herself into the front seat.

'Does the Bible ever mention God as being a noise?' Mrs Dixit asked timidly.

Mrs Rampersad looked thoughtful. '"I am the vine",' she quoted. '"I am the door." "This bread is my body; this wine is my blood." No, nothing about noise,' she decided, slamming the car door shut.

'Where are we going?' asked Mrs Dixit after they'd been driving south for ten minutes.

'Wait and see,' came the response.

'How was the church group?' Mrs Dixit was surprised to find she'd asked such a loaded question. There was no mischief in her tone, even if she couldn't help a small smile at the memory of the night before.

Mrs Rampersad kept her eyes firmly on the road.

'We were going over church matters, so the Lord would look kindly on us.'

'Seemed quite a feast you cooked.'

'It's right to be well fed when doing Jesus's work.'

'I'm sure.'

'You should eat more, fatten yourself up.' Mrs Dixit shuffled in the seat. She was self-conscious about her weight, or lack of it. 'I'll bring over some leftovers when we get home.'

'There's no need, really.'

'Chauffeur you around. Give you food off my plate. It's the Christian thing to do…'

That's a warning, Mrs Dixit thought, *I should let her have a private life and not tease.* She was being ungrateful after all the help she'd received from Mrs Rampersad, she decided, so she was quiet the rest of the journey.

'To the airport?' spluttered Mrs Dixit, as they approached, breaking her silence. She hated airports – well, hated them by proxy, because Mr Dixit had loathed them ever since *the incident*.

'You asked!' Mrs Rampersad bristled. 'Take me somewhere loud, you said.'

Mrs Dixit's stomach tensed, and she raised a hand reflexively to her jaw. They did not drive up to the terminal, however, taking another smaller road instead, which brought them to an area overlooking the runways. There were already a few other parked cars, and they reversed into an empty space alongside them.

'What are we…?'

'Hush, woman.' Mrs Rampersad nodded towards a plane that was at the end of the runway.

Suddenly, the plane accelerated. The noise was overwhelming, even within the confines of the car, the whining roar reminding Mrs Dixit of old war films her father used to like. As she watched, the plane tipped up, the front wheels lifted, and it felt like every bone in her body was vibrating, as if her skeleton would rattle out of her skin. This… this was exactly it, she realised now – to be rent apart, even momentarily, by noise and energy and the promise of heat, for whatever constituted her 'self' to be given as fuel to send this… this machine hurtling upwards. What Mrs Dixit hoped for most – and she was brave enough now, embraced by the deafening noise – was a miracle. To dislodge whatever was holding Mr Dixit back, for him to be forcibly shaken awake.

Most of all, for Naveem to have missed her, in at least a few of the strange ways she was missing him. Oh, for him to understand!

As the plane sped away, Mrs Dixit realised she was breathing so heavily she was almost hyperventilating, her hands clenched into tight fists.

'I always think of them like angels, soaring up to meet God,' Mrs Rampersad said, lifting her chin, an uncharacteristically tranquil look on her face.

'I need to get out,' replied Mrs Dixit, as she frantically unbuckled her seatbelt and fled from the car.

Outside, she felt better – the air crisp in her lungs, grass and mud under her feet – but also strangely exposed, as if at any moment a plane might descend on her head. Because of this, Mrs Dixit stooped slightly, as if walking under a low ceiling or trying to avoid gunfire, making her way over to the fence that protected the runway.

'Enjoying the view?' came a man's voice behind her, making her yelp in surprise. 'Oh, I'm sorry,' the stranger said with a sanguine bob on his toes, but Mrs Dixit did not think he seemed completely sorry. He was probably a good ten years older than her, handsome in a weather-beaten way, and wore a moustache and long, thinnish grey hair scraped back. His silver cufflinks caught the light whenever they peeked out of the sleeves of the baggy tweed coat, and he smelled of some long out-of-fashion cologne.

'It's my first time,' Mrs Dixit explained, once she'd collected herself.

'Oh, really. We'll have to be kind then,' he winked. 'I'm Magnus.'

'Hello, Magnus,' she shook his hand formally. 'Do you come here often?' she said, instantly regretting having stumbled into this cliché.

Magnus glanced back at the parked cars, and narrowed his eyes. 'As often as I can get away,' he said, still scanning the vehicles. On his finger was a gold wedding band, she noticed. 'I find I do my best thinking here.'

'Are they all as loud?' asked Mrs Dixit, nodding towards the runway. She didn't exactly mean this as a serious question, but he considered it carefully.

'Most of them, yes. It depends on the size of the plane. When you come here long enough, you can tell the make and model as soon as they start to taxi. That one there is a BA Cityflyer Embraer 170 to Edinburgh.'

'Fascinating,' Mrs Dixit said, but she was already thinking of a way to politely end the conversation and get back into the relative warmth of the car – relative because Mrs Rampersad was unwilling to turn the heating on, even though Mrs Dixit had offered to pay a greater share of petrol.

'Did you know, the world's largest aeroplane weighs over six hundred tons?' Magnus said, and Mrs Dixit feigned being impressed. 'To have that hurtling into the atmosphere, surely it's one of the greatest feats of human accomplishment.'

'I always think it's sad about what happened to the Concorde,' Mrs Dixit replied, offhandedly.

Magnus looked at her strangely. 'What did you say?'

'Concordes, how they took them all out of commission. I know there was an accident but there are plane crashes all the time and they don't stop those from flying.'

He stared at her, his face glowing with astonishment.

'You're absolutely right,' Magnus replied, and she could see there were tears starting to well up in his eyes.

'Anyway, must go,' she said, turning on her heels, the grass ripping beneath them.

'I don't even know your name,' he called after her, and despite herself, she couldn't help appreciating the filmic quality of the moment – Errol Flynn by way of *Casablanca*, with a touch of *North by Northwest*.

'Wendy,' she called back, but her voice was drowned out by the sound of an approaching aircraft.

Mrs Rampersad was blowing her nose, the abrupt honking sound still managing to carry over the din of the landing plane.

'You're letting out all the heat,' she grumbled as Mrs Dixit slid into the passenger seat and shut the door. 'Who's that, then?' Mrs Rampersad nodded towards the mystery man who was now watching the aeroplane's descent. 'You know him?'

Mrs Dixit shook her head. 'He just started talking to me, I think he's lonely.'

'You should be careful, strange men coming up to you. They might be tricksters out for your money.'

'I don't think he's dangerous.'

'There are perverts everywhere, and you're still a married woman. You ought to buy some mace.'

'Isn't that illegal?'

Mrs Rampersad sniffed. 'If you want something enough, God will provide.'

'I don't think that applies to mace, surely?'

'We should not judge His divine work.'

Mrs Dixit decided not to argue about whether purchasing pepper spray was part of God's plan – she wanted to drop all conversation about the man, because in truth, she did feel the tiniest pinprick of guilt at having spoken with him.

*

'What made you think of taking me there?' Mrs Dixit asked, as they drove away from the airport.

Mrs Rampersad tightened her lips into a pout, which Mrs Dixit now read as caginess.

'I knew a man from church, once,' she replied. 'He enjoyed watching planes.'

'Another one of your church friends?' It was out of Mrs Dixit's mouth before she realised how this might be construed.

'What are you suggesting?'

'No, I mean, you're very dedicated to your churchwork, and it can't be easy meeting men…' she was going to say 'at your age' but fortunately stopped herself. Mrs Rampersad was only in her mid-sixties, but she seemed older, perhaps because of her stiff limbs and the jerky way she carried herself. She was still a handsome woman, though, and Mrs Dixit wished she could say this to her neighbour without it sounding… odd.

'I have put everything into my church. My door is always open, especially to other parishioners to talk about His teachings.'

Yes, and especially if they were men, Mrs Dixit thought silently. She couldn't remember seeing another woman enter Mrs Rampersad's flat in all the years they'd lived below her.

'I'm not judging you…' began Mrs Dixit, but before she could finish, the car swerved to the side of the road and jolted to a halt. Mrs Rampersad stared straight ahead, her hands still gripping the steering wheel.

'Your husband was uppity,' she said, her face stony, 'and I thought you were different, but now I can tell you're just as uppity as him!'

Mrs Dixit unbuckled her belt to escape the car for a second time, scrabbling out. She was careful not to slam the door, but deep down, she really *wanted* to slam it.

With that, Mrs Rampersad drove off, leaving Mrs Dixit at the side of the road.

*

She was closer to the hospital than to home, so Mrs Dixit headed there. She reviewed the final moments in the car ride during the walk towards the bus stop, what she could have done differently, but she'd genuinely not meant to cause offence. The word *uppity* stuck with her, though. *Uppity*. She carried it to the hospital, and with her in each interaction when she arrived, whether it was a stranger's glance or a smile from one of the regular nurses, until she arrived beside her husband's bed.

'Uppity,' she repeated to herself, and tutted. It was hard not to be uppity, what with strange women in passenger seats, and unpaid insurance bills, and mysterious substances in toxicology reports! Mrs Dixit remembered that one of the other patients was possibly listening and reminded herself to be vigilant about saying any of these aloud. She tried to focus on Mr Dixit. Taking a wipe from her bag, she gently cleaned his face and ears. Next, she took a tube of moisturiser and rubbed cream into his hands. The coconut fragrance of the lotion was a nice antidote to the bleachy astringent smells of the hospital, and she enjoyed massaging his skin.

Uppity. The Dixits liked things a certain way, every couple did. That was the point. You married someone who would uphold your view of a shared life together. Mrs Dixit didn't want to be a sloppy person, the ones she saw at the supermarket with their pyjamas on in the middle of the day, the ones talking loudly on their phones, picking their noses, chewing with their mouths open. She knew it was easy to blame the young, but it was everyone! What had happened to standards? They were on a train with no driver, plummeting towards a steep cliff. Naveem believed this too; he was no more controlling than she was, they were simply *protecting* each other through order and simplicity. But if you had the audacity to be quiet and respectful in this world, you were branded as *uppity*.

The nurse came in, the pretty younger one with the freckles.

'How is he doing today?' she asked cheerily.

'I'm not sure he's going to like the world he wakes up to,' Mrs Dixit replied, solemnly.

'Yes, well…' the nurse struggled for something to say, and nurses could *always* find something to say. It came with the job. 'Can I get you some juice?' she asked at last.

It was the first time one of the nurses had offered her anything in the way of comfort – they were always, rightfully, far too busy – and Mrs Dixit had to fight the urge to sob.

She was still composing herself, when Mrs Dixit felt a presence behind her. At first, she imagined it might be the owner of the mystery voice, finally revealing himself, but when she turned, she saw instead – or thought she saw – the retreating silhouette of Naveem's mother. Mrs Dixit blinked, and she was gone, but a strange static seemed to hang in the air, like soot particles from a burnt match. *Oh, the woman's treachery!* The lies she'd told the police, and how she'd spoken to the grieving girl, Shelly. Even her comments about the hospital not taking good care of Naveem felt like a personal attack on Mrs Dixit. She wanted to give chase and confront her, but both her feet stayed glued to the floor, and a creeping sense of powerlessness fizzled out any energetic charge – and so she did nothing.

On the bus ride home, Mrs Dixit tried to welcome all the noise and discomfort she would normally attempt to block out. She imagined the screeching child was a plane landing, and actually, it helped, for a moment. But then the presence of Naveem's mother would invade her mind again, and she would feel nothing but shame for not acting when she could.

*

At home, she paused to listen if Mrs Rampersad was upstairs, but she couldn't hear anything. She'd looked for her car on the street but didn't see it. Mrs Dixit considered going upstairs and knocking on the door, but the word 'uppity' stopped her, like a hand on the chest, before she reached the first step.

The early evening was painfully quiet. Her mind ran wild, going over everything – finances, passengers, solvents; finances, passengers, solvents – like some twisted incantation.

At 7 p.m., Mrs Dixit called the taxi office.

'Wendy,' came Cliff's reassuringly gruff voice, like a gnarled Father Christmas. 'How are you? How's Naveem?'

'The same,' she replied. 'I don't need a taxi, by the way. I'm just ringing to ask something.'

'Go ahead.'

'Did Naveem ever… I don't know how to phrase this… is there anything I should know about him?'

'What do you mean, Wendy?'

She listened for something strange in Cliff's voice, an out-of-place inflection, a tell-tale sign he was prepared for this line of questioning, but she couldn't detect anything unusual.

'If he was involved in any activity that was…' she wanted to say 'illegal' but stopped herself. Cliff was Naveem's boss. She didn't want to get her husband in trouble.

'Naveem is the most honest person I know, Wendy. Is everything alright, money-wise? I know his family aren't exactly cooperative. If you need any help, I can always…'

'Everything's fine,' Mrs Dixit lied. 'I appreciate you offering, though.'

'You know, with some of my drivers, I have to take the bad with the good. A bit of overcharging here, problems with lady customers there, the occasional driving after a pint or two, but Naveem… He was clean as a whistle.'

'Would you call him *uppity*?' asked Mrs Dixit.

Cliff was silent for a moment.

'No,' he replied, unconvincingly. 'He had his specific ways, for sure. But this, I can tell you. You hear a lot of talk about wives and girlfriends, and not always the kindest of things. It's locker-room banter, you understand. Boys' talk. But Naveem never said a single bad word about you in the twenty-plus years I've known him. Not once.'

Mrs Dixit digested this. 'Thank you,' she said, her voice slightly hoarse from the sudden tightening of her throat.

'You need anything at all – just call me, okay?'

'I will.'

After she put the phone down, she listened for Mrs Rampersad but the flat above was almost aggressively silent.

Half an hour later, she picked up the phone again and called a number from Naveem's phone book. There was no answer. Relieved, she hung up promptly without leaving a message.

Well past her usual bedtime, Mrs Dixit stood outside the study. Taking a deep breath, she swung the door open and turned on the light. Inside, she kept moving, ignoring the miniature of Chomley town on the table, and bending down to access the cupboards and drawers. It was a huge invasion of privacy, and she felt terrible – *I'll explain everything to him when he wakes*, she promised the room, as if it was bearing witness. Mrs Dixit took a stack of folders and stuffed them into the bin liner she'd brought with her. Papers, a ring binder, three small notebooks, all went in too. By the time she reached the door again, she'd managed quite a haul.

Mrs Dixit sat in bed. She'd placed an old tablecloth over the bedspread to protect it, and beside her was a tub of antiseptic wipes, because she didn't like bringing dirt from the rest of the house into the bedroom (and neither did Mr Dixit, even if technically, it was *his* dirt). The first folder held eBay receipts, printed out, with annotations on authenticity and the condition of the parcels on delivery. The second folder too. The third folder held scans of trains from books. Guides on making believable trees and grass. She skimmed through the notebooks – they were a diary of progress. Very basic, and in partial code: 'Wednesday 29 July. New Washington caboose finished. PD. LPN.'

It was almost 3 a.m. by the time she got to the ring binder. More receipts for payments; email communications. Mrs Dixit yawned, and was about to close the binder, when something caught her watery eyes. *Epoxy resin.* She scanned the page. *Polyvinyl acetate.* Both bought in extremely large quantities about a year ago, much more than could be reasoned for a model of Chomley, surely?

There was something else: on another page was written the name 'Clare' and beside it, 'silver earrings'.

She snapped the folder shut, as if she'd found a particularly nasty bug crawling inside. Her mind racing, she must have eventually fallen asleep.

She woke to the sound of folders, notebooks and ring binder thumping to the ground.

*

Mrs Dixit cleared all the things to the bedroom chair, and was just settling back to sleep – trying to banish any thought of 'Clare' and what her name in her husband's ring binder could mean – when she heard noise from above. Mrs Rampersad. She looked at the clock; it was just past 4.30 a.m. There was something about the movements upstairs, they seemed *heavier*, more laboured than normal. There was an almighty bang, and then a quieter thump, and then what could have been Mrs Rampersad's querulous voice. Mrs Dixit listened, but no one answered, and she must have fallen asleep once more.

11 days since the accident

After the postman called, Mrs Dixit took up Mrs Rampersad's mail. One of the letters had American stamps, from Florida. The sender was Aiden Rampersad, who, Mrs Dixit had gleaned, was the eldest son. At her neighbour's door she listened, but there was nothing audible inside. She knocked and waited. Knocked again. After no response, she left the letters on the mat, feeling a tingle of concern creep under the outer layers of her skin.

Mrs Dixit was locking the main door behind her on the way to the hospital, when a black cab pulled up. As before, she had a momentary wobble, imagining it to be Mr Dixit, but it was Len who emerged from the cab.

'I came over as soon as I could,' he said, his elongated West Country vowels loud enough for the whole street to hear. 'I didn't see your missed call until this morning.'

'Come inside,' Mrs Dixit whispered, fumbling the keys back into the lock again, and hoping no one was watching through their net curtains.

In the kitchen, she filled the kettle, mostly to buy herself some time.

Len was wearing a pink and purple striped shirt that was vaguely shiny, giving him the impression of a city banker who had fallen on hard times, Italian cotton swapped for a polycotton blend. His belly strained against the buttons and there was a vape pen in his shirt pocket.

'Any news on Naveem's condition?' he asked, as the kettle came alive noisily.

Mrs Dixit shook her head. It wasn't a condition anyway. It was a coma.

'Len, the reason I called you last night was I wanted to ask you something…'

'Anything,' he replied a tad too quickly. 'In fact, I've been thinking about you here, all alone. I should have come by and visited more, but I wasn't sure…'

'I need to ask you about being a taxi driver,' she cut in, trying to muster more confidence than she was feeling.

'Oh.' He looked slightly disappointed. 'I mean, yeah. Of course. Ask away.'

Mrs Dixit sat down in the seat opposite him.

'Do you know of any particular goings-on?'

'What do you mean?'

'Something not exactly by the books. Anything untoward you're aware of?'

'I'm still not…'

She sighed. 'Criminal activity? Organised crime?' She lowered her voice. '*Drugs*.'

'Ah,' said Len, nodding his head slowly. 'In that case, I'll need something stronger than tea.'

Mrs Dixit took out the bottle of brandy she kept for the Christmas pudding and plonked it down in front of him.

*

'I mean, you didn't hear this from me,' Len said, leaning back in his chair, resting the glass of brandy on his round belly. Evidently, he was enjoying this – 'but some of the lads will make *deliveries*.'

'What sort of deliveries?'

'That's the catch – we don't know. We're not even supposed to ask.'

'What is it you deliver? It must be something physical?'

'Boxes.'

'Heavy? Light?'

'Depends.'

'Someone might have peeked inside one?' suggested Mrs Dixit. Len scrunched up his nose, as if he was far too scrupulous to check inside mystery packages. 'What do you think they are, then?'

'I mean, nothing dangerous. Maybe things that have fallen off the back of a lorry and need a new home? Sort of a takeaway delivery service for a special type of local business owner.'

'You make it sound almost rational,' Mrs Dixit sniffed.

'Thank you. You got to understand – with the apps and the competition out there on the roads, we're all feeling the pinch. It's not as if we only take passengers after we check their police records, is it? I've probably had a murderer in my cab, several times over, but how would I know? I've treated them the same as I would a priest. It's like these deliveries. You pick up a box and drop it off somewhere else. Don't ask questions. Badda bing, badda boom. It's a victimless crime.'

'Not for the people who originally owned those boxes.'

Len shrugged and turned his hand to the ceiling, giving a silent 'meh'. He was really enjoying his Tony Soprano moment.

'Was Naveem involved in anything like this?'

'Naveem?' Len puffed air from his cheeks, shaking his head vigorously. 'Talk about priests, he was as sanctimonious as they come. Wouldn't even be in the same room when we were discussing it.' Mrs Dixit felt a flush of pride for her husband. 'But I did have my doubts. All his train collecting, buying stuff all over the world, it don't come cheap, does it? I wondered sometimes, just how squeaky clean Naveem really was.'

Mrs Dixit put this to one side, quarantining it in her mind.

'Did one of these deliveries ever have anything to do with glue?'

Len scrunched up his face so much, he almost spilled his drink, still teetering on his belly.

'Glue?' he repeated.

'Would any of these "local businesses" require large quantities of it?'

'I don't know. It wouldn't be out of the question. There's been weird stuff before.'

'I thought you hadn't seen inside the packages?'

'Technically. But you know how it goes. Packages get ripped by accident. There was one guy said his box was full of prosthetic arms so glue wouldn't be out of the question.'

Mrs Dixit hesitated before her next question. She was afraid it might be giving too much away.

'Is it also common,' she said slowly, 'to take things while driving… to keep you awake?'

'Speed and the like?' Len shrugged, catching his glass before it toppled from its resting place. 'I've heard some of the younger guys dabble. But it's not encouraged, you know, privately even, because if there was an accident…' he trailed off. 'Oh, I'm sorry – I didn't mean… You don't think… Not Naveem?' He looked flabbergasted. 'It's always the strait-laced ones,' he shook his head. 'What was he doing? Whiz or blow?'

'He wasn't… I didn't mean to imply…'

Len whistled.

'You think you know someone…' He took a deep swig of his brandy. 'Can I have a splash more?' He wiggled the empty glass.

*

It took Mrs Dixit steering the conversation back to his wife and children a *third* time for Len to take the hint, but not before he offered a trip to the cinema. 'To help with your loneliness,' he'd added with a wink.

'The cinema gives me migraines,' she'd answered, ushering him towards the door. In truth, it was only 3D films which gave her headaches, but in the circumstances, she felt this slight fib was more than justified.

Her impulse, as she locked up for a second time, was to forgo the hospital and return to the airport. She could only partly remember what had seemed so revelatory in the dissolving rumble of the engines the day before; maybe another trip would cement it?

Mrs Dixit chided herself: *your husband needs you!* but also, she realised, on some level, she was dreading the visit.

As she approached his bed, Mrs Dixit had the distinct impression someone had been sitting in the chair moments before. The seat was even warm to the touch – or maybe it was her mind playing tricks. Mr Dixit lay as he always did: handsome profile, long eyelashes, his forehead in a slight frown, even in repose. She applied some balm to his chapped lips, smoothed down his sheets and settled in the chair, wondering if someone would shortly return to claim it.

'Do you remember that awful trip?' Mrs Dixit said finally, because it felt safe talking about a bad journey, even if someone *was* still eavesdropping. 'The weather on the flight was terrible, so much turbulence. We were diverted back to Madrid before we'd even finished taking off. What made us go to Brazil?' She chuckled, but it was not a happy memory. Mrs Dixit knew the reason they'd travelled there, of course. A lifelong dream. *His* dream of listening to bossa nova in the place it had been created, sipping caipirinha cocktails no less. Mrs Dixit had never wanted to go – it wasn't safe for tourists; muggers would rip jewellery from their fingers at gunpoint. Not that she wore much in the way of jewellery – Mr Dixit had picked up her wedding band from the Argyle Street jewellers next to a fishmongers (the words 'Clare' with no 'i', and 'earrings' popped into her mind reflexively then, and she shoved them away). When they'd landed in Rio, they'd discovered, much to their horror, it was *Carnival* weekend. Every square inch of the city seemed taken over by raucous celebrating crowds, naked most of them, their sweaty and feathered bodies gyrating all night long until sunup. The Dixits couldn't sleep, even with earplugs and both exhausted from jet lag, and they weren't able to move to a quieter area (wherever that was), because it was all booked up solid. After two days of sleep deprivation, they bought expensive early flights home, and never spoke of the failed trip again. For a time, Mr Dixit had even stopped playing bossa nova – he'd pushed through eventually though, filling the house with soporific music once again.

'Brazil,' she scoffed. 'We'd never even been to France!'

Someone in the room groaned – in response or dismay, she couldn't be at all certain.

Once home in her kitchen again, Mrs Dixit took out her address book, and dialled a number.

'Hello, it's me,' she said, when it was answered.

'Wendy?' Her sister intoned with casual surprise.

'Yes, of course.'

'Is everything alright? Naveem isn't…?'

'He's fine. As fine as you can be in a coma, I suppose.'

'Oh. Well. It's nice to hear your voice. Calling me for once.' There was a definite tone to her younger sister's voice, something cynical, which Mrs Dixit fought hard to ignore. They were ten years apart in age, and that chasm had meant they were never close growing up. As adults, the gulf had only widened, especially after Naveem. 'Did you need something?'

'No, I just thought I'd ring…' *to say hi*, she almost said, but that didn't feel right. 'To tell you not to worry. I'm coping much better than I expected.'

'Oh… good.'

'The neighbour upstairs has been very kind, she's been giving me lifts to the hospital, and really, with all the visits, and the bother with the police…'

'What's happening with the police?' asked her sister, taking the bait.

'You know, they're throwing around bizarre accusations. The police are so understaffed now, it's a mystery that they get anything done.'

'What accusations?'

'Nothing really. Nothing with any substance.' Mrs Dixit paused. 'It's ridiculous – they think Naveem might have had underworld contacts.'

Her sister laughed – no, it wasn't a laugh; it was a *bray*.

'Naveem? Next, you'll be telling me he's the Chomley cat burglar…'

'Yes, well… I told you it was ridiculous.' Her sister's mocking laughter annoyed her. 'But really, how much do we know anyone?'

'It's Naveem, though. He's so law-abidingly square…' her sister trailed off.

Mrs Dixit didn't enjoy this accusation. Being square meant you were *boring*. It was a stone's throw away from 'uppity'.

'The police have a different story,' Mrs Dixit snapped. 'There might be more to Naveem than I know. Mysteries. *Every person is a foreign country*,' she added, almost certainly butchering a quote.

'Is this about the woman in the car?' her sister asked, her voice becoming keener, as if she was leaning into the mouthpiece.

'Not exactly.' Mrs Dixit glanced around the kitchen, taking in how everything was exactly the way she'd left it before leaving for the hospital – the cutlery in its drawer, the cups and plates on their shelves, the kitchen cloth folded just so – how everything would remain spotless and ordered unless she, and no one else, messed it up. The name 'Clare' sprang into her mind again tenaciously, and she shoved it away once more. Her sister, breathing impatiently, waited for her to continue. Mrs Dixit briefly considered what she was about to say, scanned the sentence in her mind, before letting it escape. 'Her daughter called me the other day.'

'*What?*' her sister screeched.

'She wanted to meet with me.'

'What for?'

'I don't know.'

'And what did you say?'

'I told her I was busy.'

'*Busy?* You're not doing *anything*. You *must*!' Her sister's voice was too loud, and Mrs Dixit had to pull the receiver away from her ear.

'It wouldn't be appropriate. This poor young woman is grieving, she's just lost her mother.'

'Maybe she needed to tell you something important. People have secret families, you know. It's like you said before… there are things we don't know about each other.'

Mrs Dixit felt the conversation was getting out of her control. She regretted her part in the whole thing. She'd called because she wanted to… what? Impress her sister? Scandalise her? Talk to literally *anyone*, to quell her loneliness? What would Mr Dixit have thought about this conversation? *Gossip*, he'd have noted, correctly. *Gossip for gossip's sake.*

'I should go,' Mrs Dixit began. 'Love to Hen—'

'Actually, since you called me out of the blue… I wondered if I could ask you for a favour?' Mrs Dixit said nothing – she felt entrapped by decorum. She looked at her quiet empty house with longing now. 'Tomorrow I'm having new carpets put in,' her sister continued, 'and so I hoped I could drop Henry around to you in the morning. Just until lunch, maybe 2 p.m. at a push. Henry is excited already – he can't wait to see his Aunty Wendy!'

Mrs Dixit's first uncharitable impulse was to find an excuse, a lie – a doctor's appointment, a meeting with solicitors – but she faltered. She'd never before spent time alone in Henry's company and she was wary – of not being a natural enough caregiver, and conversely, of enjoying it too much and begrudging her own reproductive fate. She glanced around the flat again; it seemed less attractive than it did only seconds ago, the room appeared to be waiting, as if holding its breath. She thought about tomorrow – Mrs Rampersad still missing, her husband unresponsive on his bed, *finances, passengers, solvents, earrings...*

'That would be lovely,' Mrs Dixit replied, surprising her sister for a second time in one day.

After dinner – what constituted dinner, an overstuffed sandwich she barely picked at – Mrs Dixit went for a walk to aid digestion, which was really a thinly disguised reconnaissance to see if she could find Mrs Rampersad's car parked anywhere.

She did not.

She woke in the middle of the night and, turning on most of the lights in the flat, started to hunt for photos. There was an album in a hall cupboard, one in the bedroom, a couple of framed pictures in the living room – Mrs Dixit took everything, offloading them onto the couch. The photo albums covered the span of their whole relationship. Their wedding day. Naveem was gazing at her intently the entire ceremony, displaying only his profile. The photographer had caught them leaving the small church, but they were both shielding their eyes from the fistfuls of rice pelted at them by an overcompensating small number of guests (her parents, who had shown up after all; her sister, looking on sourly; and a friend of Naveem's who later moved to Canada). Mrs Dixit flipped through page after page. Here, he was turned away. Here, he was looking to the left of the camera. Here, he had a shadow on his face. It was difficult to get him in a photo at the best of times, so most were candid, documentary style – capturing a skittish animal about to escape in the following frame. Here, Naveem was rubbing his eyes with his knuckles. Here, he was face on, but too far away to properly see his eyes. It was almost as if he was *playing* with her.

She flipped some more. Had they never taken a photo together, the both of them, looking directly down the barrel of the camera? Here, he was blinded by the flash, eyes closed. Where were the selfies? – self-portraits, they used to be called. She checked her phone. A picture of a weird rash on his left calf that had appeared and disappeared within twenty-four hours. One of him talking to the electrician who had rigged a new kitchen light, arms folded, mid conversation. She could see the electrician's eyes clearly. Blue. She pinched the screen. Nothing but side-eye from Naveem. A video of him showing the damage to a model train he'd bought on eBay, but it was mostly his chin, chest and hands. Mrs Dixit remembered the framed pictures – *of course!* But no, his eyes were cast down here too, as if he was slightly embarrassed. *About me?* She wondered, rattled.

Had she ever sat and looked into his eyes? No, never. Except in the taxi, when they first met. Through the rear-view mirror. Only then.

12 days since the accident

Her sister dropped Henry off at 10 a.m. sharp.

'He's very excited,' she said, although Henry seemed much less than thrilled, sucking his finger dolefully.

'Come on, Henry.' Mrs Dixit shepherded him towards her front door with a gentle hand on the back of his head.

'Don't have too much fun, you two!' called her sister, diving back into her car. 'I'll catch up with all your news later!'

'Are you hungry?'

Henry shook his head. He had sandy brown hair, the same colour as his mother's as a child, and only a hint of the hereditary pointy nose, as yet undeveloped. With his large doleful eyes, he could sit for a Margaret Keane painting.

'Thirsty?'

A hesitant shake, as if he wasn't completely sure.

'Do you need to use the toilet?'

A more confident shake.

'Want to watch something on the television?'

'Do you have *BeastBotz*?' A babyish voice, as if on the verge of crying.

It was Mrs Dixit's turn to shake her head uncertainly.

'I don't think we do…'

She checked the *Radio Times*. No *BeastBotz* scheduled. Stalemate.

Mrs Dixit was considering taking them both to the hospital, but now she thought, in Henry's current state, he might find an unconscious body too frightening.

'Oh,' she said, getting up from the kitchen table that they were sitting at, 'I brought you this to play with.' She took the model train from off the countertop and placed it in front of the child. As she did so, she imagined Mr Dixit groaning loudly at the sight of one of his precious engines held by sticky fingers. Henry's hands did not look sticky though. They looked pink and dextrous, like animatronic grubs.

Henry gazed at the engine with no excitement. He rubbed his hands together like a bank manager about to deliver some difficult news.

'Look, see.' Mrs Dixit pushed the engine across the table. 'Choo, choo, choo,' she added encouragingly.

'When will my mum get back?' Henry asked plaintively, sounding much younger than his six years.

'Soon.'

'But when?'

'Very soon. Until then, we can have some fun.'

A lip pout in response. Were his eyes welling up? If he started, Mrs Dixit wasn't sure she'd be able to get him to stop.

'Why don't we go on a trip somewhere?'

'To the zoo?'

'That might be a bit too far away…'

Mrs Dixit struggled for an alternative to suggest. She thought of the planes taking off, and the memory sent a ripple through her body. But no, it was too chilly out, they couldn't stand beside the runway, however much they wrapped up.

'I know,' she said, clapping her hands. 'Henry, what do you think about celebrity waxworks?'

No, not Madame Tussauds, this was a home-grown Chomley version, created by a disgruntled ex-employee of the former establishment sixty years ago. It had been the focus of many litigious attacks by the better-known company, although none had been successful so far. The Chomley version was a bit of a local joke, while also held in fondness by the community, because almost everyone had spent plenty of time there as a child. Now it was Henry's turn. Mrs Dixit might be a good aunt after all.

They had to catch two buses, but that was fine because at least they were moving. The busywork of getting on and off the bus, finding a seat, dinging the bell at their stop seemed to invigorate Henry. The Chomley Wax Museum, rebranded as Chomley Waxworks in the nineties, and then The Chomley Celebrity Experience and Minigolf in 2004, had a distinct smell. It was familiar to Mrs Dixit immediately: old vinegary floor polish, popcorn (although they no longer sold fresh popcorn, but had plenty in foil bags at exorbitant prices), mixed with decades of damp. Henry did not appear impressed.

'Two, please,' she said to the teenager in the ticket booth, who was busy scrolling down his phone.

'Oh, for fuck's sake,' the teen swore at his screen, it seemed, and Mrs Dixit felt the sudden urge to cover Henry's ears. She clenched her teeth, letting the anger pass. The boy had a sallow look about him – as well as a pointy face, he had a sharp nose, sticking-out ears, and dark rings under both eyes. When he finally did make eye contact with Mrs Dixit, there was a glaze to his expression, as if he was gazing straight through her. She was glad she didn't reprimand him – this boy was to be pitied, sitting here, earning minimum wage, with nothing but his phone for company.

'The card machine's broken,' he said. 'Cash only.'

After receiving her change from the youth, Mrs Dixit bustled Henry towards the main entrance. She'd expected the place to be relatively empty, but inside it was overrun with children, not much older than Henry, who all seemed to be filling in a worksheet. The volume of people and the accompanying noise made Henry cringe, and Mrs Dixit felt protective of him. Should she lift him up, so he wasn't trampled? He was small, but she was not exactly strong, so she decided against it.

'Where shall we start?' she said as brightly as she could, over the din of children and harassed-sounding adults all around them.

The first room was decked out with a red carpet as if it was a special event, although the redness was muted from age and wear, shabby and frayed underfoot. It could do with a robust hoovering, too. Mrs Dixit took in the five waxwork models that stood at intervals on the carpet, smiling at invisible cameras. She could not place a single one. Avoiding a group of children who were sitting on the floor, she walked up to the nearest of the waxworks, a woman with an elongated face, to read the plaque. Angelina Jolie, apparently. Two schoolchildren sniggered as one of them reached up and honked Angelina on her waxy bosom.

'Come along, Henry,' Mrs Dixit said quickly, manoeuvring him away.

Each room was the same, however – noise, groping, a strange retinue of waxy unplaceable faces, most of which she couldn't identify even after reading the name plaques. The schoolchildren seemed bored too; a few were filling in their worksheets, but most of them were finding distractions – swapping collector cards, or playing loud games on their phones, or chasing each other. Henry seemed to shrink even more as they progressed through the building. When there was an adult (a teacher, Mrs Dixit presumed, although they seemed more like crowd control), they were reprimanding someone to one side or telling a group of children to stop mauling Renée Zellweger (Ms Zellweger's face seemed to have been microwaved for a good thirty seconds).

'Can we go?' Henry asked sullenly, pulling at her sleeve.

'Soon,' she replied, patting his hand.

Mrs Dixit felt an impending sense of failure, the same irrational one she felt whenever she accidentally dropped a blueberry and it rolled under the fridge.

*

They were almost through the waxworks, and Mrs Dixit was wondering if she could tolerate a game of mini golf to eat up more time, when they wandered into a nautically themed room. Henry was almost in tears now, sniffling and holding onto her pocket miserably. His nose was running, so she pulled him over to an unfortunate-looking Christopher Columbus with dead eyes and took out a tissue.

Beside them, a group of five children were focused very intently on something, screeching occasionally with frustration. Blotting away Henry's snot – she didn't want to hurt him, so she fought the impulse to grab his small head and give his nose a strong wipe – Mrs Dixit noticed the children were trying to tie knots. String had been hammered onto a board and there was an illustrated guide on how to make sailing knots. She remembered her knot-tying days from when she was a Girl Guide – there was a point in her early teens when she'd seriously considered the Navy. Once she'd finished cleaning Henry's nose, she folded the tissue over, still watching the gaggle of children struggle with the strings.

'Not like that!' one shouted at his friend.

'You do it then!' the other barked back, relinquishing his place.

The new child fared just as poorly, however, and soon the children around him were yelling again in frustration.

'Here, I'll show you,' said Mrs Dixit, and they turned in unison to gawp at her in surprise, one child still pulling on the lengths of string. As she approached, he duly handed them over, moving aside. 'Now... if I can remember,' but she needn't have worried, because after one attempt, her muscle memory kicked in after all these years – and she found the string before her had been fashioned into a very presentable reef knot.

'Wow!' came the collective cry around her.

'Now, you try,' she said, but the child who took the string didn't listen to her steps, and soon made a mess of it. She showed the group again, more slowly this time – over, under, through – but another child attempted it and failed too.

'Henry, why don't you come and have a go?'

The group turned to look at the smaller child who was standing nervously behind them. They parted, and Henry walked towards Mrs Dixit, almost as if he was in a daze. Fortunately, his nose had stopped running.

'Like this,' she said, showing Henry the knot-tying steps, but feeling she'd made a tactical error. If the older children couldn't get it, surely he wouldn't either, and Henry was about to be humiliated in front of his boisterous peers. He'd need therapy for years. But, fortunately, when he attempted the knot, his fingers were deft, and he listened and concentrated in a way the other children had not. After a few attempts, with some quick unpicking on her part, he had managed a pretty respectable knot.

'Wow!' came the response again, and Henry, not quite ready to smile yet, took a deep breath of satisfaction.

'Do it again!' someone yelled, and Henry unpicked the knot, and then with Mrs Dixit's gentle guidance, repeated it. This time he did smile, his eyes flashing with pride.

For the next half an hour, Henry helped teach the other kids his new skill. Some managed it, most didn't, but he was patient with each of them, helping them with his nimbler hands, as all the other children watched in quiet awe. Children would walk in from the preceding room, yelling and laughing, and soon become silent to join the hushed focus of the watching group.

Eventually, a teacher appeared, looking astounded at the huddle of quiet children.

'You're not one of the parents?' she asked of Mrs Dixit.

'No, I'm here with Henry,' Mrs Dixit replied, aware of an emerging sense of proprietorship over him.

'I got it,' shouted one of the children, and others around politely clapped.

*

When her sister arrived to pick Henry up again later that afternoon, he was sitting serenely on the edge of the sofa watching cartoons.

'How has he been? He was so looking forward to this!' she garbled, and Mrs Dixit had the distinct impression, and not for the first time, that her sister felt uncomfortable around her.

'I think we had a fun time, didn't we, Henry?'

Henry nodded emphatically, his sandy fringe flopping into his eyes, before returning his attention back to the television.

'I can't thank you enough,' her sister said, in that slightly rushed way she always had, as if she'd just remembered she'd left the oven on, with a cup of flammable liquid sitting on the cooker. 'I really want to hear all your news,' she lowered her voice conspiratorially, 'and find out everything about the daughter, you know, of the doctor…' she raised her voice again, 'but the carpet layer will be leaving soon, so must dash. Come on now, Henry!' She bustled his shoes and coat on as soon as he came near. 'Have you done something to the place?' she said, at the doorway.

'I don't think so,' Mrs Dixit replied, glancing around.

'Looks… different. Anyway, bye – love to Naveem!'

Mrs Dixit was in the kitchen, investigating how to buy *BeastBotz* DVDs on her iPad, when she heard the front door slam. The sound of boots and muttering as Mrs Rampersad levered herself up the stairs. Mrs Dixit's impulse was to stick her head out after her, but something in her neighbour's exaggerated lurching stopped her. Upstairs, another door crashed shut, and more thumping steps. The creak of metal on wood, and then silence.

After a few minutes, Mrs Dixit opened her front door and sniffed: there was definitely the smell of something heavy and alcoholic in the air.

*

When a whole silent hour passed, Mrs Dixit couldn't stand it anymore, and went upstairs to knock.

'Mrs Rampersad,' she called, rapping so hard on the door, her knuckles stung.

There was a noise, like a heavy bag sliding onto the floor, and then silence again.

'Are you there?' Mrs Dixit cried out. Heavy footfalls made their way towards her finally. She felt too exposed now, and wished she'd at least brought her neighbour's uncollected mail to hide behind. The lock rattled and the door opened a few inches.

'What?' Mrs Rampersad asked hoarsely from the gloom. Mrs Dixit could smell the booze on her breath.

'I just wanted to check you were alright?'

Mrs Rampersad laughed once, a sharp 'Ha!'

'Why do you care?' she asked, slightly slurring. 'Questioning who is allowed into *my* house for an innocent meal!'

'I'm sorry. I didn't know where you'd gone… I was… worried.'

'Not so worried all those years with your little husband downstairs.' Mrs Rampersad spat out the words. 'Not so concerned about me when I wasn't driving you all over town!'

'I'm very thankful for everything you've done,' Mrs Dixit replied, bridling. *And you offered*, she thought angrily. *Plus, I paid you petrol money.*

'You and him, judging me.' Mrs Rampersad's eyes were bloodshot and wild-looking. 'Every time I see you, whispering to each other.'

'I don't know what you mean. We were always polite.'

'Po-lite,' spittle hit Mrs Dixit in the face. 'Oh, you were po-lite, all right.' Mrs Rampersad chuckled to herself, a dark gurgling sound. 'Po-lite every day with your car tucked up, nice. While I had to park mine on the *street*.' Her Trinidadian accent was much stronger as she spoke. 'Do you know how many times my number plates have been stolen? Twice! But your car tucked up safe and sound, like a baby.'

'There's only room for one car in there, it's tiny – anyway, we own the garage, it comes with our flat.'

Mrs Rampersad wasn't prepared to see reason – she was swinging big.

'Your husband in a coma, and you don't even cry,' she laughed. 'No tears for your husband? It's like you don't even care.'

'That's not true,' Mrs Dixit pleaded, a lump forming in her throat, robbing her voice of power.

'If that was my husband, I would be there with him, day or night. Sleeping beside him if I had to.' *No, you wouldn't, not in those rigid hospital chairs*, Mrs Dixit thought reactively. 'If he was my husband, I'd…'

'But he's not your husband – you don't have one,' Mrs Dixit said pointedly, and then wished she hadn't.

Mrs Rampersad glared at her, swaying slightly.

'You come up to *my* house and judge *me* about my goings-on.' Her voice was high, raw. 'Only God can pass judgment. I *had* a husband. I had one.' She began to cry, hot angry tears.

'I apologise,' Mrs Dixit said genuinely. 'I shouldn't have…'

'You know nothing!' Mrs Rampersad turned and was still yelling as she headed into her flat. There was the crash of bottles, and the sound of breaking glass, and a noise like a chair being overturned, and Mrs Dixit thought briefly about rushing to see what had happened, but instead she crept away, scurrying down the stairs to safety.

There was loud banging upstairs for another ten minutes before things calmed down. Mrs Dixit slept fitfully that night, feeling a heaviness pressing down on her from the ceiling. Several times she felt she couldn't breathe, and had to calm herself, taking big gulps of air, and rubbing her forehead, like her husband would do, when she woke from a bad dream.

13 days since the accident

In the morning, early – a frost still on the ground – she went for a long walk. It was a Saturday, and the streets were empty, except for a few joggers and the occasional person fetching a newspaper. Mr Dixit used to subscribe to a couple of papers, before discovering he could read most of them for free using an app on his phone – an initiative from the local library. The only problem was another app reader who left inflammatory comments on the articles, many of them starting, 'I'm not racist, but…' Mrs Dixit smiled, remembering all the times her husband had nearly thrown his phone across the room.

Arriving back, Mrs Dixit made some coffee in the French press, pouring the brew into a thermos. She placed the croissants she'd bought during her walk on a plate and carried everything upstairs on a tray. Mrs Dixit was not surprised to find Mrs Rampersad's door still ajar. She knocked, but only out of politeness, entering before anyone had a chance to tell her otherwise.

The kitchen was exactly as she'd imagined it would be. Picking her way carefully through the smashed glass, Mrs Dixit went to the sink and peered inside the cupboard underneath, finding a dustpan, its brush, and a well-stocked supply of cleaning products. Putting the croissants and thermos to one side, she set about sweeping the worst of the glass, righting the overturned chairs, collecting the empty wine and spirit bottles, and wiping down the counter tops. She assumed the noise would wake Mrs Rampersad immediately, but she'd been cleaning for almost half an hour, making good progress, by the time her neighbour finally roused.

Mrs Rampersad, visibly hungover – her night shirt yanked to one side exposing a bare shoulder, hair in her eyes – stared in disbelief. She looked tired and grey and somehow smaller, as if her whole body had shrunk with dehydration. A scratch on her left arm had bled, seeping into the fabric, leaving a mottled brown splodge.

'What are you doing?' she asked quietly, as if she couldn't bear loud noises, especially not from her own throat.

'There's coffee,' Mrs Dixit said, fetching it from the far counter and placing it on the kitchen table. She took a cup from a shelf and started to fill it from the thermos. Mrs Rampersad watched wide-eyed, as if none of this was real – morning tea with the Mad Hatter.

'You didn't have to…' she began, looking around at the organised kitchen, the bin bag filled with bottles, a smaller one next to it with broken glass.

'Sit,' instructed Mrs Dixit, and her neighbour complied, settling in the nearest chair. There was an obedient childlike quality to her now; it was as if she would do anything asked of her.

'Milk?' Mrs Dixit asked.

Mrs Rampersad shook her head. 'Sugar,' she replied, hoarsely, and Mrs Dixit fetched it from the countertop. After three teaspoons were added and soundlessly stirred, Mrs Rampersad raised the cup to her mouth and gave it an experimental sip.

Mrs Dixit settled in the chair opposite her. The window was open a crack, and the frosty air was stirring. Mrs Rampersad shivered, pulling her dressing gown around her, just as Wendy Dixit began to speak:

*

I don't have many friends. I never did, even when I was a girl. My mother wasn't an especially loving person, but she told me loneliness was a phase, and it would pass. I wanted it to. I wished I could close my eyes and open them again and it would be ten years later, and I could go to pubs, and out dancing, and to the movies with my friends. But I couldn't skip, of course, I had to live each moment, and if I was a shy, nervous girl when I was a child, I became an even less confident teenager. Adulthood wasn't the salvation I'd hoped for, it felt like some cruel trick instead. I was still uncomfortable in my own skin; more so. Now I had to worry about my body too, what men thought of me – so as well as being lonely, I was scared. I'm not trying to stoke your sympathy; I know everyone's life is tough. Take Naveem – living in a crowded house, with six siblings. Two died young, a brother and a sister. Everything was a hand-me-down, his clothes, his toys, his family's ideals. He wanted to get away and find something of his own, away from the chaos, the noise, the pressure of his parents, so as soon as he could, he learned to drive. Then he realised he could make money and escape at the same time, so he became a taxi driver.

I was working at a florist shop when I met him. I'd stayed late, making three funeral wreaths, and I didn't want to walk home in the dark. It was silly, really. I should have taken the bus, but making the wreaths spooked me. When the taxi arrived, he was quiet, which I appreciated – he didn't try to chat me up or bombard me with questions. I felt safe, immediately. I liked the profile of his face when he looked at the traffic lights. It seemed like a kind face, a strong jaw, a Romanesque nose – I thought he was Turkish, maybe. When we arrived at my flat, I didn't want to get out. I kept thinking of excuses to stay, ridiculous things – I forgot something at the shop. We hadn't said more than a few words to each other, but I'd caught him looking in the rear-view mirror twice; his eyes had met mine, and stayed there for a second, but it felt – I don't know – special. I'm not sure if I believe in all that love at first sight nonsense, but I felt less alone in that taxi ride than I ever had before. Bizarre, really – saying it out loud after all these years.

The next time it rained, I called the same taxi office. I was almost thankful for the rain. I didn't want to ask for him, that felt too eager, but he was the driver again. He remembered me; I could see it in his eyes. On the third trip, his face softened for a moment as he watched me in the rear-view mirror. It wasn't a smile exactly, but it felt like a smile. Like his face was smiling. On the fourth trip, he asked me my name. On the sixth, he mentioned that he sometimes had a drink at the Gilded Cup near Flankthorn Road on a Friday, so that meant I had three full days to figure out how to show up there without looking desperate.

I roped my younger sister in to coming, we were always very different, the two of us – she's ten years younger than me, the baby of the family, she always had plenty of friends, so she resented having to chaperone me. We were both overdressed for The Cup, and Naveem didn't arrive until nine thirty, but he saw me straight away, and his face softened again, not a smile, better than a smile. He came over and asked if he could buy us a round. I hadn't told my sister he was Indian, and she was unusually quiet. He sat with us the rest of the night, and talked about music, how Brazilian music was underrated, he was keen on bossa nova even then, and when the pub closed, he gave us a lift back. I sat in the front seat with him. My sister was snoring by the time we got to mine – which was lucky, I think she would have rushed me inside otherwise, she thought he was too self-serious even then – so Naveem and I sat for ten minutes, talking together quietly and eventually he took my hand in his.

Naveem still lived with his family, because he was saving for a house of his own, so we'd always meet at mine, although he'd never take a step inside. I don't think he wanted the neighbours talking. If we ate out, it was always at an Italian restaurant, he said he didn't like curry, hated spicy food. There were a lot of things from his childhood he rejected, and I could understand that, so I never questioned it. He was sweet, and serious, and careful of his physicality so as not to scare me. I tried not to ask difficult questions about his family, and to say yes to the things he suggested, not because he had a fragile male ego I had to be careful of, but because I was enjoying saying yes to someone for once. To be fair, I didn't really know what I wanted. I'm not sure I do still. I wasn't loud, or sarcastic with him, and I tried to take things at face value, waiting for information instead of requesting it, enjoying the silences, taking comfort in the crinkling of his eyes, and the brief ripples of emotion that would pass over his face. He felt like a deep well I'd only dipped my toes in.

It wasn't long until his family started to make problems. His mother didn't approve of me. Like a chain reaction, my family started to voice their concerns. My sister wasn't supportive of Naveem, and that really affected my parents. I've never seen or read Romeo and Juliet, *but based on my own experience, I can only imagine it's full of frustrations. Closed doors, when there used to be wide-open spaces. Insanity, when there should have only been richness and love. You do start to feel mad. When everyone around you is telling you this can't happen, and you know inside yourself – It is! It must! – the fabric of reality starts to tear. How can people be so cruel? Why meddle in happiness?*

A lesser man would have given up, thrown everything away. Naveem was living at home, there was no escape for him. But he would not be swayed. It was extraordinary, to have lived such a quiet life of solitude, only to meet someone who would cast aside everything to be with you. I knew there would be repercussions. We need our family, however much we say we don't. I was ready for the fallout, or at least I thought I was. His mother was especially cruel. She went to my work, screamed at my boss. Later, she sent letters to my parents, saying horrible untrue things. When none of that worked, she cut him out completely.

With my savings too, we almost had enough for a house, so we were married – my parents and my sister came, I'll give them that

– and bought our first flat. It was tiny, but it felt like a haven after everything we'd been through. Naveem's brothers were still coming over once a week, some of them trying to cajole, others to threaten, others being the peacemaker. For a long time, it was mayhem. We just wanted to be left alone, to have an easy life.

Overnight, they stopped. We didn't receive another phone call or visit. I was relieved, but worried too. I didn't feel like they were going to give up so easily – especially his mother. I worried how being cut off from his family would affect Naveem, what would happen if there were children… but, well, I shouldn't have… There wasn't any need after all… with the miscarriages.

We closed ranks. It was a defence mechanism, to protect us from the outside world, to make the two of us enough. No children, no family – I mean there was my family, of course, before my parents died, but somehow they didn't seem to count. Naveem had always wanted to grow up in a quiet house, with order, and be left to his own devices, and so that was exactly the kind of life we built.

If we seemed distant, and unfriendly, which I'm sure we were at times, it's only because we were keeping everything contained. Where there was order and routine, there was safety. Other people were a chaos to avoid. It didn't help that Naveem drove a taxi and had to interact with the general public. It made him want to withdraw even more in his private life. With his model trains and his bossa nova. We were happy. I think we were happy. It's hard to remember now, even if it's only been a couple of weeks. Although I miss him terribly, there's something else too. Something that's always nagged at me. I'm scared to give it much thought. I can't even describe what it is, it's more a feeling.

One thing I'm certain of though is how much help you've been since the accident. I'm sorry if we weren't friendlier, better neighbours. We should have tried harder, I know that now. I'm sorry about your car. I should have offered the garage to you, for some reason I keep expecting Naveem to turn up and need a place to park his cab. If the garage is full, he'll never come home. It's silly what the brain does. Maybe I should start thinking about what happens if he doesn't...

Mrs Rampersad pounded the table with her fist, prompting Mrs Dixit to give a high-pitched mew of surprise.

'Don't say that!' Mrs Rampersad's vehemence was incredible. 'You must have faith.'

'Perhaps,' Mrs Dixit replied, trying to compose herself.

'No "perhaps". He will get up off that bed. Trust, woman.' Mrs Rampersad took a gulp of her coffee. 'And thank you... for this.' She nodded at the tidied kitchen.

'You're welcome. Now, I must go and visit my husband. Yesterday was the first day I didn't see him, and I'm starting to feel anxious.'

'I can drive...?'

'No, I think I'd like to walk today.' To be fair, Mrs Rampersad didn't look as if she should be driving anywhere that morning.

Mrs Rampersad appeared thoughtful. 'I'd wondered,' she said, 'about the children thing...'

'People often do.'

'It explains why he took your surname too... because of the trouble with his family? Or did you change it by deed poll? I mean, that's not his *real* name, is it?'

Mrs Dixit weighed up how to proceed.

'It's real,' she replied at last. 'It's his father's surname. The original form is a Sanskrit word that means 'knowledge'. Only, in India,' she shifted on her seat, 'in its original form, it's usually pronounced *Dikshit*.'

'I see...' Mrs Rampersad said gravely, no hint of a smile, which Mrs Dixit appreciated. 'Well, God does have a sense of humour. As much as the British do, so I can understand why you would *tweak* it slightly.' A smile flashed across her face. 'Heaven's be!' Mrs

Rampersad exclaimed, clearing her throat quickly to flush away any inappropriate chuckle that might be building there – much against her best wishes.

Downstairs again, Mrs Dixit was collecting her things when the phone rang. She considered not answering, but then it might be the hospital…

'I don't know what you did to Henry,' her sister's voice trilled through the earpiece, 'but you've *really* made a friend there. He can't stop talking about you. He wants to know when he can come and visit again!'

'I'm really sorry, I'd love to chat, but I must run…'

'He won't stop going on about some rope…'

'I'll call you back,' said Mrs Dixit with only the slightest of hesitations – she really did need to see her husband, her worry for not having visited him yesterday was starting to feel overwhelming – before hanging up.

Not too long after Mrs Dixit had arrived at the hospital, her mobile phone rang. She'd been humming 'Just the Bossa Nova', a song her husband disliked for being a pastiche, but one she'd always secretly enjoyed, being in English, and comparatively fun. It wasn't a number she recognised – probably one of those annoying robocallers – so she turned the phone to silent.

Mrs Dixit, warm from her walk, stripped off her coat and gloves as she made her way through the hospital corridors. She navigated herself neatly around the young families there to visit elderly relatives, holding gifts wrapped in seemingly endless clear plastic; the wheelchairs; the hobbling patients, humming as she went:

Meu amor was keen, and oh so sweet
His charm sure whipped me off m' feet
If I had stayed a single beat more
I'da let that man take me out the door

Arriving at his ward, Mrs Dixit pulled back the curtain surrounding his bed, finding it empty, the sheets made. She looked around, puzzled – all the other patients were in their beds. Her brain was flooded with conflicting thoughts. He had woken up. He had gone home. The call she'd missed was from the hospital saying just that. *Or he was d—* No. She banished that thought – fear and guilt bubbling up inside her. 'Where is he?' she muttered to herself, as if she'd misplaced him in the same way you might your keys, and quickly walked back into the hallway, to try and attract a nurse or doctor, finding neither.

Mrs Dixit rushed back to his bed, unsure of what to do. His things! – she checked inside his bedside drawer, the one she'd filled with handkerchiefs, and lotions, hand sanitiser, and throat lozenges. They were all gone. She looked around at the other patients again, and considered trying to shake one awake, but of course that was foolish. Remembering her mobile phone, Mrs Dixit called the missed number. After two rings, she heard the automated voice for Chomley Police Station. 'If you know the department you would like to contact…' Jaw clenched like a vice, she navigated the options until finally, *finally*, she was speaking to an actual person.

'You said your name was Dixit? D I X I T?'

'Yes – were you calling about my husband? He's gone missing!'

'I'm reading his file notes.' There was a pause. 'It says he was in an accident.'

'I know he was in a ('bloody' she wanted to say, but did not) accident. It resulted in him being in a coma, and now he's disappeared…'

The man on the phone responded calmly. 'If you think he's in danger, you can call 111 and speak to…'

'But *you* called *me*!'

'I can try and put you through to the officers who are handling your husband's case?'

'*Please*.'

There were holding beeps… '*It's not me, it's just the bossa nova,*' she sang manically in her mind as she waited, '*Set me free, till the music is all over*'… before going through to voicemail.

She hung up frustrated, and then regretted not leaving a message. Maybe she should call Mrs Rampersad and have her knock on their door to see if he answered? Would he have his keys? She suddenly felt an enormous surge of emotion. *Naveem!* The dense hospital air smelled of bleach and urine and decay. If she knew they weren't locked shut, she'd try to throw open a window. What was she doing? Oh yes, calling Mrs Rampersad. But what if he tried to call her and Mrs Dixit was on the other line? Where was a nurse? She should find one, why hadn't she run down to the station? They were never around when you actually…

From the corner of her eye, Mrs Dixit saw movement. One of the old chaps was no longer lying immobile in his bed – he was waving at her. The patient had unkempt dirty-white hair with a scraggly beard, and his leg was in some sort of brace. Yes, he was definitely beckoning her over. Mrs Dixit stepped forward hesitantly. She was wary – there was something about his face that spoke of hard drinking and worse.

As she moved towards him, the old man stopped beckoning her and started pointing frantically at Naveem's empty bed.

'Do you know where he's gone?' asked Mrs Dixit, her voice shrill with panic.

The man nodded frantically.

'Gone… gone…' he said in the croakiest of whispers.

'Where did he go?'

'Gone…'

'Yes, but where?'

'Woman.'

'There was a woman? What woman? The nurse?'

He shook his head.

'Woman… woman…'

'Yes…?'

'Woman took him.'

And then message communicated, he fell back into his pillows, and let out a long uncensored rasping fart.

She ran. There was no nurse at the first station, so she sprinted to the next.

'My husband's disappeared,' Mrs Dixit cried when she finally found a nurse.

'Don't panic, he can't have gone far,' the nurse replied breezily, as if this sort of thing happened every day, which of course, it probably did. Tapping at her computer, she asked: 'What's his name?'

'Naveem Dixit. He was in a coma. Please tell me he's awake and in another ward somewhere…'

'You're going to have to calm down,' the nurse said, her fingers paused over the keyboard contritely, 'you're no help to anyone like this.'

'It's my husband!' Mrs Dixit's voice was guttural, the animal urgency of it would normally have shocked her. 'He's been unconscious for two weeks. If he's awake…' A large sob released itself from her throat, making her gasp. 'Please,' she managed to whisper.

The nurse frowned at her screen.

'It says here Mr Dixit is in a stable but unchanged condition.'

'Where's he gone, then?'

'They may have moved him to another ward. Or perhaps he's being given a bath. Or in a physical therapy session. There's really nothing to worry about. They always turn up.'

Mrs Dixit felt her anguish turn to foolishness, giving her a modicum of relief. Of course – there were a whole host of logical reasons for him not being there! She was extra panicky because of not coming to see him yesterday – she'd been too tired after Henry's visit. But there was something else, too: guilt. Deep down, Mrs Dixit had been pleased to have an excuse not to come...

'This is odd,' said the nurse, scowling. 'You're his wife?' Mrs Dixit nodded. 'It says here that arrangements were made to take him into long-term care at a domestic address. Have the doctors not talked to you about this?'

'Do you mean, taking Naveem home?'

'Apparently, he was discharged yesterday.'

'But he can't have...?' Mrs Dixit felt slightly crazed. 'He hasn't. I would know!' But what did she really know for sure? Clare, whoever Clare was, popped into her mind again.

'According to his notes, Naveem Dixit is at his home. The person who authorised it was Mrs Dixit.'

'His mother!' the other – younger – Mrs Dixit said, clamping her teeth shut. She squeezed her jaw as hard as she could. So hard, in fact, one of her upper left canines popped out of her skull and skittered across the hospital linoleum.

PART TWO

35 days since the accident

The drugs… the zopiclone… had worked at last. She had finally fallen asleep.

Mrs Dixit lifted her head. It was as heavy as a bowling ball. She dropped it again, her face flomping back into the pillow, where she gave a muffled groan. As a teenager, she'd felt this groggy, unable to get up, her mother aggressively vacuuming her bedroom in an attempt to rouse her. It was the eighties, and teenagers were *supposed* to be lazy, but the change was so sudden, it was like a personality transplant – one second, she was a child, quietly waking at seven each morning without an alarm clock, the next, she was burying her head under the covers. 'Come on, Wendy,' her mother would call, turning off the vacuum, 'What man will want you, if you can't even get out of bed?'

There was commotion above – Mrs Rampersad was awake, which meant it was late morning. For the briefest of moments, Mrs Dixit considered crawling back under the covers to hide, but she knew this was childish. Instead, she manoeuvred her legs over the side of the mattress and let herself slide off.

It began again.

She was eating toast in the kitchen and wondering where all her saliva had gone, when Mrs Rampersad rapped at her door.

'You're not dressed,' her neighbour noted disapprovingly. 'Didn't you sleep again?'

The toast was like glue in Mrs Dixit's mouth.

'I did,' she managed, eventually.

Mrs Rampersad bustled past her, surveying the breakfast detritus, before ineffectively wiping the counter with a too-damp cloth. 'We should go,' she announced, throwing the cloth in the sink, and screwing the jam lid on so tightly, Mrs Dixit wouldn't be able to open it again for weeks. 'I have a feeling they might be moving him to a second location any day.'

Mrs Rampersad's new hobby, when she wasn't saving souls on the high street, was listening to True Crime podcasts, and so she saw almost everything through the lens of an American serial killer.

'Where would they take him?' Mrs Dixit asked, still trying to swallow.

'Another relative. They could know we're watching.'

And whose fault is that? Mrs Dixit thought. Mrs Rampersad's weak bladder was the answer, but of course she didn't say anything.

With an incredible clatter, Mrs Rampersad plonked the used plate and cup into the sink, and clapped her hands. 'Move, woman!' she shouted. 'Get dressed! We can't stand here all day. And remember your binoculars this time!'

Their ritual was to drive to the South Chomley McDonald's so Mrs Rampersad could buy three Egg McMuffins, and a massive Diet Coke to last her the morning (and to instigate her frequent trips to the loo). Mrs Dixit, put off by the processed smell of fast food, just like her husband would have been, had nothing. Afterwards, they'd drive to the airport, watching the planes, Mrs Rampersad eating two of the Egg McMuffins in quick succession, barely a gap between them, while they discussed strategy. This might include the possibility of police intervention (unlikely), news from the hospital (sparse), and updates from lawyers (incomprehensible). Recently, a journalist had wanted to do a human-interest piece, but Mrs Dixit was wary.

'You should think of the exposure,' Mrs Rampersad had said, between noisy sucks on her straw.

Mrs Dixit ran her tongue around the cavity of her missing tooth.

'That's what concerns me,' she'd muttered.

With a loose agenda set, the two women would drive to Naveem's childhood home and begin their stake-out.

The sky was sunny by the time they reached the airport. It was 29 March and finally a day which felt more like spring than winter. Three other cars were parked already, all facing the runway. After Mrs Rampersad yanked up the handbrake, Mrs Dixit decided to soak up the sunshine outside, leaving her neighbour to eat in peace.

She was not alone for long.

'We meet again,' said Magnus mischievously.

Mrs Dixit smiled out of politeness.

'Did I miss anything?' she asked.

'Just a BA flight – good turbines. Made a proper racket, a real teeth-rattler.'

Mrs Dixit was acutely aware that Mrs Rampersad would be watching them. She could almost feel two points of pressure on her back, like sniper lasers. The sleeping pills weren't helping either – she felt removed from her body, as if observing her own actions from a strange angle. *Disassociation*, they called it. The lethargy was even worse. If not for the roar of a plane, Mrs Dixit could have slipped into a doze just standing there.

'It's terrible about these burglaries,' she said at last, because chit-chat took the least amount of effort.

Magnus looked at her gravely.

'What do you know about them?' he asked, narrowing his eyes.

'Well, nothing. Not much at least. Only what I catch on the front of the local papers when I'm in a newsagent.'

He stared at her longer, and then nodded finally, as if this was the correct answer.

'Most robberies are committed by someone close to you,' he said. 'A burglar usually lives within two miles of your home. They learn your routine more easily, you see. Which street do you live on again?' Mrs Dixit, caught off guard by politeness, told him. 'Ah yes, the houses all have the pebble-dashed fronts, don't they? Are you upstairs or downstairs?' Again, slightly under duress, she told him. Magnus smiled, changing tack. 'And how was your evening last night?' he asked more loudly, to be heard over the noise of the engines.

Magnus always wore odd clothing combinations, she'd noticed – a hunter's jacket, the collar turned up, paired with lime-green crocs. A waistcoat with a pocket watch on a chain, complimenting what looked like pyjama bottoms. This morning he was wearing a long woollen scarf looped around his neck with a blue velvet jacket, a shredded tube of Rolos flapping in the breast pocket. 'Get into any trouble?' he winked salaciously.

Mrs Dixit thought briefly of her previous evening – a can of sweetcorn for her dinner, while reviewing notes from the lawyer.

'Trouble is exactly what I'm trying to avoid,' she replied, brusquely.

'Very sensible. People put too much stock in domestic dramas. But when you have an illness in the family…'

'How is your wife?'

'Oh yes, poor Natalie.' Her name was Natalie today, Mrs Dixit noted. Last week, he'd said his sick wife's name was Nicola. The illness changed regularly too. Sometimes it was bone cancer. Other times it was chronic myalgia. Despite the inconsistencies, Mrs Dixit found herself liking her conversations with Magnus, in a way that she didn't with, say, Len. Perhaps it was that Magnus reminded her of a favourite teacher of hers as a child (the slight dithering, and he'd also sported a moustache)? Or that underneath all the *wink wink*, *nudge nudges*, he seemed genuinely interested in what she had to say. 'She really is the light of my life, you know. When she said to me…'

But what Natalie, or Nicola, or Nina said would never be known, as the plane decided just then to launch itself down the runway. As they watched it soar into the sky – the sound reverberating pleasantly inside Mrs Dixit's skull – a voice surprised her.

'We should go.' It was Mrs Rampersad, glaring at Magnus with barely concealed contempt.

'Goodbye then,' Mrs Dixit said.

'Till next time,' Magnus replied, giving a mock bow, the shredded Rolo packet rustling in the breeze.

The most important part of a successful day's stake-out was finding a good parking spot. It should be close enough to the house to give them a proper vantage point, while being far enough away for them not to be easily spotted. Mrs Rampersad had suggested buying some smoke-tinted plastic film to darken the car windows, but Mrs Dixit felt this would only draw attention to them, so they'd settled on wearing hats and sunglasses as a precaution instead.

Today, they settled into their regimen. Mrs Rampersad lowered her seat back to give her more leg room – she was wary of deep vein thrombosis. Lately, Mrs Rampersad had decided not to wear the hat and sunglasses, as it was extremely unlikely Naveem's family knew anything about her, but she still kept them on the dashboard, ready to throw on at a moment's notice. Mrs Dixit opened the window a crack for ventilation, and to make sure the windows didn't fog up. The lawyer had suggested she pay for a private detective, but her finances were dwindling, and the lack of insurance meant nothing was coming in. She'd popped her head into a couple of florists, asking about part-time work – tempted, each time, to buy flowers to take home, the lingering disapproval of her husband stopping her – but nothing had come of it yet. So here she was.

Mrs Dixit took out her journal. The lawyer said that they were in difficult legal territory – the abductors were Naveem's biological family, and although he was estranged from them, this would be difficult to prove in a court of law. Their best move was to find something additional they could use – a way to prove mistreatment, or to show that Naveem was being held by force and against his best wishes, which considering he was still unconscious and currently had no wishes, was going to be tricky. Nonetheless, Mrs Dixit couldn't just wait around at home doing *nothing*.

So, they sat. Five days a week. In rain or shine.

But they didn't wait quietly.

Mrs Rampersad felt that music gave them an air of authenticity.

'We're just two ladies, sitting with the radio on,' she explained. 'No one will notice.' This was true. No one gave two older women sitting in a car much attention at all – it was the 'Miss Marple' effect.

Mrs Dixit didn't mind the radio particularly, but she did start to object to the mix tapes Mrs Rampersad brought to play. Banging calypso was not exactly great music to concentrate to. Occasionally, when a particularly frenetic song came on, Mrs Rampersad would get very excited, turning it up louder, dancing in her seat, making the car start to rock, and that *was* likely to get them noticed.

Today, they sat in silence.

*

'I've been thinking…' said Mrs Rampersad, without taking her eyes off the house. Internally, Mrs Dixit groaned. All of her neighbour's tinpot ideas started like this. '… about the doctor woman in the taxi. What if she was the wife of some mob boss, except she'd had enough and was running away? Your man was helping her flee the country? Or she was selling black market drugs? They do, doctors, you know. How else you think they pay back all their student loans?'

'If there were black market drugs, surely the police would have found them in the taxi?' Mrs Dixit retorted. She enjoyed debunking Mrs Rampersad's theories, because, to be perfectly honest, similar questions were often circulating in her own mind, and it felt good to publicly dismiss them. *Finances, passengers, solvents, earrings…*

'The police probably kept the drugs and sold 'em themselves. Everyone's on the take.'

'Naveem wouldn't have the nerve to commit a crime. He gets nervous when his library book return date is approaching.'

'You can never trust men – they have secret lives.'

'Not all men.'

'*All* men,' Mrs Rampersad replied forthrightly.

'Did your husband?' Mrs Dixit asked, as innocently as she could. 'Have a secret life, that is?' In the three weeks that they had been sitting in the car, Mrs Rampersad had been very liberal with her opinion and analysis of Mrs Dixit's private affairs but was still extremely tight-lipped when it came to her own. That's not to say nothing had slipped out. For thirty years, Mrs Rampersad had worked for Royal Mail, at a returned mail depot – taking an early retirement for an undisclosed reason. She had two sons, and six grandchildren between them, although she'd not met three of the grandchildren and didn't like the wives. When she wasn't listening to podcasts, or praying, or helping at soup kitchens, which she often did, Mrs Rampersad was investigating whether

Idris Elba was a practising Christian (the closest she'd come to confirming this was a lady at church who claimed that Idris had gone to the christening of her daughter's boss's aunt).

Mrs Rampersad pursed her lips, most likely planning to make one of her typically withering responses about there being 'no place in paradise for sticky beaks', when she gasped and shuffled down in her seat, prompting Mrs Dixit to quickly do the same. Remembering her sunglasses, Mrs Dixit swiped them from the dashboard, and threw them onto her face.

'False alarm,' Mrs Rampersad said, with a kiss of her teeth, as a person walked past the car. False alarms were an occupational hazard with Mrs Rampersad. Yesterday alone, there had been three: the old Korean woman who ran the shop on the corner, a man with crutches, and the postman. The postman wearing a bright red uniform jacket.

Mrs Dixit took off the sunglasses and shuffled back up in her seat, arranging her clothing so it was no longer invading her bodily creases. She already needed the bathroom, but she would wait until she absolutely had to go. And there was no way she was going to use the bottle…

The bottle was Mrs Rampersad's idea, when their frequent trips to the local café and its toilet, two streets over, had started to compromise their staking out.

'No,' Mrs Dixit had said, point-blank. 'I don't think so.'

'Suit yourself,' Mrs Rampersad had replied. 'I'm not saying we use the *same* one.'

'How would it even work?'

'"God will supply every need of yours".'

'Yes, but is he going to magically give us perfect aim?'

Mrs Rampersad gave a look down her nose.

'Please don't talk about "aim". This is not a boys' locker room.'

'I'm sorry… I didn't mean to…'

'We will use *this*,' said Mrs Rampersad, rummaging in her bag and pulling out a bright yellow cooking funnel.

'That's still a pass from me,' Mrs Dixit replied, 'divine intervention or not.'

Mrs Rampersad merely shrugged, but ominously, the funnel stayed out of the bag all afternoon.

Today was particularly slow-going. The lawyer had said that there was definitely a flight risk, she'd seen it before, where families sent their sick ones back to a 'home country'.

'Why would they do that, when we have the NHS here?' Mrs Dixit had asked.

'If they're worried about custody, that might not be their biggest concern. They may feel Naveem is safer with the extended family, with more people to look after him.'

'What if he got an infection over there and died? How would they even get him on a plane?'

'These are all valid questions, but it has happened before. They would probably need medical assistance, so if you notice a private nurse going in to the home, that might be a precursor to a move.'

'Naveem would never want to go back to India, not in a million years. What if he woke up and found himself in Calcutta? It would give him the shock of his life. It would probably put him back in a coma…'

'The chance is relatively slim,' the lawyer had said, 'but we need to consider every eventuality. An NHS nurse is still coming once a week, which is good. At least we know your husband is still in the property. Otherwise, the closer you can keep your eyes on the situation, and report anything that seems off, the better.'

*

Mrs Rampersad took the binoculars and held them up to her eyes.

'The curtains are still shut in his room.'

'Same as yesterday,' Mrs Dixit replied, 'they weren't opened all day.'

'He needs sunlight, for vitamin D. That's abuse, that is. Put it in the notebook.'

'Unless he's come round and they've moved him into the living room?'

'You know the nurse would be back with a doctor if there had been any major improvement.'

Mrs Dixit understood in her heart this was true, but she couldn't help wishing for the best. She missed Naveem. More than that, she physically *yearned* for him. Mrs Dixit had also come to understand exactly how *numb* she'd been during his weeks at the hospital. Nothing had seemed real. But now that Naveem was locked away from her, and she couldn't see him, sit with him, be with him in any capacity… The numbness was replaced with a level of emotion she did not know she possessed. Now there was a chance something could happen to her husband, and she wouldn't even have a chance to say goodbye… It was too awful.

The only silver lining was the jumble of her other concerns – the lack of money, the mystery of the doctor passenger, the name 'Clare' written in her husband's neat, deliberate handwriting, followed underneath by 'earrings', the accuracy of certain drugs in a person's system – were put into perspective. Mostly.

'You have that face again,' said Mrs Rampersad accusingly. 'Poor me, sad sack.'

'I'm fine,' Mrs Dixit insisted, feeling her voice strain.

'The nurse said he's healthy, remember? Fighting fit. Except for being in a coma, he's the picture of health. It's no use you moping.'

'I know, I know,' Mrs Dixit was glad for her neighbour's vigilance in keeping her out of a potentially bottomless well of grief.

'Right, I'm off to the loo,' Mrs Rampersad said, passing over the binoculars. 'I'll be as quick as I can.'

She was thirty-six minutes. Mrs Dixit timed her.

At 4 p.m., after a day of staking out with little of note (Naveem's father, always smaller and greyer than Mrs Dixit's memory of him, heading to the shop and back to buy an onion and gravy granules), they drove to the high street where Mrs Dixit helped Mrs Rampersad with her flyering. It wasn't expected of her, and Mrs Rampersad had appeared mildly bemused when Mrs Dixit had asked if she could join her, but the company seemed to be welcomed.

Mrs Dixit could instantly see why Mrs Rampersad had so much difficulty getting rid of her flyers. It wasn't so much the flyers themselves, as she'd previously imagined – although the devil imagery *was* off-putting – but rather Mrs Rampersad's approach. She was – how to put this gently? – physically intimidating. Instead of holding out the flyer, Mrs Rampersad kept it too close to her body, and when her mark walked past, she gave her wrist a flick, as if readying a butterfly knife, which had the result of the person stepping away. She would then grumble under her breath (still loud enough to be heard), and lurch towards them, holding the flyer now as if she was going to thwack them with it – repeating the failed process with the next person to come along.

Flick, flick, grumble, lurch.

Flick, flick, grumble, lurch.

In comparison, Mrs Dixit had much more luck. *Not like that*, she'd thought of Mrs Rampersad's technique, taking a flyer from the box and holding it out at arm's length, as if she was trying to pass on a baton. As someone walked by, she nodded her head and gave the flyer a wiggle. *Here, this is for you*, she said in her mind's eye, *take it*. Mrs Dixit knew instinctively not to smile. Only a mad person would smile at a stranger on a street. The first man walking by took the flyer from her hand – success! – glanced at it, and in one fluid motion, popped it in the nearby bin.

'How did you get him to take it?' Mrs Rampersad was aghast.

'I'm not exactly sure,' Mrs Dixit replied, blushing, 'he threw it out anyway.'

'Yes. But in the bin, as if it was important rubbish! And he looked at the flyer. The Lord's message fell upon his eyes! Even for the briefest of moments.'

'That's a good thing, is it?'

'It's a *marvel*,' said Mrs Rampersad, beaming.

From then on, it was quite fun. Mrs Rampersad even attempted to copy Mrs Dixit's method, but the head nod, flyer waggle didn't work as well accompanied with manic goggle eyes, and the audible muttering of 'take it, take it' between gritted teeth.

Between them, however, they emptied the box considerably faster each afternoon. Mrs Dixit grew to enjoy the ebb and flow of the high street; the reassuring din of people was comforting in a way that locking her door to a hushed home no longer was.

When they returned that evening, it was their most successful day of flyering yet – almost one and a half boxes. Arriving on the driveway, Mrs Dixit leapt out of the car to open the garage and help Mrs Rampersad navigate inside, closing the shutters after them.

*

It was a relief to be inside her flat tonight – her head was still thrumming slightly from the sleeping pills. The silence was broken almost immediately by the phone ringing.

'You're home! I've been ringing all afternoon again.' Her sister seemed worked up, even more so than normally.

'Is everything alright? How's Henry?'

'Henry's fine. He's looking forward to seeing you this weekend. In fact, he won't shut up about it. No, it's about your cash flow issue. I've had a brainwave…'

'Have you now…' Mrs Dixit braced herself.

'The trains…' There was a dramatic pause. 'You could sell the toy trains. They're collectors' items and some of them must be worth a pretty penny…'

'I'm not selling Naveem's model trains. He loves them. What's going to happen when he wakes up and finds I've…'

'What's going to happen when you can't pay next month's electricity bill, Wendy?'

Mrs Dixit was quiet for a moment, collecting herself. 'I thought I might borrow some money… from you.'

There was a noticeably awkward silence.

'We would love to, but with the renovations, and the redecorations and the extension – not to mention Henry's school tuition fees, the uniforms…'

'Yes, I was silly to ask.'

'You'll consider it, then? Selling the toy trains?'

'They're not toys. And I'll *consider* it…'

'Good, because I already spoke to a woman about an evaluation. She'll come over tomorrow morning and give you an idea about prices. This woman's an absolute expert, best in her field, so don't worry. I'll be in touch later in the week. Bye!'

Mrs Dixit cursed under her breath, and then remembering she was in an empty flat, cursed more loudly.

*

After dinner, she started the ceremonies of sleep. It was different now, ever since Naveem was taken. Mrs Dixit didn't sleep for two whole days after it happened. She'd begun hallucinating, she was so exhausted; her hand left a trail when she moved it too fast. With Naveem gone, she'd felt a strange sense of invasion and helplessness. But the worst emotion was guilt. Guilt she hadn't been there. That she didn't stop it from happening. Guilt that she'd not talked to him enough, as those kind nurses had always prompted her to.

After she'd swallowed the sleeping pills, she checked all the windows were locked in the front room and kitchen, before heading downstairs to Naveem's study. It had a different feel these days, it was no longer intimidating or scary – instead it radiated his *isness*, like a shrine. She came here to remember how Naveem smelled, or at least the smells she most associated with him – shellac, oil, burned copper, the tang of plastic and old smoke from the soldering iron, and the sharpness of ozone made from the sparking engines, which had the same clean aroma as the ground after it rained. Standing on the threshold, with the door ajar, she didn't turn on the lights, she simply breathed in slowly through her nose, waiting for the pills to start their numbing effect.

Mrs Dixit would think of all the times they sat next to each other, entirely self-contained: reading, watching a movie, lying in bed – such wasted opportunities. If he was here now, she would cradle his head in her hands and kiss his eyelids and the tips of each finger and thumb. She would massage his feet. She would wash him in a bath, and then dry him gently with a towel.

The pills were working, she realised, their gooeyness spreading through her limbs. Trudging heavily up the stairs again, she turned off the lights and crawled into bed, before the medicine obliterated her mind completely.

She did not dream.

36 days since the accident

In the morning the air hung heavily in the bedroom and had a sourness. It reminded her of the hospital.

The train expert knocked at 9.30 a.m.

'I'm sorry, there's been a misunderstanding,' Mrs Dixit said, when the woman explained who she was, 'I don't want to sell any of them. They're my husband's.'

'Usually it's the wife who wants them gone,' the woman replied, with an arch of her eyebrows. She had a pink, plump face, a posh accent, and was dressed in a tweed suit with straw-coloured hair combed back severely from her forehead, as if she'd walked head first into a storm. 'Whether you sell them or not, it's a good idea to get them evaluated at least, for insurance sake.' At the word 'insurance', Mrs Dixit flinched, stepping back. The woman took this as her cue to enter, so before she could stop her, the posh tweedy woman was ensconced in her kitchen.

'Would you like a cup of tea?' Mrs Dixit said out of politeness.

Above them, there were plodding stomps as Mrs Rampersad went about her morning ablutions.

'I'll just see the pieces, if you don't mind?'

Mrs Dixit took a box from under the table and placed it as reverently as she could on top. After her call with her sister, she'd rummaged around to see what was stored away in cupboards (not the study though, she couldn't bring herself to disturb anything in there again). The box contained what had looked, to Mrs Dixit's inexpert eye, like the most valuable items – based on their being either old, intricate, attractive, or some combination of the three.

The woman lifted the first train out of the box. Mrs Dixit watched for any change in her demeanour, but she had a powerful poker face.

'This one's lovely,' she said, with clipped vowels, still no change in expression. She turned the model train over and studied it, just as they did on *Antiques Roadshow*. 'A Hornby Number Two Special, if I'm not mistaken. The tiniest of rust damage, but it looks like it's been well looked after.'

'My husband's quite the perfectionist.'

'I can tell. See here…' She showed Mrs Dixit one of the wheels. 'These are replacement spokes. Sometimes people simply add modern plastic ones, but these have been selected from the same period. He'd have to do his homework.'

Mrs Dixit felt a flush of pride. She'd always thought of the trains as a quirk from Naveem's childhood – buying the toys he was never able to have when he was younger – but now she realised he had an admirable skill. She regretted not sitting with him more while he was working, asking questions, holding his hand, admiring his talent, instead of seeing it as an impediment.

'Are there more?'

'Boxes of them in the garage alone.'

'Marvellous!'

'But I have to go out in ten minutes.'

'We can reschedule for another time then. I want to bring a few catalogues over with me to cross reference anyway, now I know the stock is of high quality and not from some amateur hobbyist.' She paused for a moment, thinking. 'Did you say your husband was…?'

'In a coma.'

'Oh. That's a new one. I'm very sorry.'

'Thank you. Actually, I have a slightly unusual question. The glue that is used for model trains, is it toxic at all? I mean, would it show up in a toxicology report? From the fumes, or if you got enough of it on your skin?'

The tweedy woman seemed unfazed.

'I don't think so. Regulations are pretty tight around modern solvents. Unless you were eating the stuff, or bathing in it.' She laughed, like a small dog yapping, a terrier perhaps. 'I'll be in touch,' she said. 'Can I take this one with me?'

'Oh… well…' The thought of handing over one of Naveem's precious trains made her feel very nervous. 'Sure.'

Mrs Dixit felt instantly regretful but showed the woman out politely, nonetheless.

'You again!' said Magnus, later that same morning, beside the airstrip. He was dressed in an immaculately pressed white shirt, his coat sitting on his shoulders like a don's. Under his shirt collar ran a long pearl necklace, which had been fashioned into a sort of tie, knotting the string of pearls several times, like a bulbous sack of fish roe at his throat.

'Did I miss anything?' she replied, but her heart wasn't in the canned dialogue this morning, and he seemed to notice.

'Tough day? I have those. Moments when you realise what you miss. When it really takes hold.'

'Yes, actually,' Mrs Dixit replied, surprised at his perception.

'When my wife became ill, it was all I could do not to smash everything to pieces, and now I wish I had. I wish I'd pulled everything off the walls in fury and frustration, because at least I'd have something to be proud of. But it all goes so softly, softly.'

She nodded, staring out at the expanse of coarse grass and asphalt.

'I've been trying to remember times when my husband – I don't know – thought kindly of me.' Mrs Dixit felt disloyal talking about her marriage, especially to another man, but there was something about Magnus's non-judgemental nature that spurred her on. 'We'd hold hands, and he'd kiss me on the cheek,' her face started to flush, 'and he often told me with words – but they were fixed patterns. It would have been strange for him not to kiss me when he brought me a cup of tea, that was our way. I'm trying to think of moments when he stepped out of script, and I can't.'

'Oh, yes – *samsara*.'

'Sam what?'

Magnus smiled – she could see his fillings.

'It's a Sanskrit word. It means an endless, aimless drifting in relationships. But what about the white-hot coals? Or even the smouldering embers, eh? The *mysterious tremendium*. The mystery of being. If it disappears in relation to each other, we are lost. *Lost…*' Magnus was silent for a moment. 'We're being watched, you know,' he said, lowering his voice.

'Oh, that's just my neighbour, Mrs Rampersad.'

'No, not her – in the blue car. Have you noticed it's always around whenever I'm here?'

Mrs Dixit hadn't.

'Who would be watching us?'

'There are cunning people,' he said conspiratorially.

Peering at the blue car, Mrs Dixit tried to see who was sitting in the driver's seat, but they were holding up a magazine and the glare on the windscreen didn't help.

'My poor Nicky,' said Magnus more loudly, 'she loved the orchestra. I would surprise her with a trip to the Royal Albert Hall and she would sit enraptured. Never enjoyed it much, myself – all that racket, give me aeroplanes any day! But to see her face… that's what a marriage is for, don't you think?' He touched Mrs Dixit's hand so very gently. It was the first time she'd had any skin-to-skin contact in weeks, and the sensation made her feel a mixture of things – sadness, confusion, anger, frustration, and a powerful tug of something that felt a lot like desire.

On cue, a car door opened, and Mrs Rampersad could be heard behind them, grunting as she heaved herself out of the driving seat.

'Time!' she announced, as she manoeuvred back into her seat, slamming the door to really hammer home the point.

*

Theirs was an eventful first hour of staking out this morning. Naveem's oldest brother arrived shortly after 11 a.m., his second older brother appearing ten minutes later.

'They've been summoned,' Mrs Rampersad said, hunched in her seat, sunglasses on. 'Perhaps he's stirred?'

'They're not hurrying enough – and I think all the siblings would arrive,' replied Mrs Dixit, hunkered down herself, coat collar pulled up around her neck.

'What if the others arrived last night? I told you we should come back in the evenings.'

Mrs Dixit didn't take the bait. However much it might be helpful, she couldn't commit to nocturnal monitoring of the house as well; her sleep patterns were precarious enough as they were.

'His bedroom curtains are still closed,' Mrs Dixit responded. 'They were carrying shopping bags with food; they're only coming home for lunch.'

'What happens when Naveem *does* wake up? What do they tell him then? *Hello son, we kidnapped you from the hospital and stole you from your wife?*'

'His mother has a way of saying unreasonable things and making them sound very sensical. Do you know she told the police I was mistreating him? And that she was "concerned" I might hurt myself?'

Mrs Rampersad shook her head in disbelief.

'If anything, you mollycoddled the man,' she replied, with a snort. 'Men need to be given space, not fussed over. That's when they start to look elsewhere, when you become too much like their moth…'

She stopped, recognising that she was about to overstep a boundary, which was quite an achievement for Mrs Rampersad.

'I'm sure you're very good at giving men all the space they need,' Mrs Dixit said.

Mrs Rampersad narrowed her eyes, trying to evaluate if there was sarcasm in Mrs Dixit's tone.

'Men do not run my life, *I* run my life.'

And look where that's got you, Mrs Dixit thought silently.

Naveem's brothers left the house shortly after 2 p.m.; the older one was even patting his stomach, as if he was aware people were observing him and conferring on his actions.

It was strange, seeing them after so many years. They looked very much like Naveem, quite a bit fatter and older than she remembered, but every time one appeared, it gave Mrs Dixit a jolt, as if she'd seen a ghost. Not a ghost, a facsimile.

'Once they're gone,' Mrs Rampersad said, peering sideways over her sunglasses, 'I'm going to make a trip to the ladies' room...'

'It's her!' gasped Mrs Dixit, sliding down even further into the seat. Naveem's mother had slipped out of the house behind her sons without the watching women noticing and was now walking along the pavement towards them. Instinctively, Mrs Rampersad started the car and pulled away. You could say a lot about Mrs Rampersad, particularly when it came to her small bladder, but she did have wonderful reactions. Mrs Dixit scooted down even further, so she was practically on the floor, and peered out of the window as carefully as she could.

The other Mrs Dixit was carrying an empty shopping bag over her shoulder – she didn't so much walk as glide. If Mrs Dixit believed in auras, Naveem's mother's would be vast and purple and it would swirl turgidly. Her long dark hair – no sign of grey like her sons, was it dyed? – was fixed into a bun so large, it almost dwarfed her head. She was tiny in stature, even smaller than Mrs Dixit remembered, as if she'd shrunk in the wash, but there was a steeliness to her that belied her small frame. There was nothing soft about her face either, her nose and mouth and eyebrows were all angles, and her eyes seemed too large for their sockets, bulbous and cat-like. Those feline eyes glanced towards the retreating car, and Mrs Dixit felt them lock with hers for the briefest of seconds! – or did they?

'That was close,' noted Mrs Rampersad once they'd turned onto the next street.

'I think she saw us!' Mrs Dixit cried, mostly because she wanted this idea debunked.

'Will she call the police? Maybe we should stay low for a day or two. Or get better disguises?'

'If she's spotted the car, it doesn't matter what disguises we wear. And we can't give up. I don't care if they know we're watching. Maybe it's better if they *do*. His family can't get away with what they've done!' Mrs Dixit wasn't used to speaking so decisively, it was making her head swim.

'Or we could buy that drone, like I've been talking about. Then we can film through the windows. We don't even need to leave home.'

'I told you, no drones,' Mrs Dixit said exasperated. 'You don't even know how to turn on a computer…'

'Drones aren't computers,' Mrs Rampersad replied, sullenly, 'they're unmanned aerial vehicles…'

And that's when they had the crash.

After the bang of impact, Mrs Rampersad turned with such a recriminating look, it was as if she held Mrs Dixit personally responsible.

'Pull over!' Mrs Dixit yelled.

The car juddered to a stop.

'Oh, my days!' exclaimed Mrs Rampersad. 'Did we hit something? Or did something hit us?'

Quickly, Mrs Dixit got out. She saw what had happened immediately. Mrs Rampersad had clipped the rear bumper of a parked Nissan Bluebird and now it was hanging off in a very miserable way. She checked the front of their car – it was fine, some scratches but nothing serious. Mrs Rampersad was out of the car now too. 'No wonder,' she tutted loudly, 'it's parked all the way out here in the middle of the road. What did they expect?'

'We have to *leave*,' said Mrs Dixit, trying to contain her panic. She realised she *did* care if they were found by Naveem's mother after all, especially here, especially now. It would confirm everything the woman had always suspected about her.

'No need to raise your voice,' reprimanded Mrs Rampersad. 'I'll leave my number on the windscreen so we can sort this out, although I will be having a few words to say about their parking. Jesus was guiding us, it's lucky we only…'

'Naveem's mother is coming! We have to go *right now*!'

'I can't leave without supplying my details,' said Mrs Rampersad. 'Apart from being against the letter of the law, it's not the Christian thing to do.'

'The Christian thing?' Mrs Dixit screeched. 'The *Christian thing*? When you take the wrappers off your straws, you throw them out of the car window. Last year, Naveem caught you tampering with the gas meter. You lie and say you don't have a TV, so you never have to pay the licence fee. You almost ran over Jill's cat, two doors over, I saw it happen with my own eyes. You clomp around upstairs in the middle of the night, wearing, I don't know what, TAP SHOES, but *now* you're in a moral quandary? *Please*, let's just get in the car and *go*!'

Mrs Rampersad froze for a moment – in shock or anger, it was hard to tell – and then, as if a switch was flipped, nodded her head and walked to the driver's seat, getting in. Mrs Dixit hurried in too, and a few moments later, they were driving away in an immutable silence that Mrs Rampersad would honour for days.

*

Following their normal schedule, they drove to the town centre, parked, fetched a box of flyers from the boot each, and made their way to the high street. Mrs Dixit's mind raced the entire time, trying to think of a suitable way to apologise to Mrs Rampersad, but nothing seemed quite right, so she ended up saying nothing at all.

Their flyering, it must be said, was better than it had ever been. Perhaps it was the unspoken tension between the two women, maybe it was the adrenaline from the accident, or maybe it was that they were finally hitting their stride, but more flyers were placed in hands that day than most weeks combined. Paper *flew*. Passers-by didn't stand a chance, even when the weather turned and it began to spit. It was as if the two women had the power of telekinesis – they willed flyers into the hands of their mark, and suddenly one appeared, often the recipient blinking at the rectangle of card as if they had not themselves reached out and accepted it in their clammy paw. Forty-five minutes in, and despite the light rain, Mrs Rampersad had to fetch a second fresh box. Flyers clogged the rubbish bins, and littered gutters, but still the two women worked on, never once saying a single word to each other, the grim determination plain on both their faces.

Not a word was spoken on the trip home either, although there was a strange air of success, a job well done, amid the palpable awkwardness and the sound of rain drumming on the windscreen.

To say Mrs Dixit was relieved to get back home today was an understatement. The silence felt restorative. Taking off her wet coat, she luxuriated in it – an absence which expected nothing in return.

Henry! Her sister was dropping him off in the morning to spend the day with his (only, but apparently favourite) aunt tomorrow. Mrs Dixit had completely forgotten to tell Mrs Rampersad she had planned to bring him along, and now… She cussed under her breath, picking up the phone to call her sister to reschedule, when there was a knock at the front door.

'Hi Wendy.' Len smiled, and it was a strange smile, as if he had been practising it beforehand. 'I just thought I'd *swing by* and see how everything is. What with Naveem… It's a bloody terrible thing, him taken from the hospital. Have you talked to the police about it?'

'Frequently,' Mrs Dixit said. 'It seems there's not much that can be done when you're abducted by your own family and aren't conscious to voice your opposition. His parents have done a good job of painting me as the villain, too.' She considered telling him about the damning toxicology report but decided against it. 'It's in the hands of a lawyer though, so we'll see how that goes.'

'At the very least, it's good that someone else is changing his bedpan, I suppose!'

'What?'

'I mean, think of all the work you'd have to do if Naveem was here. They can't smell good, can they, after they've been in a coma for that long? Bedsores and what have you.'

Mrs Dixit cleared her throat.

'Can I help you with anything, Len?'

'Oh no, I just thought I'd…'

'… swing by. So you said.'

'And you told me, if I ever thought of something about Naveem. Anything out of the ordinary, to tell you. Well, I remembered something.'

He paused, and Mrs Dixit waited expectantly.

'What was it…?'

'Can I come in?'

She turned and raised her eyes to the heavens secretly, as he followed her into the kitchen.

Len sat in the same kitchen chair as he had last time, making himself comfortable. Naveem would hate the fact that Len had a preference when it came to their kitchen chairs.

'What did you remember?' she prompted.

'Could I have a cup of tea?' he asked, looking wistfully at the kettle.

Mrs Dixit sighed quietly and filled it from the tap.

'It was about his behaviour,' Len said, as the kettle began to gurgle.

'What about it?'

'Naveem was always very erratic, if you ask me.' Mrs Dixit imagined that Naveem would have been very hot and cold in his dealings with Len. Her husband was not particularly cruel in nature, but he did have a very low tolerance for idiots, and Len most certainly made the cut. 'He was also very suspicious. Paranoid, you might say. He once asked me if I'd noticed anything strange at control.'

'What sort of thing?' Mrs Dixit thought of Cliff – he'd always run a tight ship at the taxi company, she couldn't imagine him even tangentially supporting something as illegal as transporting stolen goods.

Len leaned in, lowering his voice as if someone might be eavesdropping.

'On the radio, right – we have code words. Some of them are for locations, like Parliament is the Gasworks, 'cos of all the hot air. The City is the Den of Thieves. If we're worried about a customer doing a ride 'n' run, we might say we've got a bunny.

Obvious stuff. There's some joking about too, you know if a female customer has particularly notable…' he trailed off, clearing his throat. 'Naveem asked me about some of the code words over the radio. Said he couldn't understand them.'

'Could you?'

'I got their gist. Some of them were about the special deliveries. But there were others I didn't have the foggiest about… Remember, I have my nose pretty clean, relatively speaking.'

'Did you tell Naveem?'

'Sort of. I didn't want to kick the hornets' nest. I told him it was banter – and left it at that. But he was definitely *edgy* over something.'

Mrs Dixit tried to think back. She couldn't remember a time when Naveem had seemed particularly jittery or even ruffled. He was man of order, one of habit. She would have noticed straight away if he was *erratic*. Unless he was very good at hiding parts of himself, and always had been… Her mind wandered to the woman, the doctor in the front of his cab in the accident, and a pair of earrings never meant for her… but fortunately, the kettle started to whistle.

'How are *you*, though?' asked Len, when Mrs Dixit placed the steaming mug of tea in front of him.

'I'm fine,' she said, dropping into a chair, but feeling tired. Weary. 'I wasn't sleeping well, but now the doctor has given me stronger sleeping tablets, which knock me out each night. I don't even dream.'

Len blew on his tea.

'That doesn't sound great. Not dreaming. Dreams are the way we process our emotions.' This feels like a dream, Mrs Dixit thought, Len here, in her kitchen, lecturing her on dreams. She considered pinching herself, seeing if she could wake herself up. Why was Len calling on her, really? Surely, he didn't actually want to have an affair?

Mrs Dixit felt sure that if she winked at Len right now, he'd get flustered and leave. She'd met his wife several times at company events – she was perfectly nice, if slightly vacant, which Mrs Dixit had always put down to parenting exhaustion, or perhaps having to put up with Len. 'I had a guy in my cab once,' Len continued. 'He didn't have a single dream in thirteen years. He'd seen every specialist known to medicine. Psychiatrists. Witch doctors. They all said the same thing.'

'Which was?'

'He needed to get out more. Travel the world. Lack of dreams meant a lack of imagination. We stop dreaming when we've given up on life.'

'I've stopped dreaming because I'm heavily medicated. The insomnia wasn't helping. I started to see things…' she didn't finish the sentence.

'What kind of things?'

'It's silly. I was overtired. But I would see shadows move. It was obviously just exhaustion and the light playing, but it was… unnerving.'

'You should have someone here,' Len said, leaning forward, as if he'd been waiting for this cue.

Not in your wildest dreams, Mrs Dixit thought, taking a sip of her chamomile tea.

That night, once she'd taken the two tablets out from the foil, she held them up and examined them in her palm.

'Len… I mean…' she tutted, before throwing the pills into her mouth.

37 days since the accident

She slept past her alarm clock again and was woken by the doorbell.

'I'm coming, I'm coming!' she yelled, heaving herself out of bed.

'Thanks again,' her sister said as soon as Mrs Dixit managed to open the door, 'he's *so* been looking forward to staying with his aunt again, haven't you?'

Henry nodded, and to Mrs Dixit's relief, it was a genuine one, as if he'd been asked if he liked ice cream or chocolate – his head touching his chest with each exaggerated, but seemingly authentic, nod.

'I'll be back at six. I'm going on a spa day with a few of the girls, well, it's a hen do, deferred because we lost our deposit… I won't go into it now… See you later! I'll catch up with all your news tonight!'

Henry smiled up at her.

'Can we go to the waxworks again?' he asked, his eyes large and delightfully pleading.

With Henry busy watching an episode of *BeastBotz*, Mrs Dixit quickly showered and dressed. She heard Mrs Rampersad upstairs and felt a stab of remorse. When she checked on Henry next, she opened her door so she could tell if Mrs Rampersad was on her way out. Twenty minutes later, there were the familiar banging thumps as Mrs Rampersad manoeuvred herself down the stairs.

'Hello,' Mrs Dixit said, emerging from the door on cue. 'Henry is here, I forgot. Perhaps I can bring him along too… If you don't mind?'

Mrs Rampersad grunted and shrugged, without looking at Mrs Dixit.

'Turn the television off, we're going!' Mrs Dixit called to Henry brightly, grabbing a packed bag of supplies for the day and hurrying the boy out. In the car, Mrs Rampersad proceeded to ignore both her passengers as if they weren't in the vehicle at all. They drove straight to Naveem's parents' house, eschewing McDonald's and the airport, Mrs Dixit trying to engage Henry in conversation as much as she could, even falling back on a game of 'I spy' at one point. When Mrs Dixit suggested Mrs Rampersad have a go, she received a sideways glance so withering, she was surprised the car didn't roll over with its momentum.

'My turn again then,' Mrs Dixit said, as cheerfully as she could muster.

They sat further from the house this morning as a precaution. The sky was mottled with billowy clouds, the sun poking through occasionally as a spotlight.

'Why are we here?' Henry asked in the back seat.

'We're visiting a friend,' Mrs Dixit replied. Her nephew probably wouldn't remember Naveem, he'd never been particularly present with the boy. But then to be honest, neither had she, previously. They had gone to Henry's christening, but never to birthdays, and they always hired a cottage in Wales for two weeks over Christmas.

'When can we go?'

'Soon,' she assured him. Mrs Dixit noticed a predilection for her voice going much higher and more sing-songy when she spoke to the child, especially when she was bending the truth, and she pulled herself up on it. She would talk to him like a person, he seemed to respect that.

'Are we going to the waxworks after?'

'Shall we find a picture for you to colour?' asked Mrs Dixit, trying to ignore the annoyed muttering from Mrs Rampersad beside her.

Very little occurred of merit on their watch. There were no visitors, and no one left the house. At about 11 a.m., it rained for twenty minutes, and then Henry needed the toilet, and Mrs Dixit was glad to stretch her legs and leave the suffocating confines of the cramped car. She felt out of sorts – paranoid that they'd been spotted yesterday. What if Naveem had been moved to a brother's house as a result? Or he was already on a plane?

When they returned to the car, Mrs Dixit made her pitch.

'I think you should go and knock on the door and see if he's still there.' Mrs Rampersad opened her eyes wide in surprise but didn't reply. 'You can pretend you're a charity collector. Get invited in. Ask for a glass of water, and then check his room.' Mrs Rampersad began to shake her head, but still stubbornly refused to speak. 'Please!' Mrs Dixit said passionately. 'What if they've already taken him? I need to know.' She lowered her voice. 'You can take Henry – explain you're a nanny and you need to use the toilet.' She felt ashamed, including Henry in her plan, but it was desperate measures.

Mrs Rampersad sighed and shook her head – she'd do it without Henry. Mrs Dixit was instantly relieved; it might have been putting the child in danger. Once out of the car, Mrs Rampersad zipped up her coat and without a backward glance, started towards the house.

'Good luck!' shouted Mrs Dixit, as Henry climbed into the driver's seat next to her.

'Can I have a go with the binoculars now, Henry?' Mrs Rampersad had been gone for ten minutes, each one felt like an eon to Mrs Dixit. The boy was using the binoculars to look at the clouds. 'Not at the sun, remember,' she'd had to warn him.

'Everything is small,' he'd complained.

'You have them round the wrong way.'

'That's better,' he said after she'd helped him.

Mrs Dixit watched the house intently. Mrs Rampersad had knocked, waited, and when the door was answered, talked for a few minutes, before going inside.

'When is that lady coming back?' Henry asked.

'Soon.'

'I don't think she likes me.'

'I'm not sure she likes many people, I wouldn't worry.'

'My mummy says you don't like her.'

'What? Of course I like her, she's my sister.'

Henry shrugged half-heartedly and turned the binoculars over again.

'Everything is small like ants,' he said triumphantly.

'What else does your mummy say about me?'

Putting down the binoculars, Henry thought about this.

'Your husband went away because he was so bored he couldn't wake up again. Maybe he needs to be kissed, like in *Sleeping Beauty*? And then he can get out of bed?'

Mrs Dixit, still staring at the house intently, clenched her jaw at this piece of second-hand information, although it didn't surprise her.

'Where did your tooth go?' Henry asked, tapping the lens of the binoculars with his finger, even though she'd told him he shouldn't. 'Did the Tooth Fairy come?'

She was about to respond when, unexpectedly, she caught something in her peripheral vision. At first, she thought it was a postman, because he was wearing a uniform, but then why was he was kneeling down, peering at them? She wound down the window, realising it was a *police* uniform. Her heart panged with alarm. No, he was a community officer. What was the difference? *Could they still arrest you?* she wondered. That was important.

'Hello. Can I ask you a quick question?' The officer said, through the wound-down window. He was Asian – Indian or

Pakistani – which also worried Mrs Dixit. What if he knew the family? *What if they'd sent him*?

'Come on, Henry,' she said, as gaily as she could manage.

Once they were both on the footpath, the officer stuck his head into the car.

'Is there anything I can help you with?' Mrs Dixit asked, glancing at Mrs Rampersad's yellow plastic funnel, which was still on the dashboard.

'We've had neighbours saying there's been a car with two women parked outside for a couple of weeks. There's been a burglar working in this area, so we have to follow up every lead.'

Mrs Dixit glanced across at Naveem's parents' house, which contained Mrs Rampersad, but for how much longer?

Don't come back now, don't come back, she pleaded silently.

'Is this your son?'

'He's my nephew.'

'And can I ask what you're doing here?'

'We're waiting for… a friend.'

'Do you live locally?'

'In Chomley.'

The officer asked for her home address, and she gave it, her heart racing.

'If you can move your car – the neighbours here say you're part-blocking their drive.'

'Oh, so it was these neighbours that reported the car?' Mrs Dixit said, with relief. 'Not the ones over there,' she pointed.

'Why would the ones over there report a car?' the officer asked.

'Look, I have binoculars!' Henry said. 'I can see everything close up *and* far away.'

'I think it would be best if you move along now,' the officer said.

'But, yes… we're waiting for my friend…'

'If you don't move your car, I'll have to make an official report,' he carried on. 'We can't be too careful at the minute. We're getting a lot of heat about these burglaries. I'd hate to have to take you into the station all because of a misunderstanding…'

'I understand,' Mrs Dixit said, opening the passenger door. 'Let's go, Henry.'

Fortunately, the keys were in the ignition. She started the car, nervously, as the officer watched and took down the registration number. It had been a while since she'd driven, and Mrs Dixit felt extremely rusty. She turned the wheels and pressed on the gas, and it gave a sharp jolt – she wasn't used to this clutch, it appeared to be temperamental.

Giving the officer a curt wave, she drove past Naveem's parents' house, just as Mrs Rampersad appeared from the front door, accompanied by Naveem's father. Mrs Rampersad watched as her car drove past, her mouth wide, but to her credit she didn't yell or wave, but watched impassively as Mrs Dixit rounded the corner and disappeared from view.

Mrs Dixit drove them back to the house. She didn't know what else to do, afraid the officer would see them and report them if she simply circled the block and headed back. It was the wrong decision, obviously – she should have found another place to park nearby, but she panicked. She tried calling and texting Mrs Rampersad but couldn't get through and received nothing in response. After lunch, she considered taking the car out again and looking for her, when she finally heard the front door open.

Mrs Dixit rushed out.

'I'm so sorry! There was—'

Mrs Rampersad held up her hand, her face icy – her expression could have stopped water from running. She started up the stairs.

'Is Naveem okay? Is he still there? Please, I need to know!'

Pausing on the second-to-last step, Mrs Rampersad nodded her head.

A wave of relief passed over Mrs Dixit.

'So they didn't see us! What did you find out…?'

But Mrs Rampersad continued up the stairs without a word, shutting her door firmly.

Henry was beside her when she turned, startling her.

'See, she doesn't like us,' he said and then went back to his TV programme.

In the afternoon, running out of ways to occupy themselves – and with Mrs Dixit worrying over the unknown condition of her husband, but too afraid of her neighbour's wrath to prompt any further – they took a bus to the waxworks.

The same teenager as before sat in the ticket office, picking at his cuticles and looking thoroughly fed up.

'Is it busy inside?' Mrs Dixit asked, secretly hoping it would be, wanting to be washed in a bath of sound and chatter and noise until the voice in her head was drowned out completely.

'Nah,' said the boy, checking the time on his watch, a fat gold one with a brown leather strap. You didn't often see youths wearing watches anymore, what with mobile phones so commonplace. Phones could do anything except microwave your lunch, it seemed now, although Mrs Dixit barely used the message function on hers. Mr Dixit had never been a fan of texting either, the lack of prediction in the predictive text frustrating him. 'Machine's broken,' the boy added. 'Cash only.'

It was indeed empty inside and slightly unnerving with no one else around, like a haunted house where one of the immobile figures might suddenly jump out at you. Henry seemed to prefer it today, taking his time with each room, inspecting the waxworks cautiously, investigating anything that could be interacted with: a button to start a short video about making the wax models (this was clearly a relic from the eighties, judging by the perms and mullets), flaps over celebrity quizzes that could be lifted to reveal the correct answer, an invitation to handle a tinny replica of Muhammad Ali's heavyweight champion belt.

'Would you like me to take a picture of you with…' She paused, assessing the waxy set of features approximating a human face, '… David Beckham? Or is it Johnny Depp?' The second was the safest bet as the place seemed lousy with Johnny Depps. He was obviously extremely popular at one time, and once you'd made the mould, you could clone as many as you'd like, Mrs Dixit supposed. Add some knives to the hands in one, facial hair and a pirate hat in the other…

Henry shook his head at the suggestion of a photo, so Mrs Dixit put her phone away again. She wasn't entirely comfortable with the camera function anyway.

Mrs Dixit sat down on a stool in front of the running video, really to buy her some time so they didn't rush through the place within half an hour of arriving. She considered ringing the hospital again, to see if she could be put in touch with the nurse who made weekly visits to Naveem, but so far that had proven fruitless – she was always told to refer to his GP, and his GP said to refer to the hospital. She'd deliberated intercepting the nurse as she left Naveem's parents' house, but that might become problematic, especially if the nurse reported it to the hospital, or worse, told his mother. Poor Naveem, perhaps she should go back to his parents' house right now? If she was braver, she would…

Mrs Dixit had been staring at the silent screen in a very distracted way, when something pulled her attention into sharp focus. It was a face she recognised. 'Who's that?' she muttered, peering closer. In the video, a man with a full head of curly hair was painstakingly adding eyebrows to a wax figure of a young Sean Connery, or perhaps it was Clark Gable? She watched, open-mouthed, until the answer rushed to her: *Cliff!* It was Cliff, from the taxi office – Naveem's boss! She was almost sure of it. What on earth was he doing in the waxworks' video from the eighties?

Glancing over to Henry, who was busy tying the laces of a not-quite-fat-enough Winston Churchill's shoes, she took out her phone and dialled the taxi office.

'Pick-up address?' came Cliff's familiar gruff voice.

'It's Wendy!' she said, trying not to chuckle.

'Oh, hello, Wendy. How are you? I heard about Naveem…'

'Yes, I'm doing as best I can,' she replied hurriedly, keen to get to the mystery of the video. 'I've not been sleeping, so I've been put on elephant tranquilisers. Now I can barely pull myself out of bed in the mornings…'

'I'm sorry to hear that. If there's anything I can do…'

'There's one thing you can help me with, in fact. Solve a surprising mystery I've just uncovered.'

There was a slight pause.

'What's that then, Wendy?'

'Were you ever on very personal terms with James Bond, back in the eighties?'

'I don't know what you're talking about…'

'I'm at the waxworks, and I've just seen your face come up on one of the videos here; either that or you have a twin.'

Cliff laughed then, a big bear-like guffaw. 'Guilty as charged. I can't believe they're still showing that. I worked there for a couple of summers when I was younger and thinner than I care to remember.'

'You didn't want to pursue it as a full-time career?'

'Nope, my ambition was to become a rock star, not making replicas of washed-up celebrities. It seemed sad, even then, so I gave it up. And now I have this illustrious career – although maybe I should have stuck with waxworks considering the taxi racket isn't exactly the money maker it once was…'

'Does Naveem know about your earlier career?'

'I don't think I've mentioned it. I try to keep it out of conversation, otherwise the boys give me hell.'

'I'm sure he'll find it hilarious when he wakes up.' The moment the words were out of her mouth, a lump formed in her throat.

'He will, you know – he's going to get better, Wendy. It's only a matter of time.'

'Exactly. Time… I'd better let you go, Cliff. But talking to you has given me a good giggle, just when I needed it.'

'Glad I could oblige. Look after yourself, Wendy. Sorry to hear the sleeping pills are knocking you for six, but better than not getting any sleep.'

'It's lucky I'm medicated – I think those lustrous long locks of yours might have kept me awake.'

'Ha, yes,' he said with an uncomfortable chuckle, and Mrs Dixit felt like she'd overstepped the mark. Strangely, this spurred her on.

'Cliff, can I ask you something?' Again, he was silent, but she pushed on, afraid of stopping. 'I was going through some of Naveem's things, and I saw the name "Clare", no "i"? Does that ring any bells?'

'I don't think so, Wendy.'

'I thought she might be another taxi driver?' she lied.

'No one working here with that name – none of the wives either, to my knowledge.'

That was good to know. For some instinctive reason it seemed better if this Clare, whoever she was, didn't exist in their wider circle.

She thanked Cliff and hung up, still lost in the worried chatter of her thoughts.

Ten minutes later, the teenager came over with a bin bag.

'We're closing soon,' he announced unceremoniously.

'But we only just arrived,' Mrs Dixit replied. They hadn't even made it to the nautically themed room yet.

He shrugged, completely devoid of empathy.

'Not my problem,' he said with a dismissive shrug.

Mrs Dixit started to grind her teeth, and then remembered that's how she'd lost the canine, and so stopped: 'What about the mini golf?'

'Closing too,' the teenager responded, before stomping off, giving seventies Cher a whack on her butt as he went by, causing the rock icon to wobble from side to side.

They were mostly silent during the bus ride home.

'I did shoelaces, but I didn't get to tie the ropes,' Henry noted quietly, almost to himself, and then stared out of the bus window for the rest of the journey. Mrs Dixit kept trying to think up topics to spark his interest, but nothing came to mind, and she felt, in some small way, that she had failed them both.

Mrs Dixit's stomach lurched as they approached the house – not only was her sister early, she was standing at the front door talking to none other than Mrs Rampersad!

'Come now,' Mrs Dixit said, pulling Henry along by the hand, breaking into a jog.

'We were just talking about you!' her sister called when she saw them approach.

Mrs Rampersad turned towards Mrs Dixit, but her eyes did not focus. Mrs Dixit had the strange sensation that she was partially or wholly transparent.

'Oh, really?'

'We were saying how hard it's been on you. I mean, what is this world coming to, with car accidents and comas and burglaries and the economy? I don't know how you stay so positive! I'd be a nervous wreck in your shoes, but you seem to have taken everything in your stride. A real inspiration.'

'I don't know about that…'

'Your marriage has fallen apart – there's no money coming in…'

'My marriage has not *fallen apart*…'

'Which reminds me, did the woman come to value Naveem's collection? I've spoken to a couple of people, and they all agree, you could be sitting on a goldmine here.'

'She stopped by, yes, but Naveem would never forgive me if I sold…'

'But he's not here, is he? And it's not as if he made provisions… especially with those insurance payments mysteriously stopped. And you don't want to remortgage, not in this climate.'

Her sister was enjoying airing their dirty laundry in front of an audience. Mrs Rampersad, to her credit, arms crossed over her bosom, did not seem to be enjoying this discourse. In fact, she scowled ferociously, adding barely a grunt to the proceedings.

How is Naveem? Mrs Dixit wanted to yell at her neighbour. *Tell me everything, please!*

'Even if he does get better…'

'*When* he does…' Mrs Dixit added quickly.

'… there will be questions that need answering. That doctor lady who was riding pillion with him in his cab, for a start.'

'She wasn't riding *pillion*, you only do that on a motorcycle, she was simply sitting…'

'You see, questions! When I think of you knocking around in this flat all by yourself…'

Mrs Rampersad sniffed, speaking finally: 'A woman doesn't need a man, she can be perfectly happy without one. Happier, some say.'

'I know, but…' Mrs Dixit's sister gave a look which was oozing with treacly condescension. 'Naveem took all your best years, and what did he leave you with? Toy trains.'

'He didn't *take* my best years…'

'I know, I know,' her sister replied cloyingly, but she recognised her audience was turning. 'Oh,' she said, as if surprised to see Henry there too. 'Did you have fun with your aunty today?'

Mrs Dixit braced herself, but the boy nodded.

'I can tie any shoelaces I want now,' he said brightly, but his mother didn't seem to hear. 'But we didn't get to the rope room…'

'What's needed is some realistic thinking in terms of your *situation*,' his mother said, turning back. 'Naveem is gone, and obviously, that's devastating [Mrs Rampersad tutted], but we now have to tackle the *real world practicalities*. This flat for one. Moving into a smaller place, without a garage or the need for a study, would lower your overheads, especially once you remove all the clutter…'

Mrs Rampersad made a guttural sound in her throat which Mrs Dixit knew from experience was a signal of high disapproval. Her sister, however, seemed to take this as encouragement, and continued. 'We're only thinking about *you*, Wendy. Your eyes are shut to the most important thing…'

'Which is?' Mrs Dixit was still holding Henry's hand, and the boy wriggled free of her increasingly tightened grip.

'Hope is wonderful, but if you look at the statistics about coma victims, even the ones who *do* wake up are never really the same again.'

Mrs Rampersad opened her mouth as if to say something but instead turned on her heels and stalked up the stairs.

'Strange woman,' commented her sister, under her breath. 'I hope you understand all this comes from a place of love. Really it makes no difference to me if you're here by yourself, or out there enjoying life somewhere new.'

'Where exactly do you think I should go?' Mrs Dixit asked, exasperated.

'You could move to Spain? What's keeping you here? No one is going to reward you for your misplaced sense of duty.' Her sister gave a thin-lipped smile. 'And I don't want to appear cruel…' She smiled again, a pitying smile. 'But now we're getting everything out in the open, how do you know Naveem was ever… I mean, Jim said it always looked very *convenient*. Naveem had someone to cook his meals and iron his shirts, while he was doing heavens knows what, gallivanting around London.'

'Working… He was working.'

Her sister gave her another pitying look, which made Mrs Dixit want to grab her by the hair.

'It's just… what did he ever do, to show he really cared? Jim buys me things all the time. I've lost count of the presents over the years. But, Naveem... Without real affection, how were you any different than the maid, or worse… *the mother*?'

'That's not…' Mrs Dixit started, her voice trembling with emotion.

'Correct me if I'm wrong, but I can't remember a single instance when you seemed *intimate*.'

'He was a private man,' she spluttered in defence.

'Yes, very private… Very private indeed.' Her sister lowered her voice even more. 'You've never even spoken to me about your [she only mouthed the next word] *miscarriages*. It's not that we didn't have challenges either, with Henry, but we went to all those seminars, and had multiple IVF treatments – you have to really want a baby.'

'Are you telling me I didn't *want* it enough?'

'All I'm saying is that having children would have taken the attention away from Naveem…'

Mrs Dixit was speechless with rage. Henry was looking up at them both, his forehead furrowed with concern.

'We'd better take you home,' his mother said far too cheerily, 'your daddy will be wondering where we are!'

'Can I stay with Aunty Wendy tonight?'

'Where would you sleep, silly? You have a perfectly good bedroom at home.'

'I could make a bed on the sofa…?'

She ignored her son and turned back to Mrs Dixit.

'You must start taking things more seriously. I'm only thinking about *you*.'

Mrs Dixit was reeling. *Of course there was love and tenderness!* her mind shouted. *Of course they had both wanted children once!* The miscarriages were another side of their marriage she'd locked away in the silent part of herself. There had been dark months, a winter – three years after they were married, during her second miscarriage – that was particularly painful. *Why hadn't she met Naveem five years earlier? Why hadn't her body cooperated?* There had also been quiet, shameful relief too; Mrs Dixit would not have all of the terrifying responsibility of motherhood. And Naveem had not left her, to find a woman his own age to start again. If anything, he had become sweeter, more tender. *We'll be okay*, his body language had implied, as he pulled his chair closer, made more hot drinks, did all of her regular chores. That was proof, surely?

Still, her sister's words had struck a nerve in a deep, unguarded part of herself. There must be one memory, one single irrefutable moment she could hold up as an example of her husband's love and devotion to make her sister choke on her words, but nothing came.

'Thanks again for looking after Henry.' Her sister gave Mrs Dixit a peck on her cheek as she passed. It was all Mrs Dixit could do not to rush to the sink and scrub her face with the steel wool.

That night she took an extra half of one sleeping pill.

38 days since the accident

Mrs Rampersad knocked on her door the next morning. Mrs Dixit could tell it was her, because anyone else would have given up after the fourth attempt.

'I'm coming!' Mrs Dixit yelled groggily, using the table and chairs for support as she manoeuvred herself across the kitchen.

Mrs Rampersad was holding a box of flyers.

'We should leave soon,' she announced nonchalantly, and for a moment, Mrs Dixit forgot about the recent incidents, and the fact that, until extremely recently, Mrs Rampersad had not been speaking to her.

'I thought... you were mad at me?'

Mrs Rampersad grunted.

'Your sister... Your sister is...' She didn't finish her sentence, but Mrs Rampersad's eyebrows communicated everything.

'She does mean well,' replied Mrs Dixit, but even she, her closest blood relative, couldn't adequately sell this mistruth.

'I'm not sure if she does. Family should support each other.'

Mrs Dixit nodded, but she couldn't help wondering, *what about your family? Why don't they visit? How are you so alone?* But a new imperative thought penetrated her sludgy medicated mind. 'Naveem! You saw him! How is he?'

'I'll tell you everything in the car.'

'Thank you. And I'm sorry,' Mrs Dixit said, 'for yelling at you when we hit the bumper. And also, for driving off in your car and leaving you behind. I didn't know what else to do, I panick—'

Mrs Rampersad grunted again.

'These things happen.' She turned and started towards the main door. 'I never tampered with the gas meter either, I couldn't figure out how. But I did almost run over Jill's cat, only that thing had it coming, what with getting under everyone's tyres.' She opened the front door and shrugged. 'Anyway, you do a relatively good job of handing out flyers.'

Mrs Dixit took this as the highest compliment going.

*

The two women caught up to speed on the drive to the McDonald's.

'How did you get into the house?'

'I told them I was from the hospital,' replied Mrs Rampersad proudly, 'to assess the quality of care.'

'They didn't ask you for ID?'

She shook her head.

'It seemed they had so many complaints, they couldn't wait to start.'

'What sort?'

'That the physiotherapist was always late. And they don't like his nurse – she constantly asks for a glass of water. They don't feel she should be taking drink breaks on hospital time.'

'That sounds like his mother,' Mrs Dixit tutted.

'She didn't speak much actually, it was the husband who did most of the talking. Naveem looks so much like his father, same strong nose, same brow – it was eerie.'

'How was Naveem?'

'Fine. The same. A bit thinner. It's hard to tell… The curtains were closed, so I turned on a lamp. They were both watching me carefully, and I knew they'd expect me to check things, so I examined the machines, trying not to turn off anything by accident. Hoping I gave the impression I did this all the time. His mother was staring at me suspiciously by the end, so I made a hasty retreat. Told them I had three more appointments. No money in the NHS, etcetera, etcetera. And, well, then I saw you driving off into the sunset…'

'Again, I'm so sorry about that…' Mrs Dixit quickly explained how the community officer had made her move the car because it was blocking the driveway. 'But what do we do now? We can't go back and park near the house anymore – what if the officer comes back?'

'There's no law says we can't sit in a parked car.'

'I think there is, it's called kerb crawling.'

'Not two ladies, we'll just say we're in a mobile knitting group.'

'We don't have any knitting. And the neighbour reported two women in the car – the community officer was only lenient because it was Henry and me. If he comes back and sees us sitting there, knitting or not…'

'That's not important.' Mrs Rampersad thumped the steering wheel. 'Because I discovered something in the house. A real game changer.' She smiled mysteriously, turning into the McDonald's drive-through lane. 'I think we can get him out.'

'Well…?' prompted Mrs Dixit. Mrs Rampersad had taken it upon herself, as they waited for the queue of cars to move forward, to start fishing about in her handbag.

'I'm sure it was in here…?'

'What's your idea?'

'Hold on, woman! Ah, there you are…' Mrs Rampersad pulled a butterscotch mint out of her bag triumphantly. 'Wily, this one.' She began to unwrap it noisily.

'Your plan? How do we get him out?'

Mrs Rampersad popped the mint in her mouth and moved it from cheek to cheek. 'We call an ambulance.'

Mrs Dixit's shoulders fell with disappointment.

'We've already considered that. I even talked to the lawyer about it, remember? If we call an ambulance, they'll only…'

'Hush, hush,' Mrs Rampersad said, holding up her hand, her cheek bulging with the mint. 'That was before. Now, I have some *inside information*.'

Mrs Dixit waited for her neighbour to continue.

'This isn't a chocolate éclair,' she said finally.

'*What information*?' Mrs Dixit practically bellowed.

'His parents had a problem with Naveem's ventilator. A week ago. It started beeping in the middle of the night, and they were scared it was going to stop working, or that it meant there was an issue with his breathing. They rang emergency services... Long story short, they were about to send an ambulance when the beeping stopped. When the doctor on call came over early in the morning, he said the ventilator was fine, there might have been an issue with the pressurisation, it happened all the time, but it was nothing life-threatening.'

'They told you all this?'

'Every word. We missed it all because it happened before we arrived for the day. They wanted to make a complaint. And I just happened to be the very person they could complain to. That really was a stroke of divine luck, telling them I was sent to assess Naveem's care.'

She closed her eyes and sucked the mint.

'Do you think we can tell the lawyer about the ventilator issue? Maybe we can make a case for negligence?'

'I'm not *officially* a healthcare worker, but it sounds like they did everything correctly. Ringing the ambulance, insisting a doctor came, that's not what you do if you're negligent. No, my idea is better.' She leaned closer, and Mrs Dixit could smell buttery mintiness on her breath. 'We call an ambulance and tell them there's been another issue with the ventilator. It's making a high-pitched beeping and we can hear a hissing noise – that should get them moving. They already know that a doctor gave the device the all clear, so they'll be wary of a malpractice suit. Once the ambulance is on its way, I'll return to the house and tell Naveem's parents that yes, they were right, there *is* a terrible problem with the ventilator, and we have to take him back to hospital *immediately*. The lack of oxygen might have caused irreversible problems.'

'But when the ambulance arrives, won't they quickly find there's nothing wrong with the machine?'

'That's where my plan gets inspired. In all of the chaos, I take a pin from my pocket and make a small hole in the ventilator tubing. Only when I hear the ambulance sirens approaching, and not big enough to cause any *real* issue.'

'How will you know? What if you make it too big by accident? Or something implodes or explodes? It must be highly pressurised? What if something terrible happens to Naveem as a result?'

'It will be a mere pin prick. And they'll have ventilators in the ambulance if anything goes seriously wrong.'

'Won't the staff challenge you?'

'In all the mayhem, I'll be the least of their worries – I'll slip away when they arrive.'

Mrs Dixit was still for a moment, processing.

'When they get back to the hospital,' Mrs Rampersad continued, 'you're already there, making a case for why he's safer at your house. You've hired a private nurse for twenty-four-hour care. Whatever. Maybe the lawyer can help us, finally.' She rolled her eyes as if that was a long shot. 'You'll be in a much better position to fight your case, especially in the light of the two recent mishaps with the ventilator calling into question Naveem's parents' ability to adequately look after him.'

She crunched the mint with triumphal vigour.

For a long time, Mrs Dixit was silent.

'It seems risky,' she said at last. 'He could be hurt.'

'Riskier than doing *nothing*?' Mrs Rampersad drove forward; there was one car ahead of them, giving their order of Big Macs, no lettuce over the loudspeaker. 'Riskier than sitting in a car, day in day out, hoping we're not arrested?'

Mrs Dixit covered her mouth with her hand, considering.

*

A voice in her ear – so close it tickled the canal – made her jump.

'I was saying good morning!' Magnus shouted over the wind and noisy aircraft.

'You shouldn't sneak up on people!' Mrs Dixit yelled back, clutching her chest.

'Nerves are a sign of a guilty conscience,' he hollered over the engines, wagging a finger, 'which is why you can never surprise a cat.'

This made no sense to Mrs Dixit; she was pretty sure you could sneak up on cats, but there was too much noise to argue. The aircraft beside them roared, and they watched as the plane sped down the runway and took off, rocketing up, tilting from side to side as it found purchase. Mrs Dixit revelled in the engulfing sound; the sky yielding to the explosive power.

'I didn't see you yesterday,' Magnus said, once it had gained altitude. 'You were up to mischief, no doubt?'

'Nothing of the sort,' she scoffed, which was true… yesterday. Tomorrow or the next day, she couldn't be so sure – especially if she agreed to Mrs Rampersad's crazy new plan.

'How's your wife?' she asked to change the subject. It was such a banal question: *how's the wife?* Mrs Dixit wondered what response Naveem had given to it.

'Noella,' Magnus nodded sadly. Today, it was Noella. 'As well as one can expect. Completely catatonic, poor thing.'

'Isn't it strange we both have sick spouses?'

'Not strange at all. Nothing's an accident, really. I'd say us meeting was highly orchestrated.' He smiled roguishly. 'And there are countless helpless people in this world, but they're locked away in hospitals and bedrooms. Not even physically destitute most of them – the mind is a cage too…' He looked at the cars nervously. The blue one *was* there again, Mrs Dixit noticed.

'I keep going round and round in circles…' started Mrs Dixit.

'Like a tiger,' interrupted Magnus, 'at the zoo.'

'I suppose. I keep trying to make changes, but I always end up in the same place.'

'Inertia,' he shook his head.

'I'm never sure if Naveem would…' … *approve*, she thought, blinking to let the cold air dry her eyes. 'How do you know? – if your wife would agree you're doing the right thing?'

'That's an enormous question,' Magnus said with a puff of air. 'Did they approve of everything when they were with us? Hardly. You can only imagine what they'd do in the same boat.'

Mrs Dixit considered this. Would Naveem dote on her, like he did with his trains? Sending away for more effective equipment. Medication all in a row. Systems, charts? Would he scour chat rooms for experimental treatments? Attend international conferences. Have weekly calls with health pioneers. Her heart swelled at this image. Naveem would try everything possible to bring her back, she knew he would. But in this imagining, she was with him, safe at home. Would he go through with a hare-brained scheme to rescue her, one that might put her life in jeopardy? This was harder to visualise. And even if he did get her back, would he kiss her lifeless body each night? Would he get bored of tinkering, when there was no progress, no fix, no treatment that worked? Would he yearn for her, or simply replace her, after a respectful amount of time, with a functional woman who could cook and clean again?

She fought to keep her emotions in check, her coat whipping in the blustery breeze.

'How do you maintain your… connection with your wife?'

'There are signs everywhere, if you're open to them. Reminders. A song you loved that comes on the radio, just when you needed it to. A note in a drawer. A memory from someone you both knew.'

'All I have is years and years of routine and order that *felt* safe and happy, but now it's just…' *Empty*, is what Mrs Dixit wanted to say. 'We didn't like the same songs, not even the same kind of music. Naveem only left a note on the fridge if we were running out of milk. We knew people, of course, but most of the time it was just the two of us.' Mrs Dixit stopped, realising she'd spoken much more candidly than she intended to.

'Perhaps this is karma giving you a second chance then?'

'But I don't want a second chance, I want my husband back.' *He's not gone,* she thought. *Everyone keeps talking as if he already has!*

'You misunderstand me. I don't mean move on, leave him behind. Instead, step into the reckoning of your relationship. Acknowledge you weren't always grateful. You appreciate him now. I can hear it in your voice. You're still a woman with life in her. I can see it when you watch the planes. The delight in your eyes. I noticed it the moment I met you.' He placed a hand on her shoulder, gently, delicately. 'Would you help me?' he asked, with a pleading look in his eyes. 'I think I'm mixed up in some kind of trouble.'

There was a blast of a car horn behind them.

Magnus took his hand away sharply.

'I have to go,' Mrs Dixit said, feeling confused, giving a nod to Mrs Rampersad behind the driver's wheel.

'Till next time,' Magnus said, giving the briefest flourish of a bow. 'Wherever that may be.'

'What's the deal with Errol "Mr Handsy" Flynn?' Mrs Rampersad asked as they drove after an awkward silence.

'He's just trying to help, I think…'

'These men, all trying to *help*.'

Is there a man in your life? Mrs Dixit wanted to ask. *What about the one I used to hear in your bedroom last summer? Or more recently, the gentleman friend from church who came to your flat for dinner? Are you lonely? Are you alone? Is it by choice?* But she stayed silent, having only just returned to her neighbour's good books. There were more pressing questions to answer anyway.

'I've been thinking over your plan to rescue Naveem,' she said. Mrs Rampersad arched an eyebrow. 'I'm worried it puts his health too much at risk. If something goes wrong…'

'There will be ambulance staff ready to intervene. And his health will *definitely* be put at risk on a plane somewhere, with you never seeing him again…'

Mrs Dixit flinched at this, as if her neighbour had flicked her with a rubber band.

'If his family realises what we're up to, they'll definitely take some action. We could push them into doing it. Didn't you say his mother was looking at you suspiciously in the house? She's an intelligent woman. I don't know…'

'You're happy just waiting around? Taking what comes? Letting the world beat you down? This is the chance we've been waiting for! Haven't you seen my flyers? *God is the brave man's hope, and not the coward's excuse*. I forget which part, Book of Leviticus perhaps…'

Mrs Dixit sighed.

'Can I think about it some more?'

'Take your time. It's only your husband's life at stake. But I think I've solved the problem of the community officer recognising you.'

'How?'

Mrs Rampersad gave a big smile. 'I have *disguises*.'

The disguises were a burka and a nun's habit. Mrs Dixit blinked at them.

'They were for our multi-denominational celebration performance at the church,' Mrs Rampersad explained.

'But the officer has your car registration number… And won't a nun sitting next to a Muslim woman draw more attention?'

'You're thinking about this all wrong. We can say we're praying together. We drive around and sit in streets and pray. It's beautiful when you think about it. Two faiths coming together through the power of prayer.'

'Isn't that blasphemous?'

'Why?'

'I'm not a practising Christian, and you're… not a Muslim.'

'Why do you think I would be the Muslim?'

'I… Well… I assumed…'

'Not all Muslims are black, and not all Christians are white…'

'I didn't mean to…'

'I'm making light,' Mrs Rampersad said, with a laugh. 'Your face! Anyway, the nun's costume is too small for me, that whippet Alesia Winner played her in the performance. That skinny "b" doesn't eat at all.'

'I'm not putting on a costume.'

'Why not?'

'It's too… silly. It's like a *Carry On* film. This is serious.'

Mrs Rampersad narrowed her eyes.

'You don't think I'm serious?' She clapped her lap with both hands. 'Okay, what are we going to say when the police show up then? What's your great story?'

'We can say we're a community watch team, looking out for the Chomley cat burglar. We can say we got a tip-off there was something strange happening on the street. We can say we're monitoring it as citizens. Doing our civic duty.'

'Do you think they'll believe that?'

'It's all I can come up with,' Mrs Dixit said.

'We're not doing enough,' Mrs Rampersad replied, stuffing the crumpled costumes back in the carrier bag. 'You need to risk more, quiet little church mouse.'

Neither of them knew then how prophetic her words would soon be.

*

They watched the nurse arrive at the house just after 1 p.m.

'Maybe we can go and talk to her when she leaves again?' Mrs Dixit said, her heart pounding.

'We've been over this – and say what? She'll most likely raise the alarm, or at the very least, she'd tell Naveem's parents.'

'I suppose…'

'My plan is better, face it. It will get Naveem back to the hospital, where we have many more options.'

'Okay,' Mrs Dixit said, clenching her jaw. Mrs Rampersad had been right, in a way, the costume idea was the least hare-brained of the two. 'When do we do it?'

It was an exhausting afternoon, because as well as watching the house, the two women also had to continually monitor the street. The paranoid atmosphere filled the cramped space, but fortunately there was no sign of the community officer. It was only a matter of time, though.

In her kitchen that evening, nursing a tension headache, Mrs Dixit mulled over the events of the day and her conversation with Magnus. What had he meant by being 'mixed up in some kind of trouble'? The fear in his eyes had been worrisome. Maybe there was something to the parked blue car after all?

She recalled what Magnus had said about tokens of affection, and with a sudden burst of energy, she swept through the drawers in the kitchen, the bathroom cabinet, and then – for the first time – Naveem's bedside table, looking for what, exactly? A poem? Her hair in a locket? Naveem couldn't even look directly into a camera… What if all his tenderness and romantic gestures were saved for another, someone who enjoyed receiving gifts – earrings, perhaps…

She yanked open each of the drawers aggressively. Inside, everything was just as she expected. Takeaway flyers neatly ordered and catalogued in the kitchen drawer, heartburn medications of various strengths lined up in the bathroom cabinet, books on model trains in the bedside table. She even flicked through some of these, trying to dislodge a hidden note, or something jotted in the margins, but there was nothing.

Mrs Dixit slammed the final book shut and went to bed in an awful mood.

39 days since the accident

It was a bitterly cold Saturday, and there was no food in the house, none. Mrs Dixit always liked to do her shopping as early as she could, to avoid the supermarket crowds, so she wrapped herself up and arrived at the store just after opening.

She was considering bin liners – and trying *not* to think about the online articles about patients dying in respirator explosions she'd read over breakfast – when she heard a voice behind her.

'Wendy Dixit?'

'Yes?' she replied, turning round sharply, the sudden movement causing white blotches in her vision.

'I'm Penny Marshall's daughter.'

The name registered in her mind, but Mrs Dixit couldn't remember why it was familiar.

'We spoke on the phone?'

Still nothing.

The young woman smiled uncomfortably. There was something apologetic and slightly browbeaten about her; the way her shoulders hunched, the clasping of her hands together, the inability to maintain eye contact. She wore an oversized green khaki coat, and a lumpy woollen hat which was so unflattering, Mrs Dixit wanted to yank it from her head.

'I'm Shelly?' the woman tried again. 'Penny was my mother. With your husband. In the accident…'

Mrs Dixit felt the headache from last night, dormant all morning, pulse in her temple.

'Oh yes. *Of course.* I'm *so sorry,*' and she was, so terribly sad for this poor girl, but she also felt cornered, trapped by politeness in the bin bag aisle, when all she wanted to do was run. Amid the release of adrenaline, a thought occurred to her: 'How did you know what I look like?' she asked.

Shelly gave a lopsided smirk.

'I work at the DVSA, so I brought up your licence. We're not supposed to, of course…' She shook her head as if trying to admonish herself for the bad deed.

'Considering the circumstances…' replied Mrs Dixit, shrugging – but she wasn't sure what she meant by this. Considering the circumstances it was reasonable to look at her confidential information? And was this, she wondered, simply a chance encounter or a planned one?

'I was surprised to see you here,' Shelly said, as if she'd heard this inner dialogue. 'It's like spotting a celebrity – their face seems so *familiar*, and you keep wondering where you've met them. Sorry, I'm rambling.' She scrunched up her face. 'I'm nervous.'

'No need for nerves, I'm not a real celebrity.'

Shelly chuckled at this, and Mrs Dixit was glad for the brevity. To be honest, though, she was nervous too. No – she sensed *dread.*

'I'm very sorry for your loss,' Mrs Dixit patted Shelly's arm, hoping to use this momentum to begin her departure, but the girl leaned into the arm, and before she knew what was happening, Mrs Dixit was hugging her awkwardly.

*

The hug seemed to last a very long time. Fortunately, the lumpy woollen hat smelled much better than it looked. Shelly did not exactly cry, but she sniffled audibly. The occasional shopper would wander into their aisle, and either retreat quickly, or continue to walk the length, ignoring them as if they were apparitions.

Mrs Dixit busied herself rubbing the poor girl's back.

'Thank you,' Shelly said eventually, sniffing, 'But the friction of your hand's burning my skin now.'

'I'm so sorry.' Mrs Dixit withdrew her arm.

'It's a good type of burning. Just too much of it.' Shelly wiped her face. 'Another one off my bucket list – having an emotional breakdown in the household section. I never even asked how your husband is.'

'Stable,' Mrs Dixit replied, hoping this was still the truth.

'Do they think he might…'

'They're not sure,' Mrs Dixit said quickly, and then realised she was being short with the girl, but there were questions coming, questions she did not want to discuss. There was too much going on already, without… Without thinking about the woman, the doctor, sitting there in the cab. Why she was in the front seat? Had Naveem known her? Was she simply one of his regulars? Was she in fact, Clare? A false name, a philandering name, one to hide her tracks? Did they hold hands as he drove, as she marvelled at the silver earrings he'd bought her especially? *No!* Mrs Dixit banished that thought to that deepest region of her mind, populated by leery uncles, bullies from school, and a litany of regrets and fears. Her temple throbbed.

'Would you like to have a quick coffee?' asked Shelly, shrugging and smiling disarmingly. 'I've almost finished my shopping.' She swung the basket she was carrying, which contained deodorant, toothpaste and a 56-pack of tea lights. 'We could meet in the café by the entrance?'

'I would love to, but I have lots on today…'

'Please. It would help me. I don't want to keep pestering you, but I need a few minutes to talk…'

What could Mrs Dixit say to that?

She completed her shopping in a subdued state of panic. On the surface she was choosing window cleaner, bleach spray and toilet roll, but on the inside, she was falling apart. The walls seemed to be closing in around her – Mrs Dixit felt exposed and vulnerable at the checkout, as if everyone was judging her purchases. She considered making a break for it – but how, with her packed trolley? There was usually a taxi waiting outside, but what if there wasn't? She deliberated about asking a barista to pass on a message, but of course, Shelly was already sitting at a café table. There was no escape.

'I saved a chair for you,' the girl said, patting the seat. 'They're bringing over a pot of tea. Sorry, I should have asked, but I got the impression we wouldn't have long. I can ask them to make you a coffee instead?'

'Tea's fine.' Mrs Dixit parked the shopping cart as best she could and sat down.

'I visited your husband,' Shelly announced with little ceremony.

'What?' Mrs Dixit was speechless for a moment. 'At the hospital or…'

'About a week after the accident. He looked so serene, so… I don't know… alive. After seeing Mum… well, the difference was… With Mum, I kept waiting for her to breathe. *Just one breath*, I'd think.' Shelly smiled despondently, as she took off her hat. Underneath, her hair was in messy ringlets of dyed-henna red. Although there was a fug of awkwardness about Shelly, or perhaps because of it, Mrs Dixit realised she liked the girl, despite her rising panic. Liking someone in this situation was dangerous, however. It made you less cautious.

'Why did you visit him?' Mrs Dixit asked warily.

'Shouldn't I have?' Shelly looked horrified. 'I asked permission from the nurses.'

'It's fine, I don't mind,' Mrs Dixit replied, although the idea of some unknown person hovering over her husband as he lay, unable to protect himself, was disconcerting. 'I was only curious as to why.'

'I wanted to see what he looked like. To put the pieces together in my head.'

Mrs Dixit realised she was clenching her fists.

'What do you know about my husband?' she asked, trying to keep her voice even.

'He was the last person to be with Mum. I don't blame him, by the way, for anything that happened. I know the paper said...' Mrs Dixit batted this comment away, she didn't want to know what the papers said. She wanted to leave with as little knowledge as possible. Wilful ignorance was paramount. The important thing was getting Naveem back. After that, she could deal with anything, she promised herself, dubiously.

'Did it help?' Mrs Dixit asked, 'seeing him?'

'For a moment. Because there are so many things I wanted to ask him, it was frustrating too.' She touched Mrs Dixit's hand. 'Do they think he'll recover *properly*?'

'They're... I'm not sure.'

Shelly began to cry, not sniffling this time. Proper tears.

Mrs Dixit sat, unsure what to do.

'I know it's silly,' Shelly began, 'but I felt if I could just ask your husband about those last few minutes with Mum, I could finally get some closure. There's a person out there alive, who could tell me the last thing she said,' her voice went soft, 'if it was anything about me...'

'Did you have... a good relationship with your mother?'

Shelly blotted her eyes with her palms.

'Mostly. But we'd been a bit distant. Mum and Dad split up when I was a teenager, and well, my dad has been problematic ever since: spending too much, losing his job, drinking, but he's been getting help. Mum didn't believe him though. We fought.'

'I thought your parents were still together?'

'They never officially divorced. Mum worried what would happen to Dad if she did, if he'd spiral even more. They lived separately, and she was dating people…' Shelly sniffed, ignoring, or not noticing, the flinch that spasmed over Mrs Dixit's face. 'I just wish we'd left things on better terms. I can't help thinking she might have told your husband something *important*.'

'Why do you think that?'

'My mother was a talkaholic, especially on car trips. You couldn't shut her up. The day it happened, she was going into central London to a Harley Street clinic to have a strange mole on her back checked, just to be safe. Ironically, because it was the journey there that killed her.' Shelly half-laughed, half-sobbed. 'I'm sorry,' she said, wiping her eyes.

'You don't need to be.'

'But I am – I'm sorry I visited your husband without asking you. I know that wasn't right. It was an invasion of your privacy. I was having all these crazy thoughts, and I felt like if I saw him – I don't know – he might open his eyes suddenly. I would bring him back.'

'Did anything happen when you visited him?'

'A big fat zero. I was there for an hour. That old man in the bed opposite kept flashing me though, so eventually I had to leave.'

'He what?'

'Exposing himself. The scraggly looking guy with the beard? He was really enjoying himself too. It was funny and pathetic. I told the nurses, but they just shrugged it off. I took his oranges as punishment.' Mrs Dixit stared at her quizzically, so Shelly continued. 'He had a net bag of oranges, so I pinched them.

He wasn't laughing then. Serves him right. No one wants to see his horrible gnarled old member!' Shelly wiped her face. 'Your husband was very beautiful though. Very dignified in his sleep. Like a head of state. Those old black and white photos of Nehru. What is he like?'

'Naveem?' Mrs Dixit stopped to consider this, and the image of the train books next to their bed came to mind and the thump as she'd dropped them on the floor in frustration. 'He's thoughtful, he likes talking to people, which is why he became a cabby – well, one of the reasons. That changed over the years, though. He started to test people to see if they were worth talking to. Ask them a few probing questions and depending on the answers, he'd decide whether to continue. If they didn't pass, he'd be silent. I'd often think about the passengers in his cab, the ones he didn't talk to… Then there were the nights when he would only grunt answers to me…' she laughed, but it couldn't quite mask the sliver of pain at this memory.

'How did you meet?'

'In his cab. He was my driver.'

'How romantic.'

'It was…'

Mrs Dixit felt her throat constrict involuntarily as she said this. Hadn't Shelly said something about tea?

'The accident must have been your worst nightmare. Out in his cab. I'm sure you'd always worried about something like this happening, and it came true.' Why was the girl leading her down this path? Mrs Dixit wondered. If this was an ambush, she wouldn't go down without a fight.

'It was a terrible day,' she replied, evenly.

'The only glimmer of consolation is that they had each other, your husband and my mother. It's tragic, but…'

'My husband loved me,' Mrs Dixit said as passionately as she could, but it came out sounding terse. '*Loves*. He still loves me.'

'Of course,' Shelly replied meekly, 'I didn't mean to…'

Mrs Dixit took a deep breath and began.

'If you've come here today to make accusations about the nature of my husband's fidelity, then I can say, confidently, the sanctity of marriage meant something to Naveem. I don't care how it looked, or what people have been gossiping about – what the papers or the police say. There are a lot of unanswered questions, and I'm very sorry for your loss, but I will not be made a suspect while I am dealing with my own grief…'

'But…'

'Let me finish.' Mrs Dixit had a newly found mettle to her voice. 'Naveem was not the affair type. He liked order, and he appreciated trust. More than that, he respected it. And he respected me. So, if anyone says there was anything untoward, anything less than professional in their relationship, I reject the idea completely!'

'Oh no!' Shelly said, wide-eyed and stricken. 'Did I say something… wrong? I didn't mean to… I'm always putting my foot in it!' Mrs Dixit was taken aback by how desperate the girl seemed. 'What do you mean by unanswered questions? I don't understand. But I *want* to.'

Mrs Dixit blinked rapidly.

'The fact your mother was in the front seat of the cab when the accident happened. That that might imply there was something going on with Naveem.' Mrs Dixit blinked again. 'Isn't that why you wanted to speak with me?' She lowered her voice to a whisper. 'Because you thought they were having an affair?'

Shelly stared at Mrs Dixit for a second, and then started to laugh. Mrs Dixit watched as the young woman folded her arms across her breast, as if she was trying to keep the mirth from spilling out. Crossing her own arms, Mrs Dixit waited impatiently for the outburst to finish.

'What... How...?' Shelley's nose began to stream, and she dived into her bag to find a tissue. 'What do you mean? How would that even be possible? You need to start from the beginning.'

Mrs Dixit was feeling increasingly put out – she didn't like being laughed at – but there was a growing sense that one of her worst fears was about to be allayed.

'Your mother, when the accident happened...'

'Yes...?'

'She was sitting in the front seat of the cab...'

'And...?'

Mrs Dixit let out a puff of air, as if it was obvious.

'Why was she sitting in the passenger seat, and not in the back?'

'Mum hated sitting in the back of cabs,' Shelly said offhandedly, 'she felt it was too *Upstairs, Downstairs*, like the driver was her servant. She hated talking through that little window they have in black cabs. I told you, Mum loved to chat, so she'd always climb in the front seat of taxis. If they had things on the passenger seat, she'd plonk them on the floor – that's just how she was. Your husband never stood a chance. She was probably chewing his ear off the whole journey. Did you really think... they were having an affair?' She laughed again, but then observing Mrs Dixit's expression, she stopped short. 'Oh, you did! Why didn't you ask me before? You had my number. I would have told you.'

'I said the whole thing was ridiculous. I knew it. But the police... And my sister...' Mrs Dixit felt a wave of emotion start to hit her – she realised she'd had so much worry bottled up. *What if they were having an affair? What if they'd been driving to a hotel?* But no, the doctor only wanted to chat. Naveem would have hated his personal space being invaded; he kept a box of tissues and some cleaning wipes on the passenger seat, how would he have reacted to this officious woman whisking them off and dumping them by her feet? To see the look on Naveem's face! Would he have mentioned it when he got home, this pushy customer, droning away the whole journey? Would they have laughed together about it? *Oh, Naveem!*

'What about…?' Mrs Dixit hesitated. How could she phrase this? '… about the solvents? The police said there were some traces found in Naveem's blood work.'

Shelly shook her head. 'News to me. Do they think that had something to do with the accident?' She looked thoughtful for a moment as if a new idea had occurred to her, and Mrs Dixit realised too late this was not the right thing to have mentioned.

'It's extremely unlikely,' Mrs Dixit said quickly, trying to dismiss it. 'But is there any way your mother might have come in contact with a powerful solvent? Medically or otherwise?'

'Not that I know of. She liked to have her nails done, occasionally, at this cheap local place, I can imagine whatever they used was pretty toxic – but that's the only thing I can think of. And they didn't tell me about any solvent in her blood. How would it transfer to someone else, anyway? It doesn't make any sense.'

'Would your mother be carrying any medication with her, anything that might – I don't know – leak, or be transferred by touch or through the air?'

'Not that I can think of. And wouldn't the police have found it if she did?'

Mrs Dixit nodded.

'I haven't been able to watch the CCTV footage,' Shelly said, staring into space. 'I dream about it though – always in black and white. Have you seen it?'

Mrs Dixit was about to explain she didn't have any dreams now, because of the sleeping pills, but she didn't want to bring up the notion of drugs again so soon.

'No, I haven't either.'

Shelly nodded as if this confirmed something.

'Would you watch it with me now?' she asked, almost bashfully.

'What? Here?'

'I can play the video on my phone.'

Mrs Dixit glanced around her wildly.

'But all these people…?'

'Please. I have to put this to rest. I think I'll finally be able to sleep again. And I'm sure it will help you too. You're the only other person who knows what this experience has been like…' she trailed off. 'Please?'

Shelly looked so sad – wretched even. Mrs Dixit manoeuvred her chair around so they could both see the phone. The screen was dirty with fingerprints and Shelly wiped it with her sleeve.

'Are you ready?'

Mrs Dixit didn't feel ready. She felt as if she was at the top of a very tall roller coaster, but she nodded.

The video was short, barely twenty seconds long. They watched it three times in succession.

The camera was on the intersection. The lights had obviously changed to green, because cars started to move. Naveem's cab appeared, the right indicator blinking, clear as day. To the side, pedestrians were waiting to cross. A woman with a pushchair. A man with a backpack. It was grainy, and you couldn't make out faces. A red line was drawn around the pedestrians and text came on the screen: 'Is this you? Please contact the number below'. On the first viewing, Mrs Dixit was so busy staring at the pedestrians, and at Naveem's frustratingly opaque windscreen, the appearance of the lorry caught her off guard, making her gasp. The video went into slow motion at this point, but it clearly showed the stationary cab – idling, waiting to turn – and then the hulking shape of the lorry approach. Even before it filled the screen, you could see the lorry was too far to the right. It wobbled, as if the driver was trying to course-correct, but by then it was too late. The video cut off before impact.

Shelly lowered the phone, and then silently wrapped her arms around Mrs Dixit's neck and started sobbing. A few people turned to look at them, but Mrs Dixit didn't care, not now. She would hold Shelly for as long as was required. She stroked Shelly's soft hair, and said 'there, there' quietly, and the words helped to centre herself, and stopped her from falling apart too. 'That's it. Shhhhh.' Although she didn't want Shelly to be quiet, not at all. Mrs Dixit would hold her and stroke her hair until the café closed, until night came, and the car park was empty, until the food decomposed unopened on their shelves if need be. 'It's alright,' she soothed. But it wasn't. They had witnessed the moments preceding a death, a terrible accident that was available to all. Wasn't death supposed to be sacred?

'We'll ask them to take it down,' Mrs Dixit said, resolutely. Shelly looked up, sniffling. The top of Mrs Dixit's sweater was a puddle. 'It's not right. The pedestrians would have come forward by now. I'll call the police this afternoon.'

'No!' Mrs Dixit was shocked by Shelly's vehemence. 'I'm not ready,' the girl sobbed. 'I don't want her taken away.'

'You can't even see her in the footage.'

'I know, but she's still in there. Please.'

'I won't then. Not yet.'

'Thank you. I'm sorry. Thank you.'

Mrs Dixit cradled Shelly against her chest.

'There's no rush, there's no rush at all.'

A message was waiting on her answerphone.

'Mrs Dixit?' the voice said, 'it's Lidia Millbrook, I met you the other day about your husband's model train collection. I have to say, I'm fairly impressed – initially I thought it was promising, but I can see your husband was quite the *discerning* collector. If there are more pieces like this, they could be worth a healthy sum. I would suggest moving them into professional storage space with climate control and to look, quite quickly and seriously, into either insurance or selling the items at a specialist auction. Give me a call back at your discretion to discuss.' There was a pause, as if she didn't particularly want to add the next part: 'Of course, I still have the engine you entrusted to me, so I will need to get this back to you at the very least. Goodbye.'

Mrs Dixit, who was putting the perishables away in the fridge as she listened, paused.

What would happen if she agreed to sell the trains? There would be money, much-needed, but for how long? Ultimately, she decided, she only wanted the one thing money couldn't buy.

Mrs Dixit was unable to remember the last time she'd been in his study. The sleeping pills didn't exactly help with recall. What she did recollect was a time she'd felt unsettled in the space – scared, in a strange way, but she now felt none of that. If anything, her only emotion was *annoyance*. It shouldn't have become a mausoleum, Mrs Dixit berated herself, she must start behaving as if Naveem would wake up soon! Breathe new life into it; the air was literally stale. Mrs Dixit opened the vent grate and surveyed the room. She would clean. Her husband had systems, but so did she, and oftentimes *her* way was better. Nodding to herself, Mrs Dixit started to remove the cardboard covers she'd put back over the miniature replica of Chomley, disrupting dust particles and agitating them into the air. When the tiny town was revealed, she stood back. It was so impressive; so much detail, so much *effort*. No wonder he'd been down here so regularly – in the mornings before work, evenings, weekends. That would change, she decided. Perhaps she would join him here? Naveem would loathe it, she realised. Where was a good place for her? Upstairs, keeping out of the way?

In a burst of rage, she walked to the table and knocked one of the miniature trees onto its side. Not hard enough to break it, but forceful enough to make a satisfying 'thok'. She flicked over a few more of the trees and bushes. The buildings weren't attached to a base, so she started to turn them over petulantly, on their side or upside down. She was careful not to *actually* damage anything, but creating chaos felt good, powerful. Her huge God-like hand uprooting the order of her husband's fantasy and bending it to her will, again and again, smiting the miniatures. This was for not including her. *Thwok.* This was for never bringing her flowers. *Thwok.* This was for spending their rainy-day money on toy trains. *Thwak.* This was for never leaving her a love note. For ignoring Valentine's day. For buying the most perfunctory of birthday and Christmas gifts. For all the times he didn't cradle her in his arms. *Thwok, thwak, thwuck.* For leaving her in this constant night. *With nothing.*

Mrs Dixit picked up one of the houses that looked very similar to their own, feeling the impulse to throw it across the room and see it smash to pieces, when she heard a rattle inside. It was a figurine, she realised. That was strange, none of the other buildings had miniature people inside. She fished it out through the front door and peered at it. A woman, at least it seemed to be a woman from the way the legs were tucked, was sitting in an armchair reading. There was something strangely familiar about the figurine, and Mrs Dixit inspected it more closely. Painted grey hair, the same length of her own. The eyes were green blobs, her eyes were green. The figurine was holding a book with 'Chocolat' written on the cover, she realised, a book she reread every year, her one true guilty pleasure (especially considering she didn't like chocolate). She turned over the figurine. On the base was carved either an M… or a W.

Still holding the miniature, Mrs Dixit started to inspect other areas of the town more closely. Just outside the florist, she found what looked like a younger version of herself, with longer brown hair, holding a pipe-cleaner flower. W was written on the base too. Outside the supermarket, there was a mini version of her pushing a shopping cart full of tiny shopping bags filled with tiny food. All up, there were five versions of Mrs Dixit in the town. She was everywhere, mixing with the other locals, omnipresent.

Why hadn't Naveem ever shown her his handiwork? But of course, he'd have been embarrassed… it had to be done in secret. She knew this about him. It was the same way he couldn't look down the barrel of a camera. He had populated his imaginary world with her though. That meant something. Mrs Dixit suddenly felt panicky about having ruined the miniature Chomley. She tried to put everything back the way it had been – he'd notice immediately if anything was askew – but before she left, she picked up the reading figurine from beside the miniature version of the house and took it with her up the stairs, cradling it carefully all the way.

Not much of the evening was left. Her routine was to take the pills, wash, moisturise, read a few pages before the medication began to pull at her, almost physically it seemed, into the mattress. Tonight, she hesitated. Mrs Dixit felt wide awake – buzzing, in fact, as if she'd had three espressos. Looking in the bathroom mirror, the face staring back at her was twitchy, restless, but there was another quality, especially around her eyes – a softening. Could one be both energised and more relaxed simultaneously? Picking up the figurine from the countertop, Mrs Dixit traced the smooth contour of the wooden face. The dark eyebrows and the white hair. She had to fight the ridiculous impulse to kiss it.

She lay down on the bed without taking the sleeping pills. When Mrs Dixit closed her eyes, her brain seemed to leap behind her eyelids in a not completely disagreeable way. Here she was again, at the end of another day – feeling restless, craving some greater resolution.

She wished a brass band would burst into the room and start playing to spur her into action.

Eventually, she sat up: Mrs Dixit had come to a decision.

She'd never downloaded a taxi app on her phone before, and she felt a disloyalty towards Cliff, but it was better he wasn't involved. She didn't want him getting in trouble out of loyalty to her.

A message dinged when the car arrived, and she grabbed her keys.

The driver barely said two words to her on the journey, which is exactly how she wanted it.

She'd never been there at night. The street was still, quiet, and she paused, regrouping outside the neighbour's house, fussing with her shoe. The lights were on next door, his parents were home. Wendy touched the figurine in her pocket. People in the nearby houses might notice if she stayed here like this. Commanding herself to walk, she made her way up to the front door, and stood there, hand raised, willing herself to knock.

She could not.

Peering through a side window, she could just make out Naveem's parents through the net curtain, sitting on their sofa watching television perhaps, although she couldn't hear a TV. They were so still, they seemed like mannequins, or deserters from the waxworks. How would she explain herself? Could she barge in once they answered, stick her foot in the door like some peppy salesperson, talk them into submission? Even if she did, what then? Carry Naveem away over her shoulder?

It was hopeless.

Wendy came around the side of the house to Naveem's bedroom window. She touched the glass carefully to begin with, wary of leaving fingerprints, but soon had her full hand placed against the pane. It was warm.

There are so many things I haven't told you, she thought. *Strange, sad things.* Her pain in never having their child. How trapped she'd always felt in her own mind. How proud she'd been to have Naveem. Looking at him beside her on the sofa and thinking, you married me? *Me!* With your movie-star jaw and your dark hair – he'd aged so well. She'd been scared to tell him that, in case he realised he could have it better somewhere else and left. Naveem had given everything else up – his parents, his brothers, his whole life before; she knew what he was capable of. *Was it only a matter of time before you went?*

She'd kept parts of herself ready, a mental suitcase packed, just in case. Naveem was a good man, not a perfect man. Sometimes his world was very heavy, and she knew he hurt himself with rigidness, and often she wanted to take him in both hands and stretch him out as far as she could reach, pull on his fingers until he had the wingspan of an eagle, instead of sitting so silent and hunched. *I'm sorry you hated your childhood*, she thought. *I'm sorry you wanted to leave everything behind, but only got so far as me.* She didn't know what had happened with his parents all those years ago, not everything – he'd kept that from her, and she made sure never to ask – *but I'm going to get you back*, she thought emphatically, *I promise.*

Taking the figurine out of her pocket again, Wendy held it to her chest for a brief moment and then hid it below the window, inside a shrub. She wanted to sit and close her eyes for a second, just to feel a sensation of rest with him nearby, but she was afraid of being seen, and even more afraid of falling asleep, so she picked herself up, brushed the leaves from her legs, and started to walk towards the high street to find a local mini cab office – when she heard the Dixits' front door open.

She froze, ridiculously, like a child who thinks they won't be discovered if they only hold still enough. A female voice said her goodbyes. A sister-in-law? Mrs Dixit scurried back around the side of the house to hide. As she watched, a Mediterranean-looking woman in nurse's uniform walked by. The opportunity was too great to pass up, and even though her rational brain screamed to keep out of sight, Mrs Dixit launched herself in the nurse's direction.

'Excuse me?' she called, wary of being too loud and alerting Naveem's parents.

The nurse continued walking. Perhaps she had earphones in? Mrs Dixit tapped the woman on the shoulder to make her turn round.

'Yes?' The nurse said with an inscrutable blankness. She had dark eyes with beautiful thick lashes.

'I want to ask about my husband…' Mrs Dixit began nervously. 'The patient inside the house…' she clarified.

The nurse nodded, replying: 'He's not very well.'

Panic stabbed at her.

'Is he worse than before?'

Pressing her fingers to her lips, the nurse seemed to be considering whether she should go on. Her eyes were so dark, they barely reflected the moon, even though it was a perfectly Clare night. *Clear* night, she meant. Silver crescents on each ear…

'Are you Wendy?' the nurse asked, finally.

'Yes, I am,' she replied, ignoring the impulse to hide her true identity.

'Did you know he called out your name?'

'Naveem spoke? When?'

'I suppose you weren't there?'

'Of course I wasn't, they won't let me inside the house.' Mrs Dixit's tongue snaked nervously into the empty cavity in her mouth, and she noticed for the first time the tooth next to it was loose. 'Was he in pain? Did he say anything else?'

'I can't help, I'm afraid. I shouldn't be speaking to you at all.'

So the nurse did know about the rift! Mrs Dixit shrank back, knocked by this realisation. What ammunition could possibly be given to his parents now? They would move him, for certain. But he'd spoken! She was so confused. Mrs Dixit considered chasing after the nurse and demanding more answers, but by the time she looked for her again, she was gone.

There was no need to take the sleeping pills when she arrived home. She felt genuinely exhausted, even if the events of the evening had perked up her spirits. If Naveem was speaking, it was imperative he go back to the hospital for treatment. There was a glimmer of hope at last! In the morning, she would talk to Mrs Rampersad – there was no need for her hare-brained scheme, they could escalate things themselves, now she had first-hand confirmation from a nurse that…

Mrs Dixit woke up. A noise? She glanced at her alarm clock: 3.11 a.m. Moving onto her back with a sigh, she waited for Mrs Rampersad to finish in her bathroom and return to her bed above.

What time had she returned from visiting Naveem? Taking her phone, Mrs Dixit tried to see if there was any way she might reveal this, but she hadn't sent any messages, so there was no timestamp to be found. She remembered the taxi app she'd downloaded and looked for it. Nothing. Had she deleted it? Surely not.

As the mist of sleep began to part, she had the nagging suspicion she'd never taken a taxi in the first place. What about the figurine, the one she'd left under his window? She searched for it on the bedside table, finding nothing. Maybe she had deleted the taxi app after all? The lines of reality felt murky. And then, as she rolled back to sitting, she felt something hard underneath her left thigh: the figurine. She must have fallen asleep clasping it, she'd dreamt it all. Mrs Dixit felt her chest clench – Naveem had not spoken. There was no glimmer of hope…

When the noise came again, it was in the wrong direction. If anything, it sounded like it came from *below*. Mrs Dixit froze instinctively, unsure what to do. Indecision is the greatest killer in home invasions. Our own dwellings put us too much at ease. *This is mine, nothing can go* that *wrong*. Not inside the walls where you boil your eggs and cut your toenails and brush your teeth. But we are always only borrowing this space – the walls will come down, the ceiling will collapse, one way or another. Through degradation or force, they always come down.

Mrs Dixit didn't exactly think these thoughts, her mind was still blank as she listened intently, but they floated somewhere in that place of knowing – she'd read about it in a Sunday paper perhaps or seen mention in a news story. Her pulse quickened. Something was wrong. *Very wrong*. There was a person in the house. The noises were movement, a body, in the basement study. She had a flash of memory then – the night she imagined Naveem waking in the hospital and walking home in his gown like a zombie – how it unnerved her. Now, it made her hesitate. Could it be him? But no. Deep down, she knew this noise was foreign.

As quietly as she could – and Mrs Dixit could be very quiet – she slipped out of bed and towards the door. Anyone else might have thought about sourcing a makeshift weapon – the pair of dressmaker's scissors, a large knitting needle, a vase, a paperweight, but Mrs Dixit knew her diminutive size meant that the perpetrator would most likely use whatever she held against her, so she went empty-handed, optimistic – and incorrect – in the hope that she could talk her way out of whatever lay ahead, that this intrusion had been an error of judgement or a mistake, something that could be remedied collaboratively.

In the hallway, there was a banging below her, and what sounded like someone cursing. The cursing was good – the intruder was corporeal at least, not that Mrs Dixit really thought it was a ghoul, but it was better to rule it out completely. Human – not animal or a bird that had flown in somehow and was thrashing around, trying to escape. A human, male. And young, if the voice was any gauge.

Was he alone?

At the top of the stairs, she paused. Twice in one night, Mrs Dixit was on the threshold of doing something that terrified her. The door at Naveem's parents' house, and now… She'd dreamt that trip though, she reminded herself. As proof, she slipped her tongue into the gap in her mouth and tested the neighbouring teeth. Not the slightest wiggle. Was she dreaming this too?

No. This was palpably real.

She walked down the stairs with almost a trance-like focus, counting the steps. The study door was closed, so she turned the handle, pushed it open – see, it was easy – and went right in.

*

There was a young man – a boy – dressed in grey jeans and a black hoodie with the hood down, but his back was turned so she couldn't see his face.

'What are you doing?' Mrs Dixit asked in her normal voice, at a normal volume. It might have been a clap of thunder, the way the boy swivelled to look at her. Immediately, she had the strange sensation of sticky carpet underfoot, the smell of old popcorn, and the sense she knew him from somewhere.

'Oh, fuck it,' the boy said, and launched himself at her.

He had the advantage, already facing her. Mrs Dixit's legs were not very long, but adrenaline made them fast. As she reached the middle of the stairs, she felt a hand grabbing at her right ankle, but she managed, falling onto her hands and scurrying instead of running, to evade his grasp and make it to the top. He was fast too, and young, and had adrenaline aplenty, and there were equally high stakes his side. They used no words, just grunts – the most primal and readily understandable of languages. Mrs Dixit knew now she was in danger, real scarlet-hued, razor-tipped danger, that *bad things could happen*, and most likely would, if she could not get to help. She had almost cleared the stairs when the hand came back to her foot, more assured this time, and clasped itself around her ankle, causing her to smash to the floor, hitting her chin hard, the ankle popping out of its socket.

Mrs Dixit tried shaking her leg, but the grasp was strong, and she was aware of another hand coming for her other ankle. In her mind, she pictured the rams at shearing time, bundled up by their ankles and then plonked down unceremoniously to scarper away naked and confused, except she would not be plonked down. She would be *got for good*. Her free foot made contact with the grabbing hand, and there was a satisfying crunch, and an 'Oh fuck, my fingers!', and the grasp on her caught ankle loosened. Mrs Dixit saw her moment and bucked her body with all her might, levering herself out of his clutches, and she was standing again – in fact, skidding on the linoleum – and she had possibly five seconds to decide what to do next.

Unfortunately, time did not slow down, the fight or flight response did not accelerate her decision-making process. If anything, it poured hot adrenaline onto the problem and stood back, folding its arms, job done. Should she try to get outside? Then what? What might he do in the dark when he found her? She could bang on a nearby neighbour's door. Flag down a car? The street would be empty at 3 a.m. though and he could drag her back inside before the neighbour had left the warm comfort of their bed. A weapon then: a kitchen knife.

She ran to the drawer and pulled it open with a loud clatter. She pushed away a ladle and was just about to grab a steak knife when the boy crashed into the back of her, slamming the drawer shut – fortunately, without her hand inside, but the impact crushed her chest into the counter top, smacking the wind out of her, and cracking several ribs. He was still behind her; the force had knocked the wind out of him too, it seemed, and so there were a horrible few moments when they lay crumpled together, struggling to get their breath back, racing to see who could move first. The cracked ribs didn't exactly help with breathing, and Mrs Dixit had been a softer surface, bony though she was, and so it made sense that he would collect himself together much faster. Her hand went to the drawer again, and the sharp, emancipating objects inside, but almost as she thought this, the boy placed his arm over the drawer as he levered himself up. Taking hold of her left wrist, he wrenched it behind her back, causing her to shriek in pain.

'My chest,' she said, through tears. There was a slight hesitation, which Mrs Dixit would remember later, and use to her advantage, but then he caught her right wrist and yanked it behind with the other one.

'Please!' she cried, as he led her to the kitchen table, forcing her to sit down.

'You kicked my finger,' he said petulantly, as if that justified everything.

'You broke into my house!' she rallied.

'Yeah, well, you weren't supposed to be…' but he didn't finish, and Mrs Dixit had the distinct impression he had stopped himself from continuing.

He fished in his pockets with his free hand and then she felt something going around her wrists and pulled tight, a rope, and then a final violent tug as it bit into her skin, pinching terribly – accompanied by extreme heavy breathing and mutterings of: 'She shouldn'ta been…' 'What the fuck am I supposed to do…?' 'Tells me one thing, and then…'

Eventually he was done and stood back, behind her.

She tried to turn her head to see him but failed.

'What are you doing?' she asked.

'I'm not sure.'

'You can't just lurk behind me.'

'I haven't got a blindfold for you,' he responded, sounding embarrassed, as if he'd forgotten the flowers on a first date.

'I've already seen your face,' Mrs Dixit said, and then wished she hadn't.

'Fuck it,' the boy said, and walked around to the other side of the table. He'd pulled up his T-shirt so it was covering his nose and mouth – this seemed to be a compromise he was happy with, although it looked awkward in execution and meant he had to keep his shoulders hunched. His stomach was rippled and pale and dotted with brown moles. Taking out his phone, the boy scrolled down the screen, before beginning to text.

'Take whatever you want,' Mrs Dixit said as calmly as she could muster, 'I won't call the police.'

'Yeah, right,' he scoffed, still texting. 'I've heard that one before.'

'I mean it. You have my word. Nothing you can take is of any real value.' It sounded like something that Magnus from the airport would say. *Magnus.* How strange that he'd popped into her mind now… But then again, he did say he was mixed up in 'some kind of trouble'. Like breaking and entering perhaps…? Could Magnus be involved with this?

'Everything is valuable,' the boy added scornfully, still concentrating on his phone. 'That's why I'm robbing you. Silly cow.'

Young people today, Mrs Dixit thought grimly, *always on their phone, they can't even focus when they're in the middle of a burglary.*

Magnus! Mrs Rampersad's hunch might have been right all along – Mrs Dixit really shouldn't have spoken to strange men. She'd told Magnus so many details of her life, she realised now, making her the easiest of marks. He only had to play the dithering, charming fool, and she'd told him *everything* – where she lived, her husband's coma, that he collected valuable model trains, how she was taking sleeping pills. Magnus had been so disarming. She was a fool!

But he was so nice? Maybe he was being forced to do this under duress? Perhaps there was something in the blue car after all – the driver might be his boss, or a plain-clothes detective, monitoring his movements?

The boy waited, looking at his phone. There was probably a van outside, ready to collect him – why didn't he just go, then? If Mrs Dixit had rushed outside, would a burly man have been waiting for her?

The phone made a beeping noise.

'I'll be back. Don't go anywhere,' said the boy, and even through the T-shirt, Mrs Dixit could make out the self-satisfied smirk at his bad joke.

'Wait,' she said. 'I think I know who sent you.'

That stopped him.

'Who might that be?'

She was grasping at straws, but maybe it would give her some leverage… 'He's called Magnus.'

'Who the fuck is Magnus?' Even with his face half covered, it seemed to be authentic.

'He's probably using a different name. He's a bit of a diamond geezer – moustache, wears expensive shirts and cufflinks, jewellery. Chats up lonely women, gets their details, lies about his cover story, his wife… Look, I understand why you've got mixed up with him, he's very charming.'

'I don't know anyone like that with a moustache.'

'I'll tell the police it was him. I won't even mention you, please!'

'If you don't shut up, I will find a gag. Are you going to shut your mouth?'

She nodded.

'Good.' He stuck his head into the hallway, taking the phone off its cradle.

'Where's your mobile?' he asked.

Mrs Dixit nodded her head towards the bedroom.

'You can speak,' the boy said exasperatedly.

'I left it by my bed.'

He grunted, hesitated for a moment, and then walked over to her, roughly feeling down her thighs and in her pyjama pocket, checking to see if there was anything inside. *This is not his first time doing this*, she thought, worriedly. Checking his phone, the boy headed down the stairs back to the study.

*

She was alone. Instinctively, she tugged at the cord which bound her wrists, trying to squirm free, to no avail. Her poor ribs throbbed. Mrs Dixit considered screaming, but the noise probably wouldn't be enough to wake Mrs Rampersad in her bedroom and would cause violent repercussions. Why hadn't she run upstairs to her neighbour when she had the chance? *Stupid*, she reprimanded herself. That dream had made her reckless. Standing outside his window in the soil and bushes!

What then? The boy would be back soon. She deliberated pushing the chair backwards, hoping it might break, but she would possibly give herself a concussion, splitting her head on the countertop behind. Topple sideways perhaps? She tried rocking the chair from side to side, but she was afraid she'd be even more vulnerable on the floor when the boy returned if she couldn't escape. What would he do then? There was a mean streak about the boy, and still, that familiarity she hadn't quite been able to place…

It arrived immediately then. The image of the boy at the waxworks, selling tickets at the front desk. A snippy young man, who never made eye contact, always on his phone. He was the Chomley cat burglar! Mrs Dixit considered if this new information gave her any advantage. If she told him, it was sure to be a liability – she'd not only have seen his face, but she knew where he worked too. Was her hunch about Magnus correct? The boy hadn't seemed spooked by his name. And surely he would know any of Magnus's aliases if he was involved in this?

Had she been really been Magnus's target this whole time? Was that why he kept talking to her? He didn't seem malicious in the slightest, but there was definitely something *off* about him… His obviously fictitious sick wife for one! If he was a criminal, why make such a blatantly bad attempt at fabricating a story? It didn't make sense…

Mrs Dixit shook her head, trying to stop it racing over unimportant details. Who cared if Magnus was involved, or where this boy worked? The only thing she should be thinking about was escape before it was too late!

She listened. It seemed silent – but then the murmur of a voice emerged, a phone conversation the boy was having. Perhaps he would pack up the trains and flee? Something told her it wouldn't be as easy as that. What had the boy said earlier? *'You weren't supposed to be…'* She wasn't supposed to be what? Home? That didn't make sense, who would think she was away, and why? And then it struck her. She wasn't supposed to be *awake*! The sleeping pills! This robber knew she'd be whacked out on sleeping pills, and probably wouldn't wake up even if there *was* a loud noise. Who knew she was taking the medication? Magnus. But practically everyone she'd come in contact with, she was always complaining how lethargic they made her.

Another potential culprit began to dawn on Mrs Dixit. The train woman! Lidia what's-her-face. That lying, cheating scam artist. Of course, it was her. She'd discovered how valuable the model trains were and sent someone to steal them. Mrs Dixit should never have listened to her sister!

She took two deep breaths, wincing at the pain they caused. The boy would be back soon. If he was checking in with a boss, maybe there was no one outside in a vehicle after all? If Mrs Dixit could make it out of the building, perhaps she would get away? She wiggled the cords again until they chafed her skin. He would chase her, she realised, even if she could manage to get off the chair, and he was fast.

The silence settled in again. It was now Mrs Dixit felt the most terrified. *The silence! This flat!* That she might come to an ugly end, here in this dead silence, away from anyone who loved her, as her husband lay prone. It was suffocating. She wanted to yell, to scream, not even for rescue, but so the universe would be forced to acknowledge her existence. *I'm here!* she thought, tears streaming hotly down her cheeks. *I can't be smothered like this, silently in the night.* Why hadn't she stormed noisily into Naveem's parents' house, banging pots and kicking things as she went? Why was she so afraid of the sounds she could make? Why did she have to smother herself? No! She would fight him – the boy – she would yell. She would bite at his face. Yank at his hair. She would not go quietly. Mrs Dixit was *needed* – there was Naveem, but also Mrs Rampersad now, she would be bereft without her, and Henry too. You see, there were people to make a racket for. Thank God! There were people for whom to set off fireworks, to ignite explosions, to make every possible cacophony.

Henry! His deft fingers on the cords as he tied the nautical knots, his big round hazel eyes staring up at her proudly, the gentle murmur of appreciation from the surrounding schoolchildren. *The knots!* Instead of trying to free her bound wrists, Mrs Dixit wiggled her fingers up the rope and found the bulging knot. A quick assessment showed it to be the most basic of double knots and she made short work of the first one, which was relatively loose. The second knot was tighter and would not budge. Mrs Dixit tried wiggling her wrists, to allow her to change her position, and kept chipping away at the knot with her thumb, hoping it would yield. How long had the boy been gone? Two minutes? Five? She struggled at the knot some more, but it was obstinate. She thought of Mrs Rampersad, sleeping peacefully and unawares above her, and a new idea came to her – and even in her dire predicament she rolled her eyes at the thought of it.

'Alright,' she said, quietly. She pictured the most recent flyer. '"The name of the Lord is a strong Tower; the righteous run into it and are safe". Please make me safe!' she spoke slightly louder, but still under her breath as she continued to work the knot. What else? '"For He will deliver the needy when he cries".' *And I'm crying, I'm crying here*, she implored. What else was there, oh yes – '"The poor also, and him who has no helper". And also, she whose wrists are bound by a godforsaken thief who has come into our home.' The knot gave only slightly, but she could work with that. *Hallelujah!* '"Seek the Lord and his strength. Seek his presence continually!" Untie this fucking knot!' she hissed – the swearword from her own lips surprising her, giving her an additional surge of confidence, and suddenly it was done and the biting cords loosened from around her raw wrists. She paused. He was approaching, coming up the stairs. Her impulse was to run, run! But she knew he would catch her almost instantly if she did. A bang. Not a whimper. *A bang!*

Slipping her hands out of the ropes, she stood up and turned quickly to the countertop, switching on the blender at the highest setting. It howled like an engine, but despite her flight impulse, Mrs Dixit sat back down in the same chair and slipped her hands into the noose of the rope, twisting her hands so that the cords would appear to be binding them again. The boy was leaping up the last of the stairs, his face bloodshot and angry – although luckily Mrs Dixit didn't think he'd seen her out of the chair. The blender was wonderful, sympathetic even, like the roar of a supportive crowd. Even in an absolute silence, in a vacuum, couldn't you still hear the percussion of the blood pumping in your veins, the heart beating in your throbbing ears?

The boy had reached the blender.

'How the actual…?' And then a ringing silence returned. 'What the fuck?'

'It must have been a power surge,' said Mrs Dixit as composedly as she could. 'We've been having a lot of them…'

The impact caught her on the side of the head – her ear, her cheekbone, the side of her eye – as he cuffed her with the back of his right hand. His ring would leave a small dent mark on Mrs Dixit's cheek for weeks to come.

'I told you to be quiet,' he hissed, as she gritted her teeth against the flash of pain. It wasn't exactly stars she saw dancing in front of her eyes, but little squiggles of static, virulent dust that threatened blackout. Her head swum from side to side, but she knew she must *not* pass out.

The boy roughly grabbed her hands to check the ropes were still tied securely around her wrists. She gripped the length of slack rope in her palm, hoping he wouldn't notice anything amiss, but preparing for what would happen if…

A noise from upstairs. Mrs Rampersad. They both froze, listening, eyes on the ceiling. The floorboards creaked. Mrs Dixit knew the path her neighbour was taking to her toilet. Silence. They both waited. A distant flush and more creaking. *No!* thought Mrs Dixit, *don't go back to bed! Oh, Jesus! Oh, the Saints! Please make me safe! Make me safe, Buddha, and all the prophets!* Krishna, and the Norse gods she had learned about at school, the Greek gods and then the copycat Roman versions, the ones she always mixed up in tests. Zeus and Jove and Jupiter. Neptune and Poseidon. Mars and Ares. The zippy lightning marks were going from her eyes. She almost missed them – they were like companions. The silence returned. The emptiness taking everything. The void completed.

A louder creak overhead, as if Mrs Rampersad was walking through her kitchen to her front door.

'Fuck,' the boy said in a nervous whisper. 'Fuck, fuck, fuck.'

Fuck yes! thought Mrs Dixit, and then apologised to the saints and gods she'd only moments before evoked. The sound of a door opening and the unmistakable noise of Mrs Rampersad's descending down the hallway stairs, one lurch at a time.

A drawer was opened behind Mrs Dixit, and when the boy moved to the main door, she could see he was holding a knife. She wanted to yell a warning – even though she was terrified the blade would be used against her. Instead, when it seemed Mrs Rampersad must be standing right outside the door, Mrs Dixit gave as loud a cough as she dared. The boy turned and glared at her incredulously, mouthing obscenities and drawing the knife across his neck.

They waited for what seemed an interminable amount of time and then there came a tentative, almost apologetic knock: *tap tap*. Followed by a thick silence. Mrs Dixit imagined she could hear Mrs Rampersad breathing on the other side of the door, but she dared not cough again. The boy's face was contorted in rage as he watched her, brandishing the knife in threatening swipes. Then, Mrs Rampersad started up the stairs again. Mrs Dixit was torn – her best chance of rescue was now gone, but at least Mrs Rampersad was safe.

'I know what you did,' the boy whispered angrily, as he moved to the table, the knife pointed at her chest. 'I was going to be nice, but now I'm not so sure. When the boss hears how much trouble you've been… You almost fucked this up for me.' He'd raised his voice as he spoke, and he glanced at the ceiling, but all was quiet from above. The boy checked his phone, he was obviously waiting for someone to call. 'You've made a big mistake, that's for sure.' He nipped into the living room, perhaps to check the street through the curtains, and when he came back, he was carrying one of the curtain ties.

'A fucking piece of piss this was supposed to be,' he muttered, marching behind her. Mrs Dixit felt the tie in her mouth and before she could do anything, he had it tight and wound around her head. She made a gagging sound. 'Quiet,' he said, shaking her head, using the ends of the tie like a horse's bridle. '*She'll be out fucking cold*, they said. *You'll be able do a fucking Russian dance on the bed and she won't stir*. My fucking arse.' His phone lit up. 'Thank fuck,' he said reading the message on his screen. 'Ten minutes. Is the front door double-locked?' She shook her head. 'Good. It looks like you're going to come for a ride…' Mrs Dixit shook her head again, more forcibly. 'Not up to me,' he said, lowering his voice again to a hoarse whisper. 'It's the boss. He wants this place gutted. Two blokes are on their way now with a van. Everything needs to be stripped – the trains in the garage, all the stuff down there. In a way, it's a good thing you startled me. Made me call for back-up. There's only so much I can carry on my own, and those model train fings are heavy. Didn't realise there were so many, apparently they're worth a fortune.' He opened the front door an inch or two so he could look out into the main hallway. 'When…'

The door crashed open, sending the boy reeling backwards, hitting the wall behind him. 'What the?!' he shouted in a high-pitched, childlike way, as Mrs Rampersad came through the doorway. She wore a coat over her dressing gown and was wearing workman's boots on the ends of her bare legs. Her hands were in fists and she stared down at the boy with a look of utter unbridled contempt.

'Jesus forgives you,' she announced, before giving him a kick to the ribs. He squealed like a piglet.

'I'll cut you!' he yelled, and so she kicked him again.

'Do not speak to me like that!' Mrs Rampersad yelled down at him, making him cower. 'Now, you are going to put that knife on the ground and then I want you to crawl on your hands and knees into the kitchen, very slow. I'll be behind you the whole time and if I see you make one wrong move, I'll give you another tap with the cap of these boots, you hear me?'

He nodded grimly and placed the knife on the floor.

'Crawl,' Mrs Rampersad commanded, and the boy did as he was told. She stooped down to pick up the knife from the floor, and that's when he kicked out with his foot, catching her off guard. There was an 'oof!' and then a thud as Mrs Rampersad hit the door frame.

'How do *you* like it?' The boy snarled and leapt at her, knocking Mrs Rampersad back into the communal hallway. Mrs Dixit couldn't see what was happening, but the noise was of two people using everything they had. Mrs Rampersad was heavier than the boy, but she was older and slower, and her voice came louder, in grunts, and eventually there was one last crash. It was only now that Mrs Dixit remembered her hands weren't actually bound. *Idiot she was!* She wiggled them out from the ropes, and was about to run into the hallway, when the boy appeared again, panting heavily, his face distorted with exertion and anger.

'Bitches!' he yelled.

Mrs Dixit could see there was blood in his mouth.

'Is she…?'

'Shuttit!' he shouted so vehemently that red globs of spittle flew onto the table in front of her.

'She needs to see a doctor,' Mrs Dixit yelled back, terrified Mrs Rampersad was seriously hurt.

'She's fine. The cow fell over her own boots and hit her head, I didn't even touch her… much.'

On cue, Mrs Rampersad began to moan.

The boy stomped back into the hallway. A moment later, there was the sound of Mrs Rampersad protesting woozily, and the boy telling her to keep still. Mrs Dixit craned her neck to see what he was doing – he seemed to be tying her hands together with another cord.

Where was the knife? Mrs Dixit saw it where he'd left it on the floor.

The boy returned. 'Is there anyone else upstairs?' he demanded.

'No.'

'If you're lying to me…'

'Wouldn't they have heard and come looking by now? Take anything you want, all the trains. I'll even help. And I won't say anything to anyone, I promise. I just want to take my neighbour to the hospital – I'll tell people she fell down the stairs…'

'Quiet,' he replied. 'That's enough from you. One more word and I'll give you another smack.'

Mrs Dixit wanted to hurt the boy then, and knew she was capable of it. She was going to make him pay for what he'd done to Mrs Rampersad.

The boy checked his phone before heading down the study stairs.

Quickly, Mrs Dixit ran to Mrs Rampersad. The woman was conscious, but barely, her head rolling left to right, her eyes flickering.

'I'm here,' Mrs Dixit whispered. 'I'm sorry I didn't stop him. Thank you for coming, I'm not going to let him hurt you again.'

Mrs Rampersad's head lolled.

'Skinny boys,' she slurred, not making eye contact. 'Why is it always skinny boys? Driving past in their cars and yelling? Laughing at you in the supermarket? What gives them the right? They're only children, and they're so *thin*. They should snap, like a twig, but no – they push everyone around.'

'Do you have your phone?' Mrs Dixit asked urgently.

'What did I ever do to them? I brought up my boys to be good in this world, God-fearing, respecting their mother. And what do they do to repay me? Run away overseas and leave me here all alone. Not that they're skinny anymore, that's for sure,' she laughed a strange giggling hiccup, which unnerved Mrs Dixit.

'We have to get help. But I'm not going to leave you here with him, okay? I promise.'

'They all promise, they promise they'll phone, they promise they'll come back for holidays, but you're lucky if you get a single letter once a year. It's all on Facebook, they say – well, I'm not on Facebook. Why doesn't anyone send actual photos anymore?'

Time was running out. Mrs Dixit checked the pockets of the coat Mrs Rampersad was wearing but there was nothing inside except for her keys. She could run upstairs, lock herself inside and call the police, but she didn't want to abandon her friend. There was no way to move Mrs Rampersad in the state she was in, she was a dead weight.

With determination, Mrs Dixit picked up the knife from the floor and returned to her chair. She didn't try to make it look as if her hands were still bound; instead she held the knife with her clasped hands behind her, blade pointing down.

Mrs Rampersad was still speaking woozily, and Mrs Dixit – trying to focus herself, while not wanting to think too much about the consequences of what she was about to do – gladly listened.

You know, I prayed every morning for him. Every morning I got down on my knees, and I asked the Lord to wake him up. Even though your man only ever treated me with disdain, even though my car was always left out in bad weather, even though he ignored me if I was on the other side of the road – I prayed, because it was the good Christian thing to do.

These women at church, they don't understand the meaning of the word. I know they never invite me to their Bible talks; I hear them whispering. Not one of them is out there flyering with me five days a week. There's always some excuse. Oh, I can't tomorrow, I have a dentist appointment. *Do you think Jesus couldn't visit the lepers because he was having his teeth whitened? And then they have the nerve to say I'm a bully! I don't want to be friends with those women, but I did with you. And so I prayed for him to come back. But then one morning I stopped. Because what do I have? My children don't want me. My husband only wanted to leave me. He was skinny when I met him. I thought I could fatten him, but liars never get filled up. There was a man at the church, lovely he was – a widower, a gentleman, plenty of meat on his bones – and I simply asked him over for dinner a few times, and maybe we slept in the same bed, but there was nothing unfitting, even though all those ladies at the church came whispering: 'There she goes again.' Where else am I supposed to meet anyone? To be considered some* harlot. *They would rather I crawl into bed, never to get out again. And sometimes, I do go to a bar and perhaps I drink with a man I meet, and we sleep in the same bed. I hold my hands up and ask forgiveness, but this is the only way I can be seen!*

All the skinny men in the world can't hold me down when I have that primal thirst. I shall withstand their attacks, because Jesus is in my heart, and he is here in this house! Look upon him! That glorious face, those eyes! And Jesus is in your husband too, he has a plan for him, and I would say 'Make him well again, oh Lord,' and sometimes I would cry in my room. You were practically a stranger to me then, but as we grew in acquaintance, I saw God's plan, and then I couldn't pray for him, not because I wished your husband harm, but because I'd found someone who cared finally where I was, who didn't talk to me through a frown, who didn't whisper behind my back, who I could trust – and I selfishly didn't want to lose that! I thought of coming to you and pleading, 'Let's look after each other when we're old, because, otherwise, who will?*' I was afraid I might lose what I had earned so uncertainly, and I've been disappointed in my life so many times before.*

I could have gone to Trinidad when I was younger, but there was defeat in that too. I didn't want to go back to that strange place, because although the men aren't so skinny, they can be mean and cruel in other ways, and I had cousins who were beaten by their husbands until their faces were yellow and blue. So I stopped praying, not because I wanted him gone, but because anything else was too hard to bear. I just couldn't go back… with no one caring…

What happens when we can't feed ourselves? Will Jesus show us the way? Or will he abandon us, like all those other skinny boys, driving away in the car after screaming at you on the streets, 'Fat cow!' He'll yell, and they'll all laugh together, and I'll say, 'Jesus, I can change! I don't want to die alone,' and he'll shout back: 'You had your whole life already.' And I'll call back: 'But Jesus, I always had so many problems.' I had children to feed and bills to pay, and loneliness in my heart, and oh, I was trying. I go to the high street, even though some days I am afraid when there are so many skinny boys hanging around, smoking their cigarettes and staring at me, and I'm scared I'm going to be made a martyr, and I'm scared I'll be bleeding in an alleyway, but more than that, I'm afraid I'll be forgotten! Because who will remember me, if I've even slipped the Lord's mind?

She started to get quieter, her head bobbing against her chest.

'Don't fall asleep!' Mrs Dixit hissed as loudly as she dared.

Mrs Rampersad's head bobbed up again, and she opened her eyes, their eye-line meeting at a strange angle – one of them sitting straight-backed at the kitchen table, the other slumped to one side on the floor – and seeing Mrs Dixit, she smiled, one of happy recognition, a warm, generous, expansive smile that brought a lump to Mrs Dixit's throat.

Footsteps ascending – Mrs Dixit swallowed, and clasped the knife handle more firmly. Mrs Rampersad's head was still nodding drunkenly.

The boy appeared on the stairs with a large duffel bag and put it down by the door. It made a heavy metallic clatter as it hit the ground. Mrs Dixit thought about all the expensive postage that Mr Dixit must have paid over the years, sourcing those train sets from across the world. The Dixits hadn't exactly clashed over the matter – that wasn't their style – but there were long silent evenings where they both mentally catalogued the folly of the other's reasoning. They *were* heavy, those trains. Could they be made into a better weapon than a knife? Mrs Dixit wondered. The knife was scarily definitive. A whack on the head with a train on the other hand – or better yet, a duffel bag full of them… As the boy descended the stairs again, Mrs Dixit jumped up nimbly from the chair and laid the knife down on the table. She felt instantly better now she was no longer holding it. Knives were not the answer.

Mrs Rampersad looked up at Mrs Dixit as she nipped around the table, giving her an unsteady thumbs up before her arm collapsed at her side.

Careful to bend with her knees, Mrs Dixit tested the weight of the bag. She grunted with the effort. It was too heavy to swing as it was, she'd have to remove a couple of trains, it would only take a…

She could hear the boy approaching the stairs, cursing under his breath. It was now or never. Using all her might, Mrs Dixit gave the bag a swing, almost falling backwards with the momentum – she didn't want to fly down the stairs with it. Bracing herself, she swung the bag again – the boy gave a surprised 'Wha!' as he saw her, and this time she let the bag go as he began his panicked climb. There was a crunching sound on contact, of metal, at some velocity, greeting meat and bone, the bag hitting the boy square in the chest, knocking him backwards down the stairs with an almighty crash as both bag and boy hit the floor. She waited, holding her breath. Mrs Dixit had ruled out the knife, but if he stirred…

There came a soft moan, but nothing more.

She sprinted over to Mrs Rampersad, who had her chin on her chest, her eyelids half closed.

'Come on, let's get up,' Mrs Dixit said merrily, attempting to take her neighbour's hand and pull her to a sitting position. 'Please, we don't have much time!' Mrs Rampersad groaned, which was answered by a groan from the bottom of the stairs. She remained unmoveable, even with Mrs Dixit hauling with every ounce of strength. Grabbing one of Mrs Rampersad's booted feet, she pulled as hard as she could. Mrs Rampersad moved a few inches, sliding down the wall, but then she would not budge. Mrs Dixit tried everything – pulling both her feet simultaneously, grabbing the hem of her coat, yanking on her hands – but nothing worked.

Giving it one last attempt, Mrs Dixit took hold of the tied boot laces, and there was something about this vantage that gave her extra power, and slowly and painfully, she slid Mrs Rampersad across the hallway floor and towards the front door. What was she going to do now? Mrs Dixit couldn't leave the woman here, what would happen if the boy came around? *A phone!* Mrs Dixit was about to take her neighbour's keys and run upstairs to use the phone, when Mrs Rampersad opened her eyes to say, 'You don't have to worry. See?'

There was a sudden knocking on the front door which frightened Mrs Dixit half to death. At first, she assumed it was the gang come to pick the boy up, but then through the frosted glass she noticed the flashing lights.

'I called them before I had my little fall,' Mrs Rampersad said proudly. 'I listened by your front door. I didn't know who was inside, but I didn't like the sound of them. You can never be too safe.'

'Oh, you wonderful woman,' Mrs Dixit said, tears welling in her eyes. 'Thank you, *thank you*.'

Mrs Rampersad gave another wobbly thumbs up before collapsing again.

Mrs Dixit rode with Mrs Rampersad in the ambulance as dawn broke across the sky. It was very strange to be back at Chomley hospital, but as a patient this time. After getting a dressing on the side of her face – for the cut the boy's ring had left – and some pain relief for her cracked ribs, she was discharged, only to be interviewed by the police. Once that was over, she sat by Mrs Rampersad's bed – she was being kept awake for observation. Every hour, the nurse came in with fresh coffee.

Mrs Rampersad, while still incredibly woozy, was also being extraordinarily nice to everyone. Mrs Dixit was seriously concerned about brain damage. But eventually the old Mrs Rampersad drifted back and she was soon grumbling about the state of the coffee, and the smell of the ward, and the fact the nurses were a pack of heathens. Once this rebalance had occurred, Mrs Dixit felt safe to leave her to rest.

40 days since the accident

As her home was officially a crime scene, Mrs Dixit stayed at her sister's. She would have preferred to go to a hotel, for everyone's sake, but her cards were all maxed out. She hadn't taken her mobile phone in the rush of getting into the ambulance, so Mrs Dixit simply showed up at her sister's house at 7 a.m.

Henry was amazed.

'What are you doing *here*?' he asked, as if she was the fictional faun from Narnia having just hopped out of his wardrobe.

'I'll have to make up the fold-out bed,' her sister said, clearly unimpressed with this turn of events – the drama of a home invasion not quite enough to cancel out the bother of having to do extra laundry.

'I'll just lie on the couch, if that's easier?' Her ribs were aching.

'We have the grouting being done in the bathroom, they'll be in and out all day.'

'I'm so tired, I don't think I'll notice.'

Her sister gave a look that clearly communicated: *no, but I will.*

In the end, Mrs Dixit took a nap on Henry's bed as he completed his preparations for school.

He narrated everything he was doing for her benefit:

'These are my socks,' explained Henry. There was something in his focus and movements as he dressed that was the spitting image of herself.

Despite the pain she was in, the warm milk and honey smell of him in the pillow and his bright buoyant chatter soon lulled her into a deep, and this time, dreamless sleep.

When Mrs Dixit woke at midday, her sister was gone, so she said goodbye to the workman who was grouting the bathroom and went back to the hospital. Mrs Rampersad was almost completely revived and was now enjoying the scandal of the night before.

'I heard a loud whirring noise.'

'That was the blender.'

'Ah – so I came downstairs. I could see the light was on, underneath the door, which I thought was strange, so I knocked – no answer – and went upstairs again to bed, but something didn't feel right. I asked Jesus what I should do, and he said: *Woman, go sneak down there and put your ear against the door.* So, I crept down those stairs as quietly as I could, soft as a cat' (Mrs Dixit inwardly recalled all the times that Mr Dixit had cursed the woman upstairs for her heavy footedness. 'She's doing it on purpose,' he would cry. 'She could be quieter if she tried!'). 'Then the Holy Spirit took me aside to say, *Put on these boots, there's a man's voice in there, it would not be seemly to be seen with your toes dangling out in the middle of the night.* And I put the coat on as it was cold. I listened again, and this time I heard that little man, and the terrible things he was saying, and I thought, now is the hour! I waited by the door, like a lion. When he opened the door, I was ready to save you.'

'And you did, you did!' Mrs Dixit exclaimed, wanting to reward her.

'Well, no. Not really. God's plan is unknown to us all.'

'But I would never have escaped if it wasn't for you.'

'That may be,' Mrs Rampersad said, patting her hand. 'I'm glad I could do my part.' She took a deep breath. 'You know, when I had that whack on my head, I don't remember anything else except coming round in the ambulance. But I did get a vision!'

'Of Jesus?'

'Of Tom Jones, and Mr Beasley from the church whose wife died a year ago, but best of all was Bishop Desmond Tutu. And they held me in their arms, and they were so beautiful! And Desmond Tutu sang a sweet song from my youth, and Tom

Jones did the harmony, and even Mr Beasley had a lovely voice. If I get into heaven, that's the angels' chorus I want.' She smiled mischievously. 'It was all I could do not to give that Desmond a kiss on his mouth!'

'He's a clergyman. And a married man!' Mrs Dixit played at being scandalised for enjoyment's sake.

'I'm sad for her then,' Mrs Rampersad laughed. 'He seemed to enjoy it.'

'I was scared for you, that you'd be hurt. Hurt worse, I mean.'

'I'm a tough old battleaxe.' But even Mrs Rampersad went quiet in the face of what could have been.

'I told the police about Magnus.'

Mrs Rampersad looked puzzled. 'Why?' she asked.

'I think he is connected to the robbery – he might even be the brains behind the Chomley cat burglar.'

'Magnus, a criminal? What made you think that nonsense?'

Mrs Dixit felt the sting of her neighbour's reprimand, especially coming moments after feeling so close to her.

'He's very odd. And he's always wearing expensive clothing. Watches. Cufflinks. Rings. Where did he get the money for those? But the real giveaway is how he's constantly telling small lies and trying to pump me for information every time we spoke. He really is very suspicious,' she said, flustered at having to prove herself. She'd assumed Mrs Rampersad would have backed up her story. 'The robber boy knew I was taking sleeping pills, had learned about the trains somewhere. Either Magnus told him or… well, it might also be the train specialist I told you about, the Lidia Millbrook woman…'

'Magnus is harmless, he's just a bit, you know…'

Mrs Dixit shrugged. 'No, I don't know.'

'He has a touch of…'

'Of what…?'

'His memory isn't what it used to be. He has' – she whispered – '*Alzheimer's.*'

'How long have you known this?'

'A while. I spoke to his carer, Isabella. She was always waiting in the blue car. One of those chronically cold women, shivering away with the heating turned up full blast, wasting all that petrol.'

'But why were you always quick to interrupt Magnus and me if he was harmless?'

'He might have a demented mind, but he's still a man. You have to be careful. His carer says he was in the Air Force, went to Kuwait during the Gulf crisis, an explosion gave him shell shock. That's why he likes watching the planes – because he used to fly them, and the noise cancels out the ringing in his ears. Lost his wife a few years back – Nerissa – she had an affair when he started getting ill, left him for his best friend. Didn't I tell you all this?'

'Not one word of it,' Mrs Dixit replied, flabbergasted.

'So you see, that takes him out of the running for your evil genius.'

'Oh,' Mrs Dixit covered her mouth in realisation. 'I have to tell the police. I think I got Magnus into some serious hot water.'

'I wouldn't be too worried. Nothing particularly bothers him now. I envy him.'

Mrs Dixit was reminded then of Mrs Rampersad's words when she slumped on the floor, the hurt and anger that had come rushing to the surface, but she didn't know how to bring this up without inadvertently embarrassing the woman, so she didn't. It was only when she was about to leave that Mrs Dixit turned and said, 'Those sons of yours… they really don't know what they're missing.'

Home finally; one surrounded by police tape. Everything was in disarray, and she felt in no mood to do any cleaning. Fortunately, the bedroom was unscathed, so she made a cup of tea and lay on her bed in her clothes to drink it. Mr Dixit hated street clothes on the bed. He did have a point – the world was a disgustingly filthy place.

When hunger roused her, she went to make toast, only then thinking about the answerphone. A message from her sister, pretending she was sad to have seen her go. 'It was *so* lovely to have you here,' she lied.

The second message had the unmistakable voice of the other Mrs Dixit, Naveem's mother.

'He's sick. They've taken him. I suppose you're happy now.'

With that, the line went dead.

PART THREE

48 days since the accident

Many things had changed. Naveem was in a room by himself, sealed in a protective plastic to stop unwanted diseases being transmitted to his even more vulnerable body. The nurses no longer told Mrs Dixit to talk to him, that he could hear everything she said, or implied her voice might lead him back on the path to recovery. Recovery was never discussed. His deterioration worried the many doctors and specialists, but they all agreed that it was nothing to do with the condition he was in when it occurred; the field nurse had visited only the day before it happened, and everything was medically correct. It was an unfortunate natural development, not possible foul play – this, they were sure of.

He was changed. Thinner, much thinner – gaunt and grey. His hair had been cut short, much shorter than he generally liked, perhaps the way it was cut as a child, and Mrs Dixit felt that of everything – almost everything – this was the worst transgression, worse than stealing him away, to cut off his lovely hair like that. His lips were a strange shade of beige, with dried spittle in the creases that she couldn't easily wipe away because of the plastic protection. She couldn't touch him at all, except wearing special gloves. And there was so much to tell him now, so much more he'd missed. How Henry was taking French lessons with a private tutor, and the way he spoke it, mannered and serious, was an absolute delight. Everything to do with the burglar boy's incarceration and the continued hunt for the crime boss. Her new job at the florist shop, where she worked two mornings a week, how she was thriving in her employment, and how she was always tempted to take some of the gorgeous flowers home. How she'd woken up breathless the other night, her whole body tingling from a climax – the first time it had happened like that since she was a hormonal teenager. And of course, how she was sorry for everything, sorry she'd left him alone in that study of his too long, how she should have put her foot down sooner. For what is quality time, really? It's whenever you don't want to be anywhere else. And Mrs Dixit had realised she only wanted to be right beside him.

But the biggest change was that now his mother was there too.

The other Mrs Dixit never left his side, or so it seemed. When she did go home, it was past midnight, and she would always return before 7 a.m. the following morning. She rarely took breaks – only to eat or use the bathroom, and she had never spoken to anyone in his presence the entire time.

'There are Tibetan monks on hunger strikes who are less disciplined than she is,' Mrs Rampersad had muttered one car journey home. 'What's she doing there anyway? Waiting for him to get well enough so she can whisk him away again, I bet.'

But Mrs Dixit, the younger, wasn't so sure. She'd had ample time to observe the older woman when she was seated (they both awkwardly avoided eye contact when one of them came or went from the room). Mrs Dixit, the senior, always sat straight-backed, without resting against the chair. She watched her son unwaveringly, her head covered by the wrap of a dark fabric, the sari intricately woven with subtle embellishments of silver or gold. Her hands in her lap, or sometimes one to her chest as if she was trying to channel her lifeforce through her heart into the comatose body before her. Her face had two deep long lines – grooves, really – that ran under her eyes and made it seem like she was perpetually crying.

'Like a ghoul,' Mrs Rampersad would say, uncharitably.

He's still her son, Mrs Dixit would think in response, but say nothing. The other Mrs Dixit had not earned their mutual pity, not yet at least.

This morning when Mrs Dixit arrived, the chair normally occupied by his mother was empty, which made her heart lurch with worry. But no, there was Naveem, the machines all beeping and whirring as they should be. There was a second chair that Mrs Dixit always claimed, which was slightly behind the first and to the right, allowing for the nurses and doctors to pass through, while being as close to Naveem as possible and also, most importantly, allowing her to observe her namesake. In the first few days, Mrs Dixit had felt an impulse to yell and rant at her for what she'd done, but weirdly, that rapidly passed. Perhaps it was because the other Mrs Dixit didn't seem contrite or arrogant, only profoundly sad – a deep, almost liquescent unhappiness, like a stagnant lake. So she had not spoken one word to her either.

Mrs Dixit senior appeared at the door five minutes later. Her eyes flicked to Mrs Dixit and an emotion passed lightly over her face – annoyance, disapproval, hate? One thing was for certain, she didn't like to be caught away from her bedside vigil.

'She wants to give the impression she's holier than thou,' Mrs Rampersad would snort. 'After everything she's done too! It's guilt, all guilt.'

Mrs Dixit tried not to let her face show any emotion in response to Naveem's mother, but she could feel her jaw involuntarily tightening, so she turned back to his hospital bed to hide her expression. Sitting in partnered silence, she found her mind filling with strange entertainments, random memories from their marriage, cataloguing the times they'd held hands on a beach, which beaches, the weather on those days, odd movements she noticed from his mother – the way she nodded occasionally as if agreeing with some hidden discussion, how she would shiver or shudder abruptly.

Mrs Dixit also thought a lot about her husband's childhood – what actually had he told her? He was always so unforthcoming, shutting down her questions until she'd finally stopped asking. He had lived in a house of boys and noise and domineering parents. Naveem had wanted his own bedroom more than anything else, a place for his possessions so they wouldn't get broken or stolen by one of his siblings. Four boys, what that must be like! But then Mrs Dixit imagined four Henrys and it didn't seem so bad. *Quatre*, she heard Henry say in her mind.

There were many more visitors now. The Dixit women, of course, the father popping in during the evenings to hover about, the brothers too – and their wives, and their children. Why hadn't Mrs Dixit seen them previously, when Naveem was in the hospital before? They must have stayed away, or always come later in the evening once she'd gone home.

Mrs Dixit regretted the way she'd almost tried to avoid Naveem when he'd first been in the coma. Now, she stayed for the entire day. It was a relief to no longer sit in the car in his parents' street, worrying and not knowing his condition. Sick as he was now, at least she could see Naveem with her own eyes. His extended family didn't speak to her either, although they acknowledged her with a raised eyebrow, or a polite nod of the head, the smaller children gawking at her unashamedly.

Mrs Dixit couldn't help taking sidelong glances at the kids – is this what her child might have looked like if she'd been able to have them, she thought with a pang. They resembled Naveem in the curve of the cheekbones, the bright expressive eyes, their natural inquisitiveness. They would enjoy the model trains, she felt sure, and then she experienced a sadness that these children had never known their uncle, that no inquisitive child had shared his fascinating hobby. Perhaps the model trains weren't about his childhood at all, but about lost fatherhood? She had reflected on this idea for a full two days, brimming with love for her husband. There was time for this type of thinking now – normally, Mrs Dixit would have pushed these thoughts away for being too painful; now she held them mindfully. The silence helped at times, but often it loomed heavily around her in the room and she wanted to clap her hands or make a strange animalistic screeching noise just to break its spell – and after this sensation had passed, she would feel wild and unbalanced at the intensity of this compulsion.

Other regular visitors included Mrs Rampersad, of course, who muttered derogatory things under her breath that the older Mrs Dixit must hear – and was mostly relegated to waiting in the hallway so as not to cause a scene. The younger Mrs Dixit was glad to have her there, however. It was immeasurably better knowing someone really did have her back.

'We need to corner the woman,' Mrs Rampersad had spluttered, 'demand an apology. Get it in writing that they won't try a similar thing again, when he's well.'

But the reality was he wasn't getting better, and everyone, on some level, knew it. The nurses, in their newly hushed and respectful way, no longer jolly and boisterous, struck dumb too. The doctors who stared gravely, and made private notes, and bobbed their heads when they left, averting their eyes. The woman who came to do physiotherapy was the only one to burst this bubble. 'Come along now,' she said in a broad Nigerian accent as she rotated Naveem's spindly wrists. 'Show me how to do it.' But of course, he never did.

There was one final regular visitor. No, not Mrs Dixit's sister – she was still very busy with the house renovations, and the new windows, and a dining table being delivered, although now she often dropped off Henry after school at his insistence, where he would sit on a chair beside Mrs Dixit, his feet swinging adorably as he worked on his homework.

The visitor was Shelly, the doctor's daughter, who came to silently (and sometimes not so silently) cry. Mrs Dixit enjoyed Shelly's visits, because she liked the girl, but also since she seemed to ruffle the older Mrs Dixit's feathers, and although the younger Mrs Dixit couldn't seem to channel her anger towards the woman like Mrs Rampersad could, she still enjoyed occasionally being petty.

Shelly brought vigil candles to light and essential oils to burn, which the nurses would quickly take custody of when discovered. But mostly, Shelly would sob. And on those eccentric afternoons when there were two Mrs Dixits, and Henry finishing his French grammar, and Mrs Rampersad pacing in the hallway, and Shelly weeping for her own grief as well as the grief of others, like a professional mourner at an Italian funeral, Mrs Dixit had to stop and reflect on how different it was now compared to when Naveem first had the accident, and what exactly he would think of this eclectic audience if he suddenly woke up. Sometimes – just sometimes – his potential reaction elicited a small smile.

After several run-ins with the head nurse, Shelly eventually fell back on crystals instead of candles, which she placed around Naveem on her side of the plastic sheeting, but perilously, so that they would often fall, tinkling loudly on the floor, to the consternation of the doctor on his rounds.

*

Mrs Dixit didn't spend all her time at the hospital, worrying about her husband deteriorating; she couldn't. It would have ground her down. Fortunately, she had a job now too, her first in many years. Stem & Blossom was run by a husband-and-wife team in the poshest neighbourhood of Chomley Manor. Initially, they'd asked her to come in to work a busy week during a cluster of early spring weddings, but she'd proven herself indispensable, and so she was not dispensed with. It felt good having even a trickle of money coming in again, and with the loan she'd organised with her bank manager, this at least stemmed the tide of outgoings. The flowers were worth it in themselves – they lifted her spirits, especially when she was feeling sad or frustrated. She began to see the beauty in the wilting flowers and wanted to rescue them. The owners were happy to oblige – the mangled blooms and offcuts were unusable, unwanted, but to Mrs Dixit each stem, each branch, was worth saving as long as humanly possible.

And on the occasional afternoon, Mrs Dixit still went flyering on the high street with Mrs Rampersad. She realised she could now look a complete stranger square in the eye and hold contact for an inappropriate length of time. It was quite thrilling.

She had only just returned home from the high street when there was a knock on the front door. *Oh blast*, she'd forgotten – the police were dropping by again.

Mrs Dixit tried to smile warmly at the two officers. It was not convincing. After inviting them inside, they huddled around the kitchen table. Mrs Dixit did not offer them drinks, even though she knew they'd happily accept – she didn't want to encourage them to stay.

'As you know,' the larger one said, 'we are here in two separate capacities.'

'Yes, yes,' Mrs Dixit said impatiently. She'd always been told the police force was so under-resourced, and yet these two seemed to pop by almost every other day. 'Has there been any news about the boy?'

'The suspect will have his court date soon.'

'But has he told you anything else about the burglaries? They've seemed to continue unabated, so he can't have been the ringleader…'

Both policemen shuffled in their seats at this, they obviously felt personally aggrieved the crime had not yet been solved – the amount of time they spent in her kitchen probably wasn't helping close the case.

'The burglaries are our highest priority, and we can't speak about any leads, but rest assured, our investigations are continuing.'

Rest assured, Mrs Dixit thought, no, she'd never 'rest assured' again. She slept with one eye open since the burglary. No pills anymore. It was much better to be awake than lying there, completely vulnerable. The police were no help. That was unfair. They were doing their best. She was in an unreasonable mood, she could tell. Sitting all day behind Naveem's mother did that to her. Her emotions built up but had nowhere to go. Sometimes she felt it would be much healthier if she was more like Mrs Rampersad in that regard. Radical honesty. *Unpleasantly* radically honest, but honest, nonetheless.

'Are you still questioning Magnus?' Mrs Dixit asked the officers.

The two men looked at each other.

'We have finished that line of investigation.'

'I told you it was a mistake. I shouldn't have said he was involved. He's a sweet man, who's unwell, and I've caused him and his family considerable stress.'

'It was good you told us so we could check him off our list. But obviously his diagnosis tallied with the doctor's notes and hospital records, which amongst all the other evidence, ruled him out.'

'I still feel terrible pointing the finger at Magnus, completely without foundation.'

'If it's any consolation,' the younger one chipped in, 'he probably won't remember.'

His colleague looked at his partner wide-eyed.

'I don't think that's appropriate,' he said.

'Oh, I mean… No, of course.' The younger officer was instantly remorseful. 'I'm sorry, all the stress of planning the wedding must be getting to me. I apologise.'

'You're getting married,' Mrs Dixit said politely, 'how nice.'

'In the spring. My fiancée is from Portugal, so the wedding will be in…'

His colleague cleared his throat.

'As we were saying…'

'Yes, as we were saying…' the younger one said, forcing himself to sit straighter.

'The suspect is not cooperating, even with the promise of a lesser sentence, so it was very helpful to learn about his employment at the waxworks.'

'We used to go there all the time as kids!'

The younger officer was given another look by his colleague. Mrs Dixit got the impression the older one wanted to dig the younger one in the ribs with his elbow.

'As I was saying, it seems the suspect had been working there for six months, so there might be a correlation between the burglary victims and those attending the waxworks – he was perhaps targeting wealthier customers, copying down their details when they paid by debit card to find personal information, such as addresses, on the dark web.'

'But the card machine was broken,' Mrs Dixit said.

The officer stared blankly.

'What?'

'Every time I went, the machine was out of action. He only took cash.'

The officer blinked, and then made a note on his pad.

'Very good,' he said. 'As I mentioned, we're not sure of the connection yet, but we are very close to breaking it.'

They don't have anything, Mrs Dixit thought to herself, disparagingly.

'Now, your husband,' the constable said, when the younger one had made a pit stop to the toilet. 'There's still the issue of the drugs in his system, but fortunately a new lab test has come back to confirm that although his levels were unusually high, they wouldn't have impeded his judgement and so were unlikely to cause the accident.'

'Yes, it's pretty well established by now that the cause of the accident was a great big lorry careening into his stationary cab,' Mrs Dixit responded, annoyed.

'And now we have another test to back up that theory.'

'It's not a theory if it happened. On camera.'

'Of course,' the younger one said, 'that doesn't stop a civil case being brought against your husband. By the family of the deceased.'

Mrs Dixit didn't imagine Shelly would want to press charges – especially when the claim was ludicrous. Shelly's deadbeat father, though – if he needed the money…?

'The real issue is that my husband is in hospital, surrounded by the people who kidnapped him against my wishes, and you have done absolutely nothing about it. His mother is there, day in day out, and I'm expected to sit there knowing there's been no consequence for her actions, *and* it could happen again?'

'This is a complicated issue,' the younger officer remarked, shaking his head. 'If your husband had left a living will...'

'Who does? Do either of you have one?' Mrs Dixit marvelled at how forthright she was being.

The policemen looked at each other.

'I've been meaning to...' the older one muttered.

'It's something my fiancée and I are looking into...' mumbled the other.

'Exactly,' Mrs Dixit said, vindicated.

'You see, it's a delicate private issue between you and Naveem's family. No law has been broken.'

'Kidnap? And they may do it again and this time they'll really take him out of the country.'

'If they were to make a play for moving him, then yes, that would be something we can act on.'

'What you're telling me is, until the crime is actually committed, you just sit back and twiddle your thumbs?'

'Exactly,' the younger one replied. This got considerable side-eye from his colleague. 'But we realise this must be very stressful for you,' he added, respectfully. His bedside manner had got much better over the past seven weeks – this fiancée must be a good influence.

His mother, Mrs Dixit thought, as she tried to drift off to sleep the old-fashioned way. *I have to talk to her. Make her promise she won't try to take Naveem again.* His mother was the lynchpin of the family. Making her see sense was crucial.

Mrs Dixit hadn't spoken the very first time she'd met his mother either. The moment Naveem had ushered her inside the family house, she knew his parents were unaware of their relationship. It was an ambush, but without anyone having an advantage. Both his mother and father sat calmly, albeit rigidly, teacups and saucers delicately positioned on their laps, as their son explained in a low, unhurried tone that he was in love with this woman, that he planned to marry her, to move out, to start a family of his own. Mrs Dixit, not yet a Dixit, found herself listening intently to these revelations – apart from asking her to marry him, and once saying he loved her, they had barely spoken about future plans. Eventually, his mother had stood abruptly, and Mrs Dixit had expected the cup and saucer to smash to the floor, the movement was so sudden, but still she held it and not a drop spilled.

She spoke in Hindi, but the subtext was clear:

No. We do not accept this. This cannot be. It is a mistake.

Naveem had taken his fiancée's hand then and there was a quick inhalation of breath from his parents, disdain. Mrs Dixit would have done anything to marry Naveem: changed her race, her age, her name, changed country. In a way, she hoped he'd steal her away. There was always talk of Canada, but somehow that never gained traction. They'd remained in Chomley, in the borough where they were both born and raised, once officially Essex, now part of Greater London. If she was honest – *radically* honest – she'd been disappointed when they had settled into a normal suburban life, but that too was a form of racial prejudice – why should Naveem be any different than the other men in Chomley just because he was Asian? The exotica of overseas – Naveem was interested in none of it. He craved British 'normality'. Meat and three veg; having the vegetables slightly overcooked was even preferred. Evenings in front of the TV. Holidays in July or September so they didn't coincide with the schools. He watched football, but Mrs Dixit always had the impression he was only going through the motions. And that's what had always worried her – was their marriage also *going through the motions*? He'd found a wife that suited him, one that was neither too loud nor too vivid. Had everything with vibrancy and sound been stripped away? The only thing Mr Dixit truly loved unequivocally and measurably (you could actually put a price on it) was his trains – and even then, he almost exclusively preferred them in sepia colours. Most didn't even run on a track – those were looked down upon by 'real' collectors, her husband had informed her early in their marriage. The model trains were for putting on a pedestal and observing behind glass, not running along going 'choo, choo' for some abstract sense of enjoyment.

His mother, Mrs Dixit thought again. She needed her approval in an almost visceral way – wanted her to see their years of marriage had been upright, that her concerns at the beginning of the relationship were unfounded. *We were as happy as most marriages*, she wanted to shout into the darkness. *Surely that counts?*

49 days since the accident

The next morning, she was seated behind the woman again. Mrs Dixit had not slept well – the answer to why had popped into her head the moment she opened her eyes. Of course Mrs Dixit wanted her mother-in-law's approval – for looking after her son, for washing his clothes, ironing his shirts, cooking his food. She had taken on these burdens willingly and done them *well*. But there was something else, too. There were few people who knew Naveem, *really* knew him. Mrs Rampersad obviously didn't – he'd always kept her at arm's length, as he did with most people. Strangers were an unnecessary commotion with no 'down' switch. He had far too much of that with customers. Mrs Dixit used to think Naveem became a cabby because he wanted his freedom, to be out on the road, out of his cramped house, but now she wondered if he'd really chosen his vocation because he liked having a pane of glass between himself and anyone new. Had he created a bubble in their marriage too? Which side of the glass was Mrs Dixit on? Was that why it felt so devastating when she'd learned the doctor, Shelly's mother, had been in the passenger seat? Not because it signalled an affair exactly, but because it showed someone had more effectively penetrated his defences…

If only she could talk about Naveem to someone who knew him! Reminisce. Keep him alive through their conversation. But Mrs Dixit had her own protective wrappings, and so too, of course, did his mother. Powerful ones. Like mother, like son. But how much energy would they save by pooling their resources? Perhaps that was the key? If they could find some common ground, Naveem would wake up, like a prince, woken by true love's kiss?

Mrs Dixit cleared her throat experimentally. The other woman sat completely still. Her posture was impeccable. Sometimes Mrs Dixit imagined she was sleeping, but her eyes were always open, although slightly hooded. Maybe she was reciting words of praise or a mantra? Her lips never moved, though. It was trance-like. Didn't her bottom fall asleep? Her legs cramp? Her stomach gurgle hungrily? Mrs Dixit wondered then what might happen if she took her handbag and threw it at the woman. Maybe her head would fall off – she'd be exposed as nothing more than a mannequin. *Quiet*, Mrs Dixit told herself. *Speak*. And yet, she couldn't, not one word, however much she willed it. But if not now, when? At the palliative care centre? During the funeral? In a lawyer's office fighting over the ashes?

After returning home from the hospital, Mrs Dixit decided to visit the nearby laundrette. That morning, she'd managed to spill a full cup of coffee over the duvet (she was increasingly eating meals in bed, her husband would not approve). Normally, she'd have taken it to a dry cleaner's, but she was wary of her outgoings.

On the short walk, both her sister *and* Len phoned her mobile, but she ignored them – the bag holding the duvet was getting heavier by the minute. Soon, Mrs Dixit would be dragging it along the footpath.

The confusingly named Shampoo Palace had been around since the sixties and looked it. Pushing through the heavy door was like taking a step back in time, from the chipped retro seating and the powder-caked linoleum to the ancient washers and dryers, many of them out of order. Cleverly, Mrs Dixit had brought a small fortune in coins (the Dixits maintained a change jar they sorted fastidiously) so she didn't have to break a note. Even still, it took forever to find a working machine, load the duvet and detergent, add the requisite pound coins (the prices definitely weren't from the sixties), and figure out how to make the washer work.

Her sister rang again, just as the washing machine leapt noisily into life. Mrs Dixit panicked – hers was much louder than the other three machines already going. Was the duvet too heavy? She checked, the other washing machines showed equally large loads inside. Warily, Mrs Dixit watched as the duvet slopped round and round in a growing pool of water, the noise ringing in her ears. The rhythm was hypnotic. She began to feel the vibration in her feet, climbing up her legs, making the hairs stand on end (her leg-shaving routine had gone out of the window since the accident). Was the machine getting louder?

Glancing around, Mrs Dixit wondered if she should find an attendant, but there was no sign of anyone else in the laundrette, only the spinning and sloshing and roaring. What if she ended up breaking the machine? What if she ruined their duvet and had to buy a new one? Some strange duvet – one that Mr Dixit had never read countless reviews of before purchasing. It would be solely her decision. Mesmerised by the rotating drum, Mrs Dixit realised she could buy a new duvet, and if the machine broke down, she would have it repaired. If the building burst into flames, she would escape. There was freedom in these thoughts, and it allowed to her to enjoy the spectacle – the sound of a hundred washerwomen smashing their clothes on a rock, beating their fabric in unison. The tingling in her legs travelled up her entire body, like mites creeping along her skin, as the washing machines bellowed with all their dazzling convenience.

Only then did she realise why her sister had called twice – it had completely slipped her mind. Today was Mrs Dixit's birthday.

50 days since the accident

The following morning, Mrs Rampersad drove them to the airport.

'Are you sure about this?' she asked. 'You don't owe him anything.'

'He was in police custody for two days. I think I owe him *something*. It'll make me sleep easier too.'

Mrs Rampersad shrugged.

'Suit yourself.'

Mrs Dixit bit her lip, contemplating for a second and then turned to look at Mrs Rampersad.

'Have you spoken to your sons yet?'

'No.'

'You said you'd give them a call.'

'I said I'd *try*.'

'Communication is a two-way thing. Until it's not. Just look at Naveem…'

'Okay, okay,' Mrs Rampersad said gruffly, but not without some affection. 'Although I think it's morally questionable that you're still using this information against me – info you only learned because I had a serious concussion. But fine, I'll call them. They probably won't pick up, they're always so busy. Doing what? I'm not leaving a message though. A chump's game, leaving messages. *Ooh, please call me back, Your Highness.* Do you think Jesus ever left anyone an answerphone message?'

Mrs Dixit couldn't argue with that.

When they arrived, he was standing, as he normally did, at the fence, watching the planes. It was a fine day, cold but bright. Coat weather still, but because of the sun, no longer scarf weather. Magnus didn't seem surprised to see her when he turned. *But he does remember me*, Mrs Dixit thought, *in some way, he always does.*

'Hello, you,' he said and smiled.

'Any Concordes today?'

'No, unfortunately. I don't think they can get clearance.'

She smiled. Before, she'd always imagined he was making a joke…

'How's your wife?'

'Nelle? Oh, she's good. Unwell, of course, but good.'

Mrs Dixit nodded politely.

'I'm sorry, Magnus,' she said.

'What for?'

'I told the police you were involved in this burglary stuff.'

'You did?'

She nodded. A plane – an Embraer 190: she was getting better at spotting them too – revved its engine.

'I made it very uncomfortable for you,' she said, raising her voice to match the revving, 'when you were only ever nice to me.'

'Oh well, I don't know if that's true. I'm not always nice.' He smiled vaguely and looked out towards the runway again, watching the plane go. Mrs Dixit melted into the sound as it shot off.

'You know,' he said over the departing noise, 'I've been coming here for so many years and every day, it's the same. That's what I like about it. There's always planes landing and planes taking off.' He looked her in the eye. 'Some days, I don't know how I even got here. Isn't that funny?'

Mrs Dixit put a hand on his.

'Oh, I don't think Nancy would like that,' he said, moving his away. 'She's a very jealous woman, I'm afraid.'

'Don't you mean Nelle?'

He blinked, his face showing only puzzlement.

'Nelle, of course. My mistake.'

He smiled, but it was a weak smile, as if he'd forgotten the motivation for it. He looked towards the runway again.

'The police questioning wasn't too bad.'

'Wasn't it?'

'I sometimes have problems with my memory, you probably haven't noticed.'

'Well…'

'The officers were very polite. The food was nicer than we get usually. They even showed me the police helicopter. In relatively good condition, but I've seen better.'

Mrs Dixit took a deep breath.

'I'm not going to come here much more, I think.'

'Oh, why?'

'My husband needs me. He's not well. I should focus my energy.'

'I always find that the more expansive you are, the more energy you attract.'

'I haven't been the best wife during his illness. I have an issue with intimacy. I can deal with someone being distant – that's how I was brought up, my parents weren't the kindest – in fact, I think I prefer it, gravitate towards it, but vulnerable? That's tough for me. And who's more helpless than someone in a coma?'

'I imagine you've done the best you could. It's very easy to be hard on yourself. But as my wife Nancy always says…' he trailed off, and then looked around. 'What was I saying?'

'How much you love your wife.'

He smiled, warmly this time.

'Yes, how does she put up with me?'

'How does anyone put up with anyone?'

Magnus chuckled.

'You must come visit again.'

'Alright, I will.'

'Good, good.'

She turned and walked towards the car.

In the evening, just before dinner, Mrs Dixit rang the taxi bureau.

Cliff's gravelly voice answered almost immediately.

'Wendy, how are you?'

'I'm good, Cliff. I really can't shake the image of you with those sideburns. You think you know someone!'

Cliff chuckled. 'We all have our dark pasts. Mine just wears a moustache. How are you coping after everything?'

'I'm guessing you mean the home invasion? Fine. Relatively fine. It shook me, of course, but I'm trying not to let it affect me. For Naveem's sake.'

'And they say lightning doesn't strike twice.' He tutted in sympathy. 'How is Naveem?'

'The doctors aren't very optimistic. They think he might remain in a catatonic state. They say *vegetative* – but I can't get on board with that word.'

'I'm so sorry, Wendy. I have so much respect for you – everything you've been through.'

'Thank you. I'm trying to be brave. Which is why I called, actually. I'd like to book a taxi for tomorrow.'

'Of course. Where to?'

'Chomley Young Offenders Centre.'

There was a slight pause.

'Far be it for me to question your decisions, but do you think that's the right choice? I assume you're going to see the… perpetrator?'

'Thank you for your concern, Cliff, but I've thought about this a lot, and it's the right thing to do. The police keep offering me counselling, but really, I just want to look this boy in his eye and ask him why he did it.'

'But the case is still open. You're a witness. Surely they won't let you see him before the court date?'

'I can try. I told you, I'm experimenting with being slightly braver.'

'Are you sure I can't talk you out of it?'

'No – but thank you,' she added, not wanting to seem too brash. She did realise it was easier for her to organise a visit to a criminal than it was to talk face to face with her mother-in-law.

'Oh,' Cliff said, 'I've been meaning to tell you, I looked into that name you asked about in relation to Naveem – Clare, wasn't it, no "i"? She was his passenger; I checked the call log. About three weeks before his accident. Might be another Clare, but it's around the right date, so it's likely her.'

Mrs Dixit could feel her pulse beat faster.

'Is there a surname, a contact number, an address, anything? I know you're not supposed to give details out…'

He made a low grumble.

'I'm not *supposed* to, but we all bend the rules sometimes. Clare Montgomery.' He rattled off the pick-up address and Mrs Dixit quickly scrawled it down. 'Just do something for me?'

'Anything.'

'Don't mention the mullet to Naveem when he wakes up.'

'You have my word.'

'And what time do you want the taxi?'

'Two p.m., please.'

'That's booked in for you, Wendy. Promise me you'll be careful?'

I've been careful a long time, she thought after she said goodbye and put the phone down. Now it was time to get reckless.

51 days since the accident

The taxi arrived at 2 p.m. sharp. And of course it was Len. *Of course!* Mrs Dixit berated herself – she should have specified any other driver to Cliff. *Anyone*.

'Wendy!' Len said, over his shoulder as she climbed into the back of cab. 'What a lovely surprise.'

'But you knew it was my address?' she replied.

'The surprise seeing you. Did you get my phone messages?'

'I did, I did… I've just been so busy, what with my husband in a coma, and being burgled and assaulted in my own home…'

'Don't mention it. Modern life, am I right?'

Something like that, she thought to herself.

'I just want to check I have the right drop-off address,' he said, playing with his satnav. 'Chomley Young Offenders Centre? Doing some charity work, are you?'

'I'm visiting an acquaintance,' she replied, which was the truth.

'What are they in for?'

'Stupidity, mostly.'

'I could have had a very different start in life if it wasn't for a cousin of mine. I started smoking weed, getting involved with the wrong crowd – he really pulled me up. Naveem was like that too – a moral compass. I always wanted to impress him. I think that's really why I always turned down those runs I told you about. The "special" deliveries. I knew there were two sides, Naveem was on one and those deliveries were on the other. In a way, I have him to thank for keeping me on the straight and narrow. It's not easy either – with the apps taking all our business. I've thought about going to the dark side many times. But then I see Naveem's face, judging me, and I think, *no*, Len. That's why I keep wanting to check in with you, now he's gone. Make sure you don't need anything. It's the least I can do. To repay him.'

Mrs Dixit was touched how genuine this admission seemed. She'd underestimated Len.

'I think Naveem would be very thankful.'

'I hope so,' he replied, and began to whistle along with a song on the radio.

It was a twenty-minute drive to the unassuming concrete building on the outskirts of Chomley, close to the motorway. Unassuming except for the high wire fence.

Len appeared nervous. 'Are you sure you want to be let out here?'

'Yes,' she said, although nervous herself.

'I can come in with you, if you prefer? Keep you company?'

'Thank you, but that's not necessary. I will need a ride back in an hour, if you can pick me up then?'

'It would be my privilege and an honour,' he said, beaming.

Mrs Dixit assessed the building, as the taxi beeped an excessive goodbye. Somehow a detention centre for young people seemed even more grisly than a regular prison. It looked like an internment camp, especially with the sky such a dark grey. A place of lost hopes and dreams. Mother's ruin – that's what they used to call gin, wasn't it? The Dixits were never really drinkers, Naveem would have a beer watching sport, but he never finished the bottle – she always felt it was a playing out of machismo – she'd rarely seen him tipsy, and never ever drunk. She wondered what it would be like to get Naveem drunk, really sloppily drunk. It seemed to help some people. Others, well… Her sister's first husband had been a drunk. It was fortunate she'd never had a child with him. *Henry*. Imagine Henry growing up and going to a place like this? The thought struck Mrs Dixit like a blow; it was far too horrid. She would do everything in her power to stop bad things happening to the child. She saw so much of herself in him. How strange that she'd barely known Henry before the accident.

Inside, she had to hand over her bag for a thorough inspection and walk through a metal detector. The boy's social worker was to meet her. On the phone, she'd conveyed this would a good thing for Fred (his name was Fred) – it might help him feel some remorse if he met one of his victims. Mrs Dixit had bristled at the word 'victim'.

'He's not without emotion,' the social worker had explained, 'Fred's not a lost cause… yet. He's just very stubborn. I think he feels terribly for what he's done, to you and the others. Inside. On some level. It's expressing that emotion which is the issue.'

I can relate, thought Mrs Dixit. She'd always labelled herself 'shy', but lately she'd come to consider that a lazy defence mechanism. 'Shy' meant she didn't have to *try*. It was an excuse.

Through security, Mrs Dixit put her things in a locker. The social worker had recommended she bring enough coins for the food and drink machine.

'He's usually hungry,' she explained, 'and not very forthcoming.'

'You're not saying I bribe him?'

'It's common practice for visitors to buy a few things for the lads. Don't bring too much money though. Use your discretion.'

Mrs Dixit had ten one-pound coins. The change jar had taken a beating of late. The coins were hot in her grasp, their metallic smell astringent.

A burly security officer showed her to a waiting room. It was chilly inside, and Mrs Dixit wished she'd brought a thicker cardigan. The lights were fluorescent and harsh, contracting her pupils. Sunglasses might have helped too.

After ten minutes' wait, she was about to get up and go ask the officer if they'd forgotten about her, but then there was noise and the door opposite opened, revealing the boy. *Fred*, she must stop thinking of him as 'the boy' – that wouldn't help anyone. But he *was* a boy. He looked younger than she remembered here under the severe lighting, and she was surprised how fast her heart was beating. She tried not to appear as nervous as she was. Earlier, Mrs Dixit had wondered if he would be handcuffed, but his arms swung by his sides. He avoided eye contact with her and sniffed loudly, brushing his nose with his thumb aggressively. Behind him must be the social worker she'd spoken to on the phone, a short, mumsy woman with long black hair and glasses, holding a clipboard and pen, and behind her, the brawny security officer. Fred sat down in the chair and immediately slumped down as low as he could go. He was almost under the table.

'Lovely to meet you,' the social worker said, shaking Mrs Dixit's hand.

'You too,' Mrs Dixit replied.

'Lovely,' the boy mimicked, mockingly.

'You're going to be good for Mrs Dixit, aren't you? If you don't want your privileges taken away... again?'

Eyes lowered, he nodded.

The social worker beckoned Mrs Dixit into the far corner of the room.

'Now,' the social worker said in a whispered tone that was trying to be light and fun, but came across as frenetic, 'he's going to say anything he can to rile you, just remember that. He'll want to play with your sympathy too, but don't promise to bring him anything from the outside, and don't agree to any type of communication once you leave, to him or anyone he knows. He'll try it on, they all do, but you have to be very clear with boundaries.'

'Yes, he seems to have pretty severe issues with boundaries. What with breaking into my house.'

The social worker nodded, misunderstanding or ignoring the sarcasm.

'Because this is still an open investigation, his lawyer would like you to sign a waiver saying anything you discuss can't be used as evidence. This is just a friendly chat. If you can read the disclaimer and sign at the bottom, that would be gorgeous.' The social worker had such a soft, disarming nature about her, it was easy to think she was talking about a cake sale at the local church and not a potentially violent youth offender who was sitting a few feet away.

'Shall we start?' she said cheerily, once the document was signed.

Mrs Dixit sat back down in her chair. The social worker sat to one side, tapping busily on her phone and not paying them much attention – discreetly, probably. The security officer was standing just outside the open door. *Could the boy jump across the table and throttle me before the officer could stop him*? Mrs Dixit wondered, and then tried to put this out of her mind.

The boy – Fred – was looking at his lap, his eyes glazed over with disinterest. Mrs Dixit sometimes wondered what it might be like to have a teenage son; she'd often felt that this phantom teenager would resent her – exactly the vibe she felt now. She considered how to start, to break the silence, and then remembered the coins.

'Would you like a drink from the machine?' she asked, her voice sounding strangely tinny, as if she was speaking into a metal can.

He glanced at the coins and then swivelled around to look at the social worker, who nodded approvingly. Fred seemed incredibly young then, asking his 'mum's' permission. He must have sensed the optics on this, because he immediately sat up and brushed his thumb with his nose, saying, 'Nah.' And then, after a short pause, 'Maybe after.' He scratched the side of his face. 'My lawyer says I don't have to answer anything I don't want to.'

'Fine with me.'

They sat in silence, but after ten seconds the boy started to become twitchy.

'Aren't you going to ask me anything? You've come all this way. Get your money's worth?'

He nodded at the pound coins, and Mrs Dixit was aware of the perverseness of this interaction. Why was she here, really? To make him accountable, to see him squirm? That seemed unlikely, he was too attached to his performance of 'young thug'.

Mrs Dixit shrugged. There was one good thing about a lifetime of shyness, you were better able to sit in uncomfortable silences. She would smoke the boy out.

He sniffed again.

'I'm not going to say I'm sorry, or anything like that.'

Mrs Dixit shrugged: *suit yourself. No skin off my nose* – as the hypothetical smoke continued to pour in.

'What sort of music do you like?' she asked eventually, when it seemed as if the boy was uncomfortable enough to ask the security guard to take him back to his room.

'What kind of music? What sort of a bullshit question is that?'

'Oi,' the security officer said warningly. The social worker looked up from her phone.

'My husband likes bossa nova,' Mrs Dixit said. 'Never been a fan myself.'

'I bet he likes a lot of things,' the boy said with a smirk. 'Getting sponge baths from sexy nurses.'

Mrs Dixit stared at him, stunned.

'How did you know…?'

The social worker looked up again, watching them carefully.

'Know what?' the boy replied.

'About my husband?'

'What about him?'

'Sponge baths, nurses… You know he's in the hospital – how?'

The boy shook his head.

'I didn't.'

'Why would you say that then?'

'I think I want that drink now.'

'Afterwards,' Mrs Dixit said, leaning in. 'Did you know who I was before you broke in?'

'Of course. You always got to case the joint, don't ya?'

'Yes, but did you target me for a reason? How did you find out about the trains?'

'What trains?'

'The trains you were stealing away in that bag of yours when I startled you.' *The ones I pulverised you with*, she thought but did not say. 'Come now, how did you know they were valuable? Most thieves would have taken the TV instead.'

'I saw the trains through the window grate when I was doing a recce. And you didn't startle me, I knew you were there all along…'

'You looked pretty startled to me. You can't see anything through that grating. Anyway, the light in that room's been off for weeks.'

'What are you, Sherlock friggin' Holmes?'

'Fred,' the officer warned again. 'One more, and it's back inside for you.'

'I said "friggin"!' he moaned in response.

Mrs Dixit lowered her voice. She was surprised at her steeliness, her tenacity. She didn't feel scared at all – she felt like a beagle trying to flush out a fox.

'How did you know about the trains?' she hissed.

'Look, sometimes you see things and then afterwards you google it. Stuff you never think is valuable. Old chairs. Art and junk. Model trains. People don't usually leave money lying around, and everyone has top-of-the-line TVs now, there's no money in it. But people will quite happily keep antiques out on display, a Fabergé egg if they got one, put it in a glass case in the hallway. People are idiots like that.'

'Trusting, you mean?'

He nodded.

'How did you know about Naveem?'

'I never said I did.'

'But you know who I'm talking about when I say Naveem?'

'Your husband?'

'I never mentioned his name.'

'Yeah you did, before…'

'I didn't,' she replied empathically.

'I probably saw it written down,' he said.

'Where?'

'You know, in your house.'

This was possible. Mrs Dixit considered how to phrase her next sentence.

'On the night, you were annoyed I wasn't asleep. Why was that?'

'Because everyone's supposed to be bloody sleeping in the middle of the night!'

'Yes, but you looked put out – as if you'd been *guaranteed* I'd be asleep. Had someone told you about my sleeping pills?'

'What are you, a lawyer now? I don't have to answer anything I don't want to. I'm a minor, remember?'

Mrs Dixit sat back and took a breath, massaging the inside of her mouth with her tongue to try and make it relax. The tip of her tongue nagged the empty space where her canine had popped out – she still hadn't gone to the dentist about it.

'What happened to that tooth?' the boy asked, as if reading her mind. 'Did I do that?'

She shook her head.

'It fell out of its own accord.'

'They do that then when you're old, do they?'

Mrs Dixit shrugged.

'I'm never going to get old,' the boy continued. 'Bits falling off you. I'm going out all guns blazing.'

Both the security officer and the social worker looked up then at this trigger word.

'I met you when you were working at the waxworks.'

'Hmph, that dump.'

'How long were you there?' She knew this already, but she wanted to check on something she knew the answer to.

'Too long. Six months. Minimum wage. The place is falling down. You should see the rats. They make their nests in the mini golf holes, with their squirming babies, it's grim.'

'I can understand why you turned to a life of crime.'

'Yeah, well, the pay's better. Better hours. No bloody rats – sorry,' he said, holding up his hands as the officer's head twitched in their direction. 'Sorry!'

The officer shook his head and folded his arms.

'And how do you break into that line of work?'

'Ha, *break in*,' the boy replied, 'nice.' He shifted back in his seat, obviously enjoying this part of the conversation. 'I just sort of fell into it, whatever "it" is. And I'm not specifying I was ever at these houses they said I was, or that I was even at your place. It's your word against mine.'

'The police arrested you in my property.'

'Allegedly.'

Mrs Dixit rolled her eyes.

'Okay,' she said. 'Don't you have parents? Siblings?'

'Yeah, why?'

'Didn't you feel bad for them?'

'*Bad for them*? It's their fault! If they'd given me the money like I wanted in the first place… But no, I have to get a stupid job at the poxy waxworks. My dad does metalware for shop fittings – a shop in Essex, one in China, makes a mint. Do I ever see that money? A job at the waxworks…' He shook his head in revulsion.

'Are your parents still together?'

'Oh yeah. It's disgusting! Who wants to see your parents still lovey-dovey after a million years? My mum won't stop visiting me, she cries the whole time. Can't get a word out of her. I don't know why she comes.'

'Your mother's probably trying to figure out what she's done wrong.'

'I know, right?' he agreed, exasperatedly, 'but if she hasn't figured it out by now, when will she?'

'Why did you keep your job at the waxworks if you hated it so much and you'd started on the burglaries?'

'Allegedly,' he said. '*Alleged* burglaries. Dunno, you gotta have an alter ego, right? Like Batman. Keep everyone off the trail. And I could eat all the popcorn I wanted to. Also, because…' Whatever he was about to say, he thought better of it. 'Kept my dad off my back too.'

'Have you ever heard of a woman called Lidia Millbrook?'

Mrs Dixit watched his expression for any tell as she said her name.

'Nah.'

'Are you sure?'

'Say it again?'

She repeated the antiques specialist's name.

'Nope. Sounds like a fancy bird.'

'She didn't tell you about the trains? That they were valuable? She's not taking a cut?'

'Never heard of her.'

'Well, Lidia Millbrook has disappeared off the face of the earth. Even the police can't seem to find her. Quite a coincidence she comes around to evaluate the model trains and then you show up to take them. Convenient. Then she vanishes completely.'

'I don't know what you're talking about. You're just like the newspapers, making up all these stupid stories.'

'But the burglaries have continued after they caught you?'

'I dunno, have they?' He gave an exaggerated shrug.

'So, there are others?'

'Maybe it's a copycat? A copycat cat burglar, geddit?'

'If she put you up to this, tell me. I've signed away my rights, they can't use this conversation as evidence. You're a minor, you're protected. I just want to know the truth.'

'You might have a wire on you from one of the tabloids for all I know.'

'They searched me when I arrived.'

The boy shrugged again. 'They're all in on it. I'm going to enjoy my time in court, really make my mark. I'm thinking of having a rap career after this. Putting out a line of clothing. I've got this idea for, like, you know in the movies, all the inmates wear striped clothing, Elvis and shit. What's it called, the prison one? My dad loves it. I bring out some tracksuits with them stripes, call it "Banged Up Fashion". A few ads on Instagram and Pingbubbl and you're laughing. Make a fortune, I will. That's even if I do time. Got the best lawyer money can buy. Finally, my parents have stumped up the cash.'

'You're saying you didn't work with anyone?'

'Nope, all by myself. Allegedly.'

Mrs Dixit was quiet for a moment. The boy was obviously not telling the truth, but she knew that badgering him wouldn't work. He was stubborn, and proud, and very full of himself. She needed to find a different tack.

'Do you have a girlfriend?'

'Is that why you've come? Looking for someone a bit younger now your husband's not up to the task?'

Surprising even herself, Mrs Dixit slammed both her palms down on the table. The boy gave a startled 'Huh!', the security officer stood up, body tense, and the social worker gawked at them, open-mouthed.

'Don't you ever think about your future wife? What she'll think about you having done all these things? Broken into people's homes? Shoving my neighbour so hard, she had to have stitches on the back of her head?'

'I didn't shove her, she tripped. You threw a heavy bag at *me*. Coulda killed me. My lawyer says I stand a good chance of being awarded damages. The fact that the burglaries are continuing proves it's not me. How's it going to look to a jury, two women beating up an innocent young boy, his whole life in front of him? Pushed him down the stairs and then threw a bag full of metal weights at him?'

'I never pushed you anywhere.'

'That's for a jury to decide, isn't it? Your word against mine.'

'This is ridiculous,' Mrs Dixit said. 'You're a fantasist.'

'You've got to dream big, there's no shame in that.'

'But there is shame in taking what's not yours. Can't you see that?'

'I am taking what's mine. You attacked me, and now I want compensation. I've had to have physiotherapy because of the way I fell. It's been horrible.'

For a moment the boy looked genuinely upset, and Mrs Dixit felt a pang of regret.

'I am sorry about that,' she said.

'God, you're daft. You'll believe anything I say, won't you?'

She sat more erect in the uncomfortable metal chair.

'No. I don't believe everything you've said. I know you're scared, and this place must be terrifying. I know you're not a monster – no one is. You're a child. You must wrestle with the wretched image of your mother crying every night. Perhaps you cry yourself to sleep. I'm guessing you do. I'm sure you've never had to deal with repercussions before, so this must be quite the surprise. All you've wanted is more, more, more, and now suddenly you're being curtailed. But you have a chance. And I'm here to tell you, we don't get many chances in life. Most of the time we turn away, or don't even see them. You must. Because you've been in a dream. A dream of your own ambition, and greed, and your own desire. It's not just you, I've been in my own dream, my own bubble. On the outside mine would look counter to yours – I didn't steal like you, I hid my true impulses instead, I undervalued my efforts. But it's all the same dream. We're not good enough. We constantly need more. We're all by ourselves.'

'You're talking gibberish.' The boy turned his head to talk to the others. 'Do you know what she's on about? This bird's looney.'

'You need to wake up, Fred,' Mrs Dixit said, her voice growing. 'Listen to me, for God's sake!'

'Alright, alright, calm down, luv.'

'Wake up!' she yelled, standing and slamming her hands on the table again, the coins scattering.

This time the security officer lost no time bounding over to join them. The social worker was up too, nervously trying to placate them, but the officer had the boy already and wrenched one of his arms behind his back.

'I didn't do anything!' the boy squealed. 'It was her! This crazy bitch!'

'I told you!' the officer said and pushed the boy onto the table, making him squeal louder.

The social worker had her hand on Mrs Dixit's arm now, leading her away.

'Maybe it's better if we…'

'You're insane!' The boy wailed like a stuck pig.

'I'm the sanest person you're likely to meet!' Mrs Dixit yelled back at him, astonishing herself.

'I'm going to get you for what you've done!' he yelled back as the security guard struggled out with him. 'And you're right about the other burglaries. Maybe I do have a connection. You should be careful. Wouldn't want your home broken into a second time, would you? Just one call is all it would take.'

'Quiet!' the security officer commanded, hauling the squirming boy behind him.

'I'm going to sue!' the boy yelled. 'I didn't even get my drink!'

That evening, still shaken, Mrs Dixit revealed to Mrs Rampersad where she'd been.

'Aren't you the dark horse,' Mrs Rampersad said with raised eyebrows, 'I'll make a sermoniser out of you yet.'

'I was trying to get him to see the error of his ways. I didn't succeed.'

Mrs Rampersad took a sip of her decaf coffee and shrugged.

'Doesn't matter. That's the thing about sermonising. You're never sure when a person is ready to receive. Those flyers we give people on the high street, they may sit in someone's pocket for months and then one day, at just the right moment – when they've had a terrible day, their favourite goldfish has died – wham! There it is, speaking to them.'

'I wanted to make him realise what he was doing was so… *unnecessary*.' Mrs Rampersad grunted her approval. 'How do you know you're right about things? About God?'

'Oh, I don't. Not always. Some things, yes. That Mrs Hannah has been stealing church donations for years. And that there was most certainly a coffee meeting the other Wednesday, which I was not invited to. God, I'm not certain about, but I feel curious. Constantly curious. I want other people to be curious too. So maybe I bang on about Him, but even if they take away one tiny thing, one small sliver, it could change their life. Like He changed mine when I was at my lowest, when the bailiff came and took my baby's cot with the mattress still warm, He scooped me up in His arms and told me, "Keep going, child".'

'The only thing that would change my life is if Naveem got better.'

'Have you prayed?'

'Of course.'

'Really prayed, with everything you have? Every atom of your being?'

Mrs Dixit was less certain about this.

'I'm afraid to ask with everything I have.'

'Why?'

'Because what if nothing happens, what then? What will that mean?'

'Without hope, we are lost,' Mrs Rampersad quoted knowingly.

'With too much hope, we're lost as well,' Mrs Dixit replied.

Mrs Rampersad chuckled. 'I'm just imagining the look on that young man's face. First, you give him a concussion, and then you read him the riot act!'

'He said others might come…'

'It was probably bluster. The police said they're patrolling the neighbourhood. If it's this antiques woman, she's not exactly going to be vengeful, is she? Not worth getting herself in hot water over one of her underlings. If anything happens, they'll have me to reckon with! Skinny boys don't stand a chance!'

Mrs Rampersad raised her coffee cup, and a moment later, Mrs Dixit raised hers and gave it a cautious chinking 'cheers'.

52 days since the accident

How did the boy know Naveem was in hospital? Mrs Dixit pondered, the next morning, sitting as she always did, slightly behind and to the right of his mother. She'd told Lidia Millbrook her husband was in a coma; it made sense he'd be at a hospital. Where else would a coma patient be – if not at home with his wife? Mrs Dixit hadn't told Lidia about the sleeping pills, she was almost certain about that... Was she even taking them yet when the woman had first come to value the trains?

The name 'Clare' was still haunting Mrs Dixit too. She'd googled the name, expecting, what exactly? An image of a deceitful woman? Instead, she'd only found information on Clare in Suffolk, and County Clare in Ireland. Facebook yielded better results, but even when she narrowed the search down to London Clares, there were a surprising number, a hundred at least, which had left her stymied.

There was the unresolved issue of the drugs in Naveem's system too. His mother would obviously still be thinking about this. Mrs Dixit recalled how she had told the police her daughter-in-law was a bad influence on her son. Maybe she thought Mrs Dixit was a drug addict? That she'd turned Naveem's life upside down with narcotics? Perhaps that's why they stole him away? Mrs Dixit imagined reaching over, right now, and tapping the woman on the shoulder to ask – but her hand did not move. How easily the anger had bubbled up inside her when confronted with the boy. Her voice had been so unusually loud.

*

Shelly arrived at lunchtime. She would often come on her lunch-breaks, even if it meant only twenty minutes' audience with Naveem. He had continued to reach almost mythical status with her.

'Do you want a croissant?' Shelly stage-whispered to Mrs Dixit. 'I have two.'

'I've eaten, thanks,' she whispered back, acutely aware that the other Mrs Dixit would be listening, although she never reacted to anything that was spoken. She even ignored the nurses, only coming to life when a doctor appeared.

'He looks better today,' whispered Shelly.

'What makes you say that?'

'There's some colour in his cheeks.'

Mrs Dixit stood up to get a better view, but it was difficult to see through the opaque plastic film.

'You're right,' she said, untruthfully, 'they're definitely pinker.'

'That's a good sign,' Shelly replied, taking a bite of croissant. 'All the medical journals agree on that.'

'You read medical journals?'

'Only the ones that talk about comas. It's my new hobby. You must have read some too?'

'I mean, of course – as much as I can.'

'I thought I might give him a hand massage,' Shelly whispered. 'It's good for his circulation.'

'What about superbugs?' Mrs Dixit asked, concerned.

'Those don't exist. They are invented by the press to keep old people away from hospitals.'

'Why would they want to do that?'

'So they don't get treated. To make them die quickly. It's the right-wing media agenda.'

'I'm not sure if that's… correct.'

Shelly gave her an exasperated look.

'Don't tell me they've got to you too?'

'I… well…'

'Next, you'll be telling me that you believe 9/11 was a terrorist attack and that all the bees just magically disappeared at the same time chem trails started…'

'Maybe it's not the best time to give him a hand massage. What with his mother just…'

'She won't mind.'

How do you know, have you spoken with her? Mrs Dixit wanted to ask, but with the woman herself probably eavesdropping, she steered the conversation in another direction.

'Shelly, how are you coping?'

The girl took a deep breath.

'Not so great. I have to go to Mum's place and pack up her stuff, but I just can't bring myself to do it.' She started weeping.

'You shouldn't do that on your own. I can come and help if you like?'

'Would you?' Shelly wiped her eyes. 'I'd love that.'

'It would be my pleasure.'

'I can do a tea-leaf reading afterwards, as a thank you?'

'You don't have to.'

'It would be *my* pleasure.'

Mrs Dixit smiled until her cheek began to twitch.

In the afternoon, she went with Mrs Rampersad to pick up Henry from school.

'Can we have candyfloss?' he asked, taking off his backpack and giving it to Mrs Dixit to carry, expectantly.

'As long as you don't ruin your dinner,' she replied, slipping the bag onto her elbow.

'What if my dinner *is* candyfloss?'

'They start their negotiations so young,' Mrs Rampersad tutted, amiably.

Mrs Dixit had seen the posters for the travelling fairground on trips to the high street and suggested it to Henry, as she quite fancied it herself. There was something pleasing about the transitory nature of it, and of course, the promise of commotion and noise and people, all the people. She remembered taking her sister to a funfair when Mrs Dixit was a teenager, but not being able to go on any of the rides, because her sister was too young.

'I'll be in here,' Mrs Rampersad announced, nodding towards a tent full of old-fashioned arcade games.

'Did you remember your pennies?' replied Mrs Dixit, genially.

Mrs Rampersad patted a bulging pocket, as if that was obvious.

'What shall we try first?' Mrs Dixit asked her nephew. It was an incredibly still day, not even a flutter in the bunting, and warmer than it had been all year so far.

'The big one,' Henry answered.

She smiled – he was getting braver.

She'd also smiled because she didn't think he would be allowed on the bigger rides, which he wasn't, fortunately, but Mrs Dixit was surprised to discover the ones he *was* allowed on.

'Are you sure he…?' she asked, checking with the muscular ticket collector, who shrugged indifferently and waved them on.

Mrs Dixit spent so much time preparing Henry – making sure he was belted in safely, that his limbs were all tucked in, and would stay that way – she barely had time to collect herself. When they started to accelerate – *hurtle* was the most accurate description – Mrs Dixit felt sure that they were about to launch over the protective railing and be catapulted back into the car park. But at the last moment, really the *very* last moment, they whizzed back towards the centre of the machine. It was the teacup ride on steroids.

'Ahhhhhhh!' yelled Henry, obviously terrified.

'Please! Please!' begged Mrs Dixit to no one in particular (the ticket collector had vanished in a blur).

The ride seemed to go on so long, Mrs Dixit's fear began to leave her, allowing her to settle into the sensation. Not enjoy it – that was going too far – but accept her fate. As they careened towards the fence again and again, only to be snatched away at the eleventh hour, she noticed something interesting with her hearing – if Mrs Dixit focused, she could pick out sounds before the boomerang energy flung them backwards again. A couple deciding which ride to go on next, a crying toddler near the hotdog stand, a teenager on his phone promising to wash the car tomorrow, if only he was allowed to go on the Tornado again.

If I lost my sight, I'd be fine, she thought exuberantly, ridiculously, inappropriately, for enough had been taken from her already – why should she invite more loss into her life? And what about deaf people who had no choice? Why would she want to wilfully limit herself so?

But until the ride finished, she meant it.

'Have fun, did you?' asked Mrs Rampersad, patting her (now two) bulging pockets of pennies.

Henry munched on his candyfloss happily.

'Can we make one stop on the way home?' requested Mrs Dixit, lost in thought.

'Clare?'

'Yes…'

'You were a passenger in my husband's taxi.'

Clare's eyes narrowed. She was much younger than Mrs Dixit could have imagined, twenty at the most, with large hoop earrings, highly sculpted eyebrows and bee-stung lips.

'What can I help you wiv?'

'I'm sorry to bother you, but my husband made a note of your name, he wrote "earrings" beside it and I just wondered…'

'What did you say your husband was?'

'A taxi driver. He's in a coma now.'

'Oh, my gawd,' Clare said, covering her mouth with an incredibly manicured hand. 'Stop.'

'It's the truth.'

'He never.'

'No, he is.'

'Like a *coma*, coma?' Mrs Dixit nodded. 'Are they real then?'

'Categorically.'

'Earrings, did you say?' Clare held her palms up. 'I just remembered…' She disappeared into the house. Mrs Dixit turned to see Mrs Rampersad and Henry both watching intently from the car. 'My Swarovskis,' Clare announced, brandishing two bejewelled earrings as she returned. 'Must've dropped out of my purse on the way home from the bar.'

'Oh,' Mrs Dixit said, 'I see.'

Clare tittered. 'When you opened the door, I bet you thought, who's this he's carrying on wiv? Tart! I would've!' she gave a whinnying laugh. 'No, your husband was a real sweetheart. Dropped them off and everyfing.'

'Thank you, I appreciate you telling me.'

'I remember I was joking wiv him, trying to have a laugh, flirting a bit, and he wouldn't even look me in the eye. I said, "You know you can keep those earrings, give them to your girlfriend or your wife?" I was trying to see if he'd got one, I mean, he's good-looking. And you know what he said? "My wife doesn't need to wear sparkly things, her eyes are enough." You don't hear men talking like that. He's a keeper, that one. Although I'd like to have the jewellery as well, the more the merrier, if you know what I mean!' She laughed again, and it was so infectious, this time Mrs Dixit joined her too.

Back home, after dropping a sticky Henry at her sister's, Mrs Dixit sat down at the kitchen table without even taking off her coat. She wanted to bask in this feeling of relief before the effort of getting on with life caused it to fade.

'I'm sorry I suspected you,' she said to the empty room. 'Thank you.'

She stood, slipping off her coat onto the back of the chair, and made her way down to the study. It had been left in disarray after the break-in – the boy knocking things onto the floor in his hurry and then the police processing the destruction (photographing, dusting, swabbing) – only adding to the chaos. Mrs Dixit had swept up what she could, and righted what was rightable, but what to do with the broken models? The miniature Chomley was beyond repair, at least by her ability, so she'd moved everything to one of the desks, and ordered it best she could. Now, she stood in front of the rubble, and took out the reading figurine from her pocket, the one she'd taken to carrying with her most everywhere. She turned over the figurine, running a finger over the 'W' her husband had etched into the base, before reuniting it with her kinfolk. Mrs Dixit didn't need the totem as reassurance anymore, she had something better.

In the silence, she heard music. Not music exactly, the memory of it. Her knees weakened, and a sob filled her chest, but she didn't do anything to release it. The memory came to her fully now. Naveem explaining to her in his punctilious way how music is amplified by the body, the cavities inside us; it's not only the music on the page travelling through the artist and the instrument, we become channels ourselves. Not those words exactly. But it didn't matter. She could see him, frowning with the effort to convey his concept, his serious brown eyes darting around her face, searching desperately for understanding, and softening when they found it.

Her thoughts of him were silently amplified, the soft lining aching in her throat, as she realised that memory was also a channel.

Later that night, she could hear the muffled voices of Mrs Rampersad having dinner with her man friend from church above – Mr Beasley. Earlier in the evening, Mrs Rampersad had come down to borrow a casserole dish, but really Mrs Dixit knew it was an excuse to receive praise for the outfit she was wearing. That was easy, Mrs Rampersad looked lovely in her flowy dress. Her neighbour had raised an eye at the jars and cups and vases scattered around the kitchen, each containing a slightly worse-for-wear posy of flowers or a single stem propped up against the wall to stop it from drooping – but she chose not to comment. Mrs Dixit was glad to see Mrs Rampersad so much more relaxed and genial. Although there were drawbacks too. Earplugs before bed, she reminded herself mentally…

Two days ago, however, her neighbour had appeared at her door, clutching an envelope, in obvious distress.

'My son wants me to visit!' she exclaimed.

'Isn't that a good thing?' Mrs Dixit had replied. She wiped her wet hands on her trousers – she'd been arranging some flowering branches of cherry blossom, offcuts gifted to her from work.

'Yes, but Florida! There are alligators…'

'Come now, you wanted this.'

'What if I go, and they don't let me in?' Mrs Rampersad said, wringing the letter between her fingers. 'What if they don't let me back?' She lowered her voice as if they might be overheard in their private communal hallway. 'What about *Windrush*?'

'Does that... apply to you?' Mrs Dixit asked carefully. She only knew the basics about the Windrush scandal – people, especially from Caribbean countries, being wrongly deported from the UK – from snippets seen on the news.

'I'm not sure, I haven't checked. But I haven't left the country, in case. And now my son wants to take me to Disneyland!'

'We can have a lawyer look into it,' Mrs Dixit assured her, 'it will be fine.' The possibility of Mrs Rampersad posing with her grandchildren beside Goofy was something the universe couldn't possibly deny.

53 days since the accident

At Stem & Blossom the next morning, Mrs Dixit was trying to tame a particularly finicky bouquet when a drilling sound began.

'They're refurbishing the place next door,' the wife owner complained, 'it's doing my head in! You can go early if you like?'

'Doesn't bother me,' Mrs Dixit said, which was true. If anything, the noise focused her and she was able to make the grevillea sit right finally.

'You're a marvel, all the younger girls leave if they chip a nail!'

Mrs Dixit smiled and snipped at the bigger branches with a pair of shears, enjoying the way the ends ricocheted across the room.

An expensively dressed woman entered the shop, frowning at the noise.

'Can you help?' she asked, over the drilling. This question was directed at Mrs Dixit – the wife owner was still in the back.

'Aren't these lovely?' The woman stepped forward and cupped the grevillea in her hands. 'They're so *wild*! As if they're from an alien planet.'

'Spider Flowers,' explained Mrs Dixit. 'Grevillea. People call them Toothbrush plants. They're often used as filler, but I like them on their own. Get enough together, and they're quite something.'

'How much for them all?'

Mrs Dixit gave the (in her mind, extortionate) cost, but the woman appeared unfazed.

'What's the occasion?' asked Mrs Dixit, as she wrapped them, adding some complimentary sprigs and branches to the flowers. She felt scruffy in front of the customer, with her jewellery in all the right places, and hair blown out, probably by someone fancy with no surname. She was aware of her own hands, dry and scratched from rose thorns, the nails bitten to the quick.

'It's a reward.'

'Oh, for what?' Mrs Dixit wasn't naturally so forward, but you could get away with things in a shop. Liberties.

'Getting out of bed this morning. For not throwing open the window and screaming into the void.' Mrs Dixit listened intently. She hadn't known these were rewardable actions. 'You're excellent, by the way.' The woman nodded at the burgeoning bouquet. 'Deft work.'

Mrs Dixit blushed; she was never good with compliments.

'I hope your day gets better,' she replied in her best retail voice, as she handed over the receipt.

'They never do,' the woman sighed and strode to the door brandishing the flowers like a battleaxe. 'If it's not one bell-end trying to ram it up you, it's another. Honestly…'

'Who was that?' the wife owner asked, appearing as the shop door closed.

Mrs Dixit shrugged, her cheeks still flushed.

'Someone having a slightly better day,' she answered finally, as the drilling resumed.

Later, on her lunchbreak, Mrs Dixit realised she hadn't told her employers yet that her husband was in a coma.

Shelly picked her up from work in a Land Rover.

'This was Mum's car,' she explained. 'It was in the shop when she had the accident.'

Mrs Dixit had to take a running jump to get up onto the seat, as if she was trying to mount a Clydesdale horse.

'It's very impressive.'

Shelly shrugged as she drove off. 'They're just things, aren't they, cars? Homes are different. The estate agent is coming tomorrow to value Mum's house,' she was already sniffling. 'I can't believe we're selling the place.'

'Did you grow up there?'

'Mum bought it when she left Dad,' Shelly replied. 'She wanted somewhere she could entertain – any excuse for a party. Her place was always a sanctuary I could go to if I was feeling down. Mum was my best friend, you know?'

Mrs Dixit nodded, but she didn't know. Her mum had always been a cold, distant woman before she died. She could never imagine being friends with her.

Twenty minutes later, they pulled up outside a large detached house, red brick with mock Tudor accents – *embellishments*, Mr Dixit would have called them.

'Is it upstairs, or is there a basement flat?' Mrs Dixit asked, peering at the building.

'What?' asked Shelly. 'No, it's the whole place.'

'The whole house?'

It was huge.

'She bought it before all the prices went up,' Shelly said with a shrug.

'*When, in the fifteen-hundreds*?' Mrs Dixit mumbled under her breath.

Inside, the hallway smelled of vanilla candles and spice. *And everything nic*e, thought Mrs Dixit, wistfully. The living room was swathed in peach tasselled cushions and cream sheepskin rugs – you could practically fall in any direction and not come to harm.

'Beautiful,' said Mrs Dixit, trying not to seem impolite as she ogled the deceased woman's home.

'Mum was very happy here,' Shelly said, starting to sob.

'I'm sure,' agreed Mrs Dixit, picking through the magazines on the coffee table: *ELLE Decoration*, *Country Living* and *Good Homes*! – before remembering why she was there, and beckoning Shelly over to sniffle onto her pullover. As she patted the girl's back, Mrs Dixit gazed through the far windows, sunlight streaming through.

'Does the garden go all the way back to the golf course?' she said with amazement. It was all she could do not to push the girl off and see for herself.

'Your mother never remarried?' asked Mrs Dixit as they packed up books by the television, mostly glossy ones on fashion photography and artistic nudes.

'Nope,' Shelly replied. 'She had a boyfriend – Cadillac Ken – for five years, but after they broke up, she went it alone.'

'Wasn't she lonely?'

'She never seemed to be. Mum had me, her friends – I guess there were lovers, there was always men at her dinner parties at least, sometimes they'd get touchy-feely. She was busy at her surgery, in the community. It was a full life.' Shelly crumpled again in tears. 'I'm sorry,' she moaned.

'Don't be.' Mrs Dixit felt guilty about prompting her.

'I want to talk about her – I do. It's important. I can't fall apart every time she's mentioned.'

'Did you want to go into medicine too?' Mrs Dixit asked, trying to coax the conversation into another direction. 'Follow in her footsteps?'

'I'm adopted, so I didn't inherit her healing skills. Not her traditional ones at least. I have my crystals, obviously.' Mrs Dixit nodded in polite agreement. Shelly's crystals had worked *wonders* so far. 'I did want to be a vet, but that's like being a doctor – only everything's smaller. Smaller bodies. Smaller organs. More difficult. And you spend most of the time putting animals to sleep, and I love them too much to kill them. I enjoy it at the DVSA, I know that sounds strange, but I like to see people's faces when they've passed their driving test. Their cheeks flushed with excitement. It's a very happy place really.'

She closed a box filled with books and pushed it along the floor to join the others.

'You've got me thinking now – what if Mum *was* seeing someone? And she just never replied again? I have her phone, you know.'

'Have you checked it? Surely if she was dating someone, they would have called?'

'She had Tinder, and I can see there are alerts, but I couldn't bring myself to open the app before.'

'That's probably for…' *the best*, is what Mrs Dixit was about to say, but before she could finish, Shelly had taken a phone out of her pocket and pressed the screen.

'It's loading,' she said, 'shall I read the messages?'

'I don't know if that's…'

'No, you're right, can you do it?' Shelly held out the phone with a pleading look in her eyes. 'I don't want this hanging over me.'

Warily, Mrs Dixit took the phone and stared at the screen. There were eleven messages and lots of other functions that meant nothing to her – she'd never been on an app like this in her life. The messages were all from men, of course. They seemed to start the communication, either with a cheesy opening line, or in a couple of instances, an explicit image. Shelly's mum had responded to almost all of them, with a much wittier line of her own, and in the case of the explicit images, the eye roll and thumbs down emojis. Mrs Dixit had a real sense of the woman in these messages: fun, powerful, never taking life too seriously. *Is that what I do?* Mrs Dixit asked herself as she scrolled back up through the messages again. *Take life far too seriously?*

'I don't think there were any serious connections,' she said, still scrolling down one thread from LOCALCHAP56, and accidentally adding a 'heart' to an old received message with a misplaced finger. Mrs Dixit offered the phone back to Shelly quickly, afraid she might have triggered something by mistake. Sure enough, the phone made a sudden loud noise before Shelly could take it, almost prompting Mrs Dixit to drop it on the handmade wool rug.

It was a new message from LOCALCHAP56.

i thought you'd disappeared, it read.

'What shall we do?' Shelly asked.

'Turn off the phone,' suggested Mrs Dixit.

'I'm going to tell him the truth.'

She sent the message and then they waited. The phone beeped again.

now ive heard everything. Just say you're not interested next time

'He blocked us,' said Shelly, aghast.

'Probably just as well,' replied Mrs Dixit, taking the phone and pressing it in several places until she finally switched it off for good.

*

They moved from the living room into the kitchen.

'I don't know how I'd feel about living in such a big house,' Mrs Dixit commented, as she sorted the cookbooks. 'I sometimes worry about Naveem. Being in a coma must be like getting locked in some large house you can't leave.'

'Where do you think the consciousness goes?' Shelly asked.

'I'm not sure – into the subconscious?'

'But where is that exactly?'

'The brain?'

'I mean, when you die, what part of *you* goes to the afterlife? I know it's your soul, but is that contained only in your head, or our whole body?'

'I guess it's some quality we can't even fathom,' Mrs Dixit replied with a shrug.

'Like spiritual radiation. I like that. We radiate. When we die, it's transmission complete.'

Mrs Dixit didn't quite know what Shelly was talking about, but she nodded encouragingly. It was progress to see the girl not crying.

They finished their packing and had a cup of herbal tea as there was nothing in the fridge, no milk.

'This garden!' Mrs Dixit exclaimed as Shelly opened the French doors to let in some air and the chatter of birds enjoying the sun.

'I should have given you the proper tour first,' Shelly replied. 'Mum had this old gardener who would come once a week. He always looked like he was going to topple over, his back was so crooked. I can't believe he outlived her. Mum would be furious.'

'You didn't think of keeping the house? It's big now, but when you meet someone, have a family…?'

Shelly scrunched up her face.

'I know this is tacky, but I could really use the money. Dad could too.' She lowered her voice conspiratorially. 'He wanted to sue. A lawyer said Dad might stand a chance, but I talked him out of it. I promised him a cut of this place instead. Let's just hope he doesn't drink it all away!' Mrs Dixit wasn't sure how to respond to this admission. 'I thought you should know,' Shelly continued, when Mrs Dixit didn't reply. 'About the lawyer thing. I know the accident wasn't anyone's fault. The police said that it was the momentum from the lorry's load that caused it to travel and clip the taxi. The driver feels terrible.'

'You've spoken to him?'

'He lives in Birmingham, has three kids. He says if it wasn't for his children, he would willingly swap places with my mum. I sometimes think, would I? If I could snap my fingers?' Shelly was silent, thoughtful for a moment. 'I want to travel too,' she said, coming out of her thoughtfulness. 'South America. Argentina. Chile. Oh my God!' she said so vehemently, it panicked Mrs Dixit for a moment. 'You should come with me?'

'To South America?'

'We could go trekking in Patagonia?'

'But, Naveem… When he wakes up…?'

Shelly went quiet again for a moment.

'I wasn't going to tell you this,' she said, 'but I did a reading last week during the full moon, and the cards… I don't think he's going to get better. I want him to, almost as much as you do. He's my last lifeline to Mum. But he's already gone, can't you see? They're only keeping him alive with machines. His spirit made the decision to leave weeks ago. We have to respect that. It's why he's deteriorating… The doctors say…'

'What do they know?' Mrs Dixit retorted. 'They have all these fancy scanning machines and procedures and tests, oh, the tests! The doctors don't know a thing!'

Shelly's voice was quiet, coaxing.

'I just think you need to start thinking about the next stage of your life.'

'That's all I have been doing!' Mrs Dixit replied, so loudly the birds flew from their branches. 'And so must you. All these useless tears!'

Shelly stared at her, eyes huge and moist. Instantly, Mrs Dixit started to backtrack.

'I'm sorry,' she said. 'That was… I don't know what came over me.'

'Please don't…' Shelly began.

'In your mother's house. This is very unlike me.'

But then everything was unlike her now. That worried her at night too, would Naveem recognise her? In a line-up, the version of herself he met in the taxicab, the one ten years into their marriage, the one before the accident, and who she was now – which one would her husband choose?

'Please,' Shelly said, holding up her hand and closing her eyes as if she was in too much pain. Mrs Dixit became silent, her mind still racing. Finally, Shelly opened her eyes again. 'I needed to hear that,' she said, after what felt like an interminable amount of time. 'The world keeps turning. Mars in retrograde. I've become lost in all this grief.'

'It's understandable…' Mrs Dixit started.

Shelly held up her hand again.

'It's been two months now. I can't keep going on like this. None of my make-up stays on. Mum would have said something similar to me – she would.' Tears were about to threaten her again, but Shelly sniffed defiantly. 'You know what we need?' Her face brightened. 'Music.' She marched back into the house and over to a large outdated stereo system, inspecting the CDs beside it. 'Here we go,' she said, removing one and loading it into the stereo tray. Seconds later, Yes's 'Owner of a Lonely Heart' was blaring through the speakers. 'Come on,' Shelly said, starting to dance. Mrs Dixit shrank back immediately; her impulse was to tear away into the garden and escape off into the golf course, but Shelly had her by the wrists. 'This reminds me of Mum's parties,' she spoke over the music, pumping Mrs Dixit's hands as if she was operating a forklift. 'Dance with me!' Mrs Dixit bounced on her knees as best she could, and Shelly took this as encouragement, pumping her hands even harder. Eventually, she let go of her grip, and they bopped together in the living room of a dead's woman's house, neither of them thinking what it might look like if a neighbour glanced through the window.

After Yes, they played some Queen, and then started on the dining room, taking turns to change the music. Mrs Dixit even found some bossa nova to play for Naveem, but it didn't stick. 'Doesn't really go anywhere, does it?' Shelly said, scrunching up her nose, and Mrs Dixit had to agree.

As if in answer to their earlier conversation, the two women started to find small signs of romantic life around the house. An address book in the hallway near the telephone, that was obviously a little black book (the name Spencer was underlined three times); in the bathroom was a bottle of Viagra, half-full.

'Can women take this?' Mrs Dixit wondered aloud, before Shelly googled it on her phone (they could apparently, who knew?).

The bedroom revealed a drawer with a 'neck massager' inside that Mrs Dixit – wearing gloves – tactfully washed without Shelly seeing, before putting it in its own recycling bag (although she wasn't sure if it could or *should* be recycled). Beside a television were a collection of DVDs and even a VHS or two. *Point Break*, there was also a copy of *Emmanuelle* – Mrs Dixit hadn't thought about that film in years. As well as normal everyday underwear, there were thongs, and frilly things too. It might have seemed disrespectful going through the knickers of a stranger, but Shelly was in a much better mood, and the music blaring downstairs (how nice not to have neighbours upstairs, Mrs Dixit thought briefly) kept uncomfortable thoughts at bay. They laughed, and cleaned, and treated the sorting as the celebration of a life it really was.

They were just about to leave when Mrs Dixit's mobile phone rang. Most people called her on the landline, so it was always a bit of a shock to hear the ring. It reminded her of Naveem instantly, and emergencies.

'Mrs Dixit,' came the voice, sounding concerned, and her whole body tensed in response. 'I'm so glad to catch you. I've just been talking to the police,' the woman's clipped voice was instantly recognisable, but Mrs Dixit couldn't immediately place it.

Shelly looked at her from across the room with a worried expression on her face.

'Who is this, please?' Mrs Dixit asked.

'I've just come back from a trip to Cairo – a chap there had an incredible collection, but I was there almost a month pricing everything up.' Mrs Dixit's mind raced, trying to figure out who was speaking. 'I didn't know anything about what had happened,' the woman continued, 'and the border control took me aside, and really it was quite a grilling they gave me, but I'm at the carousel now, and so I thought I'd give you a call…' As the woman continued to talk, Mrs Dixit finally twigged. 'I understand you've gone through some harrowing times, and people were concerned I had something to do with it.'

'Yes, the police were interested in talking to you and you sort of fell off the side of the planet.'

'And I still have your husband's model. I can totally understand what you must have thought, but it was a last-minute job – very handsomely paid, of course. Now I've spoken to the police, they did some calling in Cairo, and sorted everything out. But I must apologise, it sounds awfully traumatic, and I'm sorry to have added to that in any way.'

'Really, it's fine,' Mrs Dixit said, but she'd put so much stock in Lidia Millbrook being involved in the burglaries. What did it mean now she categorically wasn't?

'No, I must get the train back to you. If you're still interested in selling anything I'd be interested, and I'd lower my fee as an apology.'

'That's very kind of you.'

'How is your husband?'

'The same,' she replied, not wanting to explain he'd actually deteriorated.

'There's something else I need to clear up in terms of your husband.'

'Yes, what?' Mrs Dixit asked, concerned.

'You asked me about the glue your husband was using with the model trains. All the modern stuff is non-toxic of course, I think I said that to you when you first asked me, but I had a closer look at the one you gave me, *lent* me, I mean – I'll get it back to you, I promise – I discovered that I think your husband falls into a very particular type of hobbyist that will only use the old resins.'

'I don't understand.'

'They are pretty toxic, even the fumes are not great in a poorly ventilated room. And if he got it on his hands… Most people know the dangers, but some do it anyway because newer glues can lower the value of the older trains. So that is probably going to account for the strange toxicology report. I explained all this to the police in great detail and they took a statement, so it's all official, but I feel just terrible knowing I've been sitting on this information, and everything you've been through.'

'Er… yes, thank you,' replied Mrs Dixit, slightly overwhelmed by all this news.

'Not at all. Now I must catch the Heathrow Express before I keel over from tiredness and hunger. I will be in touch.'

There came a muffled 'There it is, the blue case,' and then the line went quiet.

Later, Mrs Rampersad and Mrs Dixit stood over the pot of glue.

'Is it just the fumes, or do you have to get it on your skin?'

'Both,' Mrs Dixit replied.

Mrs Rampersad took the screwdriver and levered the lid open. They both breathed in deeply.

'Nothing.'

Mrs Rampersad moved her head towards the can and took a big sniff.

'Oh yeah, there it is,' she said, standing up again, eyes wide. 'How can they sell this stuff if it's toxic?'

'You can still buy it on eBay. People have it stockpiled. India and China.'

'Do you think Naveem knew the health risks?'

Mrs Dixit considered this.

'He was a perfectionist, so probably.'

'You mean he *is* a perfectionist?'

'What did I say?'

'He *was* one. You talked about Naveem in the past tense.'

'Oh, did I?' She put the lid back on. 'Yes, I'm feeling a bit woozy now too.'

That night, she could hardly sleep, she even considered taking a sleeping pill again. She felt vindicated, knowing he would never take drugs. He'd barely smoked a joint. Naveem had let the doctor sit in the front seat, or at least hadn't argued when she did, because he was too polite by nature, not because anything untoward was occurring. Clare had lost her earrings, which he'd kindly returned. There were solvents in his system because he was a stickler for authenticity when it came to model trains. And of course, he hadn't caused the accident in any way, the CCTV camera showed that, the cab was stationary. She'd known, she'd known! She was proud of herself that she didn't lose faith in what she knew about him. That meant she really loved him, surely? There was another, stranger sensation though, the loss of this shadow Naveem, this bad boy who had affairs, and took drugs and was reckless behind the wheel, and it mingled into relief and shock and sexual desire, and she let her hands run along her thighs and up her chest, as she thought of Patrick Swayze and Keanu Reeves in *Point Break*, their surfer bodies, and salty hair, and when she was spent, she slept almost instantly.

54 days since the accident

In the morning, there was no residual sensation of this sexy shadow Naveem, there was only the reality. Her husband was still lifeless, in a coma. There was nothing she could do to alter that. But there was something she could change – his mother's opinion of her.

Yes, she had plenty of agency in that department.

'You are quiet today,' Mrs Rampersad said on the drive to the hospital. 'I mean, you're always quiet, compared to most. But today, you've hardly spoken a peep.'

Mrs Dixit relaxed her jaw, which was clamped shut, she realised now.

'Just thinking,' she replied, still looking out of the car window. It was sunny again today, but much colder, and she shivered.

Mrs Rampersad was too slow in the hospital.

'I'll meet you there,' Mrs Dixit called over her shoulder as she sped down the hallway.

'Do you want anything from the shop?' Mrs Rampersad yelled after her, but Mrs Dixit was already gone.

The room was empty. Except for Naveem, of course – he still counted, she mustn't start thinking of him as part of the furniture. The chair almost always occupied by the other Mrs Dixit had a scarf over it, so she was here – she must be taking one of her rare breaks. The woman either had a cast-iron bladder or was chronically dehydrated.

Walking over to the bed, Mrs Dixit took in her husband through the plastic. She really observed him; his fingers, his cuticles, the freckles and what might be a first blossom of liver spots on the backs of his hands. The coma had aged Naveem; his hair and beard were finally starting to grey, he seemed older than her for the first time, as if their ages had flipped. Mrs Dixit had always thought marrying a man ten years her junior was a prudent choice; she didn't fancy being one of those women who lived for decades after their husband died. Ten years was a good buffer. She snorted at her own hubris.

His face was still youthful-looking, if gaunt. Mrs Dixit peered closer – there seemed to be a groove developing down both cheeks, the same line as on his mother's face, fainter but true. It reminded her of one of those weeping statues – she hoped Mrs Rampersad hadn't noticed, otherwise she might start busing in pilgrims. His nose was the same, his lips too, the ends curved down, so it was always a greater victory when she could convince him to smile. But his eyes, his gaze, were still held hostage. Did he dream about her? Shelly had told Mrs Dixit that patients often reported one repetitive dream the entire length of the coma. Walking up on a staircase and struggling to open a door again and again, until they awoke thirteen years later. Thirteen years – it was an arbitrary number, but Mrs Dixit started to do the calculations. She would be sixty-nine. She let that settle. Thirteen long years. Who would she be then? An old woman. He would be older too, of course, that's how it worked, except that in this case it *didn't*. Naveem would wake up feeling as if he'd just gone to sleep. In his mind, he would be in his forties. Only now, she'd be *ancient*. Is that what she wanted, to cling to dwindling hope and misguided duty, until he came to, before taking the action she was not courageous enough to do herself? Men always fell in love with their nurses, didn't they – hadn't Stephen Hawking married his? Mrs Dixit was definitely not a natural nurse; maybe that would have been different if she'd become a mother. Perhaps this was the universe's cruel consolation prize: no baby, but a vulnerable dependent anyway…

His skin still had a waxiness to it, and he was pale, but he was very much alive. Mrs Dixit had seen both of her parents after they'd died, and once you'd seen a deceased body, you understood the difference. A corpse looked sunken and *unholy*. It was a word that Mrs Rampersad might use, but it was true. Gone from God, that's what it meant. The spirit had departed, leaving only a shell. Naveem wasn't gone, not completely, not where it mattered. Would her husband be granted the miracle of life for a second time?

She slipped her hand under the plastic cover and took Naveem's. It wasn't allowed, but she'd had so little time alone with him these past few weeks. His hand felt cool, unreal. She was reminded of the waxworks, and then Cliff with those sideburns! Naveem would find that hilarious. She wanted to tell him so much. *I should have brought flowers!* she thought. There was no excuse now she worked at a florist, even if Naveem was never fond of them. It was the gesture. Everything here was medical and bleached to within an inch of its life. There were a few of the crystals Shelly had left behind on his bedside table, but even they made the place feel less organic. Mrs Dixit had done a poor job bringing life into the room; she wasn't focused on her husband, she was distracted by all these other goings-on. She should have sat, like his mother, in focused mediation, day after day. If she had, they'd never have taken him, he might never have deteriorated. She saw that now.

Mrs Dixit squeezed his hand.

'I'm sorry,' she spoke out loud, 'I've been everywhere but *here*.' Hadn't she needed to be though? Would Naveem want her to sit by his side, day after day?

What did people think when they looked at her, she wondered. The nurses. The neighbours. *Poor dear*, probably. That's what they'd thought all her life. *Poor dear, her parents are so distant. Poor dear, her sister doesn't love her. Poor dear, she couldn't find herself a nice white husband.* Well, they were wrong. They had always been wrong. She knew. Naveem knew. It was a secret they'd kept together, their happiness, their small abundant life together. It didn't care what it looked like on the outside. What mattered was how it *felt*.

'We love each other,' Mrs Dixit said, almost to herself, as she squeezed Naveem's hand again gently. 'We do. We always have. You found me. I found you. We ignored the world. We made it together. You and me. Us.' She smiled. 'Shopping for the quietest washing machine money could buy.'

Through the plastic she watched his eyelids flicker, revealing his pupils and irises for an instant.

'Naveem?' she cried, and then shushed herself. She waited. Nothing. She considered calling a nurse, but she didn't want to leave him and hitting the emergency button would turn the place into chaos. 'Blink again if you can hear me,' she pleaded. There was no response. It was alright, though. On some level, he was here.

Mrs Dixit wasn't sure how long his mother had been standing at the doorway. Some sixth sense made her let go of Naveem's hand and turn. When she saw the woman, she gasped as if it was an apparition standing at the door, and not the diminutive form of Naveem's mother.

'Oh good, you're here,' Mrs Dixit said, when she'd finally caught her breath. 'Please, sit. I'd like to talk to you.' Her mother-in-law continued to stand at the doorway, watching the chair suspiciously, as if it might now contain a landmine planted underneath. For a moment, it made Mrs Dixit hesitate; maybe it was the woman's grasp of English, she hadn't understood? –But no, it had been fine all those years ago when they'd first met, and on the phone more recently too. Naveem's mother must simply sense what would happen if she sat. She turned her head, side to side, looking down the hallway, perhaps hoping for witnesses, or someone to save her. She reminded Mrs Dixit of her son in that action, when there were things he didn't want to do – sit by a noisy couple, take the rubbish out after dark – he would hang back, hoping the situation would change before he was forced to do the unpleasant task. 'Please,' coaxed Mrs Dixit. 'I promise this will be worth it.'

Naveem's mother took a step forward, warily, as if Mrs Dixit might pounce. She took another few paces until she reached the chair, sitting erect and flat-backed. Mrs Dixit pulled around her own chair, so they were facing each other.

Now all she had to do was speak.

*

'I know what you want to talk to me about,' Naveem's mother said in a clear voice, the words slightly clipped; it reminded Mrs Dixit of a glass being tapped with a metal spoon. The notes rang in the air.

'You do?' Mrs Dixit said, trying not to seem caught off guard to hear the woman speak in the flesh after all these years.

'You want to apologise.'

This time Mrs Dixit *was* visibly caught off guard.

'Apologise, for what?'

'For everything,' replied the woman. There was no emotion in her voice, it was the cool tone of someone imparting a well-understood fact. 'Everything that's happened over these many years.'

'Why would *I* apologise?' Mrs Dixit replied, her mind racing.

'For taking him away, like you did. Making him choose between the love of his family and...' now some emotion crept into her voice, '... *you*.'

Mrs Dixit felt slightly dazed. She knew that this would be the reaction from Naveem's mother, she had imagined this conversation so many times, but actually hearing the words was surreal. It felt like she was in a play.

'*You* took Naveem away, without *my* permission. I am his wife. *You* stole him from *me*.'

'You never asked to visit.'

'Would you have let me come if I did?'

'You never asked.'

Mrs Dixit wanted to give a curdled scream of frustration. Years of anger and resentment were bubbling up from inside her – it felt dangerous to have all these emotions emerge now. She looked at Naveem, trying to calm herself and to help her get back on track.

'I know you think I'm a terrible person, but I'm not. I love your son very much.'

'Do you?'

'How can you say that, of course I do!'

'If you love my son so much, as you say – why would you never let him see us before the accident?'

'Let him see *you*? I never stopped him.'

'Lies.'

Mrs Dixit had never felt more like hitting another person, even more so than when the boy had hurt Mrs Rampersad. Her hand twitched.

'I was always supportive of Naveem, I never forbade him to do anything. He didn't contact you because you didn't approve of me, of our marriage!'

'That is not true.'

Mrs Dixit blinked in disbelief.

'Are you telling me you did approve of our marriage?'

The other Mrs Dixit opened her mouth to speak, but then stopped herself.

'My son is very stubborn,' she said at last. 'It is the role of a wife to make her husband see the error of his ways, to bend his will. A good wife would not have let him banish himself like he did.'

'A good Asian wife, you mean.'

'It does not matter to me what colour your skin is. I am only concerned with outcomes.'

'But you blame me for Naveem's actions. He was only protecting our relationship.'

'Be that as it may, the cost was too great.'

'What did you want – for him to leave me and come back to your house? He hated it there.' There was a flicker of pain over the other woman's face. 'Naveem created the life he wanted, it was his doing, his choice.'

'Did he? You have a flat with no garden. You live in the same area he was born, not twenty minutes away. He has driven a taxicab for the past twenty years. You have no children. Is this really the life he wanted? Was it worth all the pain and suffering?'

'*Your* pain and suffering.'

(Mrs Rampersad appeared at the doorway, and seeing the two women facing each other, raised her eyebrows and made a hasty exit.)

'My son lies here in a coma, his body deteriorating over time, and it seems all you do is wait. Waiting is not the same as doing.'

'What should I do then?' Mrs Dixit asked, 'Tell me. I really want to know.'

'You never talk to him.'

'Neither do you!'

'Yes, I do. In the mornings before you arrive. I sit here and I tell him stories from his youth, when he was a precocious child, before the change. You have no stories to tell him, you are dry.'

Mrs Dixit recoiled. It was an accusation that she'd faced many times over the years, mostly from men – that she was devoid of something, not girly or playful or happy enough. 'Cheer up, love,' from builders, or 'a smile never hurt anyone' from the bloke in the shop. Dry, serious, barren. She was starting to lose the thread of her purpose. Mrs Dixit had thought she would have the upper hand, springing the conversation on Naveem's mother, but in reality, the woman was lying in ambush.

'We have a very nice life together,' Mrs Dixit said, summoning as much feeling as she was able to. 'We could have shared it with you, but we were shut out.'

'You shut *us* out.'

'I sent you a Christmas card inviting you to come over for *years*, and you never replied.'

'Naveem wouldn't allow it.'

'Naveem? I thought I was the only person at fault here.'

'I never said that. Naveem has responsibility too. When we spoke, he would say, "We can't see you at Christmas, we have plans, they cannot be changed…"'

'*You spoke*?' Mrs Dixit was incredulous at this news.

'Once a week.'

Mrs Dixit almost fell off her chair.

'You called Naveem *once a week*. And he would pick up?'

'You misunderstand, he would phone *us*.'

Mrs Dixit made a noise, a choking gurgle sound as if her oesophagus had suddenly closed.

'What would he say?'

The other Mrs Dixit shrugged.

'He would give us his news and want to know about his brothers.'

'But he *hated* you!' Mrs Dixit exclaimed, so adamantly that Naveem's mother winced again, as if the force of the words were physical.

'This is what I am talking about – the very essence of the issue. This is why there has been so much disharmony.'

Mrs Dixit folded her arms as a means to contain herself, hugging herself around her waist and rocking slightly to calm herself. She did not want to give this woman the satisfaction of seeing her cry, she would not. It seemed her husband *did* have a secret family: his own.

'Naveem called you once a week.' Mrs Dixit still wasn't sure she believed this. 'When would he call?'

'At different times.'

'I would have heard him.'

'He always phoned us in his taxicab.'

'Why didn't he tell me he was in touch with you?'

'He felt you wouldn't understand. The ties that bind children to their parents are strong.'

'So are the ties of marriage!'

Mrs Dixit tried to imagine Naveem calling his parents. Phone calls when he was in his taxi were always perfunctory, short information-imparting discussions. Mrs Dixit was usually acutely aware he was at work and so didn't want to be a drain on him. Sometimes – yes – she would have liked to be told how much he missed her, she would have liked it a lot, but she never expected it and so was not disappointed. Mrs Dixit realised now how foolish it was to have been jealous of some unknown doctor in the passenger seat – she should have been worried about his mother instead!

'You mean to tell me,' Mrs Dixit said, shaking her head, still in a haze of disbelief, 'that Naveem has been calling you every week for the past twenty years, and never once told me?'

The other Mrs Dixit nodded. 'And why do you think that is?' his mother asked pointedly.

'I don't understand...?'

'Why could he not trust you with that information? Because you would have asked him to stop.'

'No, I wouldn't have,' replied Mrs Dixit indignantly. 'I *wanted* him to reach out to you – especially in the first years of our marriage, but he put a wall up.'

'In walls, there are always doors. Only you did not seem to care to find one. You could have come to our house. You could have told Naveem: *I cannot love you if you cannot love your family.* Why do you think you never had children? Because your marriage was blocking the natural flow of things.'

'You are blaming me for things I had no control over,' Mrs Dixit said, frustratedly. 'Naveem should have told me he was in contact with you. I always thought, *I always thought...*' she spluttered. 'He was so closed off – I would never have imagined in a million years...' But now maybe she would have. Naveem had his distinct separate worlds: his trains, her, his work, his family too, it seemed.

Compartmentalisation. Everything in the place where he last left it. No one to share his toys with. He was supremely selfish. It would serve Naveem right to wake up now, in the middle of a heated conversation between his mother and his wife. Let him explain himself! But, once again, he'd avoided a difficult discussion.

She remembered something then, the whole reason for starting this dialogue in the first place – she needed to get back on track.

'Naveem never took drugs, by the way.' His mother seemed confused. 'The police?' Mrs Dixit clarified. 'Their toxicology report said he had high levels of solvents in his system, but it was from the glue he used on his trains.'

'Of course my son would never take drugs.'

'Then why did you tell the police you were worried about him?' Ah, she had her now.

'I am not clear on your meaning.'

'You told the police Naveem was in danger, and that you thought that he was…' she couldn't think of the right words, it seemed so long ago. 'I don't know, implying we were doing drugs together, which is frankly ridiculous, and unfounded and was hurtful, and could have got me into a lot of trouble if the police had taken it more seriously. And you said that I was a danger to myself and needed a welfare check!'

'I was concerned about how you were coping. I know you don't have people around you. I thought that then, at least.' She meant Mrs Rampersad, and Shelly and Henry, and the recognition of this bolstered Mrs Dixit. 'And I never said you were taking drugs, I said he was *around* drugs.'

'What do you mean?' Had his mother guessed about the train glue? If so, why hadn't she told the police as much?

The other Mrs Dixit looked hesitant. 'How much do you know about his work situation?'

'His work?' She shrugged, deciding it was better not to disclose knowing about the illegal deliveries.

'It is as I thought, he always wanted to keep things away from you so as not to make you worry.'

'Naveem told me everything.' She did not think for one moment this was true, but Mrs Dixit didn't want his mother to know that. 'About annoying customers, and how his shoulders ached from holding the driving wheel all day, and we'd laugh about the things he'd see. A pig once! In the middle of the road!' But in reality, he was mostly tired when he got home; work was the last thing he wanted to talk about, and who could blame him?

'They cut his hours.'

Mrs Dixit couldn't speak for a moment.

'They cut them. By how much?'

'By half.'

'*Half?* But he never stopped doing full shifts?'

'Naveem is very proud. Even more proud than I am.'

'Where would he go, what would he do instead?'

'He would sit somewhere. Near a park, or a supermarket car park.'

Naveem had free time, and he didn't come home? The thought was like a knife in Mrs Dixit's side. But then, she reasoned, he didn't even come home for his beloved trains. He must have been in a really bad way. Poor Naveem.

'Why did they cut his shifts?'

'They told him there weren't enough jobs anymore. It was too competitive. He needed a newer car with a sound system that the passenger could decide the music they wanted to play wirelessly.'

'Who told him this, not Cliff?'

The other Mrs Dixit nodded curtly.

'Yes, Cliff.'

All those phone conversations they'd had together over the months, Mrs Dixit thought, all the times he'd pretended to be so caring and considerate. He was duplicitous.

'Naveem also had to borrow money from us.'

'From you?' The idea of her husband borrowing money from his parents seemed absurd. He would rather have walked across hot coals. But this explained why their insurance had been cancelled. Mrs Dixit began thinking back on other things too; changes to the groceries he would pick up, cheaper alternatives instead of the brands they'd bought for years. Changing over to more affordable gas and electricity suppliers. Agreeing not to buy Christmas presents. But the planned washing machine – that would have been expensive. Mrs Dixit chewed this over – maybe it was a distraction, to throw her off the scent. Look for a new washing machine, but never commit to buying it because it's conveniently not exactly the right one. It would seem as if he *had* the money. But he still bought parts for his trains, and new ones too, they were costly.

'Why didn't he do more hours working for another taxi company? Even one of the apps?' Mrs Dixit said, thinking out loud.

'Naveem was loyal, too loyal. And he tried. He was under a lot of pressure to start additional revenue streams.'

'Like what?'

'Food delivery. Picking up laundry and delivering it. Amazon packages. But he liked being a taxi driver. There was a certain status in it. He did not want to become a common delivery person. But what other choice did he have?'

'He didn't do anything… illegal, did he? Delivering special packages?'

There was a slight change in the older woman's expression.

'No,' she said. 'You know about that then?'

'One of Naveem's colleagues said some drivers would deliver packages for extra money.'

'Fortunately, Naveem had too high morals for that. But there were pressures.'

'Not from me,' Mrs Dixit stated vehemently.

There was a slight pause.

'I believe that.' It was the first positive thing the woman had said about her and it felt like a small victory. *Not that I should be trying to win her approval,* Mrs Dixit reminded herself. 'But when your salary starts to dry up…'

'Naveem would have spoken to Cliff. They've been friends for years, they practically started the company together. I don't believe Cliff would leave Naveem so high and dry.'

'How much do you really know about Cliff?' the other Mrs Dixit asked, enunciating clearly.

'What do you mean?'

'It's his business. If it was doing poorly, don't you think that he would have to change the way he operated?'

'Are you saying Cliff was involved somehow? He'd never do something…' Mrs Dixit paused, thinking. How well *did* she know Cliff? She'd always imagined that the drivers delivering illegal parcels were rogue operators, hadn't Len said as much? Wasn't it also probable it could all be coming down from the top? Those strange code words on the radio between drivers, the ones that Naveem had been suspicious of – surely Cliff would have been privy to those? He *was* in charge of the radio.

'I don't believe it. Cliff is one of the nicest people…'

'Nice. What does nice have to do with anything? People can be nice and still break the law.'

'Are you saying that Cliff *instructed* the taxi drivers to deliver illegal packages? Naveem would never do that in a million years.'

'Which was a problem.'

Mrs Dixit shook her head. She just couldn't think of that kind man, one she almost considered a father figure, being some sort of criminal kingpin. But then she remembered the waxworks, how weird it was to see the video of Cliff there. It had stuck out to her, but she wasn't exactly sure why. She'd thought it was the ridiculousness of it all, but something else was creeping into her mind – it was a connection to the boy.

Naveem's mother folded her hands on her lap, as if this was her cue, and began to speak:

*

My son was not a rebellious child. If anything, he was the most well behaved of his brothers – studious, and bright, with a wonderful imagination. His brothers teased him, but only affectionately, they were not boisterous children – that was not allowed – no one hit or bullied each other, we made very sure of that between us, their father and I. But he was different. We could see things caused him pain. Classes he did not enjoy. Sports he did not want to play. You must push your children, otherwise all they will do is stay inside and watch cartoons, but my son seemed weary of the world he found himself in. And I understood because it's my biggest secret too.

I had always felt, even when I was a girl in Delhi, that if life was a gift, finely wrapped, mine was revealed to be empty inside. It hurt, growing up, feeling this pain, this separation from the world, so it was a small strange comfort when I birthed my third son and saw the same confusion in his eyes. Of course, I was devastated that he carried the same affliction, but I was also ecstatic, selfishly so, because I knew for the first time in my life I was not alone. But how to help him, when I could never help myself? There is no antidote for this malaise, no prescription. All I could do was offer him my arms and try to guide him away from the darkest pain.

Men are not created the same as women. They are more vulnerable, less attuned to reason. They take so very much to heart. I was afraid that he would become darker as he grew up, that he would have damaging thoughts. I remembered my own puberty, with all its hopelessness, the sensation I felt whenever I crossed a high-enough bridge or passed a fast-enough vehicle. I wanted to reach out to him more fully, but it was not in my nature. He could tell that too, the effort of my love. And it only made him retract more. Soon everything was wrong – the temperature, the carpets, his lessons at school, he could find no pleasure in any of them, and if we punished him, he seemed to acknowledge this stoically as just another indicator of a cruel universe.

How terrifying it is to see your nine-year-old child give in like this, and also know that deep down, you believe him to be true. He fought with his brothers, and his father, and the boys in his class, especially when they made fun of our name, because he was frustrated, and frustration always turns to anger. That's why I showed him the models and miniatures, I felt it was something he could focus himself on. My grandfather had worked on the railway, and so I always found the world of them magical. My son did too, it was one of the only things that calmed him, and a connection with him I loved. But soon the fights turned to something even worse: complete disinterest. Apart from his trains, he could not be roused in any way. He barely spoke, he was giving up. I had failed. Every time we crossed a high-enough bridge or passed a fast-enough vehicle, I feared for him.

When he changed, I was grateful to begin with. My son wanted to get his driving licence, it was the first thing to bring him out of his depression in a long time, so we agreed wholeheartedly. He improved. We felt it was being on the road, it gave him direction and purpose. I had never learned to drive, so I thought – perhaps this is the way out I'd never discovered? And it was, but not the one we hoped for or wanted.

Once he'd passed the test, he would go out for longer and longer drives, ignoring our curfew. There were confrontations, which led to recriminations and then longer and longer drives. We were losing him. One day, he told us he had a job, and didn't need us anymore. His father and I wondered, where? A teenage boy with no qualifications or experience. He was smart, he could have become an accountant or a teacher. But no, he was leaving school to become a taxi driver. With what vehicle, we asked? You could not be a driver without your own car. They were providing him with one, he told us, a loan, which he could pay off. Everything was organised! He bought new clothes, and barely came home, except to sleep.

We were uneasy, what was this company that would give a teenager a brand-new car? We made enquiries and didn't like what we heard. The family was known. *It was an open secret. They had several businesses in Chomley, for illegal activities and money laundering. As well as the taxi service, they owned the bowling alley, and the waxworks – still do. But my son would not even entertain the idea there was criminality – he knew better, he always did. Was I secretly happy he at least had his spirit back? Yes, I'm ashamed to say. Perhaps he sensed that – my unspoken support, however reserved. But I did not care for his new lifestyle, I only wanted him to have a life. I never desired my beautiful son to work for those people. And all the time, I was conflicted, because he had a brightness in his eyes, fuelled by rebellion.*

There was another reason he ignored us – the family were careful never to use racist language and not treat Asian drivers differently. That was very important to Naveem. It earned them his loyalty, misguided though it was.

We lived like this, in stalemate, for several years. Our son still lived with us, because his sense of family was strong, but he resented us, and we tried to make him see the people he was putting his trust in were reprehensible. He was saving for a house, he told us, especially when there were fights – any day now, he would leave and never come back. But we did not believe him. We were all so close. We fought, but so do all families. Leaving was unthinkable.

When you came along, things changed. He'd dated before, but they didn't seem serious. Then he met you just at the moment that he had enough money to feel like he didn't need us. We had all developed thick skin in our household, to survive together in that small house. His brothers were moving out and getting married, which helped ease the tension, but Naveem and I were arguing more and more. One of the men from the taxi office kept ringing at late hours asking for Naveem, and I had told him sternly not to call so late, and my son said he was in trouble because of this. We made one final intervention, his father and I, and his eldest brother and his wife, and it came to a head – we tried to show him the newspaper reports, and the stories from friends of friends who knew people, but he would not be convinced. He was moving out with you and getting married. There was nothing we could do.

I cried every night. I had failed. He was a man now, not a teenager. I had not helped him see sense in all this time. I did not think my son was involved in any wrongdoing, but I did know he was being used. He was bait, *held up as the star worker, so that others would be attracted to the taxi company. There could be no funny business, if Naveem was working there. It gave them an ounce of credibility, especially in the Asian community, especially amongst new arrivals who did not know how things worked here. Naveem was like a big brother to them. He could not see. He was asleep to anything he did not totally believe.*

But I was still torn. He was doing nothing wrong. Lawyers worked for criminals, that did not make them criminals themselves. Was it better than the alternative? The depression, and where that may have led? I had spent so many years pouring out all my energy into Naveem that I had ignored my own sadness, but it was waiting for me. I could sense it, hibernating inside.

With you, it was as if his mind was made up. Always so stubborn. You were chosen, and now we were to live with that decision. We did not know you. We were afraid. What if you were involved somehow? One night, our tyres were slashed. A man would come knocking on the door at strange times asking odd questions. I felt we were being watched. And then, just like that, Naveem moved out.

The retaliations continued. A brick was thrown through our window. Naveem's brothers tried to talk to him, to say we were in danger. But he said this was another tactic. Another ploy. He had worked for the company for years now, he knew them. They were like family. He shut us out completely for two years. After that, he would call, once a week. That's how it continued until the accident.

Mrs Dixit's head was spinning with all these new revelations.

'Why didn't you tell me about this back then?' she asked.

'He was already estranged. And it was family business.'

'I *am* his family.'

'Not then, you were not. We didn't know if you could be trusted. Naveem always did see the best in people, whether it was there or not.' This felt like a personal attack, but Mrs Dixit was still too busy reeling to respond.

'Of everything you've told me, the thing I find hardest to believe is that he called you.'

'The Dixit boys all need their mother, even when they are angry and upset. They never really grow up.' She looked softer, more maternal as she said this, the façade of the tough matriarch slipping briefly.

Mrs Dixit had built up such a story of Naveem rejecting his family, pushing them all away and building a wall around those feelings, it was bizarre to think of him as a mummy's boy still.

'I assumed you didn't approve of us – of me,' Mrs Dixit explained. 'I thought you rejected us because we married without your permission, because I was white.'

The other Mrs Dixit shook her head.

'We were not hugely ecstatic when Naveem told us you were to be married. I was concerned about your age, and that turned out to be founded, as you never did have children. My concern changed though, because his brothers have all had sons and daughters, it didn't seem as important. You know we change too, the parents, we don't stay the same. Our minds expand. I feel that if there was not this seed of unrest in our family, we would have come together and found a way through. But now, here my son lies.' She motioned towards Naveem's body.

'I thought you hated me.'

'I do not hate anyone. Not even those people he works for.'

'So why did you take him from the hospital? Why didn't you talk to me when he came back?'

'We spoke to the doctors and it was agreed that he needed twenty-four-hour home care. That would have been impossible for you to do by yourself.'

'But you could have told me at least. Discussed it! Do you know how terrible it was to arrive and find him gone?'

The other Mrs Dixit's face tightened.

'Yes, that cannot have been easy. But we felt it was for the greater good. We weren't in the habit of speaking to each other, timing was crucial, and we hoped you'd understand.' She put her hand on her heart. 'I felt if we could bring him home, if we could give him the care he needed, our son would get better. He was sick because he was separated from his family; if we were reunited again, he could become whole. But that was not to be the case.' She gazed at her son. 'He started to deteriorate, day by day. I tried everything, chanting, praying, songs my mother used to sing. I thought we would be the balm to heal him, but I failed. I did not sleep properly the whole time he was with us.'

'I couldn't sleep either,' Mrs Dixit said, lashing out. 'My husband was gone. Stolen twice, once by the accident, and then by you.'

'I'm sorry, I knew it was wrong. That's why I couldn't face seeing you afterwards. I was embarrassed and appalled by our actions. I wanted to apologise, but I didn't have the strength.'

Mrs Dixit wasn't sure if she absolutely believed the woman. There were moments she seemed so open and vulnerable, and others when it felt completely calculated.

'Naveem needs us all,' Mrs Dixit said. 'We have to put aside our differences and start thinking about what's best for *him*.' *So I can throttle him when he wakes up*, she thought to herself. *Calling his mother once a week!*

The other Mrs Dixit nodded in agreement. 'We must.'

'His eyes flickered open before,' the younger Mrs Dixit revealed.

'They will do that.'

'It was different this time. I could see his irises, not just the whites of his eyes. It felt like he was *there*, even for a second.' She didn't know if this was completely true, maybe she only hoped it to be? Perhaps Mrs Dixit was punishing his mother with false hope? Or was she torturing herself?

His mother moved to the bed, his wife following. 'When?'

'Before you arrived.'

The other Mrs Dixit spoke in Hindi and slipped her hand under the plastic to take hold of Naveem's. It was strange to see her repeat this prohibited action, the one the younger Mrs Dixit had done herself not long before. She thought of the invisible intimacies we each hold private. She thought of her husband waking now and seeing his mother's and wife's worried faces, united in their concern. She briefly imagined how it must be to die alone in a hospital bed, with no one to slip their hand under the plastic.

They watched Naveem together, his chest rising the only movement, not a muscle twitch or a flicker to be seen. Mrs Dixit felt a curious impulse to take the other woman's hand, as if their combined focus could will him back to consciousness where medical technology had failed, but of course that was ridiculous. They could no more levitate the bed.

And it was standing there, practically singing kumbaya with his mother, Mrs Dixit feeling oddly proud of Naveem for never having been on the take like the other taxi drivers, when a name leapt into her brain in bright neon colours.

'I'll be back in a minute,' she announced quietly, turning and leaving the room.

Mrs Rampersad was waiting tactfully down the hallway, earphones in, a look of growing concern on her face.

'Is everything alright?' she asked, pulling off the earphones. 'When I saw you talking to *her*…'

'I'll explain soon,' replied Mrs Dixit, not stopping, 'I need to go talk to a man about a taxi.'

*

Outside the hospital entrance, the sky overcast now, a dullness to the light, Mrs Dixit took out her mobile and dialled the number from memory.

'Your pickup address?' came Cliff's familiar gruff voice.

'Cliff, it's Wendy.'

'Wendy, what can I do for you? Would you like a car?'

'No, I'm at the hospital with Naveem.'

There was a slight pause.

'Is he okay?'

'He's just the same. Well, I saw his eyes flicker before, but the doctors always say not to get too excited about it. That's not the reason I called, though. Not the whole reason.'

There was another short pause.

'Is it about finances?' Cliff asked. 'I know how proud Naveem is, but if you need any money, Wendy, I hope you'll come to me first because—'

'Naveem *is* a proud man,' Mrs Dixit interrupted. 'He's a good man too.'

Another pause. Dead air, as they called it on the radio. It hung between them uncomfortably.

'He's one of the best.'

'Which is why I'm glad he's unconscious while I'm having this conversation.'

'I don't understand, Wendy?'

'Did you have anything to do with it?'

'With what?'

'His accident. Did you tamper with Naveem's brakes? Or did you send the man in the lorry to swerve into his cab?'

'Wendy, what are you saying?'

'*Did you?*'

'You're obviously upset – where are you? I'll send a driver…'

'Come on, Cliff, I *know*. About your family's reputation. Intimidating Naveem's parents over the years. The taxi company has always been about delivering black-market goods, hasn't it? Turning your drivers into mules?'

Cliff exhaled. He didn't sound confused by her accusations, or argue, he simply gave a long, exhausted sigh.

'Wendy, I'm sure you have good intentions…'

'Like you do?'

'I had absolutely nothing to do with the accident. That you'd even *think*…'

'Spare me, Cliff.'

'Look, I have a business to run. All my drivers have families, *children*.' The way he said 'children', the inflection, communicated this was something Mrs Dixit couldn't possibly understand. 'I'd do anything to avoid laying off a driver…'

'Even if it meant making them do something illegal?'

'It's those apps that should be illegal!' Cliff raged, abruptly. 'They should all be taken down right now.'

'But you've been doing shady dealings for decades,' Mrs Dixit said coolly, surprised at her own tenacity. 'Since Naveem started working for you. You can't blame the apps.'

'Running a business is a challenge. If you'd had one as long as I have, you'd understand. You have to be agile, take on new workstreams. But I would never harm Naveem. To even accuse me of…'

'New workstreams, like burglary?'

'What?'

'Like breaking into people's homes and stealing their things, those sort of workstreams?'

'I don't know what you're talking about.'

'Don't play coy now. You knew I was taking sleeping pills, I told you on the phone. You sent that ruffian knowing I'd be out cold. You understood how valuable his model trains were. Naveem had been collecting them for years. How could you steal from him, and put me in danger? After everything I'd been through?'

There was another silence on the other end. A thick silence, like a dark molasses.

'Listen,' said Cliff in a slightly different tone, more measured. 'I can make it very comfortable for you. Really, it's what's right.'

'Don't tell *me* what's right.'

'I know you're angry,' he said calmingly, 'but in the long term this could suit you very well. Naveem isn't going to get better, we both know that, and you'll need an income stream. I could provide that for you – get a nicer house, set you up properly. I should have offered before, but like I said, Naveem is proud. Now he's gone…'

'Naveem hasn't gone anywhere,' Mrs Dixit replied. 'And neither will I.'

'I'll give you time to think it over,' he said. 'I'm sure you're dealing with a lot.'

'You broke into my home!' she shouted. 'And for what? To steal from someone who's been a friend and a colleague for decades?'

'Mr High and Mighty?' Cliff matched her outburst. 'He's lucky I kept him on so long, especially after he started asking stupid questions about the radio. He owed *me*. I should have let him go years back. I tried to ease him out, lowering his hours, telling him there was less work, hoping he'd move on by himself, but he's a persistent bastard.'

'Yes, he's loyal,' Mrs Dixit agreed. 'Do you know, I'm not sure he ever really suspected you. He thought of you as family, we both did. He *respected* you.'

'Naveem was like a brother to *me*. An annoying, squeaky clean, pain-in-the-arse younger brother.'

'A useful one, too. Helping you groom other drivers.'

That may have been the case back in the day. But to be honest, having him around now was a burden.'

'Which is why you tried to get rid of him.'

'Not in the way you're suggesting, Wendy. I may be many things, but I'm not a…'

'That's for the police to decide,' she said and hung up the phone.

She stood for a moment, allowing her surroundings to take shape in her vision, feeling her heart thumping in her chest. Interestingly, though, she hadn't tensed her jaw during the conversation, not once.

Mrs Dixit was barely inside the hospital again when she saw Mrs Rampersad running towards her.

'I tried phoning,' her neighbour called, out of breath, as she arrived. 'God have mercy!'

'What's happened?'

'It's Naveem. He woke up.'

Uncharitably, Mrs Dixit's initial reaction, on hearing this news, was of jealousy – that his mother had witnessed this miracle alone and her untiring vigil had paid off, but as it later transpired, the other Mrs Dixit was taking one of her rare bathroom breaks when it happened. In fact, it was a nurse who had responded to the life support machinery, and found Naveem, moaning and disorientated, but very much conscious. Yes – not that Mrs Dixit was petty or anything, bygones were slowly starting to become bygones – but it did give her an ounce of pleasure knowing that, at this most unexpected and momentous of occasions, her mother-in-law had been sitting on the toilet.

After receiving the news, she grabbed Mrs Rampersad by the elbow, and the two of them raced back as best they could, only knocking into five people as they went. There was already a cluster of doctors and nurses around the bed – a coma patient returning to responsiveness was a relatively big deal, up there with a successful septal myectomy and spinal osteomyelitis surgery. Naveem's mother was in the scrum too, until a silver-haired doctor ordered everyone out of the room, and two nurses pulled the Dixits and Mrs Rampersad into the hallway.

'Will he be alright?' asked the other Mrs Dixit. 'He's not making any sense.'

Naveem seemed as if he had woken still drunk, he was slurring and appeared unable to focus. His chin would drop to his chest in the same way Mrs Rampersad's had when she was concussed.

'It can take a few hours or days for the patient to adjust.'

Mrs Dixit noticed the nurse didn't say 'get back to normal' because what might 'normal' be? A lifetime caring for a vegetative husband flashed through her mind, and whether it was just the adrenaline or her real feelings on the matter, she thought: *yes, I will. I'll do it for him. For us. For me.*

'The doctor is running some initial tests and afterwards we'll know more,' the nurse continued. 'I don't want to give you false confidence, but it's a good sign that he can vocalise and articulate his head. Let's hope for the best.'

Hope. *We've almost run out of the stuff,* thought Mrs Dixit desperately. They waited half an hour, and then the silver-haired doctor told them in a sober huddle that the early signs were promising; Naveem had responded to all the physical tests, and could understand when he was spoken to, although he was having issues with speech. Slurring was very typical of coma patients, and it might improve slowly, or it could mean he'd had an undetected stroke.

'A stroke?' Mrs Dixit said quietly. Her poor Naveem. After everything else.

'Perhaps, but we're optimistic. Now, I think you should say hello to him.'

Naveem's mother made a start towards the doorway.

'Ah, he should only see one person at a time,' the doctor clarified, before she could go any further, 'so as not to overwhelm him. Perhaps his wife can visit first?'

The older Mrs Dixit hesitated, before nodding in acknowledgement and letting the younger Mrs Dixit through.

The protective plastic had been pulled back, and he was sitting up in bed with his eyes closed, looking so… *animated.* His fingers twitched, and his lips pursed, and his legs shuffled under the sheets. *A human being is such a production*, Mrs Dixit thought as she approached, nervously. Imagine all the puppeteers it would take to control every lever, on every muscle, on every inch of a body? And yet there was only ever one puppeteer for every person, one pilot was enough.

Naveem opened his eyes, and she felt a considerable thrill at being seen by him. There was recognition in his eyes, *his beautiful brown eyes*! Or what she hoped was recognition. *Hope.* There it was again. Had they finally run out?

'Welcome back,' said Mrs Dixit, her voice oddly scratchy sounding, as she placed her hand on his.

Mr Dixit began to blow air through his lips – it was obviously taking a lot of effort. She realised he was trying to say her name.

'Yes, it's me – Wendy. It's me. I'm here.'

He nodded and relaxed his face, as if he was thinking about this, and then nodded again as if he had come to the conclusion yes, this was good. He put his other hand on hers and applied some pressure and nodded again.

'Yes,' Mrs Dixit nodded too, as the tears of relief started to flow from her eyes. 'It is good. I'm Wendy, I'm here. And you are here too.'

Naveem was to stay in the hospital for observation and more tests, and so Mrs Dixit arrived early and left late the following days. He was still sleeping a lot, but his ability to speak improved dramatically. By the third day, he was walking with help, and saying simple sentences – 'more water please', 'TV too loud' – and the prognosis was that it might take weeks, but he would most likely make a full recovery.

Mrs Dixit was overjoyed, obviously, but worry gnawed at her too. Cliff, for one. With everything that had happened, she hadn't had time to talk to the police, but she couldn't put it out of her mind. What if Cliff retaliated by sending over some heavies? Could they hurt Naveem? How would Naveem react when she told him her discovery? Even if he did become well enough to work again, there was no job waiting for him anymore, that was certain. There were concerns more subtle, too – Mrs Dixit felt changed under the inscrutable gaze of her newly awoken husband, and she wanted to explain herself somehow – if that made any sense – but she was worried about being rejected. He wasn't the same person now either, she reminded herself, he may never be. Naveem hadn't baulked at the two Mrs Dixits in the same room together at least, the women even sometimes politely speaking directly to each other. Or the fact that Mrs Rampersad often visited. But Mrs Dixit wondered if a reckoning would come, and Naveem was simply not able to give curious or derisive looks yet.

She also realised something in these strange languid days after his restoration – Mrs Dixit did not want to go back to her quiet life, not in the same way that it was before, sealed away in Tupperware boxes. But she was getting ahead of herself. For once, she wanted to tell Naveem everything, to sit and download to him all she had experienced, every hope and fear, to really deliver a treatise on her wants and needs as a person and a woman and a wife, but she understood he should be well enough to receive this information, not to be bombarded with it. So she held her tongue.

58 days since the accident

On the issue of Cliff, there was a surprising resolution.

Four days after she'd spoken to him, Mrs Dixit received a call from Len.

'He's gone,' came his West Country twang, sounding more like 'he's garn'.

'Who has?'

'Cliff. He's flown the coop. They say he's run off to the Caribbean. Shady dealings finally caught up with him. He was some criminal mastermind, apparently it was an open secret. News to me. The whole company's dissolved. We're all out of a job, with this month's pay still owed.'

'I'm sorry, Len.'

'Don't be,' he replied. 'Most of us have been taking a bit more than we should for years. A safety blanket in case such an event happened.'

'Maybe it's for the best?'

'I'll get another job shortly. Might even try one of those app guys. The internet's the future, and all that. Just lucky Naveem's still comatose, he'd have flipped!'

'I should have said! He's out of the coma.'

'Don't tell him straight away, then. You'll put him back under!'

'Yes, well…' Mrs Dixit added this information to her mental 'no tell' list. It was already concerningly full.

She'd just put the phone down to Len, when it rang once more.

'My name is Isabella, I'm Magnus's carer. We haven't met properly, but I've seen you at the airport, I was in the blue Ford Focus. I hope you don't mind my calling – your neighbour, Mrs Rampersad, gave me your number…'

'Is everything fine with Magnus?'

'Yes, in fact, that's the reason I rang – he wants to speak to you.'

There was the sound of the phone being handed over.

'Hello?' Magnus said tentatively, as if he wasn't sure who would be on the end of the line.

'It's me, Magnus. Wendy Dixit.'

'Hello you,' he said, taking his cue. There was some muffled prompting from Isabella. 'I haven't seen you around. Not avoiding me, I hope?'

'Of course not, things have been busy.'

'My wife's left me,' Magnus intoned matter-of-factly. 'Norah. Gone.'

'I'm sorry to hear that.'

'She could be quite vile sometimes. Maybe it's for the best.'

More prompting from behind the scenes.

'Ah yes, I was wondering if you'd like to come to an air show with me, old flying contraptions, fighter jets. They really cut up the sky.'

'I'm not sure…' Mrs Dixit replied hesitantly. 'My husband has woken up.'

'He's come back to you then? That's good news. Bring him as well. Isabella will be joining us too, we'll make it a quartet.'

'I'm not sure if he would enjoy it.' She already knew it would be too messy, too intense, for Naveem. The crowds in the car park. The muddy fields. They'd have to drive there, and Naveem always hated being in a car when he wasn't working.

'Thought I'd chance the offer.'

'Thank you, I appreciate it. Definitely another time though, at some point – eventually…'

There was silence on the other end of the phone, and Mrs Dixit thought that perhaps he'd hung up.

'What's the saying?' Magnus said suddenly, 'about life being only a short crash of the cymbals between one eternal silence and the next? To hear it though… To really hear it… Tabitha?'

Mrs Dixit heard a woman's voice say, 'I'm Isabella, remember?'

'Oh yes,' Magnus said. 'Must go.'

And then he did hang up.

60 days since the accident

Naveem was discharged less than a week after he awoke, having improved sufficiently, and with the hospital bed too valuable for his current condition. Curiously, Mrs Dixit felt nervous on the day of his return, her stomach churning so much, she couldn't even think about breakfast. Shelly had come over the night before to cleanse the place, burning sage into all the corners of each room, and even her sister had called to send her love – and so that Henry could practice his French down the line; he was getting very good. *Would Uncle Naveem join them on a trip now he wasn't sleeping anymore?* Henry had wondered.

'Oh, I'm sure he will,' Mrs Dixit replied, but deep down, she wasn't certain.

The next morning, she glanced at the empty side of the bed. There would be someone beside her tonight, a living, breathing person. Why wasn't she more pleased?

Mrs Rampersad knocked on the door to collect her.

'Ready?' she asked.

'I'm coming,' Mrs Dixit replied, grabbing her handbag, and trying to disguise the fact that she'd been lost in thought, anxiously straightening the painting with the flowers for the past five minutes.

She took one last look at her home. The misfit flowers and their containers had been purged from the kitchen in preparation, only a vase of simple daisies defiant in a jug on top of the fridge, tucked out of the way. It was almost back to the way it was before.

'I guess everything is going to return to normal now,' Mrs Rampersad said, as they drove to the hospital.

'You can still park in the garage – the cab is a write-off, and it will be weeks before we can think of what to get next…'

'I couldn't possibly, I know how Naveem feels about his garage…'

'It's not up to him,' Mrs Dixit asserted, 'not completely. It's the least we can do.'

The *we* hung in the air. A change in alliance. The shift.

'Well… thank you. But just until you need it again. And if Naveem objects…' Mrs Rampersad trailed off.

They were silent the rest of the trip.

Shelly had wanted to help them transition from the hospital – she'd been very patient and so far not bombarded Naveem with questions about the accident or the final moments with her mother, but Mrs Dixit knew it was taking all her self control not to grill him. Mrs Dixit had suggested Shelly go early and sit with him in the morning instead, if she fancied, before work.

Naveem seemed used to, if not slightly baffled by, the stream of unexpected people in his room, the nurses and doctors and visitors, although Mrs Dixit couldn't help feeling he would prefer his solitude, even if he did seem much less resistant to human contact than she remembered. And really, after everything she'd learned about her husband over the past nine weeks, she had cause to challenge all of her deepest assumptions.

His mother would be there too, of course; they had already discussed visits while he was convalescing, and again, Naveem had seemed, if anything, pleased that other people were making decisions for him. He came across as altogether less stubborn, younger even. That wouldn't last, though. Old habits die hard.

Mrs Rampersad tapped Mrs Dixit on the shoulder.

'We're here,' she said. 'You've been transfixed like you've seen the Holy Ghost.'

'Have I?' Mrs Dixit unclipped her seatbelt. 'How bizarre.'

She had to fight the impulse then, to ask her neighbour for a hug.

Shelly was reading a book on horoscopes, the other Mrs Dixit was sitting in her usual chair, and Naveem was seated in bed drinking his coffee when they arrived. The room had a relaxed brunch atmosphere that Mrs Dixit was almost sorry to disrupt.

'How are you feeling?' Mrs Dixit asked, but she realised as she spoke this, she really wanted to be asked how *she* was feeling.

'Good,' came the reply, Naveem glancing down at his hands, and she wasn't sure she quite believed him.

'How are you?' he asked in return, and she felt an instantaneous jolt of relief.

'Better,' she replied, truthfully.

A nurse wheeled Naveem to the entrance, Mrs Rampersad running ahead to bring the car directly outside.

'You take care of yourself,' the nurse said brightly. 'Now you've properly caught up on sleep, you must be raring to get back to your old life!'

They all smiled wanly, except the other Mrs Dixit, who rearranged her shawl.

*

It was difficult getting Naveem into the back seat, he had trouble bending in the optimal way, and Mrs Rampersad had to place a hand on his head, like a police officer trying to get a handcuffed perp in the patrol car without smacking his head. Once he was in, Mrs Dixit sat beside her husband and took his hand.

'Why didn't you let Cliff get us a taxi?' Naveem whispered before Mrs Rampersad climbed breathlessly into the driver's seat.

'I'll explain later,' she whispered back.

He looked at her strangely, cocking his head to one side. They hadn't been so close to each other since the morning of the accident.

'What happened to your tooth?' he asked, placing his hand gently on her face, 'and here?' He brushed the scar on her cheek with his thumb. 'Did this hurt?'

'Not really,' she lied. 'It can wait. Let's get you home.'

There were roadworks, gas pipes being changed, and the traffic grinded almost to a halt. Naveem had barely looked at his wife the entire journey, staring out of the window instead. They were still holding hands though, and every now and then Mrs Dixit felt a faint squeeze, or maybe she was imagining it.

When they were through the traffic jam, they started to pick up pace. Spring buds were sprouting in every direction, on every branch.

'What are you going to do when you get in?' Mrs Rampersad asked, over her shoulder.

Naveem looked as if he was carefully considering the question but gave no immediate response.

'I'm sure it'll take some time to settle in,' Mrs Dixit offered, and Mrs Rampersad nodded, even though Mrs Dixit wasn't exactly sure what this might entail. Cups of tea? A bath? Television? At what point was one actually settled?

'More gas works. I should have driven up Benton.'

'What about turning up Park Street?' Mrs Dixit chipped in.

'Jasper Ave is better,' Naveem countered.

Mrs Rampersad deferred to him, the experienced taxi driver. 'Past the stadium? I'll try.'

But they stayed exactly where they were, no one was budging. Horns started blaring, and Naveem snatched his hand away at the noise.

'Quiet, you lot!' Mrs Rampersad shouted, beeping her horn in response.

Mrs Dixit felt her jaw start to clench. She wound down the window to get some air.

'I wonder where they're going?' Mrs Rampersad asked aloud, and all of a sudden, there were high school students in varying degrees of uniformed scruffiness, swarming around the cars. 'School trip? But where are the teachers?'

They would learn later it was due to a gas leak, a problem with the new pipes, and the school had been evacuated. But for now, they watched as the children, ebullient from a day off so early, and hopped up on hormones and the coming promise of summer, shrieked and hollered and cavorted with each other around the immobile cars. Mrs Dixit wound up her window again, as if they were on a safari, and beeping horns built together into a cacophony of sound that made the children laugh and jeer.

Mrs Dixit turned to her husband, ready to soothe him, to reassure him, but instead of shrinking into the seat at the alien noise and commotion, he was sitting forward, turning his head to catch the sights all around. She took his hand again, and he squeezed it, firmly – there was no doubt this time.

'Are you…?' she began, but really, there was no need for her to ask if he was okay. His face said it all.

'It's… it's wonderful,' he replied, in awe.

Mr Dixit wound down his window now, and they watched the stream of people, listened to the excited chatter, the occasional driver yelling in frustration.

'Yes, it is,' Mrs Dixit said, almost to herself.

She was ready to go home, but she was in no rush. At some point she would finally talk to Naveem. There was a lot to say.

EPILOGUE

135 days since the accident

The steward checked their tickets before ushering the Dixits through the door. Inside, they were met by the murmur of patrons settling themselves, their expectant faces glowing in the table lamp light, making everyone seem pink and healthy.

Mrs Dixit took Naveem's hand, leading him gently behind her. It did not come naturally for the couple to be at the front. Before the accident, they would always sit in the rear so they could sneak out if they didn't enjoy a performance. It also gave them the option to flee during the curtain call and avoid the crowds. Over the years, being one foot in, one foot out like this had meant they went out less and less. Why put up with a terrible view, and all that expense, when they could sit comfortably at home?

Reaching their seats – they *were* at the *very* front, their knees practically touching the stage – Mrs Dixit took the flyers out of her back pocket. There were those she'd collected for Henry (fun ones with bright colours, and any that seemed remotely French) and a selection for Mrs Rampersad (flyers displaying good typography and design), and she stashed them in her handbag. Her neighbour had been grinning ear to ear all week; Mr Beasley had finally worked up the courage to sit directly next to her at the church service on Sunday. To the congregation, this was practically an offer of marriage, as well as a scandal on the level of Watergate.

Sitting down stiffly, Mrs Dixit felt embarrassment start to creep into her chest – the sensation of being watched by those around them, and possibly judged (such ostentatious seats, who did they think they were, royalty?). She gave this emotion short thrift. The tickets were bought with her bonus from the florists, a little extra after a particularly demanding wedding. Naveem was starting his new job next week too – as a limo driver, of all things. The idea had instantly suited him; who better to drive a luxury vehicle, one imbued with integrity and class? Mrs Dixit was proud.

Naveem was currently peering intently at a menu (it was the sort of place where waiters knelt by your table once the music started to discreetly take your order), and she could see he was also nervous by the way he chewed the inside of his cheek. Forgetting any onlookers, she reached across and brushed his earlobe with her fingers. He grinned, appreciatively and slightly bashfully, kissing her hand. It made Mrs Dixit want to bring his head into her bosom and cradle him.

The lights dimmed, and the musicians came on stage to applause. The guitarist, pianist, organist and bass player all hunkered over their instruments, but the drummer smiled broadly at the audience, making eye contact with the front row. Mrs Dixit experienced a sense of being 'caught in the headlights', but again, she tried to let the panic dissipate – if not exactly returning the smile, then at least not visibly wincing. It was loud from the off, and although she still did not technically *enjoy* the sound of bossa nova music, that was no longer the only measurement. She concentrated on the drums, absorbing each blow. Mrs Dixit could bring her awareness into each individual instrument or allow them to wash over her collectively. Her body seemed to vibrate with the music – it was the vibration that mattered, a rejigging of her molecules, reordering and realigning them. She'd heard tell of sound baths from Shelly – they were too new-agey for Mrs Dixit – but she imagined them to be a similar process to this.

As she experienced the song in her body, Mrs Dixit flicked the tip of her tongue into the space where her tooth had been. She still hadn't had it fixed. Of course she would, eventually, but it was helpful to have a reminder of what had happened, physical proof. When she woke each morning, before opening her eyes, Mrs Dixit could check the gap in her teeth, and listen to her husband's breathing beside her, and she knew, *she knew*, exactly where she was.

The band finished to a hearty ovation. And then, almost seamlessly, they began again.

A LETTER FROM DREW

Thank you for reading *With or Without You*. If you did enjoy it, and want to keep up to date with all my latest releases, just sign up at the following link. Your email address will never be shared and you can unsubscribe at any time.

www.bookouture.com/drew-davies

It was a strange time to finish a book, what with everything going on in the world. I hope you're well, and if there's any silver lining, it's that the events have helped foster a greater sense of connectedness and local community where you live. I really saw that here in North-East London, volunteers delivering food and prescriptions to neighbours they might never have spoken to before. People volunteering at hospitals. Incredible stories of charity and altruism. Not to mention the tremendous effort and sacrifices of our key workers. To say they will always have our gratitude is an understatement.

With or Without You deals with loneliness and isolation, and of neighbours helping neighbours, so it was oddly ameliorating for me in those months. I hope the book resonated with you as well.

If you'd like to leave a review, I'd appreciate it. If you fancy reaching out to say hi, I'd love that too. If there's one thing that keeps striking me, it's how important community and true connection really is.

Take very good care of yourself.

Cheers,
Drew

drew.davies.75873

@Drew_Davies

drewdavieswriter

ACKNOWLEDGEMENTS

To my incredible editor Christina Demosthenous, it's more fun working with you each time. To Hattie Grunewald, for starting this journey with me, and now building a friendship together. Mat and Jilly, for your continued support. Trinity Smith – and her mother, Veronica Smith, for research help. Thank you all.

Special thanks to all the family and local support for my nanna, who supports me so much. Louise, Norman, Suzanne from the knitting group, Dee and Andrew next door, Malcolm and Elaine for dropping off a newspaper each week, and the drivers at Waterloo taxis, who always go the extra mile: Binny, Mustapha and Veejay.

Finally, to Marios, who supports me every step of the way – I'm so fortunate to have you in my life. Thank you.

Printed in Great Britain
by Amazon

46005798R00189